Clare Nonhebel, who lives in London with her husband, decided to be a writer at the age of five, a ballet dancer at the age of nine, and a writer, ballet dancer and farmer at the age of ten. In fact she became a social worker, a public relations secretary and a freelance journalist before she wrote her first novel. *Cold Showers* was the joint winner of the Betty Trask Award in 1984, a prize awarded for the best first novel by an author under thirty-five.

By the same author

Cold Showers

CLARE NONHEBEL

The Partisan

GRAFTON BOOKS

A Division of the Collins Publishing Group

LONDON GLASGOW
TORONTO SYDNEY AUCKLAND

Grafton Books
A Division of the Collins Publishing Group
8 Grafton Street, London W1X 3LA

Published by Grafton Books 1987

First published in Great Britain by
Century Hutchinson Ltd 1986

ISBN 0-586-07005-2

Printed and bound in Great Britain by
Collins, Glasgow

Set in Times

To Robin

1

Even when it rained she walked home slowly.

'But you are drowned!' Maman would exclaim. 'Why didn't you run? Or take the bus?'

If she ran – or took the bus – she would arrive home too soon, but she could not explain that to Maman. It was not that she did not want to go home, just that she needed the twenty minutes it took her to walk. In silence and on her own, her thoughts keeping pace with the rhythm of her footsteps, she walked each day down the invisible line dividing the school-Christine from the home-Christine.

Every evening the magic process took place, like a snake shedding its skin, only to wriggle back into it the next morning. At five o'clock she was Christine Rochaud, bright girl of the English class, chatterbox of the corridors, receiver of confidences and of illicit marrons glacés smuggled under the desks.

Then with '*au revoirs*' and 'see you tomorrows' and 'don't forget to bring . . .', the class dispersed and the transformation began. As she started on her walk the voices in her head would change from Madame Scholbert's: 'Christine Rochaud, can you tell me how one would say in English . . .?' to Maman's: 'Wipe your feet, wash your hands and go and say "*Bonsoir*" to Bon Papa.' And – hey presto – by half past five she would be just plain Christine, only child and wiper of dishes, apple of her grandfather's eye and despair of her mother's tidy mind.

As she turned the corner into rue Jean-Jacques Rousseau, the home voices took over finally and completely and the school voices: 'Until tomorrow, Christine. *N'oublie pas* . . .' sank out of existence, until tomorrow.

Her feet scuffed against the flagstones, kicking up the grey Paris dust. 'The dust here,' Bon Papa once said, 'is different from the dust anywhere else in the world.' Her grand-père had a gift for sayings like that, which made one look at ordinary things – even dust – in quite a different way.

The dust, in the part of Paris where the Rochauds lived, had once been very select dust, according to Bon Papa.

'When I was a child,' he said, 'this was a distinguished suburb. Everybody had servants. Everybody knew who everyone was. There was a stability. People were not always moving about as they do nowadays. Restless, that's how they are now. No, the dust had time to settle in those days.'

'A suburb?' Christine had asked. 'Do you mean that this wasn't Paris, in your day?'

Bon Papa had paused in his walk and spat with dignity into the gutter.

'*Bien sûr*, it was Paris,' he allowed. 'But a quiet respectable place: a village within the city, one would say. But now! Anybody lives here now.'

The tall, gabled houses were mourning the past by crumbling away. The painted stucco had faded unevenly, streaked with green and yellow under the eaves, with blistering patches of black where the damp was trapped. The railings were rusted and litter blew down the streets, but in the overgrown gardens a few roses bloomed among the weeds.

Bon Papa knew the history of each of the houses. 'In number fifty-nine,' he would say, 'lived a family of nine.

They all left, one by one. The youngest son went to study at the Sorbonne. He was a brilliant child, a credit to his father; became a professor and travelled all round the world.

'The daughters all married. One went to live in Morocco, two settled in Paris, one went to Brazil, I can't think why. Then when the parents died, the eldest son returned. He loved this house. He would never allow a detail to be changed. All the furniture stayed just as it always had been, the decoration, the carpets . . . Even the curtains were never changed, though the velvet had worn quite thin.'

'Is he still living there now, or is he dead?' Christine had asked.

'He may be dead, for all I know. He left here years ago. Married a night-club dancer from La Pigalle. She never liked the old house, but he refused to let it go.'

'When did he move away then, Bon Papa?'

'Eh? Oh, I don't know. His wife ran away with a Chinaman from the laundry, and the next thing we heard, the house was sold.'

Christine liked to think of the stolid old houses standing silently through generations of change. Bon Papa and Bonne Maman, who had died before Christine was born, had lived in their own house all the years of their marriage, and Maman and her sisters, Tante Léonie and the unknown Tante Sophie who lived in England, had grown up there too, walking home from school each day as Christine did now.

Once when Christine had come home late from a party, she had stood outside the house in the dark and looked in through the unshuttered windows at Maman and Papa and Bon Papa in the lighted salon, talking and yawning and getting up to fetch things, just as they always did, quite unaware of being observed. It was as though they

9

were actors on stage, with Christine in the audience, watching them. After that she had sometimes felt – even when she was inside and part of the scene – that they were all just acting and had nothing to do with real life at all.

Sometimes, when Maman and Papa had one of their rows, the actors seemed almost too well rehearsed in their lines; the pattern was so familiar that Christine could have prompted them.

Maman would start shouting first while Papa, smugly relaxed in his armchair, murmured sarcasms in a reasonable voice. If Maman prepared to retreat, however, leaving him – lone and ridiculous – exposed to Christine's gaze and Grand-père's silence, he would raise his voice and bark an insult to her outraged back.

In act two, before the curtain fell, Maman would re-enter the fray and the noise would rise to a crescendo of discord till the supporting cast withdrew, upstaged, to the shelter of the wings.

'Upstairs,' Bon Papa would say firmly, ushering Christine before him, and they would shut themselves away from the drama in his dark, cluttered, safe little room.

Christine had preferred it when Bon Papa's room had been at the top of the house, up the second flight of uncarpeted stairs. As she climbed them, she would run a finger along the rail and, as a record of her passing, flake off a crumb where the wall turned the corner, so that over the years her visits to Bon Papa's room were marked by a white-toothed bite in the peeling brown paint.

But since he had become older, and shaky on his legs, Maman had ordered him downstairs, and now they all had bedrooms on the same floor. 'You'll be nearer the bathroom,' Maman said, but he grumbled about the arrangement.

'You'll hear me snore,' he said.

'We'll put up with that all right,' Giselle had replied not understanding.

Christine knew he had meant that his snoring was private. Giselle oversaw her father's daily life, provided his meals, tidied his room and did all his laundry – even knocked on the door when he was in the bath, to make sure that he had not fallen asleep and drowned. The least he expected was privacy in his nightlife, to snore without being heard.

Thinking of Bon Papa, Christine quickened her pace.

'*Bonsoir,* Christine!'

Madame Rouvieux, the old lady who lived opposite, spent most of her life, it seemed to Christine, stationed by her garden gate.

'*Bonsoir,* Madame Rouvieux.'

'How was school today?'

'Fine, thank you.' Christine tried to think of a more imaginative answer and failed. 'It was all right.'

Madame Rouvieux nodded her head approvingly, and a hairpin hanging loose from her bun swung precariously over one ear. Christine watched it, fascinated.

'Your grand-père is not back yet; I haven't seen him return.'

'He's probably still at the park then,' said Christine, 'watching the game of boules.'

Madame Rouvieux clasped her hands in glad surprise, though she knew – and Christine knew she knew – every detail of her neighbours' daily lives. One could not sneeze, in rue Jean-Jacques Rousseau, without Madame Rouvieux enquiring after one's cold the next day.

'Watching the boules! Well! Does he play, your grand-père?' The hairpin dangled coyly.

'Not usually,' said Christine, her eyes fixed on a point above the lady's left ear. 'He used to play, but he's too old now.'

11

'Old? *Mais non*,' Madame Rouvieux protested. She shook her head decisively, and the hairpin detached itself and flew into the mimosa bush.

Christine sighed regretfully. 'I'll have to go home now,' she said. '*Au 'voir*, Madame.'

'*Au revoir, ma petite*. See you tomorrow. My best regards to your family.'

'Of course.' Christine would not bother to pass on the best regards, for if she did Maman would click her tongue impatiently and say, 'That old busybody! Nothing better to do than gossip all day.'

Then Bon Papa, drawing his eyebrows together, would peer at Maman and say reprovingly, 'She is a good neighbour, Giselle,' and Maman would purse her lips tightly and clatter the dishes in the sink.

Christine waved goodbye to the old woman and ran up the garden path. Pushing open the back door, she heard the plaintive voice of her Tante Léonie above the kitchen clatter of pots and pans.

'I don't know what is wrong with the child, Giselle; her little brother is no trouble – a perfect angel, I assure you. One brings them up in exactly the same way, treats them absolutely alike . . .'

Then came Maman's voice, muffled by steam and clatter: 'Nothing to do with it, *chérie*. Christine is just the same – girls are always more difficult. Jean-Luc always wanted a boy; perhaps he would have taken more interest in a son.'

'But Christine is quite a help in the house now, *n'est-ce pas*? Girls, when they get older . . .' the sentence trailed off. 'And so pretty.'

'But yes' – Maman again – 'everyone remarks on how much she resembles me. Look at photos of me at the same age. Identical twins, one would say! Christine – is that you? Come and say "*Bonsoir*" to Tante Léonie.

Regarde, Léonie, her hair. Beautiful, *non*?' Her hands reached out, possessively, to Christine's long dark hair.

Christine bowed her head defensively. '*Bonsoir,* Tante Léonie.'

Sometimes she resented her resemblance to Giselle. 'One can tell you are mother and daughter!' everyone would exclaim.

Giselle had had them photographed together. They had sat side by side on a rose pink sofa in the studio of the photographer, Monsieur Henri Trichard, who was the father of one of Christine's schoolfriends. He had smiled from the time of their arrival until the time they left, except when he disappeared behind the camera.

He had complimented Giselle on her perfect complexion, on her perfect teeth and hair, and even on her figure, though he was only taking pictures of her face.

Every time Christine saw that photograph now, with its mother and daughter likeness of olive skin, dark eyes and hair, she recalled the discomfort of that occasion. Normally, people looked at you for a while and then looked away. They did not stare and smile and make remarks.

They did not order you to sit close to your mother, to let her wind an encircling arm about you, to press her cheek against yours, to blend olive skin and dark hair until two people, daughter and mother, became one image, trapped together forever in a silver frame.

'Giselle!' Léonie's voice reached a pinnacle of reproach. 'The recipe for the *pot-au-feu* – you never gave it to me! Admit now, you don't want to give away the secrets of your cuisine.'

'What are you saying, *mon chou*? I forgot completely. Wait, find a pencil; I will tell you from memory. First, nothing but the purest ingredients . . .'

Christine went out through the dining-room, scooping

13

a Brazil nut out of the bowl on the buffet to appease her appetite, which had been aroused by the tantalizing smell of Maman's celery soup. If Papa knew Maman had her sister for company he would be even less likely to come home on time, and supper would be late again.

'Can't we eat without him?' Christine would plead. 'We'll die of starvation if we wait any longer.'

'We'll leave it a few more minutes,' Maman would decide. 'He said the meeting wouldn't go on so late tonight. Not that one can believe it.'

Maman liked them all to eat together. Eating supper together was the sign of a united family, she had once said.

'Are we a united family?' Christine had asked curiously, and Maman had snapped, 'Of course. Why not?'

Christine thought of the evenings she spent with Bon Papa in his room while Maman and Papa argued downstairs, of the re-heated meals taken alone with Bon Papa when Maman went out; of Papa working late at night in the dining-room with his papers strewn across the table, muttering irritably as Christine tiptoed through on her way to bed. It seemed that united families only ate supper together; the rest of the time they spent in different rooms, or even different houses.

'Marie-Louise's father plays Scrabble with her,' Christine once told Papa, in the middle of one of his working sessions.

'Henri Trichard?' he said contemptuously. 'Henri Trichard doesn't know the meaning of the word "work".'

Papa knew the meaning of work all right, Christine thought. It was a shame that he didn't know how to play Scrabble too.

She wandered back into the kitchen now. 'Is Papa going to be late tonight?'

'. . . So I said to her, "*Chérie,* what do you expect? I

14

am simply not free as you are, to go out for a whole day on my own pleasure; there is Grand-père to see to and then when Christine comes home – '

'Maman,' said Christine.

'Christine, you will not interrupt me when I am talking. What do you want?'

'Is Papa coming home late?'

'No. Why?'

'I just wondered.'

'For heaven's sake! I am trying to talk to your aunt. Go and wonder somewhere else. And lay the table while you're about it,' she called after Christine's retreating back.

Christine took another nut from the bowl and began to count out knives and forks. She broke off as she heard the garden gate creak, and rushed to the window.

'*Salut,* Bon Papa!' she called, waving frantically.

He stopped and waved his stick in greeting before continuing his shuffling walk up the path.

Christine flung the cutlery back into the open drawer and rushed out through the kitchen, causing Tante Léonie to exclaim disapprovingly.

'Bon Papa! Guess what happened at school today? Something awful!' She hugged him with such enthusiasm that he staggered.

'*Ouf*! You knock the breath from me,' he complained. He kissed her on the top of the head. 'So – tell me.'

'Madeleine Guirac got an A for geography homework,' she gabbled, 'and I only got a B – and she copied off me, Bon Papa! She copied my work and she got higher marks than me!'

Bon Papa considered the matter gravely. 'How did she copy it, if it was homework?'

'She asked to see my book this morning because she hadn't done the work. I couldn't say no, could I?'

15

'Then you have only yourself to blame.'

'But to give her higher marks for the same work!' Christine protested. 'That's what isn't fair.'

'Life is not fair,' said Bon Papa. 'School is as good a place as any to learn that.'

Christine shrugged philosophically and squeezed his arm. Perhaps, after all, it didn't matter so much.

'Who won the boules, Bon Papa?'

'I didn't stay to the end. I was getting cold.'

'Is your chest bad again?'

'*Mais non*. But it doesn't do to sit around in the cold, just the same. What is for dinner?'

'Tante Léonie.' Christine giggled. 'Cooked in the oven, with shallots.'

Bon Papa grunted. 'Who is looking after the children?'

'I don't know. The neighbour, I suppose.'

They went into the house together.

'There you are, Papa.' Giselle barely looked up from her cooking.

Tante Léonie came over and kissed him briefly on either cheek. 'Papa. You look well.'

'And you. You are deserting your husband again? We see you here more often these days.'

Tante Léonie flushed slightly. '*Au contraire*. He deserts me. May I have a drink with you?'

'Help yourself. I'll have a small Ricard.'

'I'll have a large one,' said Maman. 'Christine, make yourself useful, *mon lapin,* and pour the drinks.'

As she went into the dining-room, the open drawer of the buffet reminded her that she had not yet laid the table, and she took out the cutlery again. Spoons for soup, knives and forks for the main course, one set extra for Tante Léonie, and another chair to be brought to the table. Maman had replenished the fruit bowl, but with yellow apples. Christine liked green apples, hard and

16

juicy. Papa liked the yellow ones. They were easier to peel, he said.

Just as she was thinking of Papa, she heard his car draw up outside, and moved to the window to watch him get out. He locked the car door and tested the handle with his usual deliberation, then checked the tyres, the oil and the water. It was a nightly ritual. If he returned late at night, he would carry out the routine by torchlight.

Christine did not rush out to meet him, as she had Bon Papa, but stood by the window and waved when he looked up. He raised his hand perfunctorily, and glanced round as if embarrassed by the gesture. He was safe, however, Madame Rouvieux had deserted her watchpost in favour of a lonely supper, and the greeting passed unnoticed.

He looked tired, Christine thought, and preoccupied. There was a crease between his eyebrows that meant he would not like to be disturbed tonight. He would eat his supper, and then they would all wait for him to announce whether he would take possession of the dining-room, to work – or the salon, to relax.

If it was the salon, he would lie back in his deep armchair, his eyes closed and the furrow deepening in his brow, while his fingers tapped in time to nothing.

They would turn on the wireless or chat amongst themselves, glancing at him from time to time, and Christine would go to bed at the same time as Bon Papa, so that Papa was only disturbed once to say goodnight.

Sometimes, lying in her bed, Christine would hear Maman and Papa talking downstairs. Occasionally there would be laughter, but more often nowadays there were bursts of angry shouting interspersed with lulls of talk in softer voices, becoming almost inaudible. If, when the voices were raised, she heard her own name, Christine would creep out of bed and sit on the stairs, hugging herself to keep warm, and strain to make out the words.

Here again, she felt poised between two worlds. Above her she could hear the intermittent coughing and snoring of Bon Papa, whose private world of memories could shut out all arguments and atmospheres and excluded even Christine at times; below her were Papa and Maman in their own little when-Christine-is-in-bed world, a world of sudden rows and reconciliations, of honeyed sarcasms and violent embraces. Then the Christine on the stairs would feel as the Christine walking home from school did, belonging to neither one world nor the other but divided between the two.

'Where are the drinks, Christine?'

With a start, she realized that she had been day-dreaming. The drinks were not poured and the table was not laid, and Papa was home early for once and would want his supper.

'I'm just coming.' What had they wanted? She could not remember. Brandy for Bon Papa and Ricard for Maman? Or for Tante Léonie? Ricard for somebody anyway. She poured a small glassful and left it on the buffet.

'Maman' – she interrupted the kitchen conversation – 'was the Ricard for you?'

They turned to look at her. 'Say "*Bonsoir*" to Papa,' Maman chided her.

'*Bonsoir*, Papa.'

'Are you all having drinks?' he interrupted. 'Have we time, Giselle? The meal is not ready?'

'*Mais si*,' she said. 'It is ready. If Christine had fetched the drinks when we had asked for them . . . Will you join us in a drink, or shall we eat?'

'We will eat now,' he decided. 'All right with you, Papa?'

18

Grand-père spread his hands. 'It's all the same to me.'

Maman opened the oven and a cloud of delicious steam gushed forth, redolent with herbs and garlic. Christine sniffed appreciatively.

'Christine, go and wash your hands, *mon chou*.'

'I haven't finished laying the table.'

'Then go and finish it! *Nom de Dieu* – what have you been doing all this time?'

Christine returned to the dining-room and wondered what to do with the Ricard she had poured. On the one hand, Papa would be annoyed to see it left there, going to waste. 'Why didn't you say you had already poured it?' he would demand. On the other hand, if she tried to tip it back into the bottle she would surely spill some on the polished surface of the buffet, and that would upset Maman. She opened the cupboard door and pushed the glass right to the back, behind the bottles. She would give it to someone tomorrow.

She now had everything: pepper, salt, two kinds of mustard, wine, water jug, glasses, bread knife.

'*Tout le monde à table!*' cried Maman, bearing the tureen of soup before her in a way that reminded Christine of the three wise men bearing precious gifts.

'Gold, frankincense and myrrh,' said Christine softly.

'Have you washed your hands, Christine?

'I'm just going.'

When she returned they were all seated, their eyes fixed expectantly upon Maman. Maman held them all by the apron strings, playing on the family stomach with ingenious nuances of herb and spice. At supper time, by tacit consent, it was Maman who played the leading role, eating quickly, talking constantly, tearing at a piece of bread with long, nervous fingers, jumping up to fetch a dish, to replenish an emptying plate.

'Jean-Luc, Papa, a little more salad.' It was a command

19

rather than a question, the glistening lettuce scooped on to the plates as she spoke. 'Don't eat all your bread, Christine, keep it to wipe up the juice on your plate. Too much bread is bad for the figure. Léonie, a most extraordinary thing, I must tell you who I met today, of all people . . .'

The soup bowls were whisked away and Christine rose to help Maman bring in the next course.

Bon Papa picked at his food mechanically, growling at the unsolicited extra helpings, spearing each morsel with resigned deliberation. Papa tackled the meal with measured efficiency, as he would have a business contract. Food was a serious affair, not to be disturbed by unnecessary chatter. When he wanted to interrupt Maman's flow of conversation he would carefully prop his knife and fork against the edge of the plate, wipe his moustache, and then, with premeditated vehemence, he would expostulate: 'But you are ridiculous, Giselle! What are you saying? You are not logical in your arguments.'

When Tante Léonie came to dinner, as she often did when Oncle Pierre was working late and the neighbour could be prevailed upon to babysit, Maman had an ally against Papa's interruptions. Tonight Maman was in full spate.

'Truly, a face from the past. An old neighbour from our childhood days, who moved to Rennes – you know who I mean, Papa?'

Grand-père looked up, hearing his name. '*Hein*? *Non, non, je sais pas.*'

'Madame Dubarry!' Maman announced triumphantly. 'You remember Madame Dubarry, Léonie, who lived down the road in the Guillaumes' house? She's back to visit her sister, it appears. I wouldn't have recognized her; she has aged terribly. She knew me at once though, said I hadn't changed a bit – just imagine, in all these years! And such delight when she recognized me! Jean-Luc, you will have heard me mention Madame Dubarry – *non*? – we used to laugh at her, but she was kind to us really. She never had children of her own and . . .'

'Well, go on,' Papa interrupted irritably, 'continue the story of your meeting; we are all agog.' He took up his fork again and with deadly accuracy speared a morsel of meat which he chewed with deep concentration.

'Well, she didn't seem to have heard much of us since she left Paris; she had heard of Maman's death it seemed, and she enquired after Sophie. Imagine how awkward for me! I tried to turn the subject, and she was content to talk about Maman for a while – what a marvellous woman she was and so on . . .' Bon Papa looked up briefly '. . . but then she came back to the subject of Sophie – her "dear Sophie". She had heard she had gone to England – "to study, *n'est-ce pas*?" – and how was she, had she returned, and so on. I said as little as possible, but of course I couldn't pretend there had not been some kind of scandal. Sophie was always Madame Dubarry's favourite. Poor old woman, she must be a bit gaga; she didn't seem to understand, kept saying her "*pauvre petite* Sophie" couldn't have done anything wrong, and she did so hope her life was a happy one – '

'Maman,' said Christine. 'What scandal was there? What did Tante Sophie do?'

Grand-père crashed his fist down on the table. 'Giselle! I will not have such things discussed in front of the child. Keep your talk of scandals for a more suitable time.'

Christine wondered when was a suitable time for scandals. It was unusual, she reflected, for Bon Papa to get angry. She could remember only one other occasion when it had happened. It had been when Papa was away in Amsterdam for a conference, and Maman had seemed

21

more carefree somehow, gayer, with an air of reckless-ness. She had taken Christine to the zoo with Henri Trichard, the photographer, who was also the father of Marie-Louise, one of Christine's friends at school. Sometimes he had come to collect Marie-Louise when she had been playing at Christine's house and once or twice Christine and Maman had encountered him by chance in the park, when Maman had decided that Christine needed fresh air and had taken her for a walk. And of course, he had taken that photograph of them.

He was nicer out of the studio, Christine decided. At the zoo he had paid for them all to go in, and had bought ice-creams for Christine and a Martini for Maman in the little café. He had even bought nuts for the bad-tempered-looking gorilla whose name, he had said, was Jean-Luc.

'That's Papa's name!' Christine had exclaimed, and Henri Trichard had laughed uproariously. Maman had laughed a lot too, that day, and Christine had laughed in sympathy, though without understanding the jokes. And Henri had teased Christine, and dared her to ride on the camel, and she had had three rides, one after the other, without getting down. Drunk with elation and fear, she had – on the third ride – risked taking one hand off the moulting hump to wave at Maman and Henri, but they had not seen her. They were standing close together and Henri had his arm round Maman's shoulders and Chri-stine had thought it was a pity Papa never did that, because they looked nice smiling at each other like that.

Then there had been the bears, and the snake house, and another ride, on an elephant this time, and a few sleepy lions, and a succession of unknown animals with strange names, and then much later, when it was getting dark, the three of them had walked through the streets and wandered from café to café, and Christine had almost fallen asleep while Maman and Henri sipped their final Martinis and talked in muted voices. They had driven home, and Christine was dropped off at the gate and let herself in at the back door, very quietly so that she would not wake Bon Papa.

But Bon Papa had been awake, and had appeared at the top of the stairs in his dressing-gown.

'Do you know what time it is, Christine?'

'It's late, I think.'

'Where have you been all this time?'

She had flung her arms round him, partly in ecstasy and partly for support. 'We went to the zoo, and I rode on a camel and Henri bought me ice-creams, and – '

Grand-père pushed her away from him roughly and held her at arm's length. 'Who is Henri? Henri who?'

'Monsieur Trichard. He's – '

'Where is your mother? Why didn't she bring you home?'

'She did – they're in the car outside. She'll be in in a moment.'

As she spoke, they heard the engine start up and the car drive off.

'There! She's coming in now.'

But Maman had not come in, not until much later. Christine had been asleep and was awakened by the sound of an angry voice which at first she had not recognized: she had never heard Grand-père shout like that before. She had put on the light to see the time. It was five o'clock in the morning. She had fallen asleep again soon afterwards; but some of Bon Papa's words had stayed in her mind: 'Remember what happened to Sophie. These things do not go unpunished. You are playing with fire, my girl.'

The next day Giselle had said, 'You will not tell Pápa about yesterday, Christine. He doesn't approve of zoos.'

'Christine! Tante Léonie has asked you three times to pass her the salt.'

Christine started. 'I'm sorry.'

'It amazes me,' said Jean-Luc, 'how anyone can spend so much time day-dreaming. What do you find to think about?'

Christine looked at her plate. 'I just think,' she said.

'Other people,' said Giselle, 'manage to think and eat at the same time. Eat.'

Christine ate.

2

People said of Giselle and Léonie that it was good to see two sisters who got on so well. It was only the naïve or the malicious who remarked, 'But surely there were three sisters, weren't there?

Christine sat looking at the old brown photo in Bon Papa's room, at the three little girls wearing stiffly starched frocks and smiles to match. When she was little, Christine had asked who they were. One was Maman, she had been told, and one was Tante Léonie, and the middle one was Tante Sophie, who lived in England.

'Is Tante Sophie dead?' Christine asked. She swung her legs against the old iron bedstead and watched Bon Papa as he shaved, his shaky hand carefully scraping the foam from his chin. His hand jerked upwards and a thin red crack appeared in the suds. He swore under his breath.

'No, she is not dead. Why do you ask?'

'Why doesn't she come to see us?'

'She lives in England.'

'So?'

'It's a long way. Do you expect all the English to pop over for an apéritif before dinner?'

'Is Maman Tante Sophie's sister?'

Bon Papa shook the razor and began the delicate manoeuvre round the left edge of his moustache.

'Mm-hm.'

'Why doesn't Maman write to her?'

'You don't know that she doesn't.'

'*Mais si.* Maman doesn't write letters.'

'Your Maman has no time. Are you ready for school?'

'Yes. We're a bit late, I think, Bon Papa.'

'All right. I'll have breakfast when I get back.'

At the age of eleven, there was really no need for Christine to be escorted to school, and waiting for Bon Papa often made her late. Christine had pointed this out to Giselle, but she said, 'Let him walk you to school, *chérie*. It makes him feel useful, and old people need to feel useful.'

Christine accepted that, but stern-faced Mademoiselle Dubois who took the late list did not accept it. Every inch of the way to school, the uncompromising voice of Mademoiselle Dubois would echo in Christine's ears: 'Late again, Christine Rochaud. If it happens once more I shall speak to your parents.' It was not that the reprimand mattered to her parents – Maman did not even think it important enough to tell Papa – but it mattered to Christine. The fear of being late niggled in her mind like a maggot in an apple, eating its way into her pleasure in the early morning streets.

The first sound that assailed their ears as they came out of the front gate, the young girl arm-in-arm with the old man, was that of Madame Rouvieux's wireless, tuned loudly to penetrate her deafness. Often they would hear the old woman's voice too; while it was still too early for her to begin her street-side vigil, she addressed herself to the disembodied radio voices, chiding and arguing with them as though they were in the room with her. 'Enough music now!' Christine would hear her cry. '*Allez-y*! Time for the news!'

Down to the end of the rue Jean-Jacques Rousseau, round the corner and up the hill they went. Sometimes Christine had dreams in which she reached the end of the road, in a hurry because she was late, and then found herself back again at their own front gate. Time and

26

again she set out, counting off the landmarks: Madame Rouvieux's mimosa bush; the Guillaumes' dog which pushed its head through the gate; the house which had been made into two, with two front doors with white-on-blue number plates: 14 and 14 *bis*, and finally the plane tree on the corner. And then just as she was about to turn left, there she would be again in front of the Rochaud house with its wooden letterbox attached to the gatepost. It was as though the house was reluctant to let her go and leave it alone all day to its emptiness.

It was always a relief to Christine to turn that corner at the end of the road and prove that real life was stronger than her dreams.

The first landmark in the next street was the rusty water hydrant by the broken paving stones. In the early morning the street cleaners would come and turn on the hydrant, diverting the stream of water with twists of old rag till it flowed down the gutters and into the drains. Once, Christine had found a doll lying in the gutter, overlooked by the man with the broom, swept away in the tide, naked and drowned amid the fallen plane leaves.

Then there was the *tabac* where Bon Papa had bought the same brand of tobacco for his pipe for more years than he or the owner, old Monsieur Froissart, could remember. There was dust in every corner, and the Gauloises display in the window had been bleached by sun and neglect, till the packets were pale and wrinkled and speckled with dead flies, as if the *tabac* were issuing its own health warning.

Two, three, five metres further on was the Bar Vichy, with its Café Rombout sign and its faded menu with little pictures of the fare. 'Oeuf sur le plat' was Christine's favourite, with its perfectly symmetrical yolk-on-white, not in the least bit browned around the edges as ordinary fried eggs always were.

Inside the Bar Vichy, which even in the morning was always dark, the few breakfast-time customers stirred sugar lumps into their thick green coffee cups, leaned on the counter and crumbled croissants. The rack of hard-boiled eggs never seemed to diminish, and Christine sometimes wondered if they were ever eaten and replaced, or if perhaps they, like the Gauloises packets, were hollow and marked 'For Display' and stayed there for weeks and months and years.

The clink of coffee cups and the greetings called from the doorway of the bar were soon lost in other sounds from the waking street: dogs barking, dustbins clattering, the banging of doors.

But the early morning sights and sounds and smells were always dominated by the cars, selfishly nose-to-bumper so that no one could walk between them to cross the road. Citroën, Renault, Peugeot, red, brown and green, revved their engines, seethed and snorted, hooted and belched fumes.

The drivers of the big cars won on manoeuvres, edging the humbler vehicles out of the way, but the little Citroën Dyane, with its feeble deux chevaux engine power, won on verbal tactics, for the front-seat windows were conveniently hinged along the middle, so that the driver's elbow could push it open ready for him to shout: 'Salaud! or 'Espèce de con!' or other rush-hour insults, then withdraw rapidly, slamming the window shut before the other drivers replied. 'Designed by a Frenchman,' Bon Papa always said, 'Who else would invent such windows in a car?'

They crossed the road, squeezing between the impatient cars, paused in the middle, and arrived on the opposite kerb where the flower seller stood.

Christine always slowed down going past the newspaper kiosk with its hundred fluttering journals tacked all over the walls, inside and out. The newspaper headlines shouted disasters and scandal about politicians and English royalty, while the magazines depicted glossy smiling faces. Some of the magazine covers showed not only faces but complete bodies clad in a puzzling assortment of scanty clothes. One lady pouted ferociously, brandishing a whip, clad in nothing but knee-high boots and a black suspender belt. Christine was not surprised that she looked indignant: anyone would be angry if somebody took a photo of them looking so ridiculous and then sold it to a magazine.

Round the final corner, up the hill three more streets to Ma'mselle Dubois, her late list and her frowns. 'Christine Rochaud . . . you are late again . . .'

'We'd better hurry, Bon Papa.'

He grunted, quickened his pace and then as they started up the hill, slowed down again. His feet dragged and his breath was heavy on the dusty morning air. Feeling his weight on her arm, Christine looked up into his face.

'*Ça va pas?*'

He gasped. 'No. No, I don't feel too well, suddenly. I'll stop for a few minutes. Will it make you late?'

She hopped from one foot to the other, torn by the dual anxiety. 'Yes. Maybe. I think so.'

'You run on,' he decided. 'Will you be all right on your own?'

'What about you, Bon Papa? Can you get home?' She felt responsible for him, here on the street.

'Don't worry. I'll rest a little while and then go back. Off you go now.'

'Look – up here, a little wall. You can sit there and recover your breath, yes?' She led him to it, protective as a guide dog to a blind man.

He kissed her on both cheeks – twice, instead of his usual three times. 'Go quickly. Have a good day.'

'*Au 'voir.*' She ran, her bag flying from her outstretched hand. Halfway up the hill she paused and looked back uncertainly. He sat motionless on the wall, his shoulders hunched against the noise and bustle of the morning and she felt a sudden pang of desolation, as though it were she who sat there, waiting for the life to flow back into her veins.

She hesitated, then decided. Following the wafting aroma of hot bread she turned off into a side street, pushing her way between the gossiping groups in doorways and the bicycles perched by one pedal on the crumbling kerb. Counting out her money, feeling in her pockets for the stray *centimes,* she tipped the requisite sum on to the pâtisserie counter. '*Un croissant.*'

'You want it wrapped?'

'*Non. Merci, non. Merci bien, Madame. Au 'voir, Madame.*'

The next customer smiled at her haste. 'Hungry again? It's a long time since breakfast, *hein?*' She and the *pâtissière* laughed indulgently, with the slow richness of adults who have a whole day ahead, gloriously free from scolding, clock-watching Ma'mselles.

Christine ran again, her heart pounding in her chest. If he had gone, cutting short his rest, starting from home and the breakfast she had caused him to miss . . . As she rounded the bend, she saw him rise painfully to his feet and steady himself with one hand on the wall.

'Bon Papa!' she shouted, but her voice, breathless, came out a whisper. Instead she ran, her feet clattering on the cobbles.

She caught him by the arm as he was taking his first steps. 'A croissant,' she gasped, holding it out to him in explanation. 'You must sit and eat it. To give you strength to go home.'

He took it, and a faint warmth crept into the pallor of his skin.

'You have made yourself late for school,' he said.

She kissed him hastily, on one cheek only. 'Sit down till you've eaten it,' she begged. 'Promise'.

He nodded his assent and she fled once more up the hill. I don't care, she thought ferociously. I don't care if I am late. She would tell herself that while Mademoiselle scolded and Mademoiselle, exasperated by her indifference, would threaten to tell her parents, her form mistress, and Madame Scholbert herself . . .

But at least it was Thursday, and Thursday was half day. The displeasure of the gods had to end at midday on a Thursday, and when the bell rang for the end of school, Christine would be free as air.

However, midday finally arrived, she dawdled for a few minutes in the playground, waiting for Marie-Louise, for Maman would not be at home this afternoon. 'Don't come home,' she had told Christine, 'because no one will be in and I don't want you in the house by yourself. If you can't spend the afternoon at the house of one of your friends, go to your Tante Léonie's.' An afternoon at Tante Léonie's was something to be avoided; it was imperative that Christine should spend the afternoon at Marie-Louise's house.

Marie-Louise had golden hair and had stayed behind to comb it in front of the cloakroom mirror. Now she emerged, calm and satisfied, from the school door.

'Maman says I can wear nail-varnish at weekends from now on,' she announced to Christine.

'What for?' Christine asked. She linked her arm through her friend's and they passed through the school gates, bidding a brief *au revoir* to the surly concierge.

Marie-Louise looked at Christine with contempt. 'Because I'm nearly grown-up,' she said. 'That's what for.'

'Maman is out this afternoon,' said Christine, 'so I'm not going home.'

'My papa is out too,' said Marie-Louise. 'I was going to go to his studio but now I can't.'

Christine was glad of that. The photography studio in the centre of Paris was a holy of holies wherein only Marie-Louise was permitted to tread. Many a time Christine had waited outside, her nose pressed to the window, while Marie-Louise was feted inside as the daughter of *le patron*. A huge colour photograph of Marie-Louise stood in the shop window, and there were a few girls in her class who had not been taken to see it. When Marie-Louise organized one of these pilgrimages to the studios, Christine somehow did not feel that she liked Marie-Louise as much as usual.

'I'll come home with you then,' she said now. 'Or we could go swimming if you like.'

'No' said Marie-Louise, 'I'm going to my sister's. You can't come too, this time, because we're going out shopping.'

Christine felt betrayed. 'Couldn't you go shopping another time?'

'She's buying me a new dress,' said Marie-Louise simply. 'You can get the bus with me if you want, though.'

'*Merci*,' Christine refused, hurt. 'I'll walk. See you tomorrow.'

'*A demain.*' Marie-Louise waved airily. Christine hoped she would have to wait a long time for her bus.

Christine walked faster than usual, striding purposefully as though for her too the afternoon held promised delights. She was halfway home when she remembered that she was not meant to be going home. She could have asked Bon Papa to forgo his visit to the park and stay at

32

home with her, she realized now; or she could have redoubled her protests to Maman that she was old enough to stay in the house alone.

Still, there was nothing much to do there, after all. She could of course go down and join Bon Papa in the park, but that would mean sitting still all afternoon and, freed from her classroom bench, she felt restless. An afternoon with Tante Léonie and her children held even less appeal. Too young to be exempt from Tante Léonie's scoldings and too old to qualify for the ice-creams and bonbons she bought her own children, Christine found her role on these occasions became one of nursemaid.

'Take the children to the park, Christine,' Tante Léonie would say, 'while I just go round the shops.' And for hours, it seemed, Christine would try to keep them together and happily occupied, while Fabienne was invariably cheeky and ran away and little René screamed for his maman.

On impulse, she decided to spend the afternoon out on her own. She would take the usual bus but, instead of getting off at Tante Léonie's, would go on into the centre of Paris. I'll be a tourist, she thought happily. Bon Papa always said that the tourists saw all the finest sights in Paris, 'while we who live here go round with our eyes tightly shut'. This afternoon she would see Paris alone and with her eyes open.

When she was small, Papa had taken her to see the Eiffel Tower – as an excursion and just in passing. They had not gone up the tower. 'It's ridiculously expensive,' Papa had said, 'and besides you'd probably be sick.' So instead they had walked up and down the long avenues, had stopped to watch the boats chugging down the Seine and had gone to a place whose name she could not remember, full of fountains and steps. It had been a golden day. She remembered walking back, her legs aching, but hand in hand with Papa, trying to stride as he did, delirious with the adventure of it all.

Maman had not been happy, though. 'Are you mad?' she had cried at Papa, on their return. 'The child's exhausted. Fancy dragging her all that way! Do you call yourself a father?'

The bus arrived and she chose a window seat, looking out on the passing streets, craning her neck to see down an alleyway, or into a shop window, scanning the faces of the people waiting at a crossing. Hungry for details, she absorbed everything, and was startled to be recalled by the voice of the bus driver.

'Off you get, we stop here.'

The surroundings were unfamiliar.

'Are we near the Tour Eiffel?'

'You'll have to get another bus if you want to go there. Or the Métro. St Michel is right down there.'

She had no more bus tickets in her *carnet*, and no money for the Métro. 'Is it far to walk?'

'*Oui*,' he said briefly, climbing out of the cab. 'The other end of the Quartier Latin – get yourself a streetplan.'

The Quartier Latin! But Papa's office was quite near, just over the river. He often mentioned that he had dined at midday in a restaurant in the Quartier. Without any clear intention, but with a vague, mingled sensation of loneliness and hunger, she began to walk in the direction of the river.

The church of Notre Dame, viewed from the bridge, she recognized, for they had driven past it many times, and Bon Papa sometimes used to take her there on Sundays, when they were both younger. 'Just for a change from the local church,' he said, 'and to discover that God is everywhere.'

Christine had liked the cathedral's gloomy interior lit

34

by many candles. 'A light shining in the darkness,' she quoted soulfully, and felt suitably religious in the cool, hushed building, while the agnostic traffic roared outside.

Over the second bridge, away from the Ile de la Cité, she followed the quays, scanning the shops and the street names for remembered landmarks, and just as she began to fear she was lost she arrived at the big double doors with the brass plate on the wall: Parnassier S. A. Once there, she halted, unsure of her purpose. She realized now that she had been half hoping to see Papa coming out of those doors, or in the street outside, so that she could pretend the meeting was accidental.

Now she was faced with a choice. She could go in and ask for him, weighing the possibility of his giving her some money for lunch – or even, dare she hope it, taking her out for lunch – against the certainty of his anger. Or she could simply go away, off on her lone adventure which suddenly did not seem so exciting now that she was here, a stranger in the unfamiliar centre of her home city.

She hesitated for a long time, hopping from one foot to the other. A group of businessmen, all looking exactly alike, pushed their way through the doors, chattering like rather solemn, overgrown schoolchildren released for the lunch break – but Papa was not among them.

Christine watched them go down the street. No doubt, she thought, if Papa did come out he would not be alone but with a similar group. With a sudden pang of horror she imagined his embarrassment at finding her waiting for him, shaming him in front of his colleagues, or even his *patron*. She turned and hurried away down the street, feeling that she had had a narrow escape.

Of course, Papa was a *patron* – a boss – himself now, for he had been promoted, but he in turn had a boss above him. It was all quite complicated, and Christine had only understood when Bon Papa had likened Papa's firm to Christine's own school with its hierarchy of pupils and junior, senior and head teachers. If Papa had explained it like that in the first place, Christine would have understood it straight away, but Papa could never explain things that were perfectly clear to him and would usually give up, saying, 'You'll understand when you are older; you're too young,' as if knowledge was something which came automatically with age, like bosoms.

When she was younger and had heard Maman say that Papa was working for promotion, Christine had thought that 'promotion' was the name of the company. Now she knew that it was a kind of reward for hard work, like a school prize. Papa had won one of these promotions last year, just before Christine's eleventh birthday. When he came home and told her, she was very excited, and he seemed pleased and amused by this.

'What will you get,' she had asked, 'for your prize?'

He had laughed. 'Some more money in my salary cheque,' he said. 'Not a great deal more, but some. Perhaps I'll buy you a bicycle, to celebrate. Would you like that?'

'Will they let you come home earlier now?' she asked. 'You won't have to work late now you've won it, will you?'

She remembered how the smile had faded from his face when she said that.

'*Au contraire*.' he said stiffly. 'I'll have to work harder than ever now. It's a position of great responsibility.'

Soon afterwards, he had gone away to Germany for three whole weeks, for the company. He had not mentioned the bicycle again, and Christine did not remind him.

She wandered back now the way she had come, over

the river, unconsciously following the group of business-men from Papa's firm. They stopped, eventually, in front of one of the larger restaurants on the Boulevard St Germain and settled themselves at a pavement table without even consulting the menu outside. They know they can afford anything they want, Christine thought enviously; anything at all.

She turned out the contents of her own pocket – *centimes* rather than *francs*, she saw with disappointment. With any luck, there would be enough for a hot dog from one of the little stands in the Boulevard St Michel.

Christine cast one last look over her shoulder at Papa's colleagues. I wonder what they would do, she thought, if one of their daughters turned up? And then she made her way down the *boulevard*.

What a good thing she had not seen Papa, after all! She could imagine, now, not only his all-too-probable embarrassment at seeing her there, but also the scene that would erupt later at home.

'What are you doing, Giselle, to allow the child to wander round Paris on her own?' he would demand of his wife, and Maman would retaliate: 'You dare criticize me as a mother? When you take no interest whatsoever in the child and leave all the work of bringing her up to me!'

When they talked like that, it always seemed to Christine that they must be talking about someone else, a strange, inanimate 'child', and not about the Christine standing there right in front of them.

The food stalls in the Boulevard St Michel were tempting: hot dogs and *croque monsieur*, rolls and crêpes with all kinds of fillings: shrimps, jam, cheese, chestnut purée – anything you could want, if only you had the money. Or there were *gaufres*, deliciously fried on the waffle grid, dipped in sugar or drenched with golden syrup. Or a variety of *beignets*: crisp batter-coated morsels served hot in a napkin. Christine liked the cauliflower beignets best. But everything cost so much! Even the ice-creams were expensive, because of the tourists, and boring vanilla flavour cost almost as much as the more exotic mocha, praline or raspberry sorbet.

'How much is a hot dog?'

'Two *francs*.'

She counted out the *centimes*. 'I've only got one *franc* eighty.' The vendor shrugged and turned to his next customer, a fat man in tartan trousers, a short-sleeved shirt and a camera. Christine stared at him fascinated. A real live tourist, looking just as a tourist should.

The man caught her eye, grinned, and said something in American to the vendor, who grunted and slid a hot dog across the counter to Christine. She hesitated.

'I haven't got two *francs*,' she said.

'*C'est l'Americain qui paie.*' He added something under his breath that sounded hardly complimentary to the American.

Christine looked up and saw the American smiling at her. She picked up the hot dog, gingerly, as if it were stolen property.

'*Merci beaucoup*, Monsieur,' she muttered, scarlet with embarrassment, and fled towards the park.

The Jardin du Luxembourg was full of children sailing boats on the pond and students sitting in groups under the trees, discussing serious things and munching hot dogs and ice-creams which they had paid for themselves.

She could imagine what Maman would say if she knew Christine had taken money from a stranger. Her guilt quite spoiled the hot dog; it tasted dry and sawdusty and she threw away the last frankfurterless mouthful of crusty bread.

Groups of students were gathering round the bandstand

in the park, obviously suspecting that the three men plucking disharmoniously at their guitars were about to launch into something more musical. Christine drew closer.

There was an expectant hush as the men continued tuning up, and the twanging strings were accorded a respectful silence. Finally the men broke into song, strumming enthusiastically, and the crowd relaxed, began talking, laughing and arguing amongst themselves. Now the real music had begun there seemed to be no need for listening.

Christine pushed further forward to hear the music but her attention was distracted by the crowd. She stared enviously at all the chattering groups, safe in their quarrels and their companionship, and was overwhelmed by a sudden awareness of being alone and speechless in a world of rapport. Abruptly, Christine decided to go home.

With an urgency akin to panic, she elbowed her way back through the crowd of faces, and half walked, half ran to the park gates. Idiot, she chided herself furiously as she went; what use is an adventure if you run home to Maman? But, adrift in an unfamiliar Paris, it was Maman and home she wanted.

Standing at the bus stop, she fought back the urge to burst into tears. What a baby! scolded the sensible Christine, while the babyish Christine bit her lip and glared fiercely at a passing motorist; anyone would think you were a two-year-old, instead of eleven.

When the bus came, she paid her fare quickly and went to the back, hoping that the driver would not notice if she went further than the destination she had asked for. It was a good thing, after all, that she had accepted the American's hot dog, otherwise she would not have been able to take the bus at all.

The journey seemed long, the bus hot and stuffy, and the streets were grey and dreary. A sense of lassitude came over Christine. She might just as well have gone to Tante Léonie's after all, she thought. How pointless it was to trail round the city alone, in the hope of finding adventure or meeting Papa; the one event was as unlikely as the other: both were doomed to failure.

The bus drew up outside the school and Christine hopped off hastily, before the driver could comment on her budget-price ride. She cast a quick glance at the school gates and wondered what the time was; it did not seem so very long, now that she was back, since she had walked out of those gates.

'*Pardon*, Madame, have you got the time?' she asked an old woman with a shopping basket.

'Quarter to three,' said the woman briefly and hurried on without looking at her.

A quarter to three! She could not go home so early, or Maman would know she had not been to Tante Léonie's. But suppose Maman was home by now, from wherever she had been? Christine could always say she had been to a friend's house and come away early – couldn't she? She began to walk towards home, slowly at first, then quickening her pace.

As she turned the corner into their road, Christine saw a car parked right outside their gate, an opulent-looking beige sports car. As she came nearer, Madame Rouvieux appeared miraculously at her gate.

'*Bonjour*, Christine; you are home early. Are you well?'

'Yes thank you, Madame. It's Thursday – half day.'

The old woman frowned. 'But you are expected home, yes? You don't usually come home at this hour.'

'I went to a friend's house,' Christine lied, 'but she had to go out shopping with her sister so I came home early.'

She hated herself for lying to Madame Rouvieux. Added to the fact that she had not paid for her hot dog and had cheated on her bus fare, it had undoubtedly been a bad day for the soul of Christine Rochaud.

'I see.' Madame Rouvieux still looked worried. 'Listen, *ma chérie* – why don't you come in? I have no gâteau today, but we could play draughts . . . what do you say, *hein*?'

'It's very kind of you, Madame,' said Christine politely, 'but I think I'll see if Maman is in. I'm a bit tired today.'

'Wait,' said Madame Rouvieux. 'Your Maman is not in. I saw her go out and she has not come back. Your grand-père is also out.'

'Oh.' Once again, Christine felt on the verge of tears. I must go home, she thought almost desperately. She really wanted to be at home. She knew she was being silly, but the desire to be in their own kitchen, with the old house ticking and creaking comfortingly around her, had become overwhelming. She did not feel like spending a couple of hours over a slow game of draughts with Madame Rouvieux.

As the day was a write-off anyway, morally speaking, she perjured herself once again. 'But I have a key,' she said. 'I can let myself in, even if there's no one there.'

'*Mais non, non, non!*' Madame Rouvieux protested, throwing up her hands. 'You cannot be alone in the house. Your Maman would be very angry. I insist that you come to me, I insist! Come now, no more argument.'

Christine felt trapped. Searching round for some way out of the dilemma without being rude, her eyes fell once more on the car.

'Look at that car,' she said, staring at it with assumed interest. 'Fancy parking it right in front of our house like that. Do you know whose it is?'

A strange look, almost of fear, came into Madame

Rouvieux's eyes. 'No,' she said. 'No, I don't know,' she looked away.

'It had better not still be there when Papa comes home,' Christine said.

'No,' said Madame Rouvieux. 'No.' She stared fixedly at Christine, as though searching her soul. Christine felt uncomfortable. Remembering her motive for introducing the subject of the car, she made good her escape while Madame Rouvieux seemed so transfixed.

'*Au 'voir, Madame; à demain.*' She was halfway across the road before the old woman answered.

'*Au revoir, chérie.*' There were no more protestations that she should stay.

To Christine's surprise, she found that the back door was open. So there was someone in, after all! A great tide of relief flowed over her. She was home safe and secure; the clock ticked and the kitchen smelt of warmth and food, and Bon Papa's shoes stood ready for cleaning by the stove.

'Maman!' she called, 'Are you there, Maman?'

There were noises of footsteps upstairs and Maman appeared at the top of the stairs, her face flushed as though she had been overdoing the housework again. 'You take everything too fast, Giselle,' Papa always complained. 'There's no need to attack the place like that.' Maman in the midst of a cleaning blitz was a force to be feared.

'What are you doing home at this hour?' Maman snapped.

Some of Christine 's relief at being home evaporated. 'I left Marie-Louise's early.'

Maman came slowly down the stairs. 'You went to Marie-Louise's house?'

Christine fidgeted and nodded her head in what she hoped was neither a yes nor a no.

'Was her mother there?'

'No – I don't know, I mean, I went to her sister's house, not Marie-Louise's own house.'

'I see.' Maman stood there and looked through her. 'Why are you home so early? I told you I wouldn't be in.'

'But you are,' Christine pointed out.

Maman seized her by the shoulders and shook her so that her teeth chattered together. 'You are a rude, disobedient little girl,' she hissed. 'Why don't you do what you are told? Why didn't you go to your Tante Léonie's?'

Christine laughed. Afterwards, she could not have said why she laughed; certainly she was not amused. The nearest she came to explain it was that it was something to do with having felt lost and wanting to come home and then Maman suddenly shaking her and saying those words.

It was not what she had expected, and it was not . . . not quite right, Christine thought. The words were not right. Would Maman, for all her scolding, normally have said – or hissed like that, between her teeth – 'You are a rude, disobedient little girl'? Would she have stared at Christine like that, with her eyes popping and her face red?

She felt suddenly and inexplicably frightened. Her adventure had not been an adventure, Maman was not Maman, and now home did not seem like home either; there was an unnatural, hushed atmosphere. Even the clock seemed to be ticking uneasily, at an uneven pace.

When Christine laughed, Maman slapped her face, and Christine burst into tears. Maman caught her by the elbow and led her to the foot of the stairs.

'Go up to your room,' she shouted up the stairs, as though Christine were already up there, 'and don't come down until I tell you.'

'I'm not a baby!' Christine protested tearfully.

'Well, don't behave like one,' said Maman more calmly. 'Go on – do as you're told for once.'

Christine climbed the stairs, rigid with protest at the injustice of it all. Slamming her bedroom door as hard as she dared, she lay down on the bed and stared at the ceiling. What a day, she reflected; what a wasted, miserable day. She heard Maman going downstairs – or was it upstairs? Christine listened. No, the footsteps, rather slow and heavy, were going down.

Outside in the street a car started up and drove off noisily. Christine hoped it was the car that had been outside their gate; Papa would have been angry if he had come home and found someone in his parking place. Not that Papa would be home for hours yet – nor Bon Papa either.

She sat up. Whatever would Bon Papa say if he could see her now, lounging about, feeling sorry for herself?

'Tired?' he would say. 'Sore feet? Time enough for these ailments when you're a hundred; don't start grumbling when you're eleven, or you'll have another eighty-odd years of it.'

Christine kicked off her shoes and slid her feet into another pair, battered and comfortable. Forgetting Maman's instructions to stay in her room, she clattered downstairs and into the kitchen, where Maman was pulling faces in the mirror over the sink as she plucked the little hairs from her eyebrows, squinting with concentration.

'I'm going down to the park,' Christine said as she sped through, 'to meet Bon Papa.'

Giselle turned in time to see Christine's feet disappearing out of the door. 'Christine, those shoes . . .!' But Christine had gone. 'Oh, *putain*!' Giselle shrugged, and turned back to the mirror. She had worse things to worry about, and Grand-père, after all, would not notice even if the child turned up barefoot.

3

He was sitting as he always sat, on a bench in the tree-lined avenue, leaning slightly forwards with both hands resting on the handle of his walking stick. From there he had an uninterrupted view of the boules pitch, though Christine could never be sure whether he actually watched the game – which did not rate very highly as a spectator sport, certainly, consisting as it did of leisurely discussions of tactics, amicable arguments and slow, shared cigarettes – or whether his vague, watery eyes were focused on some far distant memory, beside which the present-day public garden paled into unreality.

As always, it gave her that odd tugging feeling in her heart to see him sitting there, motionless and alone. She hurried towards him, guilty at being the unseen observer of his loneliness.

'Bon Papa!' she called, when she was within earshot, and his head turned slowly, as if she had awakened him from a dream. Christine did not run today. She felt tired as she had never been tired before, with an aching weariness.

The old man waited patiently, his eyes never leaving her face.

'You are early,' he said. 'Ah – Thursday.'

'Yes,' she said, and kissed him. 'A good game?'

'They are waiting for Jacquot to return,' said Bon Papa, indicating the lounging group of men puffing lazy smoke rings into the misty air. 'He has gone to the *commissariat*.'

'Is Jacquot in trouble?'

'*Mais non* – he has gone to see his brother, the policeman.'

'Oh yes, of course.' Christine had forgotten about Jacquot's brother.

'Do you want to go home straight away or shall we stay a while longer?' Christine asked.

'As you want.'

'Not yet then,' she said. 'As long as you're not cold.' She settled herself beside him on the bench, and he took her hand in his. Christine felt that she was too old to hold her grand-père's hand in public but she had not the heart to tell him so. After all, there was no one there to see, except the boules players.

'*Salut, la petite*!' One of the men waved at her, and she waved back at the whole group as they turned slowly round to witness this new diversion.

'*Ça va*?' they chorused, and she called back, '*Ça va*!'

Their voices ranged from the young to the very old and gruff. Jacquot, strolling towards them, back from a hectic afternoon of socializing at the *commissariat,* laid a rival claim to their attention, and the group about-turned in regimental slow motion to receive the prodigal.

'What do they do all day?' Christine wondered. 'Apart from playing boules?'

'They recover from the effort of playing boules,' said Bon Papa, 'or they gather their forces for another game. It is a vocation.'

Christine giggled. 'Why don't they work? And how do they have any money?'

'They have no time to work,' Bon Papa replied solemnly, 'and no need. Men who are not interested in the making of money are rarely interested in the spending of it. The bare necessities suffice; besides, the nation owes it to itself to support such dedicated passers of time. They

46

remind us that time is something not to be devoured but to be savoured gently, like a good wine.'

On the road beyond the park gates, cars hooted their resentment of the crawling traffic jam.

'Not like them,' said Christine, nodding her head towards the noise. 'They are devouring time, *n'est-ce pas*? Because they want to be home as soon as possible, they're all stopping each other from getting there.'

Grand-père turned his head to look at her. 'Were you late for school this morning?'

'A bit,' she admitted.

'The Mademoiselle told you off?'

Christine shrugged. 'It doesn't matter.'

'If it would help,' he suggested, 'Giselle could telephone and explain it was my fault.'

'It wasn't your fault!' Christine was indignant. 'Mademoiselle Dubois doesn't worry me, anyway,' she lied. 'She always lets Marie-Louise off if she's late, did you know? I don't mind her being nasty – Mam'selle Dubois – but she should be equally nasty to everyone, don't you think?'

'Why does she let Marie-Louise off?' Bon Papa asked.

'I don't know. Véronique says it's because her father is on the school committee.'

'That man!' Bon Papa snorted.

There was a short silence.

'Maman likes him,' Christine said.

Bon Papa looked sharply at her. 'Why do you say that?'

'It's obvious. Why don't you or Papa like him?'

'It does not concern you,' said Bon Papa shortly.

Christine was too used to Bon Papa to be put off by his brusquerie. '*Mais si,*' she argued. 'Your opinion is as good as Maman's, isn't it? So why should I know one and not the other?'

The corners of his mouth softened. 'You have an answer to everything,' he grumbled.

'Answer my answer to everything then,' she cajoled. 'Why don't you like Monsieur Trichard?'

'He is no better than those men there,' said Bon Papa, looking at the boules players, and his mouth was hard again. 'Only he is not honest enough to let the world see his shirking.'

Christine frowned. 'But Monsieur Trichard doesn't play boules instead of working.'

'He would do better to do so,' Bon Papa said, almost inaudibly, and his stick stamped a relentless bruise on the gravelled path.

Christine was still trying to unravel the riddle. It did not do to ask direct questions, for she knew from experience that to reveal one's incomprehension to an adult had the effect of reminding them of one's childishness, and the source of information would dry up abruptly.

'Papa says Monsieur Trichard doesn't know the meaning of the word "work",' she hazarded.

'Monsieur Trichard,' said Grand-père sternly, 'does not know the meaning of a great many things.'

'What sort of things?' Christine coaxed, but she had gone too far now.

'It is time to go home,' Bon Papa decided, struggling to his feet. 'The mist is rising.'

Sure enough, the mist was curling, stealthy as sleep, round the base of the furthest trees. The air gritted its teeth and nipped Christine's ears with sly malice.

'Yes, she said, 'let's go.'

The last of the boules players were disappearing beyond the park gates. The day was over, with nothing left to do but to go home and pass the hours till bedtime.

Christine hooked her arm through Grand-père's and for once it seemed that he was supporting her. Her legs were heavy as lead, as heavy as her sore eyelids and her aching stomach.

'I'm not well,' she told Bon Papa.

'How, not well?' He looked at her.

'I don't know,' she said listlessly. 'I ache everywhere.'

'It is your age,' he said, and they walked on. Christine did not see why it should be her age. One did not expect to be particulary unhealthy at the age of nearly twelve. At Bon Papa's age, perhaps. But she said nothing.

Madame Rouvieux was in her small front garden, raking up the fallen leaves.

'Go past quietly,' Bon Papa said. 'She may not see us. It is too cold to stand around talking.'

Christine felt guilty about having evaded Madame Rouvieux earlier. 'You go in,' she said, 'and I'll just talk to her for a few minutes. I've dodged her once today already.'

'All right,' he agreed. 'I'll tell Maman where you are.'

Christine waited till Grand-père had made his slow getaway.

'*Bonsoir,* Madame,' she called.

'Christine! *Quelle belle surprise!*' Madame Rouvieux made it sound as though she had not seen Christine for months, instead of just an hour or two ago. Then she seemed to remember and gave Christine the same searching look again.

'All right, earlier? You found no one at home this afternoon?'

'*Si,*' said Christine. 'Maman was in.'

'Ah.' The old woman hesitated. 'Just Maman?'

'Bon Papa was down at the park,' Christine explained.

Again Madame Rouvieux stared at Christine. Usually she pressed Christine to come in, to have gâteaux, to do the crossword. Today she seemed to have nothing to say.

Everything about today was odd, Christine thought. She stared back at the old woman, in silence.

'In my day,' said Madame Rouvieux, shaking her head with sad solemnity, 'the innocence of children was regarded as something precious – sacred, even.' She sighed heavily. 'Innocence is a great gift, Christine.' Christine continued to gaze at her. 'But then,' the old woman reasoned, 'loyalty is also a great virtue. You are a good child.' With that she turned and hobbled back to her house. Christine watched her, her hand half raised to wave goodbye, but Madame Rouvieux did not turn back. The door closed behind her.

Christine shook her head. 'Senile,' she said sorrowfully, and went home.

The back door was ajar, and Bon Papa's shoes were in the doorway. Christine stepped over them and leaned against the wall of the little porch to take off her own shoes.

The voices of Maman and Bon Papa reached her from the kitchen and she listened while tugging at her shoelace.

'Where are you going tonight?'

'Just out with the Bénauds; probably to a little *boîte* somewhere. I shan't need to eat before I go, and Christine will have had a school lunch . . .'

'Not on a Thursday,' Bon Papa reminded her.

'Well, lunch with Léonie then. So I'll leave you to make yourselves an omelette – all right? Jean-Luc can help himself to a sandwich when he comes home.'

'Jean-Luc is not going with you?'

Giselle gave a short laugh. 'I have given up asking him. Monsieur is too occupied with his so-important career. Where would Parnassier S.A. be if Jean-Luc Rochaud took his wife out for an evening? I tell you, if I didn't know him better, I'd suspect him of having another woman, with all these late nights.'

'Giselle, you go too far!' Bon Papa's tired old voice produced a flash of anger. 'If you and Jean-Luc are not close, you should look to your own behaviour as a married woman . . .'

'My behaviour, as you put it, is a result of Jean-Luc's behaviour – not the cause of it.'

'It can hardly help the situation, *ma fille*.' The voice was stern, but weary again, as though the words were old ones, dragged out with great effort for the occasion.

'How can it make any difference, if he doesn't know?' Maman again. 'Don't I deserve some happiness, with someone? Jean-Luc is not the only one with a life to lead.'

The stone floor was cold on Christine's stockinged feet. She was about to push open the door into the kitchen when Bon Papa spoke again.

'And what about Christine? Have you thought of the effect it has on her, to have a mother who prostitutes herself?' The bitterness of the unknown word made Christine flinch. She hesitated, shifting her weight from one foot to the other and wriggling her toes to warm them.

'Don't talk to me like that!' said Giselle sharply. Her voice sounded breathless, as though she too had been shocked by Grand-père's violence. 'I am not a child to be admonished by my stern Papa.' She tried to speak lightly, 'You don't have to take responsibility for my moral welfare any longer, you know.'

'As a father, I am responsible for all my daughters, whether I wish to be or not. Though I sometimes wonder what kind òf father I have been, with Sophie and now you . . .'

'Oh, don't bring Sophie into this! You know it's not the same thing.'

'How – not the same thing? To me it seems the same.'

51

'She was unmarried!'

'And you are married! And that makes it better – *hein*? The fact that you are married to one man makes it more acceptable that you should . . .'

'Oh Papa, you know I didn't mean it like that.' Giselle sounded sullen now.

There was the sound of a chair being scraped back.

'I will tell you,' said Bon Papa with ponderous severity. 'The only difference between you and Sophie is that she had the courage to face up to her responsibilities.'

There was silence. Even from the porch, Christine could feel the atmosphere crackling. She wondered whether to go out again, perhaps back to Madame Rouvieux, but she was tired.

'Anyway,' Giselle continued, 'you can't honestly claim that it affects Christine when she knows nothing about it.'

'She's is no fool, Giselle. You cannot continue like this indefinitely. And I would not say that you had been discreet, even now.'

'Papa, even if Christine did notice something, she is far too young to understand. You talk as though she were a grown woman, instead of not yet twelve years old.'

There was another silence. Christine's feet ached with cold, but to go into the kitchen would be to face an atmosphere more glacial than any stone floor.

'And what about the school holidays?' Bon Papa continued.

'It's only October: the school term has only just begun! And by the time it ends – who can say?'

'You should think seriously about it, Giselle. You will not be able to turn the child out of doors in the Christmas holidays as you could in the summer. It is, after all, her home as well – and Jean-Luc's – and mine.'

52

Somebody dropped something and it clanged noisily on the hard kitchen floor.

'There is no need for you to go out every afternoon, you know, Papa,' Giselle said, and her voice sounded breathless again. 'I don't want you catching cold, Papa!' Her voice rose. 'At least stay and listen to me!'

Bon Papa's voice, quite faint now, said, '*Ma fille*, it has all been said before. I am too tired and too old. As you say, it is your life.'

Silence. Christine, almost fossilized with cold, shook herself into action, banged the outside door and kicked her shoes around, making a noise. 'I'm home, Maman!'

Giselle was standing by the sink, staring at her reflection in the mirror, as though she had never seen it before. She turned as Christine came in.

'*Bonsoir, chérie*,' she said meekly, almost politely.

'*Bonsoir*, Maman.' Instead of brushing her face briefly against Christine's cheek, as she usually did, Maman stooped and kissed her properly, once on each cheek and once more for luck.

'Did you have a good day at school?'

Christine did not remind Maman that she had seen her already this afternoon and that, far from concerning herself with school, Maman had said – no, hissed at her, like a snake – 'What are you doing home at this hour?'

Fearful that her eyes would betray that she had been eavesdropping, Christine turned her head away and said, 'It was all right.'

'Are you hungry, *mon chou*? I will make you a nice little *goûter – non*? There is only an omelette for supper – which is quite nourishing enough, but still . . .'

'No, I don't want anything, thank you.' Christine held out first one foot then the other in front of the stove.

'You are cold, *ma petite*?'

'Not really, just my feet.'

Giselle sighed, as if in exasperation, and the corners of her mouth tightened momentarily. 'You look a little pale,' she said, with renewed solicitude. '*Ça va pas*?'

'I'm all right. I ache though, here in my stomach – and my back. Bon Papa says it's my age.'

'Nonsense!' said Giselle. 'You're much too young!' She sounded cross again.

'Too young for what?' Christine asked, but Maman turned away.

'Go and wash your hands, Christine. I'm in enough of a hurry as it is.'

'What time are you going out?'

'Who said anything about going out?' Giselle countered, over her shoulder.

Christine hated her. 'You're always going out,' she said.

'What nonsense!' Giselle snapped.

'Always,' Christine repeated, backing out of the kitchen. 'Always, always, always,' she chanted, going up the stairs. She thumped her stockinged feet on each stair for emphasis. '*Toujours, toujours.*' She knew she was being horrible, but the achy feeling made her want to be horrible. '*TouJOURS!*' she concluded on a crescendo.

'Get out of my sight!' Giselle screamed from the foot of the stairs, though Christine was already out of sight. 'Do you hear me?'

Bon Papa emerged from his room. 'Giselle,' he said. 'Please.'

'That's right!' she shouted back to him. 'Don't tell Christine off! Pick on me! the prodigal daughter – *hein*? Worse than the wicked Sophie, *hein*? All I can say, Papa, is that you've changed your tune over the years. You've certainly changed your tune!'

But Bon Papa had retreated into his room and Christine into hers. Giselle, scornful of their cowardice, retired to

54

the bathroom and soothed her pride with scented face cream.

Christine sat on the floor and spread out her homework. There was less space in the bedroom than in the dining-room, and no table, but in her own room she was left alone, to work or to day-dream undisturbed.

'What are you doing now?' Maman would demand, if Christine took up her post at the dining-room table. 'Haven't you finished yet?'

'I'm thinking,' Christine would say, defensively. 'Just thinking.'

'Dreaming,' Maman would snort. 'It's about time you woke up, *ma fille*. You live in a little world of your own.'

Here in the small bedroom, she could inhabit her own world without interruption. Shaking a drop of ink from her pen on to the scruffy fragment of blotting paper, she prepared to start her English exercise.

Rire, she thought. She thumbed her English book to the vocabulary. 'To laugh,' it read.

'I have laughed, you have laughed, he/she/it has laughed,' Christine recited under her breath. 'We have laughed, you (plural) have laughed, they have laughed.' Maman's laughter, brittle as thin ice cracking. They have laughed – Maman and Henri at the zoo. Why did Bon Papa disapprove of him? I have laughed, you have laughed, he has laughed.

Henri Trichard always laughed. He laughed when he came to the house. Christine, upstairs, would hear him downstairs with Maman.

'Monsieur Trichard has called in on his way home from work, Christine.' Then: 'Go upstairs and get on with your homework, Christine,' or 'Go up and see if Bon Papa is all right, Christine.' Maman's tinkling laugh would have started before she was halfway up the stairs.

But at other times, Maman did not laugh. 'Why are

you home so early? I told you I wouldn't be in.' But Maman had been in.

Henri Trichard laughed when he talked to Christine. She liked his laugh, but she wondered sometimes what he was like when he was not laughing. He laughed with Marie-Louise and tickled her under the chin teasingly, when he came to meet her from school in his sleek, beige car.

Christine had seen him once, driving up rue Jean-Jacques Rousseau in that car as she was walking down it, home from school. He had not been laughing then, but scowling, his hands gripping the wheel as he swerved round a bend, as if he were in a great hurry.

Maman had not been laughing that day, either, when Christine arrived home.

'Is something wrong?' Christine had asked, looking at Maman's red-rimmed eyes and heavily powdered cheeks, and Maman had said: 'No, nothing. Go and get your homework done early for once tonight.'

There had been something funny about the atmosphere in the house that day, too, Christine remembered. Remembering that made her feel better. Today had been a strange day, but in the past there had been other strange days.

'I have laughed, you (singular) have laughed,' repeated Christine.

In his room, Bon Papa coughed and thumped his chest, and downstairs Maman shouted, 'I'm just going, Papa.' Then, more loudly, 'Papa!'

Her footsteps, heavy with impatience, on the stairs. 'Papa!'

Bon Papa's door opening. 'You called me?'

'Several times. I'm just leaving. I've got a key, so you can lock the door but remember not to put the bolt on.'

'All right.' His voice sounded flat and tired.

Christine guessed that he wanted to ask Maman what time she would be coming home, but that he was too tired for discussions and arguments, so he did not ask.

'See you in the morning.' The sound of three kisses, quick and impatient. Christine always kissed Bon Papa slowly. At his age he preferred things to be done slowly.

The door opened. 'I'm going, *chérie*. Be a good girl.' Another three kisses, so swift that the lips barely touched her cheek.

'*Au 'voir*, Maman.'

'Finish your homework, now.' And the hasty footsteps went down the stairs and the back door slammed.

The coughing started again. Christine picked up her pen and began to write out the English sentences. The coughing became convulsive, interspersed with wheezing.

She jumped to her feet and threw open her bedroom door. 'Bon Papa?'

She knocked on the door of his room and went in. He was almost doubled up with the effort of coughing, one hand holding a handkerchief to his mouth and the other supporting himself against the bureau. Beads of sweat glistened on his reddened skin. For a moment Christine held back.

'*Ça va pas*, Bon Papa?'

When he shook his head, she moved forward and took him by the elbow.

'Sit down in the chair. Shall I bring you a brandy?'

He leaned back in the chair and closed his eyes. Christine, watching him, wanted to shake him, to keep him awake, to make him talk to her and tell her everything was all right. He looked so old like that!

'Bon Papa?' she said, and her voice cracked. 'I'll get you some brandy – yes?'

He opened his eyes. 'With a little hot water,' he asked. 'Can you boil a little water?'

'Of course.'

'Be careful now,' he warned. 'Don't burn yourself, *hein*?'

'No.' She wanted to give him a kiss, but his skin was all wet. Tiny drops trickled into his beard. She hesitated, then slipped out.

As she waited for the saucepan of water to boil, she realized that she had not asked him what he meant by 'a little' water. And could she pour boiling water into the brandy glass, or should she put the brandy into a cup? Jean-Luc's arrival saved her from having to go and ask Bon Papa.

'*Bonsoir,* Papa.'

He stood in the doorway and looked at her, frowning. 'Where is Giselle?'

'She went a little while ago. Bon Papa is not well; I'm making him some – '

'Went where?' His lips were a thin, pale line in his white face.

Christine shrugged. 'Out for the evening. I don't know where.'

'How – you don't know where? You don't know where your mother is?'

Christine turned her eyes away from him. 'I think she told Bon Papa where she was going.'

He strode through the kitchen and into the dining-room. 'Papa!'

Christine followed him. 'He's upstairs. He's not very well.'

Jean-Luc grunted and she stood out of his way as he made for the stairs. She waited, hearing the brusque, questioning voice, and the pauses as Bon Papa made his replies, inaudible to Christine.

'*Nom de Dieu*!' Jean-Luc shouted, hurtling downstairs two at a time. 'Does nobody wonder about what she

58

does? Does it make no difference to you whether she is here or not?'

He landed at the foot of the stairs, almost on top of Christine, and she took a step backwards. A hissing noise made itself heard from the kitchen. 'The water!' she said.

He followed her into the kitchen. The gas was extinguished, and water trickled down the front of the stove in a cloud of steam. Christine grabbed a cloth.

'Turn the gas off, for God's sake!' said Jean-Luc and grasped the handle of the saucepan.

'It's hot . . .' Christine began.

With a bellow of pain and rage, he dropped the offending saucepan on to the floor and kicked it across the kitchen with such violence that it crashed against the opposite wall.

'*Salaud!*' he shouted. '*Salaud! Le salaud!* His face, so white before, became purple, and his eyes bulged. Christine froze, her mouth half-open and her hands squeezing the dishcloth against her chest.

'What the hell were you doing in here?' Jean-Luc shouted. When she did not answer, he continued, at the same pitch, 'Are you cooking something or what?'

'Boiling,' she said, her voice a whisper. 'Boiling some water for brandy.'

Although he was shouting at her he did not seem to be seeing her. His eyes stared opaquely.

'Who picked her up?' he said abruptly.

'What?' She could not follow him

'Who came to collect her – your mother? I'm talking about your mother.'

Why did he refer to Maman as 'your mother', Christine wondered?

'No one. She just went on her own. I think,' she said, remembering the conversation she should not have heard, 'that she was meeting the Bénauds.'

59

'Why didn't she tell me she was going out?' he demanded.

Christine was silent. He did not seem to expect her to answer.

Bon Papa came heavily down the stairs. 'Jean-Luc. What is the matter?'

'Nothing,' said Jean-Luc roughly.

'You are tired,' said Bon Papa. 'Have you eaten?' His voice was soothing. His eyes took in Christine, pressed against the side of the sink.

'Yes, I am tired,' said Jean-Luc his voice rising again. 'I am tired and hungry because I have been working all day without a break and when I come home I expect a meal and I expect my wife to be here, or at least to have left me some explanation . . .'

'I can make you an omelette, if you like,' Bon Papa said placatingly. His chest heaved with the effort of talking, and the knuckles of his wrinkled, brown-spotted hands were white as the naked bone. Christine shivered.

'No,' said Jean-Luc. 'You had better go to bed, if you are not well.'

'I'll make you something, shall I?' Christine offered. 'I haven't eaten yet either.'

'You have made enough mess for one day,' said Jean-Luc. 'I can do it quite well myself. Which is just as well as it turns out,' he added bitterly, 'because I am having plenty of practice.'

Bon Papa was already at the door, relieved to be dismissed, and Christine followed at his heels. She wondered if Jean-Luc would remember that she had said she had not eaten and would make her something too. Christine would have liked to cook supper for him. She knew how to make omelettes, if only Maman and Bon Papa ever gave her a chance to try it alone. They would help so!

60

'*Très bien fait, ma chérie* – but let me do this next bit,'
Maman would say. Or, when Maman went out in the
evenings and Bon Papa was cooking he would caution:
'Don't touch the spoon, Christine, it is hot. Don't lift the
pan, it is heavy,' till she longed to prove that she could
do it all unaided.

Still, Jean-Luc was cooking his own, and that was that.
It meant that she would have to stay out of the kitchen
till he had finished rummaging for things and crashing the
pans about and spilling things and swearing. If he did not
remember – or was in too bad a mood – to cook something
for Christine too, it would be a long time before she
would eat. And it seemed a very long time since that
half-eaten hot dog in the Jardin du Luxembourg that
afternoon.

'Good night, Bon Papa,' she said at the top of the
stairs. 'I'm sorry about the brandy – I let the water boil
over. But I'll do it as soon as Papa's finished in the
kitchen.'

He shook his head. 'Don't bother with it. I shall be
asleep by then.'

She looked crestfallen and he added, 'My cough is
much better now; I don't need the brandy. Thank you
anyway.' He kissed her on top of her head and she
hugged him.

'Sleep well, Bon Papa.'

'And you, *ma mignonne.*'

Christine sat on the floor of her room and wondered how
she was going to fill the hours until bedtime. Bon Papa
was going to bed so early these days, just as she had
begun to be allowed to stay up a bit later. Only the very
young and the very old went to bed at this hour.

There was always the homework of course, but English

never took her very long. Besides, Christine was so hungry that she didn't think her brain would work any more until it was fed. The rumbling of her stomach drowned her thoughts and her head felt alternately feather-light and heavy as lead. If Papa were not in a bad mood, she could have been eating supper by now. If he were a more sociable type of father perhaps they could have eaten together, in the kitchen or with trays on their knees in the salon.

Jean-Luc was not a trays-on-knees sort of person, though. Christine imagined Marie-Louise's father, laughing, and eating his supper by the fire with Marie-Louise sitting at his feet. Christine had seen them like that sometimes, when she went to Marie-Louise's house. The firelight would cast soft shadows across the room, and Henri Trichard woud run his fingers through Marie-Louise's ringlets and tease her by pretending to tug them.

Then Marie-Louise's mother would come in to see what all the laughter was about, and the idyll would be spoiled. Christine did not like Marie-Louise's mother, who had a sharp, pointed face and never laughed at all. Maman was much better than Madame Trichard, on any score. Even Monsieur Trichard seemed to think so.

She picked up the English book again. I have laughed, you have laughed, the man in the brown overcoat has laughed . . . the man in the beige car has laughed . . . it was no good, she was too hungry. She rolled over on to her front and dug her elbows into her stomach to fill the aching void. 'The aching void,' she said aloud. The phrase pleased her. 'I, Christine Madeleine Rochaud, am an aching void,' she proclaimed to the flowered curtains. In his room, Bon Papa coughed and spluttered and spat into his handkerchief. Christine stopped reciting. The phrase sounded sinister.

* * *

When would Papa be finished in the kitchen? She was certain now that he would have forgotten to cook anything for her. Otherwise, he would have asked what kind of omelette she wanted, surely? Maman made *omelettes fines herbes*, with tiny, fragrant shreds of parsley and shallots and other delicious things. Tonight, though, Christine would have chosen something more substantial – ham, perhaps. What she would really like would be an enormous stew of beef or horsemeat, bubbling with garlic and onions, with tantalizing, floating morsels of all kinds of *légumes* bobbing and dipping in the sauce. Her mouth watered with nostalgia. It seemed so long since she had eaten that the taste of food was a memory, dying to be rekindled.

She laid her head on her folded arms. The musty smell of the carpet made her nostrils twitch. She wondered how old the carpet was, whether it had been in the house since before she was born, since Maman and Tante Léonie were born. And Tante Sophie. That was a long time ago, far back in the mists of time, like the mists swirling in the park . . .

Christine woke with a jolt that ran through her body like an electric shock. The light stabbed her eyes and cramp attacked her legs.

'Christine,' said Jean-Luc again.

She propped herself up stiffly on one elbow and stared at him stupidly, her eyes still wide with shock.

He crouched down on her level, awkwardly apologetic.

'I didn't realize you were asleep.'

'Yes.' Her mind grappled with reality.

'Listen, Christine.' He held out a flat brown object on the palm of his hand. 'Listen to me a minute. I found this – in the bedroom, under the bed.'

Christine stared at him, uncomprehending.

'Can you tell me . . .' he continued, but his voice

quavered and dried up. He cleared his throat. 'Can you tell me,' he repeated, hoarsely, 'to whom it belongs?'

Christine heaved herself into a sitting position and took the wallet dumbly.

'It's not yours?' she said, and Jean-Luc shook his head. They had both forgotten the scene in the kitchen earlier. This was another Papa, the Papa she remembered when she was very small – younger, less confident, more approachable than the stern businessman she knew today.

No, it was not Papa's wallet. Papa's wallet was black. Bon Papa had given it to him for his birthday and had had his initials stamped on it: J-L. R.

She opened the wallet and found herself looking at a faded photograph of a little girl with ringlet curls and missing front teeth; a younger version but still easily recognizable. 'Marie-Louise,' said Christine.

Jean-Luc held out his hand for the wallet and studied the photo for a long time.

'Marie-Louise Trichard?' he said finally. Although it was a question, his voice was flat and expressionless.

Christine's eyes ached. She did not answer.

'Yes,' said Jean-Luc. 'Yes, I thought so.' He turned the wallet over delicately with his fingertips and found a small back pocket. He pulled out a business card and Christine read, upside down, the elegantly fancy lettering: *M. Henri Trichard, Artiste Photographique.*

The card slipped through Jean-Luc's fingers and fell on the carpet.

'Christine,' said Jean-Luc in a whisper. 'Do you know anything about this?'

His eyes were dark and despairing and as she looked at them a film of water welled up over the brown irises. The rims of his eyes were raw and red and his whole face was dragged downwards, haggard.

Christine burst into tears and flung her arms around his

neck. For several minutes he hugged her tightly, crouched there on the floor, and she could not be sure whether it was her sobbing that shook them or whether it was Papa who was shaking. Finally, he released her gently.

'Go to bed, *ma fille*,' he said. 'You have school in the morning. Have you eaten?'

She shook her head and sniffed convulsively.

'Shall I bring you a sandwich?' He stood up, awkward again, the Papa she knew.

'No. No thank you. I'm not hungry any more.' She sat in the middle of the floor.

'Here.' He picked up her nightdress from the chair. 'Get into bed now. Sleep well.'

'Papa,' she said, and he turned, his hand already on the door handle.

'Yes?'

'Papa – what are you going to do?' Her fears were all the more acute because she only half understood the situation. The two figures of Maman and Monsieur Trichard, linked in some mysterious way she could not comprehend, seemed to fuse into a force that threatened the family, the fabric of the house, and the whole world as she knew it.

Papa paused, his eyes hopeless.

'Do?' he repeated dully, 'What can I do?'

4

Christine awoke the next morning with the sensation that something was wrong. The house was silent, with an uneasy, restless kind of silence. At first she thought it must be very early, that no one was up yet, but a glance at the bedside clock told her it was late.

It was so late, in fact, that it was a wonder Maman had not called her several times, or even, as she had sometimes done before, ripped back the bedclothes, leaving Christine suddenly stripped and shivering, cuddling protestingly into the last little patch of warmth.

Christine did not feel like getting up this morning. Yesterday had been exhausting, rushing to school, trailing round Paris and to the park and back with Bon Papa. Exhausting on the mind too, she thought, recalling the strange behaviour of Maman and Papa, and even Madame Rouvieux.

Remembering last night, she felt even less inclined to get up. How tempting to wriggle under the bedclothes, cocooned in the warmth and the darkness, and sleep till awoken by good news, laughter and sunshine. Instead there was rain pattering on the window and she would be late for school again, and Papa had cried last night and there was this ominous silence in the house . . .

She threw back the bedclothes, grabbed her dressing gown and ran down the stairs.

'Maman!'

'In the kitchen.'

Giselle, still in her dressing gown, was seated at the

kitchen table, a cigarette between her fingers. The ashtray in front of her was overflowing.

'Aren't you well, Maman?'

'Of course I'm well.' She did not look up.

'You aren't dressed.'

'No,' said Maman. 'No, I am not dressed. I don't think the world will collapse because of it, do you?'

Christine stared at her. 'Is something wrong?'

Maman looked up and Christine was shocked to see that she did not look pretty this morning, not at all. One would think she had never been pretty, to see her now.

'What could be wrong?' Maman said, and Christine was not sure if she recognized sarcasm in her voice.

Christine thought of Papa last night. 'You could have had a row with Papa,' she suggested.

'Yes,' Giselle agreed. 'I could have.'

Christine waited – to be told what to do, scolded, admonished for being late, anything – but Maman continued to stare at the smoke worming its way out of the cigarette end, and said nothing.

'Has Papa gone to work?' Christine asked finally.

'Of course. Have you ever known Papa not to go to work? The roof could fall and kill us all,' said Giselle bitterly, 'and Papa would still go to work.'

'And Bon Papa?'

'Bon Papa is still in bed.'

Christine sneaked a look at the clock.

'Yes,' said Giselle, 'it is late and no, he has not had his breakfast. No one has had breakfast. Breakfast has ceased to exist in this house. This cook is on strike.'

'Shall I take him his breakfast?' Christine offered. Giselle shrugged.

Christine put the pan of water to boil and cut two small slices off the end of yesterday's loaf. The coffee jar was empty. Christine took the electric grinder from the cupboard, keeping her eyes on Giselle's face. Giselle watched her without interest.

'I'll have to grind some more coffee,' said Christine apologetically. She gently tipped beans into the grinder, trying to keep them quiet, and pressed the switch softly. The machine whirred and died. She glanced at Maman and pushed the switch harder and the beans sprang to life, whirling and clattering, beating angrily against the imprisoning container.

Christine watched them fearfully, her hand hovering over the switch. Finally they surrendered into powder and, relieved, she cut the current.

'Do you want coffee, Maman?'

'I have been drinking,' said Giselle, 'half the night. I have smoked a packet and a half of untipped cigarettes. My mouth is an ashtray and my stomach is a dustbin.' Two tears rolled out of her eyes and ran dismally down her cheek into the corners of her downturned mouth, the lips naked and cracked without their lipstick. 'My skin is like an old woman's,' she said, on a final note of despair.

'Why?' asked Christine appalled. Her fingers tugged nervously at the packet of coffee filters. 'Why have you been up all night?'

'You may well ask that question,' Giselle said. 'What has been achieved by it all?'

Christine said, 'I don't know.' She did not know what Maman was talking about.

'It's all the same in the morning,' Giselle continued, in the same hopeless voice. 'Jean-Luc goes off to work . . .' – 'Jean-Luc' Christine noted, not 'Papa' – '. . . and I am left here to get Grand-père his breakfast and get Christine off to school . . .' – but I am Christine, and I am here, Christine thought, so why did Maman talk as if she were not there? – '. . . and do the shopping and get the lunch and clean the house,' Giselle went on, 'every day, every day until – when? All my life?' She stubbed out the spent cigarette and another two tears chased each other down her nose and plopped unchecked into the ashtray. 'Alone,' she sobbed. 'With no love, no laughter, no fun – nothing. Nothing at all.'

'I'll clean the house' said Christine. 'Do you want me to? When I get back from school?' She did not know what to say. It was difficult to know what Maman wanted.

Giselle drew another cigarette out of the packet then threw it back on to the table. 'Give me some coffee,' she said.

Hastily, Christine poured coffee into the filter and versed a few drops of water over the paper.

'You're very tired, I expect,' she said tentatively.

'It's not surprising,' Giselle said bitterly. 'He never thinks of me, that I have a full day's work to do. He thinks it does not matter keeping me up all night, with his shouting and his accusations. He thinks women sit around all day doing nothing.'

Christine filled the filter and set the coffee jug in front of her. 'You could go to bed now and have a sleep,' she suggested. 'I'll tell Bon Papa and he won't disturb you.' Then, on impulse, Christine put her arms round her and hugged her, as if Maman were the child. 'Go to bed,' she urged. 'You will feel better afterwards.' She did not know what she would do if Maman continued to sit there and cry.

'All right,' Giselle said meekly.

'I'll bring your coffee up to you,' Christine added.

When she carried up the tray, however, Maman was already asleep, her face pressed into the pillows, and her breathing heavy with exhaustion. Christine was surprised, when she went into Bon Papa's room, to find him also asleep. Normally, he would have been up, shaved and in his dressing gown long before this hour, waiting patiently for his breakfast, which he ate alone in his room.

'Bon Papa,' she said softly, and his eyes opened immediately. 'It's quite late,' she said.

'Yes,' he said. 'I know.' The words came out with effort, and Christine noticed how pale he was.

'You're not well?' she said quickly, and her heart contracted at the thought. Oh God, she prayed, let somebody be all right today.

'My chest,' he said. 'A touch of bronchitis. You'd better tell your mother I'll spend the morning in bed.'

'She's asleep,' Christine told him. 'She was up all night, she says.'

Bon Papa heaved an enormous sigh. 'That I know,' he said. 'Did it disturb you, the shouting?'

Christine shook her head dumbly. What had happened last night? 'What was it about?' she asked.

'Who can tell?' Bon Papa said. 'When you are my age, *ma petite fille*, you will realize that it does not matter what people argue about. If they want to argue they will never lack a subject.'

Bon Papa's answers were not answers at all, Christine reflected: they never told you what you wanted to know. Bon Papa struggled to sit up and coughed painfully, clutching the front of his pyjama jacket.

'Drink your coffee,' Christine said. She held the bowl out to him and he accepted it with hands that shook as they raised it to his mouth.

She wondered if she ought to wake Maman up to tell her that Bon Papa was ill. But Maman needed to sleep, to sleep away the exhaustion and the emotion and to wake up miraculously restored to the Maman Christine knew. Christine was afraid – afraid for Maman and for herself – to reawaken her to her morning self.

Probably Bon Papa would not need Maman till lunchtime anyway. Even when he was ill, he hated anyone to help him to the bathroom and would somehow struggle out on his own, clutching the walls and the door handles for support and gasping painfully with the effort.

But if he fell? Christine flinched at the thought. If he fell on the bathroom floor and could not get up and Maman was asleep and didn't know . . .? She wanted to ask him, to make him promise, that he would be careful, that he would not die. His skin was yellow and waxy, his lips blue and his cheeks hollow. His hands trembled and the coffee bowl tipped perilously. Christine rescued it.

He gave up the bowl without protest; his eyes closed and his breathing became heavy.

'I made you some *tartines*,' Christine said, holding out the plate with its two modest discs of stale buttered bread, with the marmalade and its teaspoon by the side. She often stayed to watch Bon Papa eat his breakfast. He would spoon the marmalade into his mouth and follow it with a bite of the brittle *tartine* which would leave crumbs in his moustache.

Bon Papa shook his head weakly. 'Not today,' he said. He slid down in the bed again, his head falling awkwardly against the headboard and his pillow at an angle under his neck. Christine tugged at them inexpertly and he tried to help but his head fell back wearily again.

'Leave them,' he said. '*Ça va*. They are all right.'

Christine looked at him fearfully. 'Should I call the doctor?' she asked.

'No,' he said faintly. '*Mais non*. What can a doctor do for old age?' His eyes closed. 'You go along,' he said. 'I'll be fine.'

Christine picked up the tray and went out very quietly. Snores came from Maman's room on the top floor, and heavy wheezing breaths from Bon Papa's. Tears welled

71

up in her eyes. She wondered what to do. Obviously, she would have to stay at home until Maman awoke, but what would Mademoiselle Dubois say when she finally got to school? What would Maman be like when she woke up? And what if Bon Papa died there in his room, with only Christine to know?

While the wheezy breathing continued, of course he was still alive. As long as she stayed there at the top of the stairs, Christine could hear him. She laid down the tray, went into her own room and hastily pulled on her school clothes, keeping her ears attuned to Bon Papa. Then she returned to the landing and sat with her back to the wall, opposite Bon Papa's door, keeping vigil.

She looked wistfully at the *tartines* on Bon Papa's tray but it seemed treacherous to eat his breakfast. Finally, however, hunger overcame her and she wolfed down both the *tartines*. The marmalade – Maman's own plum variety – was sweet and sickly and made her feel better but eating the frugal meal only emphasized the emptiness of her stomach and finally she succumbed and went swiftly downstairs, returning with an apple and a slice of sausage.

She brought out the pillow from her bed, too, to cushion her backbone against the wall. Even from here she could faintly hear the old kitchen clock. '*Qu'est-ce-qui-arrive – er – a?*' it ticked. 'What-is-going-to-happen?' the words repeated themselves in Christine's head. What is going to happen?

She wished she were at school, sitting safely in class, one child among many, answering questions, writing in her book, reciting poems by Verlaine, trying to be the first to solve the mental arithmetic problems, trying to finish her painting before the bell went – it was all so secure and predictable.

Christine pictured them all sitting in their places:

Madeleine Guirac on the left, under the picture of the Blessed Saviour with the bleeding heart, then Marie-Louise Trichard and the new girl Carine, with Christine's empty desk between them.

She and Carine were in the same group, with Madeleine, for the play-reading in today's French class. They had been rehearsing for days in the lunch breaks. The class was studying Sartre's *Closed Doors* and was halfway through it by the time Carine joined, so Christine had undertaken the task of telling her the story.

'It's about these three people trapped in a room for ever more,' she had explained, and Carine's dark eyes had widened behind the black-rimmed spectacles she wore.

'Why can't they get out?' she asked.

'It's meant to be hell,' said Christine with relish. 'However much they hate each other – and they do – they can't get away, and they can't kill each other because they're already dead.'

Giselle, at home, had not understood the play. 'Jean-Luc, we saw this years ago with Janine and Victor Seiner – do you remember?' she said. 'It's absolutely unsuitable for children of Christine's age. An eternal triangle with one of the women . . . well, not normal. You understand me. I won't have the child reading it!' she declared but Jean-Luc only shrugged.

'The school knows its business. Perhaps all the implications are not explained. A child would not know what it's all about.'

'It's all about sex!' said Giselle. 'It's perfectly obvious to anyone of any age.'

'It's not, Maman,' Christine said. 'It's all about hell.'

'Even worse!' Giselle proclaimed. 'What did I tell you, Jean-Luc? Completely unsuitable for children.'

Christine and Carine liked the play, though they were

sad that they were not given the attempted murder scene. Marie-Louise, Bernice and Véronique were given that one. They rehearsed in the lunch breaks and Christine could see Marie-Louise at the other end of the playground, plunging imaginary daggers into Véronique's neck. She seemed to be enjoying herself. After a while she tired of it, however, and wandered over to join them, but Christine said, 'We haven't finished yet; Carine and I've got another two speeches to do.' Marie-Louise had glared at Carine and said, 'It must be the first thing she's said of any interest since she came here then.'

Carine had flushed and turned away and Madeleine had exclaimed, 'Leave her alone, Marie-Louise! She's only shy. Not a big mouth like some I could mention.' So Marie-Louise had aimed a kick at Christine and declared, 'Well, if you prefer that boring little girl with the spectacles, Christine Rochaud, then you needn't think you're my friend any more, and you needn't expect me to give you a bite of my *brioche* at break time either.'

Now Carine and Madeleine would have to do the play-reading alone, with Mademoiselle Javine reading Christine's part, and Carine, Christine knew, would be sick with embarrassment at being made so conspicuous. She fidgeted wretchedly. If she left now, and ran all the way to school, she might just be there in time, if . . .

Bon Papa's straining breaths ceased for an instant and Christine sprang to her feet, but by the time she was in his room he had started coughing, and she felt herself go weak with relief.

She was silly to worry, she told herself; Maman certainly never spent all morning listening outside the door when Bon Papa was ill. That was different though. When Maman was around, Christine did not worry about Bon Papa either, because then it was Maman's responsibility and she would automatically cope with any crisis.

Thinking of her sitting weeping into the overfilled ashtray, however, Christine wondered uneasily if Maman really could cope. The thought frightened her beyond words, for if Maman who was so brisk and self-assured coud not manage, then who could? Certainly not Christine, who was only a schoolgirl and who, Maman often said, had no more idea of things than a blind kitten.

'Ça va, Bon Papa?' she whispered, but he did not hear her, and she tiptoed out again, half closing the door.

Sitting there on the landing, without any other distractions, her mind wandered over last night's events and struggled to give them some interpretation. It was obvious, Christine reflected, that Maman had done something wrong, for although it was by no means uncommon for Papa to have a row with Maman, it had been a shock to overhear Bon Papa scolding her as he had done yesterday.

That it was something to do with Henry Trichard, Christine did not doubt, and the certainty made her deeply suspicious of him. She might not understand all the implications of the situation but she could sense danger in it. Inexplicably the ever-smiling Henri was a threat to the whole family; Christine knew it without being told.

Then there was the wallet under the bed. Christine found it hard to believe that Maman, who took her to church some Sundays and was so particular about cleaning shoes and brushing teeth, could ever do anything seriously wrong. Her mind shied away from the fact, but returned to it in ever-narrowing circles. Why was Henri's wallet under Maman and Papa's bed? Christine covered her eyes with her hands and tried to think of explanations which would leave Maman free of blame, but there could be only one conclusion: Maman had *stolen Henri Trichard's wallet*!

A little moan of distress escaped her. No, it couldn't

be true! He must have dropped it by mistake – but under the bed? Or, perhaps he had called round, carelessly dropped the wallet, and Maman was keeping it for him – but why would she put it under the bed? Why not tell Papa, or even give it to him to drop into Henri's studio on his way to work?

True, Papa did not like Henri. They were so different, the two men – Papa serious and hardworking, Henri carefree and flippant. For a little while after that time when Henri had taken them to the zoo, Christine had thought, secretly and guiltily, that Henri was nicer than Papa, that in fact it would be more fun to have someone like Henri as a father.

Now, without knowing why, she did not think so any more, for was it not, indirectly, Henri who had made trouble for Papa, who had made Papa look so anguished and despairing last night? And Christine could never remember Maman, even after the worst rows with Papa, ever looking as terrible as she had this morning, so that must surely be Henri's fault too.

But why had she stolen his wallet? Was Maman's depression this morning due to guilt – or fear of being arrested perhaps? Christine determined that if they came to arrest Maman, she would hide her, cover up for her, pretend that she had not seen Maman for a long time.

It surprised her a little that she was prepared to do these things, for lately she had not always seen eye to eye with Maman. But, now that Maman appeared to have committed this crime, Christine could not find it in herself to blame her. It was Henri, she felt, who was the villain of the piece, who had caused all this trouble.

It was odd, though, Maman, far from regarding him as a villain, had seemed to like him so much. So why would she steal his wallet . . .?

Maman woke up at about midday. Christine heard her

opening and shutting the drawer of her dressing table, and she went downstairs. When Giselle came down – dressed and with her make-up on, Christine was relieved to see – Christine was sitting at the dining-room table, reading, as if she had been there all the morning.

'You didn't go to school, then?' Maman said.

'Bon Papa is ill,' Christine said, in explanation. 'I thought I'd better stay.'

'*Oh Bon Dieu*,' Giselle exclaimed. 'What other calamities are going to befall me, I wonder? It's his chest I suppose?'

'A touch of bronchitis, he said,' Christine told her. 'He doesn't look well.'

'I'll go up and see him in a minute,' Giselle decided, 'but I'll get the lunch started first or we'll be late for everything today. God knows how I'm going to catch up as it is. You'd better go in to school, Christine.'

'Can I have lunch first?'

Giselle clicked her tongue against her teeth. 'Can't you have lunch at school? I have paid for it, after all.'

'I'll have missed it,' Christine said, 'by the time I get there. And anyway, I'll have been marked absent so I'd have to go and see Madame Scholbert first. Will you write me a note for this afternoon?'

'I'm sure it's not really necessary, just for one morning,' Giselle reasoned. 'Surely they don't expect a note every time someone misses a morning?'

Christine sighed. Maman did not understand about school. She could never see why it mattered if Christine was late or if she did not have a clean gym shirt or why she, Giselle, should be expected to attend parents' evenings which were long and boring and required one to stand in queues.

'People don't miss mornings at school,' Christine explained patiently.

'Oh, come on,' Giselle argued. 'For dental appointments, say.'

'They still have to bring a note,' Christine insisted. 'Besides, I haven't had a dental appointment.'

'No,' Giselle considered, 'but it is not a bad idea to say that you have. If you say that you were ill they will wonder at your miraculous recovery this afternoon.'

'I wasn't going to say that!' Christine protested. 'I'm not ill, am I?'

'Well, what were you going to say?' Giselle demanded. 'That your parents spent all night arguing and your mother retired to bed?'

Christine pursed her lips thoughtfully. 'I could say Grand-père was ill and you weren't around to look after him,' she suggested.

'*Merci*!' Giselle exclaimed. 'And have everyone thinking I neglect my responsibilities? No, Christine, I'm sorry but you will have to say that you had to go and see the dentist.'

Christine grew red in the face. 'But it's not true,' she objected. 'I can't say that if it's not true, can I?'

'Don't tell me,' said Giselle icily, 'that you always tell the truth because I know that is not the case, *ma petite*. Or is it that you only lie to suit yourself?'

Christine twisted her hands uncomfortably. Had she not vowed, back there on the landing, that she would, if necessary, lie to help Maman? Only she would have preferred a heroic, worthwhile lie to this petty deception which seemed somehow mean and also unfair to Madame Scholbert, who would not expect Christine to be dishonest. 'All right,' she said finally. 'All right, I'll say that.' It was something, anyway, to see Maman back to her normal self. Christine had not liked to see her sitting so meekly in the kitchen this morning. It was not like Maman at all.

'So,' said Giselle briskly, 'if we have finished making a nonsense out of a nothing, perhaps I can prepare the lunch now. Just pop upstairs and ask Grand-pére what he would like.'

Bon Papa did not want anything, but he insisted on dressing and coming downstairs. 'Am I to stay in bed waiting for death?' he said.

Christine wished he would not talk about death.

'*Ecoute, mon enfant*,' he said seriously, seeing her turn her head away, 'everyone has to die sometime. You know that.'

'There are lots of people older than you,' Christine said, adding callously, 'Let them die first.'

Giselle was not pleased to see Bon Papa downstairs. 'You would do better to stay in bed, Papa, till the germs have gone,' she told him.

'I shall not be in the way,' he said. 'I shall sit in the salon, with the crossword.'

Giselle glanced at him out of the corner of her eye, without pausing in her task of mincing the herbs. 'I have friends coming this afternoon. They will not stay long,' she said.

'Ah,' said Bon Papa. 'So you wish me to stay in bed – till the germs have gone.'

'It's for your own good, Papa,' Giselle said angrily.

'Of course,' Bon Papa agreed. 'But perhaps we have reached the stage where the infection . . . may be more easily banished by my presence down here. The germs appear to have multiplied thanks to my exposure to the open air of the park. Perhaps I no longer want to encourage this sickness.'

Christine had the impression that Bon Papa was talking about something quite different from the apparent subject. He was clever with words, Bon Papa. He manipulated them and gave them meanings beyond their ordinary

79

definitions. Christine did not always understand what he said, but she never failed to admire the way he said it.

Giselle seemed to understand him, however, for she became flustered and would not look at him. 'It is not what you think, Papa,' she said. 'It is over. Simply a case, this afternoon, of banishing the infection, as you say, for good. I suppose that makes you very happy.'

Christine was shocked to see that Maman was crying again. She looked at Bon Papa, silently pleading with him to make the words mean something different, so that Maman would not be upset. If Maman kept crying, as Papa had cried – almost – last night, and if Bon Papa did not make haste to make everything better . . . Christine shuddered. It seemed to her that the whole world was sliding downhill and without Bon Papa who would save them all?

Do something, Bon Papa, she begged wordlessly, trying to infuse strength into his frailty by her own willpower; do something to make it all right – and live to be a hundred, she added, just to make sure that it stays all right.

As if he had heard her Bon Papa said, more gently, 'I am pleased, and sorry, for you, *ma fille*. But you will not regret it.'

'You don't think,' said Giselle, turning to him piteously, 'that it's too late, Papa?'

But here Bon Papa would not console her. 'That I cannot tell you,' he said heavily, and Giselle's head dropped again, and her mincing of the vegetables grew less determined.

'Maman,' said Christine.

'Lay the table, Christine,' said Maman in her old voice, and Christine knew better than to argue.

It was a silent lunch. Although she was hungry, having eaten next to nothing yesterday, Christine found that she could not eat. Her stomach cried out for food but her dry mouth and constricted throat selfishly refused to convey the food.

After lunch, Bon Papa said, 'I shall go out, Giselle, as usual, but I shall return in an hour.'

'Papa!' Giselle protested. 'You are not well.'

'I shall not stay in the house,' he repeated. 'That I will leave to you.'

Giselle hung her head. 'It will be the last time,' she said.

Christine was shocked. 'You should not go out, Bon Papa,' she said. 'Your bronchitis . . .'

'Christine,' said Maman, 'you will help me with the washing-up, and then you will go to school.'

Christine dried the plates in mutinous silence while Bon Papa shrugged himself painfully into his thick coat and, with grunts and gasps, pulled on his shoes. Then he left, leaning heavily on his stick.

'You shouldn't have let him go,' said Christine defiantly.

'Oh be quiet, Christine!' Giselle snapped. 'You try my patience.' She swabbed the draining board, viciously.

'On your way to school,' she began again, after a few seconds' silence, 'you will be so good, Christine, as to call into the photography studio of Monsieur Trichard, Marie-Louise's father, and you will inform him that due to family trouble my appointment this afternoon will have to be made earlier. Can you remember that?'

'I don't know,' Christine said sullenly. She resented Maman's referring to Henri as 'Monsieur Trichard, Marie-Louise's father', as though the man were a perfect stranger to them both.

It was obvious that Maman could not both be expecting friends, as she had told Bon Papa, and have an appointment at the photography studio, which meant that Maman was not being entirely truthful. Christine felt that to be entrusted – or rather burdened – with this unwelcome mission she should also be entrusted with the truth. So she shuffled her feet and stared out of the window and told Maman she did not know whether she could remember the message.

'What do you mean, you don't know? Maman cried, her anger, which she kept permanently available, springing into use. 'A child who is as clever at school as you reputedly are cannot remember such a simple message?'

'It isn't on my way to school,' Christine pointed out. 'I'll be late.' She was prevaricating, and Giselle knew it.

'You are already half a day late,' she said sardonically. 'You cannot make it half a day and a few extra minutes?'

Christine looked obstinate. 'I don't want to,' she said.

Giselle flushed angrily and looked uncomfortable. 'So,' she said. 'You will not do this little thing for your Maman?'

'It's not that I won't do it for you,' Christine said awkwardly, for had she not vowed that she would do anything for Maman?

'Of course,' said Maman pursuing her advantage, 'if you are unwilling to put yourself to such a slight inconvenience for the sake of helping me, I cannot force you. However, it would be well to consider all the many things I have done for you, *ma petite ingrate*, and if your conscience dictates that it is not necessary for you to make any kind of return – '

'All right!' Christine shouted. 'All right! I'll go!' She stamped her foot, and the tears rose in her eyes. She would do anything for Maman, anything if only it would help to restore everything to normal. Only let everyone behave as before, only let the house return to its old uneventful rhythm and she would take part in any of Maman's truth-or-dare games.

Perhaps Maman was going to make amends, to give back the wallet – and this was Christine's fear as well as her hope, because how would Henri receive her as the bearer of stolen goods? Would he perhaps think that she was the culprit? And, if so, would Maman defend her as Christine had been prepared to defend Maman?

There had been that time, Christine remembered, when Marie-Louise had come to play and had spilt Coca-Cola all over the rug in the salon, and when her father – Henri, as Christine thought of him now – had come to collect his daughter and had offered an apology for the stained rug, Maman had said not at all it was Christine's fault. Christine could not be sure, if Henri got the wrong impression of her about the wallet, that Maman would bother to correct it.

Sure enough, Maman slipped the wallet into the envelope she gave Christine and followed it with a short note which she then took out and re-wrote, at much greater length. Tears plopped on to the paper as she wrote, and she brushed them away impatiently. Christine stared at the floor.

'For the love of God, don't stand there looking over my shoulder, Christine,' Maman said. 'Go away and do something; I'll call you when I'm finished.'

Christine went and stared out of the dining-room window instead. She would miss the whole lunch break now and part of the first afternoon lesson.

'Maman,' she said, returning to the kitchen, 'you won't forget to write me a note for school?'

'I'll write one tomorrow,' Giselle promised, folding the squared notepaper and slipping it into the envelope. 'At the moment, I feel I have written my whole life history.' She took the letter out of the envelope again and ran through it, her lips moving as she read, then with an impatient gesture she crumpled it into a ball and, lifting the lid of the boiler, threw it in.

Taking another sheet of paper, she scrawled a few hasty lines on it, folded it roughly and put it in the envelope quickly, as though afraid she might change her mind again.

'*Ecoute, Christine*,' she said. 'You will give this to Monsieur Trichard personally, do you hear?' Christine nodded without enthusiasm. 'Couldn't you phone him instead?' she said, in a final hope for reprieve.

Maman pursed her lips primly. 'It is not for me,' she said, 'to ring Monsieur at his studio. Go now.' She kissed Christine dismissively and pushed her towards the door.

Christine walked slowly, dragging her feet, and wondered what it would be like, starting school in the middle of the afternoon. She would be somehow an alien, she thought wistfully; while everyone else was established in the warmth of the day's camaraderie, which was built up of shared croissants at break time and illicit chatter during the double biology period, she alone would have the chill of arrival still on her.

By now the imprint of home would have worn off her classmates and they would have fused, as they always did, into an amorphous 'school' group into which the home-Christine, carrying with her not the shared school events but Bon Papa's illness, Maman's tears and Papa's grief – and perhaps Henri Trichard's anger – would fit awkwardly.

She hesitated when she reached the studio, peering through the polished *vitrine* into the dark interior to see if the villain was there alone, but she saw only the reflection of her own face mockingly partnered by the smiling portrait of Marie-Louise. For a few moments longer she lingered, finding in Marie-Louise's picture a likeness to her father and weighing the guilty envelope in

84

her hand. Then she took a deep breath, pulled open the door and walked in.

The receptionist, an elegant lady with rouged cheeks and an immaculate chignon, looked up as Christine came in. Henri Trichard, who had been leaning over her looking at some prints on the desk, straightened up and motioned to the receptionist not to get up. '*Ma petite Christine!*' he said, moving quickly towards her and smiling with determination. 'What a pleasant surprise.'

Christine held out the package dumbly, and his smile wavered a little as he slit it open with a ruthless forefinger. The smile faltered completely and became a frown as he pulled out the wallet then quickly returned it to the envelope. The brief note he read in seconds before crumpling it as Maman had its predecessor, and stuffing it into the pocket of his expensively cut trousers. He turned on his heel abruptly and said, without the trace of a smile this time, 'Tell her I have to work this afternoon. I'll phone later,' and hurried off through the swing doors marked 'Studio'.

The receptionist was studying the prints with great concentration, as though anything which took place beyond the smart little desk had no significance for her. Christine murmured, '*Au revoir, Madame,*' not in any expectation of being heard but for the sake of politeness, and found herself once more in the rainy street.

Outside she recalled that Henri had given her a return message for Maman. She could, of course, deliver it when she came home from school, but as the message concerned this afternoon, surely it should be given straight away. She turned towards home.

'Tell her I have to work this afternoon.' Most people worked every afternoon as a matter of course; certainly Papa did, but then Papa was not a photographer, or as Marie-Louise called him, a photographic artist. If Maman was expecting friends, as she had told Bon Papa, then no doubt it would make little difference to her whether Henri worked or did not work this afternoon, unless he was one of the friends expected. But then why would Maman have this appointment to see him? Christine's mind refused to function. Think of something else, she instructed it. There was something about the subject of Maman and Henri that repelled her thoughts, as one magnet repels another. Images rose, unbidden, of Henri speeding down the rue Jean-Jacques Rousseau in his beige car, of Maman flushed and distraught, greeting Christine. '*Non, chérie*, no one has called today.'

'What nonsense!' said Christine aloud. 'What rubbish you think, Christine Rochaud.' To empty her head of the rubbish, she began to run but even her feet betrayed her, pounding a rhythm on the pavements. 'Hen-ri, Gi-selle.' To exorcize the foolish words she whispered her own. 'Jean-Luc, Gi-selle,' she repeated firmly, 'Maman, Pa-pa,' then, 'Chris-tine, Grand-Père,' over and over again till she reached home. 'Chris-tine, Ma-man, Chris-tine, Pa-pa, Pa-pa, Ma-man, Ma-man, Hen-ri . . . *non*!' she said aloud, and Madame Rouvieux, pottering along under the dripping trees in her front garden, looked up and scuttled inquisitively to the gate.

Maman heard the message in silence, then turned abruptly and walked upstairs.

'Maman' said Christine after her. 'Do you think it's worth going in to school now?' She did not feel like another long walk, and Carine would have had to recite her piece alone by now; it was too late to save her.

When Maman did not answer Christine said, 'I think I'll stay at home – *tu penses*?' but again there was no reply, so she sat down on the bottom stair and thought about Papa at work with his papers in the evening, frowning with concentration, and then of Papa last night, his eyes dark, whispering, 'Do you know anything of this, Christine?'

Lost in her thoughts, she jumped when the back door was flung open and a rough voice cried, 'Anyone there?' Maman, whose hearing was impeccable, emerged from her room, her face blotched, and ran lightly down the flights of stairs to see who it was. Christine preceded her into the kitchen.

It was Jacquot, the champion boules player, now looking awkward and ill at ease in the Rochaud kitchen. Bon Papa, silent and haggard, with beads of sweat trickling like blood down his pallid forehead, sat slumped over the kitchen table.

'I brought him home, Madame,' Jacques explained, his voice unnaturally hushed as a mark of respect to Maman, whom he had never met. 'He was taken ill.'

'Thank you,' said Maman faintly, then, quickly pulling herself together. 'May I offer you some refreshment?'

But Jacquot refused, patently anxious to free himself from the embarrassment which locked his tongue and his limbs, making him a stiff, comical puppet. His head was tilted awkwardly to one side and his arms were rigid as spillikins.

'*Eh bien*,' he said, several times in succession, '*Eh bien, j'vous quitte*,' and shook hands with them all, violent with relief.

'*Merci beaucoup*,' Bon Papa thanked him and Jacquot struck him gently on the shoulder. 'Go slowly,' he told him. 'We can't do without an audience, we champions!' and Bon Papa raised a faint smile at this sally. Nodding apologetically to Giselle as if to excuse his levity, Jacquot shuffled out of the back door, grinning with embarrassment until the porch mercifully shielded him from sight.

'Christine,' exhorted Maman. 'Help me to get Grand-père to bed,' and between them they helped him up the stairs and into his room, the old man staggering and coughing till Christine feared he would collapse.

He insisted on undressing himself, without aid or witnesses, and Giselle disappeared downstairs to fetch brandy while Christine hovered outside the door.

'Can I come in yet, Bon Papa?'

'Yes, come in.'

'Maman is getting you some brandy,' Christine told him. 'Shall I help you into bed?'

'No, no, I can manage.' With some effort, he hauled himself on to the high, old-fashioned bed which he would never allow to be replaced. 'We've grown used to each other's lumps and bumps,' he would say. He let himself be tucked in like a child, closing his eyes in grateful relief at the comfort.

'You were always a good child,' he murmured. 'Always the best. A kind heart. You're a good girl, Sophie.'

'Christine,' she corrected him. 'It's Christine, Bon Papa.'

He opened his eyes. 'Of course,' he agreed. '*Bien sûr.* Christine.' He closed them again and sank into the dozing stupor of the sick and the very old.

'He called me Sophie,' Christine told Giselle when they were both downstairs. 'He didn't know who I was.'

'I expect he just got the names muddled up,' Giselle told her. 'Old people get confused. And he always says you remind him of Sophie.'

Usually so busy, Giselle was sitting at the kitchen table, idly tapping a pencil on its scrubbed wooden surface. As she seemed inclined to talk, Christine settled herself in the chair opposite.

'What was she like – Sophie?' she asked.

Giselle put her head on one side and considered. 'She was a funny girl,' she said musingly. 'Not pretty or vivacious, rather reserved. A terrible day-dreamer – like

88

you, you see, it's true. She used to drive Maman mad with her endless reveries, also like you – *hein*?'

'Did you like her?' Christine asked.

'Of course I liked her!' Maman said indignantly. 'She was my sister. Mind you,' she continued, on reflection, 'once Léonie was older it was always the two of us who were close. Sophie was so different. She was never interested in the same things.'

Christine edged her chair closer to the table, 'What kind of things?'

'Oh, parties and clothes and dressing up and shopping – all the usual things that young girls like,' Giselle said. 'Maman used to give marvellous parties with all kinds of people – she knew half of Paris.'

'Like you,' Christine said.

'Don't be ridiculous! I don't know half of Paris,' Giselle contradicted, but she looked pleased. 'They were really great occasions, Maman's parties,' she continued, 'and we always had new dresses for them. Maman was very good like that.

'But Sophie was never grateful; she used to say, "I look stupid dressed up like a mannequin; I don't feel like a person." And she would hardly say a word all evening, never indulged in even the mildest flirtation, and if Maman didn't watch her she would disappear upstairs and we would find her there, reading a book, when the guest went home.'

Christine was fascinated, 'And you think I resemble her?' she asked. The idea that someone else in the world was like her gave her a sense of companionship.

Giselle shrugged. 'Grand-père thinks so; I don't see it so much myself. In looks you are like me. But she used to get great enthusiasms; she was quite impulsive. For all her quietness and her watching people, she would suddenly get inflamed over some little issue that anyone could see was of no importance.'

'Like what, for example?' Christine urged.

'Oh, I don't know.' Maman stood up, bored with the subject. 'It's all such a long time ago.'

Christine looked sideways at her and dared the question. 'Why don't we see her now?' But it was over; Maman's communicative mood was whisked away like the dust that she banished so briskly with her efficient broom.

'You know very well, Christine,' she said. 'It's because she lives in England. You have been told that before. It was her own decision to leave her family and live abroad so she had no one but herself to blame. Haven't you any homework to do?'

'No,' said Christine simply. She ventured one more question. 'Do you still love her? I mean, she is still your sister, isn't she?'

'It's natural to love one's family, isn't it?' Giselle said snappishly. Then she considered for a moment and said slowly, 'To be honest, I don't know what she would be like now. I haven't thought about Sophie for years.'

Carine came around after school to see Christine. 'I thought you might be ill.' she explained.

Christine was touched. 'I'm not ill,' she said awkwardly, conscious of Maman listening from the kitchen, 'but it was kind of you to come. Did you have to do the play-reading on your own?' she added.

'No, I was let off!' Even now, recalling it, Carine heaved a sigh of relief. 'I thought I would have to read it with Mademoiselle Javine – I was terrified!'

Christine was relieved too. 'I thought you'd hate me for not turning up,' she said.

90

'Go and play upstairs, children,' Giselle called from the doorway. 'I'm going to clean this room in a minute.'

Christine shrugged an apology to Carine for being addressed as 'children'. 'Can you stay?' she asked. Carine shook her head. 'I have to get home,' she said. 'My mother worries if I'm late.'

'It's a long way to walk,' said Christine concerned. 'Wouldn't your father come and collect you?' Then she remembered, and clapped her hands over her mouth in horror.

Carine laughed. 'Don't worry,' she reassured Christine. 'I don't mind.'

Christine looked at her curiously. 'Why did he leave home, your Papa?'

'The usual reason,' said Carine casually. 'An affair with another woman.'

Christine was shocked. 'It must have been awful, when he left you,' she said.

Carine's small mouth made a *moue*. 'Not really,' she said judicially. 'It was worse when he was there, with all the rows and everything. When he left it was much better. Maman takes me out everywhere now and has more time for me at weekends, and when I go to see Papa it's like a birthday every time. He's always buying me dolls and bonbons and gâteaux. When he was at home all he did was tell me off.'

Christine was wide-eyed with disbelief. 'But it can't be a good thing,' she said, 'to lose your father.' Maman always talked with condemnation of 'broken families', who split up and led their separate lives instead of living as a united group, as God had ordained and the Rochaud family practised.

Carine grinned wickedly. 'Don't believe it,' she said. 'Both parents are so afraid that you'll like being with one more than the other that they'll give you anything you

91

ask for. Even if Maman says no at first, if I say I will ask Papa she gives in straight away.'

'Christine,' said Giselle coming in with the dustpan, 'I thought I asked you to go upstairs?'

'Carine can't stay,' Christine explained. 'This is Carine,' she added, by way of introduction.

Carine ducked her head nervously and said, '*Bonsoir*, Madame,' inaudibly.

Giselle nodded briefly and said, 'There are some plums in the kitchen, Christine, if you and Carine would like some,' whereupon Carine decided she could stay a few minutes longer after all.

While they were in the kitchen, Jean-Luc came in.

'*Bonsoir*, Papa,' Christine greeted him, her mouth full of plums. 'You're very early.'

'Yes,' he agreed briefly.

Giselle, hearing his voice, said the same. 'Why are you so early?'

'Because,' he said, through his teeth, 'I had no sleep last night and I am very tired. That surprises you, *hein*?'

Giselle pursed her lips. 'I have had a tiring day myself,' she said. 'Grand-père is ill. That reminds me – Christine, just pop upstairs and make sure he's all right, will you? If he wants anything else,' she added in a weary voice. 'I will come up.'

'I won't be a minute,' Christine told Carine, and Carine nodded dumbly.

Bon Papa was huddled beneath the bedclothes, grey in the face.

'Are you no better?' Christine enquired softly.

He grunted, 'I am so cold,' he complained. 'I cannot seem to get warm.'

'Shall I bring you up some more covers?'

'Yes,' he said piteously. 'That would help.'

She returned, carrying the duvet from her own bed.

92

'This will keep you warm, Bon Papa,' she said, tucking it round him tenderly. He looked so ill! Christine could remember when she had had flu, lying aching and feverish beneath the intolerable weight of blankets for two whole days and nights. It was not good to be ill like that. 'Can I bring you anything else, Bon Papa?'

'*Merci, non.* I will sleep now, thank you, *mon chou.*'

'*De rien.*' She wished she could do something for him, to make him better. 'You are sure?'

He nodded, his eyes already closing again.

The shouting began as Christine closed the door softly behind her – Giselle first, then Jean-Luc. Fearful equally for Papa and for Carine, stranded in the kitchen with two strange adults fighting, Christine took the stairs two at a time.

'I will not have it!' Giselle screamed, as Christine entered the kitchen. 'I will not have you taking your petty revenge by ruining my health like this!'

'Where is Carine?' Christine asked.

They looked round. She was not there.

'Damn you!' shouted Christine, the tears springing into her eyes, and Giselle flinched.

Christine ran through the open back door and down the path. She caught up with Carine just outside the gate.

'I'm sorry,' she blurted, oblivious to the undisguised interest of Madame Rouvieux across the road. 'I'm so sorry!'

Carine smiled at her. 'It's not your fault,' she consoled. 'Besides I'm used to it. My parents were like that all the time before they split up.'

'Before they . . .' Christine hesitated. 'Listen,' she said suddenly. 'Something awful happened.' She felt that she could not go on any longer without telling somebody.

Carine halted in her tracks. 'What is it?'

Christine shook her head in vexation, 'I don't know

exactly,' she said wretchedly. 'Papa found this wallet –
not his – in the house. Maman gave it back, but . . .'

Carine looked bewildered. 'Whose wallet was it?'

Christine blushed. 'It belonged to . . . to another man,'
she said. 'I don't know how it got there, under the bed.'

'Under the bed?' Carine stared. 'Your Papa found
another man's wallet under the bed?'

Christine nodded.

'Then it is your mother who is having an affair?' Carine
asked. 'I thought it was always the father who did.'

Christine went hot and then stone cold. 'Oh no!' she
said. 'Oh no, no, Maman wouldn't do that. She wouldn't!'

Carine averted her eyes, embarrassed. 'I'm sorry,' she
said. 'I thought that was what you were telling me – with
the wallet and everything. I'm sorry.'

'It doesn't matter,' said Christine.

'Perhaps,' said Carine anxiously, 'perhaps I've got it
wrong.'

Christine shook her head. 'It can't be right,' she whispered. 'It can't be.'

Carine bit her lip. 'There is probably some other
explanation,' she said pleadingly. 'I'm sure there must
be.' But Christine had turned away.

'I'm sorry,' said Carine again. Christine waved her
apologies away but the words would not come out, and
eventually Carine said, 'I'll have to go. See you tomorrow
at school then?' and started off down the road, looking
back over her shoulder every few paces.

Christine clung to the gatepost and the tears poured
down her cheeks. 'It can't be,' she whispered. 'It can't be
true.' But she knew it was, for hadn't she searched for
another explanation – any other explanation that would
exonerate Maman? She leaned against the cold steel of
the gate and sobbed till she thought her chest would
burst open, spilling out her heart on to the stony path.

When Giselle came and took her by the arm, she followed blindly, her sobs drowning Maman's words of comfort.

Jean-Luc stared as they came in. 'Is she all right?'

'She is over tired,' Giselle said. 'Obviously someone prevented her from having any sleep last night, with his shouting.' As Christine became almost hysterical at this, she added hastily, 'It's all right, Christine; just calm down, will you? I'll put her to bed, Jean-Luc. Open the door for me.'

But Christine, at the foot of the stairs, fell to her knees and sobbed so heartbrokenly that Jean-Luc said, 'I will carry her,' and picked her up in his arms like a baby. She hid her face in his shoulder, comforted by the faint smell of the aftershave he always wore and ashamed that he should have to carry her. 'I'm too heavy,' she said between sobs, and he said, 'Not at all,' but rather breathlessly.

'Where is your duvet, Christine?' Giselle demanded as Jean-Luc deposited his burden on the uncovered bed.

'Bon Papa,' Christine gulped. 'Bon Papa . . . was cold.'

'I'll fetch the spare blankets,' Jean-Luc said.

Giselle stood looking down at Christine. 'You are very tired, *ma fille*,' she said, and it sounded almost like a command. 'I will bring you your supper up here, when it is ready.'

When Giselle came up later with the tray, however, Christine hid her face under the blankets, and did not move. She heard Maman say to Papa, '*Voilà*, she is asleep. As I told you, she is just over tired.'

Then the footsteps retreated and Christine was left alone.

5

No one at La Sainte Vierge school worked very hard on a Saturday. With the freedom of Saturday afternoon within a few hours' reach, the children could not take the morning seriously.

Half the girls in Christine's class were perched on the school steps, watching from this lofty position the break-time activities of the other half.

Carine, as new girl, had been allowed first turn in the skipping game. It was not entirely a matter of courtesy; the established champions – notably Marie-Louise – were anxious to size up their new competition.

The girls sitting on the steps clapped their hands in time to the slow thud of the skipping rope on the tarmac.

'. . . *huit, neuf, DIX*!'

The rope speeded up. '*Onze, douze, treize . . .*'

Carine's solemn, elfin face showed no emotion. She jumped the rope neatly and without any apparent effort. Only the black-rimmed glasses showed any agitation, rising and falling on the bridge of her small pink *retroussé* nose.

'Let me take the rope,' Marie-Louise demanded.

Véronique, holding the rope, resisted. 'It's not your turn.'

'You're not doing it properly,' Marie-Louise objected, tossing her blonde curls. 'It's too slow.'

'It's all right like that,' Christine said. 'It's not meant to get any quicker till after *vingt*.'

'. . . *dix-neuf* . . . *et VINGT*! *Et plus vite!*' chorused the supporting cast.

The rope speeded up again.

'*Plus vite! Plus vite encore!*' clamoured Marie-Louise. 'Let me take the rope.'

'No!' said the girls with the rope.

'No!' said Christine, and 'No!' said Carine, a trifle breathlessly. Already Carine knew Marie-Louise well enough to suspect that in her hands, if her supremacy should be challenged, the skipping rope could become a weapon.

Christine knew it.

'. . . *vingt-neuf . . . et TRENTE!*'

Faster still.

'. . . *trente-huit . . . neuf . . . QUARANTE!*'

The spectators on the steps sat forward expectantly.

When the count reached a hundred, the voices hushed reverently. The rope was spinning so fast that it could hardly be seen. Carine's perspiring face showed extreme concentration. Finally she gasped, 'That's enough!' and sat down precipitately.

'A hundred and forty-two!' exclaimed Véronique admiringly.

'Fantastic!' acclaimed Christine.

'My turn,' said Marie-Louise.

Carine took her place on the steps, beside Christine. Her thin chest heaved from the effort.

'That was really good,' said Christine, and Carine smiled radiantly.

'Start the rope,' said Marie-Louise.

The rope turned and the chanting began slowly again.

'*Un . . . deux . . . trois . . .*'

There was a sense of anti-climax.

At '*dix-neuf*' Marie-Louise stumbled and the rope came to a halt.

'Only nineteen,' said Véronique.

'You speeded up too soon!' Marie-Louise accused. 'You're not meant to speed up till *vingt*.'

'I didn't,' Véronique protested.

'You did!'

'She didn't,' other voices affirmed.

'She did! Suddenly, *on dix-huit*, she speeded up,' Marie-Louise insisted.

Christine glanced at Carine and saw the delight in her victory draining from her face.

'Carine is better than us, anyway,' Christine said. 'The highest anyone ever got before was ninety-something.'

'The highest I got was twelve,' said plump Suzanne, and giggled helplessly.

'I got to eighty-six once,' said Véronique, 'but I was younger then.'

'I've done hundred and sixty before now,' claimed Marie-Louise loudly.

'Oh, Marie-Louise, you haven't,' Véronique remonstrated.

'I have! I have!' said Marie-Louise wildly.

'I would have remembered it,' insisted Véronique.

'It was one time when you were away.' Marie-Louise's face contorted with the effort of making herself believed. 'That's why you don't remember it – but I did it.'

'I don't remember it either,' said Christine, 'and I haven't been away for ages, apart from yesterday.'

Marie-Louise, maddened, turned on her. 'You're not much of a friend if you can't remember that!' she shouted. 'It's Carine now, is it? "Well done, Carine! You're better than Marie-Louise, Carine!"' Her voice rose to a shriek.

Carine twisted her hands together and stared at the tarmac.

'I didn't say that,' said Christine. 'But she is good, you have to admit it.'

The others murmured assent.

'A hundred and forty-two!' Suzanne repeated. 'And it was going really fast at the end!'

Christine nodded. 'I couldn't do it,' she told Carine.

'You couldn't do anything, Christine Rochaud!' shouted Marie-Louise, and the class sat forward expectantly once more. When Marie-Louise lost her temper, it could be more exciting than any skipping contest. 'You can't skip at all, hardly! You sing flat! And you look like a rag-bag!' She paused for further inspiration, and the heads turned hopefully towards Christine to await her response.

'At least,' said Christine coldly, 'I don't screech like a crow.'

A ripple of amusement spread through the group and a few elbows nudged each other furtively.

'At least my father has his own photography studio!' Marie-Louise countered.

Christine hesitated. 'At least my father works harder than yours,' she said.

Marie-Louise's eyes shone as she found a trump card. 'At least,' she said, dwelling lovingly on the words, 'at least my mother doesn't go around with other men!'

A gasp went up. Marie-Louise had gone too far. Eager eyes turned upon Christine's face. Carine edged furtively nearer to her new friend, her elbow touching Christine's in tacit moral support.

Christine felt herself go hot all over.

'That's not true,' she said, and her voice cracked.

'*Mais si*!' Marie-Louise insisted triumphantly, 'It's the truth! I know! Someone told my mother.'

'They were wrong,' said Christine. Her cheeks burned, and the pressure of threatening tears made her eyes ache. 'You are lying.' She could not believe at that moment, that she had ever liked Marie-Louise. She searched for something to say to stop Marie-Louise's accusations and

99

prevent the hated emotions rising in her throat. Her mind flickered over the vision of Marie-Louise's father receiving Maman's note yesterday and turning so abruptly away.

'My maman says so,' Marie-Louise continued smugly. 'My maman says that when your father is away your maman goes out with other men.'

'And did your maman say who all these "other men" are?' Christine asked, with dangerous calm.

Marie-Louise shrugged. 'What difference does it make?'

'Oh,' said Christine, 'it makes a lot of difference.' She looked at Marie-Louise, at the smile – so like Henri's – on her pretty, self-satisfied face, and she thought of the words that could wipe off that smile and make Marie-Louise share her own sufferings of last night.

Knowing that Marie-Louise could so easily be hurt made Christine suddenly pity her. If she only knew! But Marie-Louise, whatever her behaviour now, had been her closest friend. So instead of shattering forever the complacent smile and the complacent faith in the father who had his own photography studio, Christine merely shrugged and said firmly, in unconscious imitation of her own father, 'This is silly. I won't discuss it, it's too ridiculous. Let's have another game.'

The others still hesitated, waiting for Marie-Louise's response, but Christine took one end of the skipping rope and Carine picked up the other.

'It's your turn, Madeleine,' Christine said, and the skipping resumed, slowly and doubtfully at first, but then, as they all became engrossed, fast and furious as before, and the argument was swept aside.

Later, as they were coming out of school at midday and Marie-Louise, defiantly arm-in-arm with Madeleine

Guirac, had gone on ahead, Véronique whispered to Christine, 'But it isn't true, is it, about your mother?'

'Of course it isn't,' Christine answered with only a second's hesitation, and Carine supplied: 'It was just that Marie-Louise was running out of things to say. It was obvious she was making it all up.'

'Oh, *bien sûr*,' Véronique agreed promptly. 'Me, I never believed it for a minute. She will say anything to cause a sensation, that one.'

With her new-found knowledge, Christine was half-afraid she would find Henri at home when she returned, but Maman was alone.

'Tante Léonie is coming round after lunch,' she told Christine. 'She's leaving the children here and going shopping.'

'Oh. How is Bon Papa?'

'He seems a little better,' Giselle said, 'but I'm keeping him in bed.'

Christine nodded, 'I think you are right,' she said seriously.

Giselle looked at her with some amusement. 'Oh, you do? Well, that's something anyway.' She sighed, from the heart. 'I haven't done much right recently.'

Two days ago, Christine would have gone and hugged her but now, somehow, she held back, and Giselle continued: 'Go and change out of your school clothes. Papa's coming home early again this afternoon.'

Bon Papa, when Christine went to his room, did indeed look a little better.

'Yes,' he said, 'I am better. Madame Rouvieux came in this morning to see me.'

Christine perched on the edge of the bed. 'How did she know you were ill?'

'How does Madame Rouvieux know everything there

is to know?' he responded. 'She has antennae, that woman, like a bat – a private radar system.'

Christine giggled. 'Did Maman let her in?'

'How could she refuse?' Bon Papa said. 'It was a neighbourly thing to do. She is a kind woman, Madame Rouvieux. When she saw I was well enough to sit up, she went and fetched the draughts board and we had a few games.'

'Who won?'

'Eh?' asked Bon Papa. 'Oh, she did. I let her win the last couple, poor old woman.'

Christine smothered a smile. Madame Rouvieux was at least five years younger than Grand-père.

'She asked after you,' Bon Papa added.

'After me?' Christine was flattered. 'Why?'

'She likes you. She says you always stop and talk to her on your way home from school.'

'She stops me, usually,' Christine said. 'Every day she says the same things.'

'She is lonely,' said Bon Papa. 'She talks just to hear the sound of a voice.'

'Really?' Christine tried to imagine what that would be like. 'Why don't we invite her here one evening?'

'Your mother wouldn't like it,' Bon Papa answered mechanically. '*Regarde* – I found you a new word today.'

He picked up the newspaper and held it very close to his eyes. '*Voilà*! Read me this one.'

Christine got up and peered over his shoulder. '*Une mé-ta-mor-pose*,' she articulated.

'A-ha!' Bon Papa was triumphant. '*Métamor-PHOSE*! And what does it mean?'

Christine shook her head. 'I don't know. I think I've heard the word before but . . .'

'*Alors*,' said Bon Papa. 'Fetch the *Larousse* and look it up.'

Christine ran downstairs to the salon.

'I told you to change out of your school clothes, Christine!' Maman called.

'I will,' she promised. 'In just a minute.'

She ran back into Bon Papa's room with the heavy volume.

'Just let me find it . . . *voilà! Métamorphose* . . . change from one form into another; transformation. I still don't know what it is!'

Bon Papa's brow puckered with concentration.

'Well, for example – a butterfly. When it is born it's a bug, a small ugly thing. Then one day – whoosh! – it hatches into a butterfly. *Voilà une métamorphose.*'

'Oh, I see. What about a kitten becoming a cat – is that a metamorphosis?'

'No-o.' He was uncertain. 'It is the same form, you see, only bigger; and it happens gradually. A metamorphosis is a sudden transformation.'

'Like Cinderella,' Christine said. 'It was a metamorphosis when the rats changed into footmen.'

'Exactly,' said Grand-père, satisfied.

'Find me another word, Bon Papa.'

'You find one,' he said. 'Look at the newspaper and pick out one that you don't know.'

She scanned the page. '*Comité* – no, I know that one. It's a group of people deciding things, *n'est-ce pas*?'

'More commonly,' said Bon Papa, 'it is a group of people talking about deciding things and in the end deciding nothing. But you have the right idea, yes.'

'*Trilingue!*' Christine exclaimed. 'That's one I don't know.'

'*Mais si!*' Bon Papa admonished. 'You know it.'

'No I don't.'

'*Mais si, si!*' he insisted. 'It is being able to speak three languages.'

'Oh! Like *bilingue* is speaking two?'

'Of course.'

She thought for a minute. 'And what is someone who speaks four languages?'

'A freak.' They both laughed appreciatively, which set Bon Papa coughing again.

'I wish you would see the doctor, Bon Papa.'

'What can the doctor do?' he wheezed.

'He can keep you . . . keep you well,' Christine said.

'Keep me alive, *hein*?' Bon Papa looked penetratingly at her. 'Is that what you mean? *Non, ma fille*, the doctor cannot do that. One lives when it is time to live and dies when it is time to die.'

Christine did not look at him. 'I expect you'll miss me,' she said nonchalantly.

He took her hand and patted it. 'Not at all,' he said, 'I shall be keeping an eye on you, up there. So mind you behave now!'

She half smiled. 'It's not the same though, is it? I won't be able to talk to you – or at least you won't be able to answer.'

Grand-père hesitated a minute. 'Listen,' he said seriously, 'I will tell you this for you alone – understand? If ever you are in any trouble after I'm gone – trouble that Maman or Papa cannot help you with – then you can always contact your Tante Sophie.'

'Tante Sophie?' Christine said in bewilderment. 'But she lives in England, and Maman doesn't even know the address.'

'I have the address,' said Bon Papa, 'and I will give it to you. In the bureau – go and look – in the inside drawer, a piece of paper.'

Wondering, Christine fetched it. 'Madame Sophie Broon,' she read. 'Is that her name? Broon?'

'Brown, it is pronounced,' Bon Papa said. 'Copy out

the address now, carefully. And then perhaps you can write it out again on an envelope you will find there.'

'Are you writing to her?' Christine was astounded. The elusive, long-lost Tante Sophie was suddenly miraculously near at hand. Bon Papa knew her!

'I don't write now,' Bon Papa said. 'My eyes are not good enough. But I send her a little money every month. You will also find that in the bureau and you can put it in the envelope when you have addressed it.'

Christine was doubtful. 'I don't think you can send money through the post,' she said. 'Maman says – '

'I have been doing it for fifteen years,' said Bon Papa brusquely, 'so don't tell me that I can't.'

'Fifteen years,' said Christine in amazement. 'Before I was born!'

'Ah yes,' said Bon Papa and his eyes twinkled. 'Believe it or not, *mon enfant*, the world turned even before you were born.'

'But Bon Papa!' Christine exclaimed, struck by a sudden thought. 'I could write a letter for you! If you told me what to say, I could write it down.'

'Of course,' he said slowly. 'Yes, of course.' His old eyes shone suddenly. 'You will tell her that her papa has a secretary now. Your best handwriting now!' he warned.

Christine was hunting through the desk for some writing paper. 'I'm ready, Bon Papa. What shall I put?'

He sat back against the pillows and closed his eyes. 'Begin "*Ma bien chère Sophie*,"' he said. 'It is almost two years since I have been able to write to you, because of the cataracts in my eyes. As before, *ma petite*, I think it best that you do not write back, but I am glad to know that you will receive these few words from me, through my little granddaughter Christine, Giselle's daughter, who resembles you in many ways.'

He was going much too fast, Christine thought. Her

hand was aching with the effort of keeping up. Bon Papa seemed to have forgotten that he was dictating a letter and was talking to himself, much of it not making sense; he was lost in the world of the past.

She couldn't put in the letter all about how he had met Grand-mère and everything. Tante Sophie would want to hear some news, after two years.

'Ah,' said Bon Papa, 'those were good times.'

'Bon Papa,' Christine said, 'Tante Sophie will want to know how you are, won't she? What shall I put?'

'*Hein*? Oh, the letter,' he said, remembering. 'Yes, you write something, Christine. Can you do that? You will say things better than me.' His face was white again, drawn with the effort of talking.

'I'll do it, Bon Papa. Why don't you lie down?'

He moved painfully down the bed. 'Say what you think. You write a good letter. Tell her about us.'

Christine fumbled through the *Larousse* for the spelling of 'cataract'.

'How much will the stamp cost, Bon Papa?'

'There are some in the drawer,' he said.

Christine wrote steadily, telling Tante Sophie about Bon Papa's bronchitis, about Maman's outings and Papa's work and about Tante Léonie and Oncle Pierre and her small cousins, Fabienne and René.

Grand-père stretched forward and caught her hand as she was writing. 'She will receive it next week,' he said, and there were tears in his eyes.

Christine spent the afternoon trying to amuse Fabienne and baby René.

'They will be no trouble to me, Léonie, I assure you,' Maman had said, and they were not. Giselle shut herself in the kitchen for the afternoon and cooked. Delicious aromas floated through to the salon – vegetable soup, ratatouille, and little spice gâteaux.

'Give me one, Tante Giselle,' Fabienne begged, but Maman was hard-hearted.

'Later on, when they are cold,' she said. 'In the meantime, out of my kitchen.'

Fabienne pouted. 'But I want one now!'

'You won't get any at all,' Giselle said, 'if you make faces like that.' Fabienne was not Maman's favourite. René got the last piece of chocolate from the dining-room buffet, and a brisk hug and kiss, which made him cry.

'I don't like Tante Giselle,' said Fabienne. 'She's just like my maman. My papa gives me anything I want.' She swung her long hair defiantly, a seven-year-old woman.

'You'll have a cake later,' Christine promised. 'They make you burp when they're too hot, anyway.'

'I don't care,' Fabienne claimed. 'I like burping. If I scream,' she said, 'will Tante Giselle give me one?'

'No, she won't,' Christine said, with conviction, 'but you might get a smack.'

Fabienne decided against it. 'Will you get your dolls' house out, like last time?'

'If you like. It's upstairs, though. You'll have to stay down here and watch René while I fetch it.'

'No, I'll come and help you,' Fabienne decided.

'You can't help,' Christine told her. 'The stairs are too narrow for two people to carry it down at once.'

'I'll come up anyway, and see your room,' Fabienne said. 'Have you got any new things?'

'No, it's not my birthday yet.'

'My papa buys me things,' said Fabienne proudly, 'even when it's not my birthday.'

'Yes, I know. Stay down here with René, Fabienne, just while I fetch the dolls' house.'

'No, I'm coming with you,' the child insisted.

Christine gave in. 'All right then, but don't make any noise because Bon Papa's ill and he's having a sleep.'

'Will we see him?'

'I expect you can see him when he wakes up,' Christine said, like a mother promising a treat.

'I don't want to see him,' Fabienne said.

Christine was shocked. 'Why not?'

'He smells,' said Fabienne dismissively. 'I don't like people who smell.'

'He does not smell!' said Christine in a furious whisper, for they were outside Bon Papa's door now.

'He does,' said Fabienne unperturbed. 'Haven't you noticed it?'

'No,' said Christine shortly. To be sure, Bon Papa had his own particular odour, a unique blend of tobacco and old man and the garlic cloves he loved to chew, but that was an intrinsic part of him. Almost from babyhood, Christine could remember that unmistakable aroma of Bon Papa, pungent and comforting.

'Don't forget the furniture for the dolls' house,' Fabienne prompted. 'Don't forget the sofa with the little cushions.'

As it happened, it was the dolls' sofa with the little cushions that caused the trouble when Papa came home.

'What is all this mess?' he demanded, coming into the salon and finding it strewn with tiny articles of furniture.

René, who had been peaceably chewing the legs of one of the dolls' house occupants, burst into lusty howls at the sound of his voice.

'For God's sake!' Jean-Luc supplicated. 'Get all of these things out of here, Christine. Go and play in your bedroom.'

Christine lifted the dolls' house, with Fabienne still trying to push her hand through the windows to salvage a favourite item. 'Let go, Fabienne, we've got to take everything upstairs. Will you pick up some of the things?'

'I'll bring René,' Fabienne said and, catching him none too gently round the neck, began to drag him across the floor. René's screams redoubled.

'*Nom de Dieu!*' Jean-Luc swore. 'Giselle! Giselle! Giselle!'

Maman came and removed the children by promising spiced gâteaux.

'Can't a man have any peace in his own house?' Jean-Luc demanded.

'The house happens to belong to Grand-père,' said Giselle acidly, 'and your love for peace has never been made particularly obvious, to me at least.'

Christine returned to gather up the rest of the toys, packing them meticulously into the box.

'Come on, Christine!' Jean-Luc urged her. He scooped up the fragile things roughly and trod on what looked like a miniature sofa. 'Get this rubbish out of my way!' he shouted, flinging the offending article into the waste-paper bin, and Christine gathered up an armful of toys and fled, scattering tiny chairs and tables in her wake.

'My papa never shouts at me like that,' Fabienne declared, her rosebud mouth bulging with gâteau. 'My papa is nicer than yours. He's the best papa in the whole world.'

'You only think that because he is yours,' Christine asserted, while Maman stooped, precipitately removing a stray cigarette end from René's questing fingers which hungrily combed the floor.

'Why?' Fabienne asked. 'Do you think your papa is the best in the whole world?'

'Yes,' said Christine, with only the slightest hesitation, 'of course I do.'

Giselle let out a snort of sardonic laughter. 'Then God preserve us from the worst,' she said.

Jean-Luc relinquished his solitary possession of the salon only when Tante Léonie had come and gone, irritable after her unfruitful shopping for bargain-priced clothes to make her look like a millionaire's fancy.

'They're so sly, these manufacturers,' she told Giselle. 'They make clothes which look marvellous in the shop then once they are put on a real person – hey presto! Lumps and bumps and bulgy seams everywhere. It's a disaster.' And she left in a state of high discontent, dragging her two protesting children home to a repeat of last night's supper.

'Has she gone?' Jean-Luc enquired, emerging from the salon.

'Well, look who it is!' Maman exclaimed, facetiously. 'The last of the protected species. Join the real world, *mon brave*. I have had the most exhausting afternoon.'

'I am going out,' said Jean-Luc.

Giselle stared at him. 'Out where?' she demanded.

'For a drive.'

'Oh, marvellous!' Giselle applauded. 'Monsieur tells me I am not to go out, my life is not my own, my body, my soul, are not my own and then he, Monsieur the Independent, takes it into his head . . .'

'SHUT UP!' Jean-Luc roared and Christine flinched at the agony in his voice. He sounded, she thought, like a wounded lion she had seen once in a film.

'I'm telling you, Giselle, don't force me, don't force me . . .' His whole head flushed red as blood and a bulging vein strained against the skin on his temple. Trembling with emotion, and with tears flooding down his cheeks, he wrenched the back door open and flung himself out.

Christine watched him, aghast.

'Papa!' she cried, but he had gone.

'Let him go, Christine,' said Maman in a flat voice. 'He'll be back when he's got over it.'

But Jean-Luc was not back for supper, even though they waited until later than usual.

'We'll have to start,' Giselle said finally. 'The ratatouille will be ruined as it is.'

They sat, the two of them, in lonely splendour in the dining-room, while Bon Papa ate his supper on a tray upstairs.

'He'll be back, don't worry,' Giselle said, though Christine had not uttered the question.

They cleared away the plates and swept up the crumbs and left the table as if it had never been used. The washing-up was completed in silence.

'Where are you going?' Giselle demanded, as Christine left the room.

'To do some homework,' she said, surprised.

'Can't you do it down here?'

Christine shrugged. 'All my books are in my room.'

'Then bring them down here,' Maman said.

So Christine brought the books down and spread them out on the dining-room table, while Maman paced back and forth and smoked cigarettes and twisted the flowers into different arrangements in the vases.

'He is doing this to worry me,' Giselle said, wrenching the neck of a gold chrysanthemum to make it face the other way. 'He thinks he will have me gnashing my teeth with jealousy at what he is doing.'

'He said he was just going for a drive,' Christine reminded her.

'That's all he will do,' Giselle said. 'He thinks he will make me jealous, but I know.'

'Where can he drive to, though?' Christine wondered. 'He's been gone three hours.'

When he had been gone four hours, Giselle said, 'He is staying out for the night, that's obvious. Well, I'm not waiting up for him.' But she stayed up, and Christine stayed too. Once, when she stood up, Giselle said helplessly, 'Don't go to bed,' and she answered, 'I'm going to the bathroom. I won't be a minute.'

At twenty to twelve, Christine placed a glass of Ricard at Maman's elbow and Giselle drank without tasting it. Then they sat in silence again, Giselle staring at her fingers and flaking off the bright red polish with her thumbnail, while Christine yawned and widened her eyes in an effort to stay awake.

When the phone rang at half-past twelve, it was a relief to both of them. An accident, Maman said, replacing the receiver. Papa was not badly hurt but in a state of shock. They could go to the hospital if they wished.

The smell of the hospital corridors made Christine shudder. The scoured stone floors echoed death and disaster; doors clanged on shuttered rooms, ringing with ordeals too terrible to mention.

Despair hung over the place like a yellow fog.

'Come along, Christine!'

In the admissions ward, a row of inert bodies lay inhaling through tubes, bags of blood suspended ghoulishly above them like a vampires' tavern. Christine kept the back of her hand surreptitiously in contact with the folds of Maman's skirt.

Papa, unconscious and unrecognizable, was the third body from the door. Whereas the other bodies gasped and whistled through their throats, Christine could not hear him breathe.

'Is he breathing?' she asked the white-coated attendant.

'Of course he's breathing,' said Maman angrily. 'He's not dead.'

The attendant moved away to adjust a tube in an adjacent arm.

'I want him moved,' said Maman, 'to a single room.'

'Tomorrow,' the man promised. 'He is only in this ward for the night.'

The doctor arrived. 'Madame Rochaud?'

Maman extended a hand. 'Your husband will be all right,' the doctor assured her. 'He has a couple of cracked ribs and some bruising and he is suffering from shock.'

'What happened?' Giselle asked. 'Was there a collision?'

The doctor shook his head. 'He drove into a wall,' he said.

Giselle was stunned. 'Had he been drinking?'

The doctor looked embarrassed. 'It appears not. Is there any reason . . . had your husband any particular problems, Madame – financial perhaps, or . . . ah . . . marital?'

'Certainly not,' said Maman, with such indignation that the doctor ducked his head apologetically. 'Naturally,' Maman added, 'he has a very demanding job.'

'Had there been any trouble at work, do you know?'

'It's always possible,' said Giselle dismissively. 'He doesn't talk much about his work.'

Christine spoke up. 'But how,' she asked, 'could he drive into a wall? He always drives so carefully!'

Maman answered her quickly. 'It is impossible to tell how it happened, Christine. Probably he swerved to avoid something.'

The doctor nodded vigorously. 'Of course,' he agreed. 'It is impossible to tell. There were no witnesses. I am sure, however, your husband will be able to tell you himself tomorrow, Madame. The injuries are not serious.'

He scurried away, relieved at having discharged his

task without causing any of the hysteria so often associated with it.

Maman and Christine remained staring at Papa's inert form, one in an identical row of humps under identical bedclothes.

'We might as well go home,' Giselle said. 'We can come back tomorrow.'

Christine remembered climbing into a taxi beside Maman, then sleep engulfed her like a thick black shroud.

6

'But why?' said Christine. 'Why have you arranged for me to stay at Tante Léonie's?'

'It's only for a few days,' Giselle promised. 'It will be much better for everyone. For one thing, you will not be exposed to the risk of infection.'

'You can't catch bronchitis from someone else,' Christine asserted.

'Pardon me, but you can,' Giselle contradicted.

'I've never caught it before, the other times Bon Papa has had it. Neither have you, or Papa.'

'Christine, you will accept that your Maman knows a little more about medical matters than you do,' Giselle told her.

'Well, I don't care if I do catch it,' said Christine rebelliously. 'I want to stay here with Bon Papa.'

'I have quite enough to do, Christine, looking after Bon Papa and now having to run back and forth to the hospital to see Papa,' said Giselle, 'without having you under my feet as well. Now do try to be grown up and understanding, *chérie*. You know it's a lot of work for me.'

'But I can help you!' Christine protested. 'I can take Bon Papa his meals so you won't have to go up the stairs all the time, and . . .'

'No! I have said no, Christine, and that is all there is to it.'

'But Bon Papa needs me!' Christine burst out. 'He likes me there when he's ill! He says I cheer him up.'

Giselle laughed. Christine's woebegone face at this moment did not look as though it would cheer up anyone.

'Don't be so ridiculous, Christine! What is so terrible about a few days' holiday at your Tante Léonie's? You've been there often enough before.'

'I know,' said Christine dismally. 'That's why I don't want to go again.'

But it had been no use, and by the evening she was here in Tante Léonie's house, unpacking her suitcase in the cluttered room she would have to share with her cousin Fabienne. Slowly and reluctantly, she laid her clothes on the narrow camp bed and opened the wardrobe. It was crammed tight with Fabienne's frilly dresses, skirts, elegantly tailored little coats, and several flounced dressing gowns.

Christine closed the door again and tried the chest of drawers. The drawers stuck, packed too full with Fabienne's cute little jerseys and blouses, petticoats and spotless underwear. Fabienne did not appear to have cleared much space for her cousin. Every available surface, from the pink satin-ruffed dressing table to the small, unused desk, was overflowing with fluffy toys, dolls' clothes and painted china ornaments. Christine looked round the room, shrugged, and put her clothes back in the suitcase.

She had a particular dislike for this fussy little room, for some of her unhappiest hours had been spent here, lying awake on the ridgy camp bed worrying about whatever crisis was happening at home and wondering how long she would have to remain in exile. Christine was determined not to stay long this time. On purpose she had packed very few clothes so that she would have an excuse to go home to collect clean ones.

She felt absurdly guilty at leaving Grand-père to the mercy of Maman when he was ill. Giselle would carry trays up to his room and stay in when the doctor called, Christine knew, but she lacked patience for the extra little attentions which could make him feel – what was the word she wanted? – not pampered exactly, but, cherished, perhaps. She felt that Bon Papa needed constantly to be reminded that there was some reason for hanging on to life, else he might give up the awful, unequal struggle to keep breathing, wondering whether it was all worth it.

Christine's train of thought was interrupted by sudden, piercing screams from the direction of the salon, and the sound of feet running down the passage. The door burst open and Fabienne rushed in, shrieking, and flung herself on the bed.

'What's the matter?' Christine enquired after a few minutes, when her small cousin showed signs of running out of breath.

'Maaa-maan!'

'What has Maman done?' Christine pursued patiently.

'She HIT me! I was painting a picture in the salon and the jar of water just fell over. It RUINED my picture!' Fabienne opened her mouth to howl again.

'I don't suppose it did much for the carpet either,' said Christine practically. 'Come on, don't cry – show me all the new toys Papa has brought you since the last time I came.'

Fabienne refused to be consoled. 'When Papa comes home I'm going to tell him Maman hit me,' she said vindictively.

'What for?'

'So that Papa will tell Maman off for being so mean,' said Fabienne righteously. 'And he'll give me some bon-bons to make up for it, and Maman will be furious,' she concluded triumphantly.

117

Christine was scandalized. 'But you can't make trouble between your parents like that!'

Fabienne shrugged. 'Why not? I always do.' She lost interest in the subject. 'Look at my dress! It's got paint all over it.' She opened the door and bawled: 'Maman! Maa-man!'

Christine watched her, perplexed. Tante Léonie came into the room, carrying René. 'What is it now? Fabienne! Just look at your dress!'

'It's the paint,' explained Fabienne unnecessarily. 'You'll have to wash it.'

'You wicked child!' screamed Léonie. 'As if I hadn't got enough work! Take it off immediately.'

Fabienne ducked out of range of her mother's avenging hand and began undoing the buttons of the dress.

'Come here!' Léonie dropped René, who howled in protest. She grabbed Fabienne, pulled the dress roughly over her curly head, and slapped her bare leg resoundingly, leaving a dull red patch. Fabienne clutched her mother's hand to restrain it and let out an ear-splitting scream which had the effect of maddening Léonie even further.

Christine picked up René, who continued to cry for his mother. The noise was appalling. Oh Bon Papa, thought Christine in desperation, why have they sent me here?

The sudden entrance of Oncle Pierre caused an immediate, miraculous silence. 'What the devil is going on?' he enquired. 'Honestly, Léonie, I wish you would control your temper with the children. *Bonsoir*, Christine – how are you enjoying yourself in this madhouse? Léonie, for heaven's sake put some clothes on Fabienne; she'll freeze to death.'

'Do it yourself,' Léonie retorted furiously. 'I've got better things to do. I've been trying to prepare supper for the past half hour.'

'Well, you go and get on with it then. I'm ravenous.'

'You needn't expect it on time, after all the interruptions I've had from Fabienne.'

'Don't waste any more time then,' Pierre replied, infuriatingly calm. 'Viens, *mon chou*, let's find you a clean frock. What about this one?'

'Yes, lovely!' Fabienne was all smiles for her father, dimpling prettily and clinging affectionately to his hand.

Christine found Tante Léonie in the kitchen, poisoning the food. She threw bitter chicory into the salad bowl and mixed it with stale herbs. She hatcheted the lettuce with a blunt and rusty knife until the green leaves turned brown around the edges. The watercress had wilted under her baleful gaze.

'Pierre says he's got an ulcer now,' she said. 'I don't know why I bother to cook at all. It must be from all that restaurant food at lunch times.' She took a bottle of rancid oil from the cupboard.

'Shall I make the salad dressing? Christine offered.

'If you like. There should be some vinegar somewhere. How he expects me to have everything ready by the time he comes home . . . It makes a change for him to come home at all, instead of spending his time – his family's time and money – with stupid so-called business associates who have nothing better to do than to get drunk and tell dirty stories . . .'

'This vinegar is all cloudy, Tante Léonie. Is there a new bottle?'

'*Hein*? Oh, it'll be all right. If you want to put mustard in it, there's some on the table. I usually add a pinch.'

Christine took a look at the jar and decided against it. René sat on the floor and played with an eggshell he had found in the bin.

'Does Giselle put mustard in?' Tante Léonie asked.

'I don't think so,' Christine said. 'She puts a tiny bit of sugar in it.'

'Sugar? In salad dressing? Whatever for?'

'She says it sweetens the acid, or something.'

'What do you want sweetness for?' demanded Tante Léonie, unanswerably.

'Léonie!' Pierre called. 'When is dinner going to be ready?'

'Oh really!' Léonie snatched René up from the floor, confiscated his eggshell and plonked him in his high chair where he screamed. She stalked out of the room and Christine could hear her haranguing Pierre in the salon. She went and picked up a toy monkey from a pool of water on the draining board. 'Look, René – see the monkey!'

The little boy stopped crying and looked at her doubtfully, finger in mouth.

'Look, he's dancing!' Christine bounced the toy up and down on the tray of the high chair. René smiled.

'Shall I make the monkey dance on your arm, René? Here he comes then: are you ready?'

He giggled. The toy monkey jumped from the tray on to René's jersey, then disappeared mysteriously over the edge of the chair. René waited with bated breath. As the monkey crept slowly up the high chair he craned his neck to watch, gurgling with excitement and beating his hands on the tray.

'Really, Pierre, you are quite impossible!' shouted Léonie, walking backwards into the kitchen. 'I don't know how the hell you expect me to manage – because I just can't.'

'So you keep telling me!' Pierre yelled back from the salon. 'I thought that was the whole idea of having Christine here – what more do you want? We'll get a Swedish au pair girl if you like – I don't mind!'

The monkey paused momentarily in its antics, and René tapped Christine's hand reproachfully.

'Sorry,' she apologized. 'OK, here he comes again – ready? *Un, deux, trois . . . attrapé*!'

René burst out laughing.

'Oh, don't get him all excited, Christine,' said Léonie irritably. 'He'll be infernal later on and I've got a splitting headache as it is.'

René crowed and waved his hands.

'I thought you were doing the supper, Christine. Haven't you done anything else apart from the salad?'

'I didn't know what we were having,' replied Christine, stung by the injustice.

'Well, it's all in the fridge. You can take out the rest of the pâté; we'll start with that.'

Christine took out a crumpled package and peered at it doubtfully. 'I think it's gone off, Tante Léonie.' She sniffed at the pâté and wrinkled her nose at the smell.

'*Merde*!' swore Léonie loudly.

'*Mè! Mè!*' mimicked René delightely, waving the toy monkey.

'Look, take René and go into the salon. I can get on better by myself,' said Léonie, tight-lipped.

Christine was not sorry to be dismissed. She wandered into the salon, carrying René. Pierre was lounging in a corner of the low-backed sofa and waved a languid hand at her.

'Come and sit down. Make yourself at home.' His sweeping gesture put at her disposal the whole of the dark, high-ceilinged little room. 'Wait – I'll put a record on. You like music?'

Christine nodded and sat down. René clambered on to her lap and Fabienne, ever jealous, left her dolls on the floor to come over and pull him away.

'No, leave him, Fabienne,'

'Come and play with me, Christine.'

'Why don't you get a book and I'll read you both a story?' she suggested.

'All right. He's too little for stories anyway.' Fabienne ran off to her room to fetch a book.

Pierre winked at Christine. '*Ça va*? Don't take any notice of my wife; she has her off days. All women are the same.'

'Men have their off days too,' Christine retorted. 'All the time, some of them.'

Pierre laughed. 'You're growing up, *ma petite*. The eternal battle of the sexes, *hein*?'

Fabienne returned, her arms full of books. She leaned against Christine. 'Which one shall we have? This one's about a rabbit – it's a bit babyish: we won't have that. What about this one – no, what about *Astérix*?'

'All right. Are you listening, René? don't push him away, Fabienne – he can look at the pictures.'

The baby leaned forward to see the page and Fabienne settled herself on the sofa, one arm possessively round Christine as she began to read. Christine felt a sudden wave of affection for them. They were spoiled, certainly, but that was not their fault. She would have liked to have younger brothers and sisters to play with and look after and read to.

The music from the record-player rose and swelled round the down-at-heel room, engulfing the dark corners and the peeling paint with smooth, liquid streams of sound.

Pierre sank back into a chair, kicked off his shoes and draped his legs over the chair arm. He looked thoughtfully at the little group on the sofa, engrossed in their story . . .

'"Watch out!" cried the Big Fat Uglies – look, there they are, René – "here comes Astérix the Gaul."' Pierre's

122

expression relaxed and the corners of his mouth curved slightly, and Léonie, appearing in the doorway, looked quickly, suspiciously, towards her husband. 'You all look very settled,' she said brusquely. 'Don't you want any supper, then?'

The hands of the clock stood at ten to nine when they finally sat down to eat. Fabienne and René had dark circles under their eyes and were beginning to grizzle.

Pierre reached for the small pot of greasy *rillettes* which had replaced the ancient pâté as the first course, and inspected it silently for several minutes. Léonie looked at him with venom in her eyes.

'We had a superb lunch at work today,' he commented tactlessly. 'The hors d'oeuvre was delicious – in fact,' he chuckled at the recollection, 'Françoise ordered a second plate of it and didn't bother with the entrée at all.'

'So you had lunch with your secretary?'

'*Chérie,* it was a business lunch – don't worry yourself, there were four other men there to chaperone us!'

'And she was the only girl? I've no doubt she enjoyed that.'

'I think it was more fun for the men,' Pierre said speculatively. 'Not many business lunches are enlivened by such decorative company.'

Argument was averted by the sound of the phone ringing. Léonie hesitated, then got up to answer it.

Christine smeared a tiny amount of *rillettes* on to a piece of bread. Pierre grimaced at her. 'Disgusting, isn't it?' he remarked cheerfully. 'My wife only buys revolting food so that it lasts a week instead of three days. This time she's excelled herself; we'll probably be eating these *rillettes* for the next couple of months.'

'Who was it?' he enquired as Léonie came back into the kitchen. 'Not the Pope again, I hope. He always

123

reverses the charges,' he explained to Christine, who choked on her bread.

Léonie ignored him. 'It was Giselle.'

Christine stood up quickly. 'Can I have a word with her?'

Léonie looked at her with mild surprise. 'She's rung off now. Was it anything important?'

'I wanted to ask when I could go and see Bon Papa. Did she say he was any better?'

'Much the same, I think. You couldn't have gone over there tonight anyway, because she's going out in ten minutes. She rang to ask if she could borrow my shawl.'

'Going out? Who's looking after Bon Papa?'

'I really don't know. She didn't say. Fabienne, don't put so much in your mouth at once. Probably the neighbour – what's her name? Anyway, Papa can't come to much harm in bed and I expect he's had his supper by now. Fabienne! What did I just tell you!'

'But I could still go round,' protested Christine wretchedly. 'If he's on his own . . .'

'I didn't say he was on his own. I don't know. And look at the time! He'd probably be fast asleep by the time you arrived.'

Christine toyed miserably with the food on her plate and relapsed into silence.

'By the way,' Léonie added, 'you won't mind babysitting tomorrow night, will you? Pierre has temporarily run out of names in his little black book so while you're here he might as well take his wife out, for a change.'

Pierre raised his eyes to heaven in mock supplication.

I'll never be able to see Bon Papa at this rate, thought Christine in desperation; I'll be stuck here every evening. Instead of replying to Léonie's question, she asked, 'Did Maman say whether the doctor had called?'

'*Chérie*, I really didn't have time to ask. She'll be

popping in for the shawl in a few minutes, so you can ask her all these questions yourself.'

By the time they had ploughed their way through the meal as far as the cheese course, both René and Fabienne were wailing with fatigue, and Christine felt like joining in. Léonie cleared the table.

'Put them to bed, can't you?' said Pierre. 'They'll be impossible in the morning.'

'Why don't you do it? They're your children too.'

'I'd be extremely surprised if they weren't. But I must just read to the end of my chapter. I've got to a juicy bit. So you put them to bed and I'll do the washing-up when I've finished – OK?'

'I don't mind doing the dishes,' said Christine.

'Well, there's no point in both of you doing them,' said Léonie. 'You wash up, Pierre, and Christine can put the children to bed. Just see that Fabienne cleans her teeth, Christine; apart from that she can look after herself.'

'Will you let me know when Maman comes?'

'Oh – you'll need a clean nappy for René. There's a pile of them in the cupboard in our room.'

Pierre went into the salon and Léonie followed him. 'I thought you were going to wash up?'

'Later – I said I would do it later.'

'I know you. They'll be left in the sink . . .'

Christine picked up René. 'Come on, Fabienne, you go in the bathroom first.'

Several times while she was changing René she thought she heard a knock at the door, but when Giselle did eventually arrive, Christine was in Fabienne's room and did not hear her.

'Your stairs are terrible; they kill me!' said Giselle breathlessly, kissing her sister perfunctorily on both cheeks. 'And that woman downstairs has let her children

125

leave toys all over the place again. It's like an obstacle race. You must be very fit, living here!'

'I'm not fit, I'm exhausted,' Léonie claimed. 'Who's taking you out?'

'Monsieur Guillaume and the Bénauds. I have instructions not to be more than two minutes.'

'Well, come on in,' Léonie said. 'The shawl's in the salon. You will excuse my husband. He has his nose in a trashy book and the world revolves without his noticing.'

'Never mind, *chérie*. He could find worse things to occupy his mind – at least he's at home.'

'I tell you frankly, *ma petite,* as long as he leaves me alone he can do what he likes,' said Léonie bitterly.

'*Chérie*, we've picked the wrong husbands. You should be married to Jean-Luc – he'd never look at you! A husband like Pierre would be a welcome change sometimes!'

'I thought you said Pierre wasn't your type.' Léonie looked sharply at her sister.

'I was only joking, *mon chou.*' Giselle laid a hand on her arm with a touch of impatience. 'Look, I'd better hurry, or they will go without me.'

Léonie pushed open the salon door. 'Pierre, throw me that shawl on the table, will you?'

'*Hein*?'

'The shawl. Oh, never mind, I'll get it myself. It's like being married to a stone wall,' Léonie commented to Giselle.

Pierre pinched Léonie's bottom as she passed. 'Better than an ice-maiden,' he said, and Léonie looked annoyed.

Giselle watched them with amusement. 'By the way, where's Christine? Gone to bed?'

'No, not yet. Do you want to see her?'

'I haven't got the time. It took me ages to persuade old

126

Madame Rouvieux to babysit for Papa; she wanted to wait in for some telephone call or something.'

Christine appeared in the doorway. 'Maman,' she said, 'is Bon Papa better?'

Giselle laughed. 'Charming, *n'est-ce pas,* Léonie? *Bonsoir,* Maman, lovely to see you, how are you? Oh no, just "How's Bon Papa?"'

Christine flushed.

'*Non, chérie* – he's about the same. The doctor's coming again tomorrow lunch time. I must go. Even with the speed Paul Guillaume drives we'll be horribly late.'

'Well, I only hope his driving is better than Jean-Luc's,' Pierre said, and Giselle and Léonie laughed. 'How was he this evening, by the way?'

'Oh fine,' said Giselle. 'I must fly, darlings. Drop round tomorrow, Léonie, after taking Fabienne to school, and we'll go to the market.'

Christine followed her mother out on to the stairs. 'Maman,' she said in an urgent whisper, 'let me come home – please.'

'*Ma petite* Christine, you haven't been here five minutes!' Seeing the woebegone expression on Christine's face, Giselle added, 'Don't worry, it isn't for long and you'll be the first to hear all the news. Just be patient, there's a good girl.' She dropped a kiss on Christine's head and hurried downstairs.

'Giselle!' Monsieur Bénaud's voice floated up the stairwell. 'Are you going to be all night?'

'*J'arrive, mes enfants, j'arrive!*'

Once Giselle had left, Tante Léonie dispatched Christine to bed. She lay stiffly on its uncompromising hardness, listening to Fabienne's breathing and studying the forms of the furniture in the moonlight.

Finally, abandoning attempts at sleep, she knelt up on the bed and parted the curtains slightly. The moon, luminously white and distant, made her feel cold and lonely, an insignificant speck in a giant universe. It seemed only natural that such a tiny organism should be forgotten in the great scheme of things. What difference could it make to anyone, after all, whether she stayed in one house or another, whether her mother slept with one man or another, or her grandfather lived for a few more years or a few more minutes?

But it makes a difference to me, Christine thought desperately. Puny and powerless, she could only wait and – since she had only been taught to say prayers and not to pray – repeat over and over again the formalized words, '*Notre Père, qui es aux cieux* . . . Our Father who art in heaven . . .' But heaven was far away and she could not see the God she had heard of in school, only the cold white face of the moon.

Back in bed, with the curtains closed, the world was cosier, and she remembered other words of the prayer. 'Give us this day our daily bread.' A God who cared about whether his creatures had enough bread could not, surely, be a cold God, distant like the moon? Wasn't there something, too, about knowing every sparrow that fell? Christine began to feel vaguely comforted. She might only be a speck in the universe but she was at least bigger than a sparrow.

She stopped her frantic recitation of prayers and prayed, from the heart, 'I want to go home where I belong!' and the answer came, surprisingly easily, 'Then go home.'

Tomorrow, she decided, after school, she would simply go home and tell Maman that she must see Bon Papa, and Maman in the face of such conviction would not refuse her.

* * *

School, Christine reflected, was for children with nothing more important to fill their minds.

Madeleine Guirac was drawing noses in the margin of her book. Madeleine had an uncle who was an artist, and he had taught her to draw the most wonderful noses with shadows around the nostrils and everything. Madeleine's noses were the envy of the class. Other people drew faces, but Madeleine specialized in the nose.

He had been going to go on to teach her to draw the whole face, Madeleine's uncle, but while he was staying with her family he had inconsiderately introduced himself, with the same thorough attention to anatomical detail, to a blond-haired youth in the Bois de Boulogne. The youth, in his ignorance of the artistic spirit, had introduced Madeleine's uncle to the police, who had encouraged *le bon* Oncle Marc to leave Paris in a hurry, never to return. So the artist had departed, leaving his young niece a legacy of perfect noses without a face.

Every child in the class had a story. The grown-ups don't realize, Christine mused, looking around her, how different we are. We come into this school with eleven years of life behind us, all from a different family with a different history, and they think we'll all get on just because we're all the same age.

There was Martina, now. Martina's grand-mère could tell you things that would curdle the blood if you believed them: fairy tales of a gruesomeness unrivalled by anything you could read. After her first visit to Martina's home, Christine had relayed these stories to her parents one supper time, and they had been amused by her wide-eyed credulity in the horror tales.

'There was this man, you see,' Christine told them, astounded by their placid indifference to her account, 'who baked babies in gas ovens. Really he did! Martina's grand-mère told me, and she knew him. And then, do you know what he did?'

'Finish your beef, Christine. Don't talk with your mouth full.'

'Yes but, Maman, this man . . .'

'Pass me the onions, Jean-Luc. Yes, all right, we're listening. Which man was this?'

'But I'm telling you! This man that Martina's grand-mère told me about. I can't remember his name, but he stole all these little children away from their mothers and he made bedspreads out of their clothes – I think that was it – and then he baked them in ovens, just for fun.'

'Not to eat for his supper?' Maman said.

'The child will have nightmares,' Bon Papa growled.

'No I won't,' said Christine indignantly.

'You're too old to believe all that rubbish,' Jean-Luc had said. 'The old woman wouldn't have told you if she'd thought you would swallow such fables and take them to heart like this. Now, enough talking. Eat up your beef.'

'But Papa, it's not a story; it's all true! I tell you, Martina's grand-mère knew this man. He did it to one of her babies, that's how she knew.'

'Oh what rubbish, Christine!' Giselle had exclaimed.

'But he did, I tell you! Martina's mother said so too. She said that if Martina's grand-mère hadn't run away from Poland and come to France they would all have been put in gas ovens and killed too.'

There was a terrible silence. The family froze.

'Christine,' said Jean-Luc slowly. 'This Martina, what is her surname?'

'Godard. Why?'

'Her grandmother's surname, what is it?'

'How would I know? Oh yes, I do. Madame Something-Inska. Something funny.'

'And so the family is Jewish.'

'*Hein*? No, Polish, Papa. They're Polish.'

Maman had put her fork down. She said, 'Polish Jews,' and Jean-Luc had nodded, and Grand-père too.

'Now listen, Christine,' said Maman. They were all very solemn. 'Listen carefully, *mon chou.* You are never to talk to this child again, do you hear me? And never, on any account, to go to her home.'

Christine was aghast. 'But why? She's my friend! And her family are so nice. Her mother was the one who mended my dress when I tore it – you remember, Maman? It took her a whole hour to do and you said how beautifully it was sewn, and how kind – '

'The subject is closed, Christine,' Giselle had said. 'Pass me your plate and go and fetch the cheese.'

Later, Christine had approached Bon Papa. 'Talk to her, Bon Papa! Martina's my friend. She hasn't done anything wrong.'

But Grand-Père on this occasion had supported Giselle. 'There are matters you cannot understand, *ma fille.* The Jews have caused a lot of trouble in Europe.'

'Please, Bon Papa! Do something. Please. I didn't believe those fairy stories really. Really I didn't. Of course not. Who would?'

'Leave the matter now, Christine. Your generation cannot understand these things. We have lived through it; we know.'

And Christine had gone away saddened by the knowledge that even Bon Papa was not perfect.

At the school gates that evening, Christine found Maman.

'Is something wrong?' she asked, amazed at this unprecedented event.

'Bon Papa is still not well,' Giselle said, 'and Madame Rouvieux can't – or won't – sit with him this evening. I was going to take you to the hospital now but I can't leave him, so you'll have to go on your own and then come home and stay with Bon Papa while I go. It's a great nuisance.'

Christine did not like the idea of going to the hospital on her own. 'Can't Tante Léonie sit with Bon Papa while we both go?'

Giselle looked displeased. 'I did ask Léonie,' she said, 'but she seemed quite annoyed. Apparently they're going out or something and wanted you to babysit.'

'Yes. I'd forgotten about that,' Christine admitted.

'Well, she'll just have to be annoyed,' Giselle said. 'She must understand your first duty is to your own family, and it's more important that you should look after our own babies!'

Christine did not think Maman should refer to looking after Bon Papa as babysitting, but she said nothing except, 'Do I have to go to the hospital on my own? I don't even know where the ward is.'

'You can ask. You have a tongue and a voice! Don't you want to visit your papa when he is unwell?'

Christine hung her head and muttered a hasty denial. 'It's just that I don't like hospitals,' she said.

'No one likes hospitals; do you think I like hospitals?' Maman demanded, and again Christine shook her head. 'Well then, off you go and don't stay too long. Remember that I have to go as soon as you get back.'

'What time will supper be, then?'

'Oh, we'll just have a snack, Christine. Bon Papa won't want anything and I ate at midday with Léonie. I'll make something for you when I get back from the hospital.'

Christine grimaced. 'That won't be for hours! I'm starving! We only had ravioli for lunch.'

Giselle took out her purse. 'Buy yourself a hot dog on the way to the hospital, then. Only a hot dog, mind, no bonbons or rubbish.'

132

'All right. Thank you, Maman,' Christine agreed duti-fully. There was nowhere near the hospital where food of any description was sold, but with any luck the *charcuterie* round the corner from the school would have some slices of pizza left. '*Au 'voir, Maman.*'

'*Au 'voir, chérie.*'

Christine walked decorously to the end of the road, then, out of sight of Maman, ran all the way to the *charcuterie* and emerged munching a wedge of quiche, cupping her free hand under her mouth for fear of dropping the precious morsels.

The single ward to which Jean-Luc had been moved was several long corridors away from the entrance. Fol-lowing the directions she was given, Christine walked quickly, looking straight ahead, inwardly flinching at the hospital odours.

She knocked tentatively on the door which bore a white card with the single word 'Rochaud', and turned the handle. Jean-Luc, in pyjamas but no dressing gown, stood by the windows looking out on a dismal panorama of walls, pipes and fire-escapes. As Christine moved towards him, she saw that his shoulders were shaking. She stopped in her tracks, uncertain. Should she go out again? Or would that attract his attention more than if she stayed where she was?

Finally, he blew his nose heartily and turned away from the window. 'Christine!' he exclaimed. 'I didn't hear you come in.' He looked confused. 'How long have you been there?'

'I've come in just this minute,' she lied.

'Well – take a seat.' He made a show of rummaging for something in the bedside locker, hastily dabbing his eyes with his handkerchief at the same time, while Christine perched herself on the very edge of the chair. Jean-Luc straightened up, pulled on the dressing gown lying on the

133

bed and tugged the bedclothes straight before sitting down in the second chair, on the other side of the bed.

Across the scratchy-looking blankets they regarded each other timidly. Christine felt that one of them should have moved a chair nearer to the other, but to do so now, deliberately, would create a physical closeness which would require an intimacy of conversation to equal it. So they remained divided by the high bed and conversed as strangers.

'Have you come straight from school?'

'Yes.'

'Your maman is busy, I suppose?'

Christine hastened to explain, 'She's going to come and see you later. Bon Papa is ill; she has to stay with him.'

Jean-Luc looked concerned. 'He is no better?'

Christine shook her head. The sight of Papa crying had unnerved her; she felt poised on the brink of tears herself. There had been a time when she had prided herself on never crying. Now, just at the time when she was expected to have outgrown such childish things, she found it harder to be resilient.

'What is it?' Jean-Luc pursued. 'His chest?'

'He has bronchitis,' Christine said. 'And old age, he says. How are you?' she added quickly.

He shrugged. 'As you see,' he said, 'the injuries are not grave. Cracked ribs,' and he patted his left side which was visibly padded out under his night-clothes, 'and bruises across my chest and head. It is remarkable, when you consider, that such an impact could have so little effect. The doctor tells me,' he added bitterly, 'that I have been very lucky.'

'It must have been terrible,' said Christine, with sympathy. 'Frightening.'

'Oh, it was not that that frightened me,' said Jean-Luc.

'It was not the prospect of death, and certainly not these ridiculous injuries. What a farce, *hein*?'

Christine looked at him, wide-eyed. 'What was it,' she asked, 'that frightened you?'

'Life,' he said simply. His eyes looked through her. 'Living can be much more frightening than dying. You think that you stand on solid rock, strong, secure – brave, you believe. Then suddenly you see it is all an illusion. You stand on the edge of a precipice, too weak or too cowardly to move either forwards or back.' His eyes focused on Christine's unhappy face. 'Never mind,' he said more gently. 'I don't expect you to understand. I hope you don't.'

'*Mais si, je comprends*,' she asserted. 'It is terrible to be afraid.'

'What are you afraid of,' he said, 'at your age? You are too old to be afraid of witches and too young to fear reality.'

'I'm afraid that Bon Papa will die,' she said, and her voice shook, 'and I will be left alive.' Her hands closed over the edge of the blanket on the hard bed and gripped it tightly, till the knuckles showed white.

'Yes,' said Jean-Luc. 'You have your troubles too. I was forgetting. I am sorry.'

They sat in silence.

'How is Maman?' he asked eventually. 'Is she coping all right, with Grand-Père ill?'

'I don't know,' Christine said honestly. 'I've been sent to stay with Tante Léonie.'

Jean-Luc frowned. 'Why?'

'So that Maman will only have one person to look after, she says.'

'Then,' he said slowly, 'you are not seeing Bon Papa at all?'

'I'll see him tonight, when Maman comes here, but he

135

might be asleep,' she said and added in sudden desperation, 'I don't want him to die when I'm not there.'

'He is not necessarily going to die yet,' Jean-Luc said. 'He is a tough old man, you know.'

'He didn't know who I was, the other night,' Christine told him. 'He thought I was Tante Sophie.' At the back of her mind she registered faint surprise that she should be telling Papa things like this.

'Sophie?' repeated Jean-Luc. Christine waited for him to say something else, but he fell into silence. She waited.

'Are you going home now?' he asked. 'Or to your Tante Léonie's?'

'No, home.' Feeling she was being dismissed, she stood up.

'You have to go now?'

She looked awkward. 'Maman told me not to stay too long,' she recalled.

'Of course. And you will be hungry, I expect, if you have come straight from school,' he said unexpectedly.

Christine was touched that he should think of her. 'I bought some quiche,' she explained concisely, fearful of boring him with such mundane details.

'Ah, I see.'

'Well,' she said, gauche once more. 'I'll go.'

'Yes.' He stood up and went to open the door for her, as though she had been a real visitor. As he held the door open, she felt it was imperative to go out of it as quickly as possible, without keeping him waiting.

'*Au'voir*, Papa.'

'*Au'voir*.'

She had moved a few paces down the corridor before she realized that she had not kissed him goodbye, so she turned and gave a half-wave, but the door had already closed behind her.

When Christine arrived home, Giselle was waiting for her. 'How was he?' she asked.

Christine hesitated. 'I don't think he's very well,' she said.

'Of course he's not well!' Giselle snapped. 'Why would he be in hospital if he was well? He has had an accident, you know.'

Christine felt that Papa's particular sickness was less to do with the accident and the hospitalization than with Papa himself, but she did not think that Maman would like to hear that, even if she could have put it into words. But Giselle seemed to divine some part of her meaning for she added, after a minute, 'In what way, not well?'

Christine spread her hands expressively. 'I can't say,' she said. 'You will see for yourself, when you're with him.'

'Talking of which, I had better go,' Giselle said. 'Pop upstairs, Christine, and tell Bon Papa that I'm leaving now.'

'What shall I do if there is something wrong with him?' Christine said, suddenly anxious.

'With who?' Giselle asked frowning.

'With Bon Papa.'

'If he needs anything, you can take it to him, surely?' Giselle said. 'And he can get to the bathroom by himself, if that's what you mean, and even if he can't, I've left a pot in his room.'

'No, I didn't mean . . .'

'Then what?' Giselle demanded. 'Come on, Christine, I'm in a hurry. Is this one of your prevarications?'

'No! I meant, what do I do if he . . . gets worse?'

Giselle shrugged. 'Wait till I get back, I suppose. I shan't be very long. There's no guarantee that the doctor will come out at this time anyway, and nothing much that he can do if he does come. Grand-père has his pills to take if he needs them.'

'They don't seem to do much good,' Christine said.

'There is nothing else they can give him,' Giselle said. 'And there is nothing I can do for him, by sitting by his bedside all the time, if you are implying that I neglect him because I go out.'

'I'm not, Maman! I just wanted to know what I should do, just in case . . .'

'Well there is not much that can happen while I'm out,' Giselle said, slipping on her coat and lightly brushing the sleeves. 'If his breathing gets too difficult he can take another pill.' As Christine still looked wretched, she added, 'And if he dies, *chérie*, there is nothing that any of us can do.'

In the event, Maman did not stay long at the hospital and Bon Papa slept peacefully all the time. In the absence of Maman, Christine took her homework into the warm kitchen and staved off hunger with a hunk of cold *saucisson* and fresh crusty bread. It was good to be at home again, she thought, and remembered to thank God for her easy deliverance from Tante Léonie.

She added a mental postscript to those thanks when Maman returned, dripping with rain, and said, 'Your father, in his wisdom, has ordained that you should come back and stay at home, Christine. What it has to do with him I really don't know – he's not the one with the extra work – but there you are. The master of the household has spoken so we must all obey.'

7

Christine sat at the kitchen table, her head on her folded arms, listening to the noises of the house. Upstairs Maman, getting ready to go out, trotted briskly back and forth, the carpeted floor dulling the sound to a series of muffled thuds.

In her mind's eye Christine pictured Maman peering into the mirror, dabbing powder on her cheeks with a swift practised hand, turning her head from side to side to see the effect in profile, then leaning forward, pursing her lips and dabbing at a stray smudge of lipstick. Christine wondered why Maman took all that trouble, just to go to the hospital, but then Maman never went out anywhere, even to the post box on the corner, without putting on her 'street face'. 'You never know whom you may meet,' she told Christine.

Contrasting with the quick thud-thud of Maman's footsteps were the downstairs noises: the stolid tick-tocking of the old kitchen clock, the sudden shifting of coals in the boiler, and the occasional creaking of timbers as the old house settled itself more comfortably in its foundations.

The house was a bit like Bon Papa, Christine thought: Its bones creaked at every movement, and although its rooms reverberated with past, remembered noises – children's shouts and laughter, conversations and clinking glasses – it had somehow become less able to tolerate present sounds, as if their rude newness disturbed its memories.

Christine's noise did not disturb the house, she knew.

Even when she came home from school, calling out to Maman or shouting her news up the stairs to Bon Papa, the old bricks did not flinch. Bon Papa did not disturb it either; he and the house had grown old together and understood each other.

With Maman, it was a different matter. Without even raising her voice, she could jar the nerves of a room by the way she whirled through it, whisking a newspaper off a table, flicking at the flowers in a vase or rattling cups on a tray. The house pricked up its ears on her approach, rather as Bon Papa, sound asleep in his chair – though he snoozed undisturbed while Christine played around his feet – would stir as soon as Giselle appeared soundlessly in the doorway.

Still, Maman did not threaten the house. She goaded it, but it did not resent her, Christine felt, because the offence was unintentional. Maman simply did not recognize that the house had a spirit of its own. While Christine and Grand-père winced at the tactlessness of interrupting its rhythmic breathing with her sudden, brittle laughter and clattering footsteps, she was complacently unaware of her *faux pas*.

In Papa's case, though, the offence was deliberate. When Jean-Luc shouted suddenly into the evening calm, or without warning hurled an object across the room, the house cowered deep in its roots. For Papa understood the house, and in his darker moods the knowledge of his crime could give him a bitter satisfaction.

Christine knew that Papa understood it because sometimes he would sit completely still in his armchair, his fingers tapping lightly in time to the sonorous breathing of the house. When Maman flurried through the room talking as she went, he would start irritably and snap at her. It was not that he was annoyed with Maman – though Maman thought it was – but simply that she

140

disturbed the harmony, jolting the sleepy old house into sudden wakefulness.

Most of the time Jean-Luc liked the house and respected its old bones. The two co-existed peacefully, not bothering each other, sitting in companionable silence. Sometimes, though, the very stolidness of the place, and his dependence on it, would irritate him beyond endurance and he would lash out, piercing its peaceful cocoon and searing its age-old memories. When this happened, Grand-père would retire to his room ruffled but unresentful, till the storm had blown over.

'Christine! Christine!'

'*Oui*, Maman?'

'Are you ready?'

'*Oui*, Maman.'

'Really ready? We must leave immediately,' Maman called as she ran downstairs, without modulating her voice as she came nearer. 'Christine! I asked you twenty minutes ago to get ready.'

'But I am ready!' Christine protested.

'In those shoes? Have a bit of sense!' Giselle scolded.

Christine looked at her feet. 'They're quite clean.'

'They don't match your clothes! Black shoes with a brown skirt?'

'Oh, Maman does it matter? We'll miss the bus if we don't hurry.'

'That wouldn't be my fault, would it? All right, come on. Remember to tuck your feet out of sight when you sit down, that's all.'

'Papa will be offended that Grand-père hasn't come,' said Giselle, when they were on the bus.

'He won't expect Bon Papa to come when he's ill, surely?' Christine said.

'I know that,' Giselle said, 'but he could just come to

141

give me some moral support. It's a great strain, hospital visiting.'

'His chest is still very bad,' Christine excused him. 'He can hardly breathe sometimes.'

'His chest is never good. But given the circumstances, with Jean-Luc so ill . . .'

'But Papa's getting better – *n'est-ce pas*? The doctor said so.'

'Oh, you're too young to understand, Christine! An accident is far more than bruises and cracked ribs. It's the shock, the worry – the whole system is upset, body and mind.'

'Papa's mind was upset before the accident,' said Christine thoughtfully.

'His mind was upset! What do you mean, his mind was upset?' hissed Giselle in a furious whisper, so that the old lady with the deaf aid should not hear.

'Well, all those rows and rages, for one thing. He never used to be like that, did he?'

'Mind upset, indeed!' Giselle seethed. 'Don't you ever say that to anyone ever again, do you hear me? People will think I'm married to a psychiatric case!'

Christine sighed and was silent.

Giselle, when they reached the hospital, swept ahead through the chill, antiseptic corridors with Christine following, head lowered and steps dragging.

'Come along, Christine! *Dépêche-toi*!'

Outside Papa's room, Giselle hesitated.

'I'll just go in first,' she said, 'and see how he is.'

The door closed behind her and Christine stood in the corridor outside, her nostrils assailed by the fearsome hospital smell, her eyes averted as overalled porters wheeled rattling trolleys bearing – who knew what?

'When I die,' Bon Papa had once said, 'it will be in my own bed and not in hospital.'

Christine flattened herself against the wall and strained to catch Maman's voice from the other side of the door.

'Just for five minutes,' said the voice, surprisingly near, and Maman emerged again.

'Christine, Papa is not feeling very well today, so I think if you go in just for five minutes at the end . . .'

'I don't have to wait out here all the time, do I?' Christine protested.

'*Chérie*, just for twenty minutes or so . . .'

'Why can't I go in for five minutes and then wait for you at home? Please, Maman – *je t'en prie.*'

'Oh, very well, I don't suppose it makes much difference. Just wait one minute while I tell Papa.'

Exactly one minute later she beckoned Christine in, hissing 'Just for five minutes now! Don't outstay your welcome.'

Christine felt that any welcome was bound to be shortlived.

'*Bonjour*, Papa,' she said politely. '*Comment vas-tu?*'

'Not so good,' grunted Jean-Luc, remote and unfamiliar in the high hospital bed.

Christine could never be sure about kissing people in hospitals so she stood, hands behind her back, till Giselle frowned at her and gestured towards the chair.

Christine perched on the edge of it and wished Maman would help out with the conversation rather than rushing about with flowers.

Jean-Luc's eyes were also fixed on Giselle. 'Come and sit down,' he said. 'The flowers can wait.'

'Have you a knife, *chéri*? These stems are much too long. I suppose there isn't another vase?'

'No – I don't know.'

'I'll go and see if I can find one,' Giselle decided.

'For heaven's sake, Giselle, sit down! Have you come to see me or to decorate the hospital?'

But Maman had already gone.

Christine and Jean-Luc eyed each other warily, unsure of how to converse in this tête-à-tête situation, with Giselle as an occasional third.

'What have you been doing?' Jean-Luc enquired.

Christine thought. 'I went to school this morning,' she said and hesitated. 'Maman asked if I could have the afternoon off, as you're coming home soon.'

Jean-Luc grunted. It was not much of a conversation so far. Christine searched for inspiration.

'When will you be coming home, exactly?' she asked.

Jean-Luc looked at her with more interest.' 'Why do you ask that?'

Christine looked blank. 'I just wondered.'

'Oh. Does it seem – different at home without me?' he pursued.

Christine considered the matter. 'It's just like when you're away on business,' she said honestly. 'No different, really.' Seeing his expression, she sought to make it better. 'I'm sure Maman misses you a lot,' she said.

'And you?' said her father. 'Do you miss me?' His mouth curved sardonically.

'This vase will have to do,' said Giselle, pushing the door open with her foot. 'There simply isn't anything else. Christine, time to go, I think. Papa needs his rest. Now go straight home on the bus, do you hear me? No wandering about. Jean-Luc, are you quite comfortable? These sheets don't look too clean to me . . .'

Christine found herself outside the door. Not worth coming for, really, she thought resentfully. 'How are you, Papa' and out. I should hardly think that tired him out too much. More likely to tire me, all these buses and things, just for that.

It began to rain as she stood waiting at the bus stop and she remembered that Maman had the umbrella. Just

144

as well that Maman had not asked Bon Papa to come, Christine thought. He always wheezed more when he went out in the rain. She would go home and make him a bowl of black coffee, just as he liked it.

The bus drew up and a stout woman elbowed Christine out of the way, tut-tutting angrily as Christine stumbled and caught her arm to save herself.

'No manners, the kids today,' the woman remarked to the bus driver, who stared reprovingly at Christine. 'Just watch it,' he said. Christine went to the very back of the bus and stood up all the way home, swaying against the bar, even though there was a spare seat in front of the stout lady. A dozen pairs of eyes bored into her back as she got off at the stop where, freed from their collective disapproval, she skipped down the street to show she didn't care. The garden gate clanged shut behind her.

Bon Papa was shuffling about in the kitchen, looking tired. 'There's a woman here,' he said, 'to see your mother.'

Christine kissed him twice on each cheek. 'You look awful, Bon Papa,' she said solicitously. 'Go back to bed.'

'All right,' he said. 'Can you talk to this lady?'

'Who is she?'

'Me, I don't know her,' said Bon Papa dismissively, 'but you might.'

Christine found Marie-Louise's mother in the salon, sitting bolt upright on the edge of a hard chair, her handbag clutched in both hands. She reminded Christine of a woman she had once seen in a dentist's waiting-room.

'*Bonjour*, Madame Trichard,' said Christine politely.

'*Bonjour*, Christine,' responded Madame Trichard in a high voice. There was a moment's hesitation, then they both spoke at once.

'Did you want to see . . . ?'

145

'I was just passing,' said Madame Trichard, speaking louder than Christine, 'and thought I'd drop in and see your mother.'

'She's not here, Madame.'

'Your grand-père thought she would not be long. I've been waiting . . .' Madame Trichard glanced at her watch and shifted restlessly, '. . . a little while already.'

'It depends on the buses,' explained Christine, 'because sometimes when she comes out of the hospital the rush hour is still bad.'

Madame Trichard started. 'Hospital?'

'Maman goes to see Papa every evening,' said Christine.

'I didn't know he was ill.' Madame Trichard twisted her long string of beads round and round her finger, till Christine thought they would snap.

Christine was surprised. 'I thought you would know,' she said. 'He had a car accident.'

Madame Trichard moistened her lips. 'Is he badly hurt? How long will he be in hospital?'

'The doctor won't let him home till the concussion is gone, but it should be quite soon now.' Christine remembered her manners. 'Would you like a drink while you're waiting? We have Ricard and vermouth and something else.'

Madame Trichard uncrossed her legs and leaned forward as if to stand up. 'Perhaps after all, I'd better not wait,' she murmured, as though to herself. She did not stand up. Christine waited.

'So you thought I would have known about your father's accident?' Madame Trichard said with sudden sharpness. Her small bright eyes reminded Christine of a bird – a hawk, she thought, eyeing up its prey. She suddenly felt afraid of Madame Trichard. 'Why did you think I would know, Christine?'

. Christine was confused. 'Everyone seems to know,' she said.

Madame Trichard stared her straight in the eye, holding her gaze. 'Did you think – perhaps – someone would have told me? My husband perhaps?'

Christine hesitated. 'I thought Marie-Louise might have told you.'

Madame Trichard narrowed her eyes, and her gaze roamed restlessly over Christine's face as though searching for something. 'But my husband would have known too, wouldn't he?' she said. 'Being such a good friend of the family?'

Christine turned away and knelt in front of the open door of the buffet where the apéritifs were kept. Madame Trichard came silently up behind her and stood looking down at her lowered head.

'Because he does come here, doesn't he, Christine?' she said, still in the same silky voice. 'He comes quite often.'

Christine turned to face her and held out the bottles. 'Ricard or vermouth?' she asked.

Madame Tricard bent down so that her face was almost touching Christine's, their eyes on the same level.

'He comes to see your mother, doesn't he?' Her voice was barely above a whisper, but the hawk's eyes were hard and glittering.

Christine pushed the bottle into Madame Trichard's hands, and she glanced down at it briefly as Christine rose precipitately to her feet.

'He used to come here sometimes to pick up Marie-Louise,' Christine said.

Madame Trichard stood up more slowly. 'And why do you think he comes here now?' she asked.

Christine felt a shiver run down her spine. I don't like

147

you, she thought; go away, I don't like you. Aloud she said, 'He doesn't come now.'

'Not while you're here, no.' Madame Trichard had a tinkling laugh like Maman's: the sort of laugh that made one feel that there was nothing really funny. 'But you're not here during the day – *hein*?'

Christine turned back to the buffet to retrieve a glass. 'Maman is not here either,' she said. 'She goes shopping every morning, or to see friends sometimes.'

'And what does Maman do in the afternoons?' asked Madame Trichard, with slow emphasis.

'She goes out with my Bon Papa,' said Christine. 'He likes to go to the park to watch the boules, and Maman goes to keep him company.' She poured a tumblerful of neat vermouth and returned the bottle to the buffet. The bottle hit the edge of the shelf, and she grabbed the neck to stop it from toppling.

'So,' said Madame Trichard drily. 'Madame Rochaud spends every afternoon in the park with her old father, watching the games of boules.'

'Yes,' agreed Christine.

Madame Trichard picked up her gloves and handbag and moved towards the door. 'You are very loyal to your Maman,' she said. 'Either that or you're a little imbecile. I'll see myself out.'

Christine watched from the window as Madame Trichard marched briskly down the garden path, her shoulders squared like a general going into battle. For some time after the general had gone, Christine stayed at the window, staring at the empty road, till the sound of Bon Papa's coughing awoke her from her reverie.

Going to the foot of the stairs, she shouted up to him, 'I'll bring you some coffee, Bon Papa.' She noticed with surprise that she still had the glass of vermouth in her hand. She sipped it tentatively and screwed up her nose in disgust.

'Has the woman gone? I heard a door slam.'

'Yes, she's gone. I thought you were going to lie down, Bon Papa.'

'I am better sitting in the chair; lying down I can't breathe. You are a good child to bring me coffee. It will warm me up.'

'Are you cold? Your hands are like ice, Bon Papa! Here, I'll put the duvet round you. What about some brandy?'

'No, the coffee will be fine. Why didn't the woman stay? She said she wanted to come in and wait.'

'She decided not to, after all. *Regarde* – I have brought some bread and chocolate in case you're hungry. Do you want it?'

'*Merci* . . . no, I'm not hungry. You eat it. Did you know the lady?'

'Mm,' said Christine, through a mouthful of bread. 'Marie-Louise's mother.'

'Marie . . . you don't mean Trichard's wife? Madame Trichard?'

'*Si.*'

Bon Papa leaned forward, the bowl tipping in his hands. 'What did she want?' he asked anxiously.

'Bon Papa – you're spilling the coffee. I don't think she wanted anything. She was just passing.'

'Did she seem angry – upset?'

'*Mais non*,' said Christine airily. 'I think she came to sell lottery tickets.'

'Lottery tickets? Are you sure?'

'For charity,' Christine explained glibly. 'She was passing this way and she thought Maman might like to support it. It was for . . . for wayward children.'

149

Bon Papa had a sudden fit of coughing and Christine took the opportunity to change the subject.

'Bon Papa, what are those elephants made from? The ones on top of the bureau.'

'They are ivory,' he said. 'A present from an old friend who travelled a great deal.'

'What is ivory made from?'

Bon Papa considered a moment, then smiled. 'From elephants!'

'No! Truly, Bon Papa? What is it really made from?'

'But I have already told you! From elephants – from the tusks of elephants. Truly!'

'How do they make it go yellow in the corners?'

'That is from age. They are quite old, those elephants. Antiques.'

'Did somebody carve them?'

'Yes, yes, somebody carved them.' Bon Papa leaned his head against the high back of the chair and closed his eyes.

'Bon Papa.'

'*Oui.*'

'Are you tired, Bon Papa? Do I ask too many questions?'

'*Non. Pas du tout, non.* I was thinking about Duvier – the friend who gave me the elephants. You may have them if you wish; I would like you to have them.'

'*Mais non*, Bon Papa! They are yours! They belong in here, on the bureau.'

'We will leave them there on the bureau if you prefer. But they are yours, I have said so: you are to have them when I am gone.'

'Don't say that!'

'Why not? You must face the fact, *mon enfant*. I am an old man.'

Christine rubbed the back of her hand across her cheek.

'I wish you could live forever.'

'*Bon Dieu*! I don't wish it, me.'

'What do you wish for, Bon Papa? If you had three wishes, what would you have?' Christine hunched up her knees and threw her arms round them.

'What would I do with three wishes at my age?'

'Oh, but you can't refuse them if they are offered to you!' said Christine, shocked. 'You have to wish.'

'Well, then . . . for a peaceful death, I suppose.' Seeing Christine's face, he changed his mind quickly. 'All right then, I would wish for . . . for you to be a brilliant lawyer when you grow up.'

Christine was intrigued. 'Why a lawyer?'

He opened one eye. 'Because you argue so much.'

'No!' she protested. 'Besides, you can't use your wishes for me – it's cheating. Wish again.'

'You make too many rules,' he grumbled. 'Aha, but I have you! I would wish for my three wishes to be given to you! Now you have to decide how to use them.'

'That's easy! I would wish for a motor bike.'

'You are too young!' Bon Papa objected.

'Well, for a magic motor bike that I won't be too young to ride. And then for . . . for a trip to England to see Tante Sophie – without Maman being annoyed. And for the third wish. I would wish for Papa not to come home just yet.'

'Christine! What are you saying?' Bon Papa slapped his hands against the threadbare arms of the chair.

'Oh, I wouldn't want him to get worse or anything,' Christine said hurriedly, 'but perhaps he could go on a holiday or something, to put him in a good temper with Maman before he comes home.'

Bon Papa looked disturbed. 'You mustn't take your father's tempers too seriously, Christine. He doesn't mean the things he says.'

'Why would he say what he didn't mean?' Christine reasoned. 'Maman says Papa doesn't like me.'

'What nonsense, Christine! Your Maman never said that to you!'

'Not to me. To Tante Léonie.'

'You shouldn't eavesdrop,' said the old man uneasily. He shook out his handkerchief and wiped his forehead.

'I don't eavesdrop!' said Christine indignantly. 'I can't help it if people think I'm not listening when they talk. I can't make myself deaf, can I?'

'Your father does not dislike you: that is nonsense,' said Bon Papa emphatically. 'If your mother said that, she was wrong.'

'Christine!' A shout came from downstairs.

'There's Maman home,' said Christine, scrambling off the bed. 'She told me to do the *haricots*, and I forgot all about it!' She kissed Bon Papa swiftly on the top of his head. 'Wait, I'll take the coffee bowl down. Do you want any more, Bon Papa?'

'No thank you. Are you sure you don't want to take the elephants now, to put in your room?'

'No, I'd rather leave them here; they've always been here.'

'You don't like changes, do you, Christine?' He raised one eyebrow teasingly at her.

'I would if things changed for the better,' said Christine sadly,' but usually they don't.'

'You might have done the *haricots*, at least!' Giselle complained. 'What have you been doing since you got home?' Without waiting for an answer, she continued: 'The traffic was murder; the bus hardly moved. It would have been quicker to walk except that I was almost too tired even to stand. Of course, no one offered me a seat.'

'You're not old enough,' said Christine. 'You have to be an old lady before people give you their seat.'

Giselle looked at Christine and laughed suddenly. 'So you don't think I am an old lady? That's something, anyway.'

'Do you feel old when you're your age?' Christine enquired with sudden interest. 'Or do you still feel young?'

'At the moment,' said Giselle, 'I feel ninety-nine. Pour me a drink, would you, *mon chou*. A large one.'

'All right.' Christine abandoned the *haricots*. She was about to open the buffet in the salon, when she caught sight of the full glass still standing on the table.

Giselle, when she tasted it, puckered her face. 'Sweet vermouth! You know I usually have dry.'

'I know,' Christine apologized, 'but it was left over and I thought you wouldn't want to waste it.'

'Left over from what?'

'I poured it for Madame Trichard but she didn't drink it. Madame Trichard came to see you,' she added, by way of explanation.

'Madame Trichard? Why didn't you tell me?'

'I just have told you,' Christine pointed out.

'What did she want? She's not still here?' Giselle looked round hastily.

'No, she left. I told her you were at the hospital. She didn't know Papa had had an accident.'

'Christine, what did she come for – what did she say?' asked Giselle urgently. 'Tell me what she said.'

'She said she was just passing,' said Christine uncertainly. 'Then she said she'd better go – when I told her about Papa; but she didn't go.'

'What did she say? What else?'

'She said . . . she asked me what you did in the afternoons,' said Christine slowly.

153

'Oh my God,' said Giselle faintly and sat down. 'What did you tell her?' she asked dully. 'That I did the housework?'

'No,' said Christine.

'No?' Giselle's head jerked upwards.

Christine sliced the heads off the remaining *haricots* in slow motion. 'I said that you went out in the afternoons,' she said, 'to the park, with Bon Papa, to watch the boules.'

Giselle stared at her. 'But Christine, you know that's not true.'

Christine shrugged. 'I don't know what you do,' she said defiantly. 'I'm at school.'

'You know I never go out in the afternoon,' Giselle repeated in bewilderment. 'Why did you say it? Why, Christine?' Her eyes, fixing Christine's gaze with her own, reminded Christine of Madame Trichard's hawk-like eyes, boring into her soul.

She shrugged again, and slipped out of her chair. On her way to the door, she said, 'I just thought you might sometimes go out with Bon Papa, that's all. I don't know what you do.'

Giselle detained her. 'Wait – Christine, do you think Madame Trichard will call again?'

'I don't know,' said Christine. 'She didn't say.'

'Perhaps I might start going out in the afternoons,' said Giselle softly. 'Christine, *ma petite*, without realizing it, you have helped Maman a great deal.'

'I'm going to lay the table,' said Christine.

'I thought if I made the soup while you were here, you could tell me where I go wrong,' said Léonie, hacking at an onion. 'Last time I served it, Pierre absolutely refused to believe it was the same recipe as yours. Now is one onion enough?'

'That depends on the onion,' said Giselle. 'You're throwing half of it away, it seems to me.'

Léonie looked surprised. 'Oh, that's only skin and things, it's too fiddly to mess around with the outside layers. I'll take another one.'

She pulled an onion off the string hanging by the cupboard and guillotined it noisily. Christine, sitting over her homework next door in the dining-room, winced.

'Anyway,' Léonie continued, 'go on with what you were telling me about Madame . . . what's her name?'

'Trichard. Well, that was all really. She didn't stay long apparently, and Christine didn't tell her anything. She was just trying to stir up trouble, the jealous old . . .'

'You're not still seeing him?' Léonie scraped the heap of mutilated vegetables across the table to Giselle. 'Here, you do it. I'll watch you.'

Giselle took up a knife and began slicing with neat, rhythmic strokes. 'It's all over with Henri,' she declared grandly. Then she added in a sudden rush, 'Anyway, he hasn't been near me since before Jean-Luc's accident, the bastard. Not even a phone call to say how are you.'

'Like all men,' said Léonie contemptuously. 'You don't think perhaps he wondered if the accident *was* an accident? If he thought Jean-Luc had found out about you and him and was so upset that . . .'

'No!' said Giselle loudly. 'The idea is quite ridiculous. I am not seeing Henri any more, anyway, so the matter is completely closed. When Jean-Luc comes home, everything will be quite different.'

'You could well be right there,' said Léonie with feeling. 'Especially if Madame Troublemaker goes to Jean-Luc with her stories.'

'She was trying to warn me off, that's all,' said Giselle confidently. 'She will not go to Jean-Luc.'

8

The class room was stuffy and airless. Christine sat idly watching a fly which buzzed continuously against the window pane, climbing up then slipping back in sonorous frenzy. The sound was just audible to Christine, three desks away, even through the rise and fall of Mademoiselle Javine's voice.

Mademoiselle Javine talked excitably about rivers and rainfall, waving her hands to emphasize salient points. The diamond ring on her left hand caught the light. To the class, the ring was a symbol of security. The course of Mademoiselle Javine's engagement never had run smoothly, and on the days when the ring was absent her pupils knew they had to tread carefully; one foolish answer or out-of-place giggle, and the culprit would find herself before Madame Scholbert, without a second chance.

On the diamond days, however, Mademoiselle Javine was all sweetness. Wearing her most feminine attire, she would address the class in a clear, soft voice, with girlish enthusiasm, making wide, generous gestures illustrating rock formations or weather patterns. The girls, youthfully insensitive to the finer nuances of romantic attachment, delighted in mimicking her voice on these occasions, with each sentence slipping into a ladylike whisper at the end.

The delicacy of articulation was accorded scant respect, for the class was only too aware of the strident possibilities of that gentle voice which could swell to the volume of a sergeant-major's on the non-diamond days. So they would, one after another, raise a polite hand when the voice was in mid-sentence, and request, 'Could you speak up a little, Mademoiselle? We can't quite hear you today!'

'Can anyone tell me,' Mademoiselle Javine's dulcet voice continued, 'the major factors affecting rainfall? Christine Rochaud?' On good days, Mademoiselle picked on the brighter, less troublesome girls so that the hour flowed smoothly, as befitted a teacher described by her lover only the night before as 'a little sugar angel, a delicately scented flower'. On bad days, eager for conflict, she would confine her attention to those most likely to annoy her.

Today, she waited patiently for the answer to her question, the diamond glittering as she fluttered her hand prettily in Christine's direction.

'Christine?' she repeated, in a slightly higher voice.

'Christine!' Carine hissed, and Christine jumped, her attention distracted at last from the doomed fly.

'*Pardon*?' she said startled. 'I didn't hear the question.'

The class tittered appreciatively.

Mademoiselle Javine repeated it, with touching patience. ('What grace, what charm you have, *mon bijou*. How your little pupils must model themselves on you!')

Christine shook her head, as one who wishes not to waste time on unnecessary issues. 'I don't know, Ma'mselle.'

A tiny frown ruffled the porcelain smoothness of the angel's brow. 'Well, just name me one significant factor then.'

Again, Christine shook her head, and the girls held their breath. Surely she was not going to carry on with the joke and jeopardize the mood of the mercurial Ma'mselle Javine?

'You cannot name me just one factor affecting rainfall?' Ma'mselle Javine cried, her voice soaring like a lark on a clear day. 'Not one?'

'*Non*, Ma'mselle,' Christine replied absently.

'Stand up!' cried the angel – she who could so swiftly become the avenging angel – and Christine stood. 'Christine Rochaud!' Ma'mselle declared. 'Are you telling me that you cannot make any reply to this simple question on a topic which I have been discussing for nearly sixty minutes? Are you?'

'Yes,' Christine admitted.

'What have you been doing, for the whole of this lesson? It is obvious you have not been listening to me, Christine Rochaud, so what have you been doing?'

Christine wondered whether to mention the fly, now in its death throes on the windowsill, but thought better of it. 'Nothing, Ma'mselle.'

'Nothing! Exactly!' Ma'mselle Javine declared, and there was more than a hint of steel now in the candy-floss voice. 'Nothing at all! You have wasted a whole hour of your time, of my time, of the class's time!'

Christine did not see how that could be, but said nothing.

'What have you to say, Christine?' The steely edge to the voice was unmistakable now. ('I'll bet that your little girls are terrified of you, my magnificent gorgon!')

Christine was unsure of the correct answer to this one.

'Nothing, Ma'mselle.'

'Nothing?' the gorgon shrieked. 'Not an apology – nothing?'

'I'm sorry, Ma'mselle,' Christine amended.

'It is too late to be sorry,' the gorgon declared. 'Too late, when you have wasted a whole hour of my time. You will go and be sorry to Madame Scholbert, *mon pauvre enfant*, and you will stay behind tonight and spend your time in some profitable but uninteresting exercise,' she concluded triumphantly.

'But I can't . . .' Christine began, but the gorgon ('If

158

you scream at your pupils like that, no wonder they all detest you!') proclaimed, 'Go! Go!' with such dramatic insistence that she rose and left the class without further protest.

Madame Scholbert received her graciously. 'Ah, Christine. I was meaning to see you later on. How is your father?'

'I thing he is better, Madame. They say he'll be home soon.'

'That is good news. Is he still in pain?'

Christine thought of Papa standing sobbing at the window of the dreary little room. 'No,' she said doubtfully. 'He has concussion still, they say.'

Madame Scholbert nodded. 'And your mother? How is she managing?'

Christine hesitated. It was difficult to know the answer to that question. In her mind's eye she saw Maman, depressed and exhausted, smoking cigarette after cigarette; then she saw her, sparkling and vivacious, laughing at jokes about Jean-Luc's driving and rushing off to dinner at a night-club with her friends.

'I think,' Christine said, 'that she is managing all right, thank you. My grand-père is ill,' she added.

Madame Scholbert clicked her tongue sympathetically. 'What a lot of trouble for your poor maman! Is he very bad, your grand-père?'

Christine nodded, and her eyes filled. If you cry, she threatened herself fiercely, I'll never speak to you again.

Madame Scholbert rearranged the papers on her desk. 'Was there anything in particular you came to see me about?' she asked.

'Oh yes,' Christine remembered. 'Mademoiselle Javine sent me.'

'What for?'

'For not paying attention in class,' Christine confessed.

159

Madame Scholbert pursed her lips. 'Why were you not paying attention, Christine?'

'I don't know.'

'Well,' said Madame Scholbert slowly, 'I must ask you to ensure that it does not happen again.'

'No, Madame.'

'I will not punish you this time, Christine.'

'Madame,' said Christine, 'Mademoiselle Javine said I had to stay behind tonight, but I can't – really.'

Madame Scholbert tapped a pencil on the desk and frowned. 'If Mademoiselle Javine has already said you must be punished . . .' she said. 'Why can't you stay tonight?'

'My mother said I have to visit my father after school,' Christine explained. 'She can't go herself because my grand-père was ill again in the night and she doesn't want to leave him.'

'I see. I will have a word with Mademoiselle, Christine, and you may be excused detention this time. But in future, please pay attention in class.'

'Yes, Madame,' Christine agreed.

'You may go now.'

'Thank you, Madame.'

Reprieved, Christine had a sinking feeling of disappointment. How much easier it would have been to sit at a desk for half an hour after school, studying rainfall, than to wait about for buses, cold and hungry, and then to brave the hospital and visit Papa on her own. She dreaded the moment when she would push open the door and find him there, perhaps withdrawn and indifferent, perhaps sobbing with fear, or maybe angry and bitter. 'Your maman has crushed me underfoot like a snail,' he would say. 'Oh no, Papa,' she would reply, 'I'm sure she didn't mean to.'

In spite of Grand-père's reprimand, she still wished

that Papa would not be allowed home till he was strong and confident again. She had thought, at first, that he was nicer when he was shaken, unsure of himself; he seemed so much more approachable than the business-like, taciturn Jean-Luc. But now he was almost too approachable: like a frightened child, he seemed to be looking to her for help and Christine, in her turn, was scared.

If Papa and Maman could not cope, then who could? If Bon Papa was no longer strong enough to hold them all up, then how could life go on, and who could help them?

'The bell has gone, Christine! Don't you want to go home?'

'Oh yes.' Christine had not heard the bell.

'Papa is taking us to the ballet tonight,' Véronique continued, 'and afterwards to eat onion soup at a little place he knows near the theatre. I probably won't get to bed till terribly late.'

'Lucky you,' Christine said.

'Oh, I don't know,' Véronique complained. 'I'll be exhausted tomorrow and my maman will make me get up at the usual time and go to school. She never lets me off. You're the lucky one: your mother isn't strict about things like that.'

'She's strict about other things,' Christine said.

'Such as?' They were in the changing rooms now, pulling on their coats.

'Oh, about wearing the right colours together and not bothering Papa and things like that.'

'Doesn't sound too bad,' Véronique decided. 'You should hear my mother, always nagging. She spends the whole evening, usually, telling me to do my homework. Does yours?'

'Sometimes,' Christine agreed. 'But quite often she's out in the evenings anyway, so I don't see her.'

Véronique grimaced. 'Do you have to have babysitters? I hate babysitters.'

'No, we live with my grand-père so he's always there. But he goes to bed very early – straight after supper sometimes.'

'What do you do all evening then, if your parents are out and your Bon Papa goes to bed?' Véronique asked. 'Watch television?'

'We haven't got a television. Sometimes I listen to the radio,' Christine said, 'or read, or . . . well . . . do my homework.'

Véronique looked pitying. 'Don't you get lonely with nobody there?'

Christine shrugged. 'I'm used to it,' she said shortly. Véronique's questions were beginning to upset her; they seemed to imply that her life was lacking in something, and was a bit pathetic. 'I don't mind,' she repeated defiantly.

'Well, I would,' said Véronique. 'Anyway, see you tomorrow.'

'*A demain*,' Christine responded. 'Have a good time at the ballet.'

'Thanks, I will. *Ciao!*'

At the bus stop, she found Carine. 'I thought you'd gone.'

'Yes, I told Maman I'd be home early,' Carine responded, 'but I might as well have waited for you: I've been standing here for ten minutes.'

'Are you going out then?'

'No, Maman invited some neighbours in. The children are about the same age as me – well, one is older and one is younger. They're really nice. We usually all end up playing Monopoly and things.'

'That sounds fun,' Christine said wistfully. 'Our neighbours are quite nice but they haven't got any children.'

'But you've got cousins,' Carine reminded her. 'You're lucky having relations. I don't have any at all.'

'There's just my aunt and uncle near us,' Christine said. 'At least, there is another aunt but she lives in England and I've never seen her.'

'What's your aunt like – the Parisian one?'

'She's all right,' Christine said, without enthusiasm.

'Does she buy you things?' Carine pursued.

'Birthday presents, you mean? She usually gives Maman some money to get me something,' Christine said.

Carine looked at her. 'I thought aunts were meant to spoil you. Yours doesn't sound much fun.'

'She's all right,' Christine said again. 'She complains a lot, though.'

'What about?'

'Everything,' Christine spread her hands expressively. 'About my uncle, about socialists, foreigners, veins in her legs, foreign cooking – everything.'

'I'm glad I haven't got an aunt, then,' Carine said fervently. 'Here's my bus – no, it's the wrong one again.'

'I'm getting this one,' Christine said.

'It doesn't go your way!'

'No, I'm going to the hospital to see my father.'

'Do you have to go every day?' Carine sympathized. 'How boring. Can't you get out of it?'

'Oh, I don't mind,' said Christine loyally. 'Except that I get so hungry,' she added as an afterthought.

The passengers began fighting their way on to the bus. 'Hold on!' Carine said. 'I've got half a brioche left from break time if you want it.'

'Please!'

'Get on, quick! I'll hand it to you.'

Christine poised herself on the step.

'Hurry up, please!' demanded the driver.

Carine thrust the half-eaten brioche into Christine's hand.

'Thanks! *Au'voir*!'

'*Ciao*!' Carine shouted after her. '*A demain*!'

'*A demain*,' Christine called.

'*Au 'voir*!'

'*Au 'voir*!'

'For the love of God!' muttered a woman sitting by the window and, abashed, Christine made her way to the back, then waved vigorously as the bus drew away.

The hospital corridors were mercifully free from trolleys and patients today and Christine's nose was becoming accustomed to the smells.

Jean-Luc answered promptly when she knocked and Christine hoped that was a good sign.

He was sitting in his dressing gown, in the chair beside the bed with the newspaper open on his lap.

'*Bonsoir*, Papa.'

To avoid a repetition of their last conversation across the great divide, she did not take the other chair, but kissed him first then perched on the edge of the bed on his side – not too near, not too far.

'I didn't know you were coming,' he said.

'Maman can't come this evening,' Christine explained, 'because Bon Papa was ill last night.'

'Is he still bad today?'

'I don't know. He was asleep when I left this morning and I've come straight from school now.'

Jean-Luc looked worried. 'You should have gone home,' he said.

'Maman told me to come and – and of course I wanted to come and see you,' Christine amended hastily.

'But of course.'

Christine did not like it when Jean-Luc was sardonic. 'How are you?' she remembered.

'Oh, excellent,' he responded. 'I had another visitor late yesterday evening. 'Madame Trichard.'

Christine's stomach, sensing trouble, performed a quick somersault.

'Why did she come?'

'No doubt to cheer me up,' Jean-Luc said drily. 'Unfortunately, she did not have much success. I gather that you were also a recipient of her mission of duty?'

Christine hung her head. 'Yes.' She wriggled her toes inside her shoes and watched them attentively.

'She asked you questions about Maman.'

'Yes.'

'And you told her that Maman goes out with Grand-père in the afternoons.'

Silence. Christine lowered her head so that her hair partly hid her face.

'I am glad that you protected Maman, Christine,' Jean-Luc said unexpectedly. 'I hope you would have done the same for me.'

Christine felt the weight of her responsibility bearing down on her thin shoulders like a physical burden. She had protected Maman and she must also protect Papa, and Bon Papa too. They were weak and so she must be strong. But she did not feel strong; she felt small, frightened and inadequate for the task.

'Does Maman know,' Christine asked, 'that Madame Trichard came?'

'No. I am not going to tell her,' he replied, 'and I would prefer that you did not tell her either.'

Papa always gave orders like that: 'I would prefer . . .' If he wanted to make the point more emphatically, he would increase the level of sarcasm in his voice and say, 'I would much prefer . . .' The phrase recalled to Christine a tiny incident of a few years ago when Papa, returning from work, was welcomed enthusiastically by his small daughter. 'I would much prefer, Giselle, that when this child wipes her fingers across my suit they should not be covered in jam.'

'Damn her!' Jean-Luc declared forcefully. 'I suppose I should not speak ill of the mother of a schoolfriend of yours . . .'

'I hate her,' Christine said. 'She's a horrible old witch.'

Jean-Luc did not correct her. 'The trouble is,' he said softly, 'that while others imagine one to be in ignorance there is no obstacle to behaving as though one were. But once the charade is exposed, one no longer has a pretext for cowardice.'

Christine's eyes strayed to the fruit bowl on the bedside cabinet. Jean-Luc followed her gaze. 'Have an apple.'

Christine looked confused. 'I didn't mean to . . .'

'Go on, help yourself.'

She hovered over the bowl, uncertain whether to ask a further favour.

'And so,' Jean-Luc continued with a sigh, 'one is forced to act, whether or not one considers it prudent, for in the eyes of society, prudence and courage are not at all the same thing.'

'May I have the banana instead, Papa?'

'Yes, yes,' he said impatiently. 'I had another visitor,' he added, 'at midday today. Marc Boisseau from the office. He came in his lunch hour.'

'That's good.' Christine peeled the banana. She preferred apples really, but bananas were more filling, and if Giselle had been busy, supper could be very late. She wondered how Bon Papa was.

'Thank you,' she remembered, thinking of Bon Papa, 'for telling Maman I could leave Tante Léonie's.'

He grunted, embarrassed.

'Has Tante Léonie been to see you?' she asked.

'No,' he answered. 'Did she say she was going to come?'

'No,' said Christine. She finished the banana. 'Where shall I put the skin?'

'There is a waste-paper basket over there.' He indicated it.

'Won't it make the room smell?' she asked, solicitous for his comfort.

'Yes, perhaps. There is a paper bag in that drawer. Put it in there and take it home with you.'

Christine opened the drawer and found the bag. Lying on top of it was a set of keys. She took them out and held them up for a second, examinging them.

'Put those back!' said Jean-Luc sharply. 'They are not your affair.'

Hurt, she dropped them back in the drawer.

'I think I'd better go home now, Papa.' She kissed him briefly on each cheek and leaned forward for her customary third, but he had turned his head.

'I'll see you tomorrow, Papa.'

'No.' He hesitated, and she looked at him in surprise. 'Don't bother to come tomorrow,' he muttered awkwardly. 'It is too much for you, after school.'

'I don't mind,' she said. 'It's not too much.'

'I may not be here,' he said. 'That is – they are talking of letting me out soon. It may well be tomorrow.'

'They will have to give you more notice than that,' Christine reasoned. 'Maman will have to know when to bring your things.'

Jean-Luc was silent. Another explanation occurred to Christine.

'You don't want me to come,' she burst out. 'You don't like me coming to see you!' She remembered Maman telling Tante Léonie that Papa was not interested in her. 'Perhaps he would have taken more interest in a

167

boy,' she had said. Papa evidently found her boring, a waste of his time.

'No, no,' he said hastily. 'It's not that,' but he hesitated and did not advance any other explanation.

She went to the door.

'It's not that,' he repeated helplessly. 'I swear it.'

'OK,' she agreed tonelessly. '*Au 'voir*, Papa. She closed the door behind her.

'Monsieur Rochaud's daughter?'

Christine swung round.

'Are you the daughter of Monsieur Rochaud?' the doctor asked again.

'*Oui*, Monsieur.' Should she call him *Docteur*, she wondered?

He began to walk down the corridor with her. 'Is your mother coming in this evening?' he asked.

'*Non*, Monsieur.'

He frowned. 'It is not possible for her to come in, later on?'

'My grand-père is ill,' Christine explained. 'She can't leave him today.'

'I see.' The doctor stopped walking and Christine stopped too. 'I shall have to ask you to convey a message to her then,' he said. 'I don't like to do it but there is no alternative.'

Christine was offended at being considered a last resort. 'I can give her a message,' she assured him.

'You must tell her,' the doctor said, 'that I am not in favour of Monsieur Rochaud going alone to his flat when he comes out tomorrow. Whatever the difficulties, I believe he should go home first for a period of recuperation, until we can be perfectly certain he is no longer concussed.'

Christine went cold with shock. 'What flat?' she said.

'His flat. He tells me that he and your mother have

recently separated, but under the circumstances I think he needs a short period of . . .'

Christine thought the doctor had made a mistake. 'Monsieur Rochaud,' she emphasized. 'I am the daughter of Monsieur Rochaud.'

'Yes,' said the doctor patiently, 'Monsieur Rochaud – your father. I want you to tell your mother that when he comes out of hospital tomorrow I would prefer him to go home.'

'I didn't know he wasn't going home,' Christine whispered, her vision of the doctor becoming blurred. 'I didn't know he was coming out tomorrow.'

The doctor cleared his throat, embarrassed. 'I had no idea,' he excused himself. 'I really had no idea that you had not been told.' He cleared his throat again. 'Don't cry,' he said.

'I'm not crying,' Christine said. She clenched her fists in an effort to control herself.

'Can I do anything to . . .' the doctor enquired helplessly. When she shook her head, he said, 'I think you had better go home and talk this over with your mother. All right?'

Christine nodded dumbly. He moved a few steps away. 'Sure you're all right?'

When she said yes, he walked quickly away as though anxious to put as much distance between them as possible.

Christine, with the same instinct, began to walk in the opposite direction. Recollecting herself, she realized that the exit was the other way, but by this time she was once more outside Papa's door and, without thinking, she pushed it open and went in.

He looked up from his newspaper, startled to see her again. 'What is it?' he asked. 'Have you forgotten your bus fare?'

'Why didn't you tell me?' she cried. 'Why didn't you tell me you weren't coming home?'

Slowly, he let his head sink into his hands, 'Oh, dear God!' he said.

Christine regarded him without compassion. 'Why aren't you coming home?' she asked. 'Why?'

He raised his head. 'Who told you? You saw the doctor?'

She nodded. 'I didn't even know you were coming out tomorrow,' she said piteously. 'You didn't tell me – nor did Maman.'

'Maman doesn't know,' he said quickly.

Her eyes filled with hot tears, scorching the lids. 'Why?' she repeated.

'Come here,' he said, and she moved towards him unwillingly, not trusting him any more. He took her hands but she stood uncompromisingly at arm's length, as if to approach him further would involve her in this plot against Maman.

'As you know,' he said, 'your mother and I have not been getting on well recently, and – '

'No!' she interrupted. 'No, I don't know that!'

'But Christine, you do know,' he reasoned. 'You cannot have been ignorant all this time of the rows, the arguments?'

'There have always been rows,' she said stubbornly.

'Not like this,' he said. 'Not since . . . You know it was never like this before.'

'Maman is tired,' Christine defended her. 'She has a lot to do looking after Bon Papa and everything.'

'I am not blaming her,' he said, shaking her hands in his to emphasize his point. 'Not for anything, do you understand? It has all been as much my fault as hers. I have not been a good husband – nor a good father.'

Christine choked on a sob. 'You have!' she protested.

The ground seemed to be sliding away from her. She struggled to keep her balance.

'No,' he said. 'I can see that now. What man can get away with neglecting his family as I have done? A wife and a child need to be looked after, cared for. Now can a man do that if he is always away on business or occupied with his work?'

'We are all right,' Christine asserted. 'Bon Papa looks after us.'

He gave a wry smile. 'Yes,' he said. 'Perhaps it was made too easy for me.'

'You can't look after us at all,' she pointed out, 'if you don't come home. The doctor said you had your own flat!'

He sighed. 'Yes,' he said, and his voice sounded very tired. 'Marc Boisseau arranged it for me. He brought the keys today.'

'The keys in the drawer?'

'Yes,' he said. 'The keys in the drawer.'

Christine looked with loathing at the cabinet.

'I was going to go there straight from the hospital tomorrow,' Jean-Luc continued, in the same fatigued voice, 'without telling Giselle that I had been discharged.'

'But why?' said Christine again, tearfully.

'Because,' he said. 'I thought a *fait accompli* would be easier for everyone to accept . . . or simply easier for me, perhaps. I don't know. One often finds altruistic reasons to justify one's selfishness.'

'But why can't you come home?' she repeated. The tears, unchecked now, poured down her cheeks till she could not see him.

'I may come later on,' he consoled. 'I think it is best to give this way a try, though, for a little while, then see how your mother and I both feel.'

'For how long?' Christine demanded.

He shrugged. 'We would have to see how things worked out,' he said.

'A week?' she insisted.

'A week, perhaps,' he said, but she did not believe his tone of voice. 'A month. Maybe longer. It would be a . . . an experiment, if you like.'

'I don't want you to make experiments!' she wailed. 'I want you to come home!' She forgot that she had wished for his homecoming to be delayed until his temper improved. This was different. This was worse than anything.

For the first time, his logic began to falter. 'Do you?' he said. 'I have not been much of a father to you, have I?'

In reply, she flung herself at him and wound both arms round his neck. 'You must come home,' she sobbed. 'You must! Everything will get worse and worse if you don't come home.'

'It may be far worse if I do,' he said soberly.

'Please Papa!' she begged, her tears leaving blotches of damp on the collar of his dressing gown. 'Please!' And she howled like a small child, a howl of complete desolation.

'Listen,' Jean-Luc said desperately, holding her at arm's length, and shaking her gently so that she was forced to listen to him. 'Listen to me, Christine. I will tell you what I will do. Are you listening?'

She nodded.

'The doctor thinks that it would be better if I went home for a while, first,' he said. 'So, if it would make it easier for you, I will take his advice and then we will talk about the matter later on. What do you say?'

'You will come home tomorrow?' she asked. 'You won't go to the flat?'

'No, I will come home.'

'You promise?'

'I promise.'

'And you will stay with us?' she said. 'You won't go away?'

He hesitated. 'I cannot say how long I will stay, Christine,' he said, and she was quiet. 'But I promise that I will stay for a while.'

She thought about it, her tear-stained face solemn. 'But you will tell me, next time?' she pleaded. 'You won't go away without telling me?'

'No,' he said. 'I will tell you. I should have told you this time,' he acknowledged. 'I didn't realize how grown up you are now. You have a right to know what affects you, too.'

She nodded, trusting him again.

He took a large handkerchief out of his pocket. 'Blow your nose,' he said, 'and dry your eyes, and then go home and have your supper.'

She blew her nose obediently. 'What shall I tell Maman?' she asked, her voice thick.

'Tell her,' he said, 'tell her that I am coming home tomorrow and that I will be ready to leave the hospital any time after ten o'clock in the morning. Tell her to take a taxi.'

'Is that all?' Christine asked.

'Yes, that is all,' he said heavily. 'Everything else can be discussed later, when we are settled.'

'She will see that I've been crying,' Christine pointed out, and he clicked his tongue.

'Yes, of course. Well,' he considered, 'I suppose you will have to tell her that your clumsy, tactless father has upset you again. No doubt,' he added drily, 'it will not surprise her in the least. Now, will you be all right on the bus?'

'Yes.'

'You have enough money for the fare?'

'I have my *carnet* of tickets.'

'Would you like an apple to take with you?' Remorseful at causing her such distress, he wanted her to accept something, but she shook her head. What she wanted from him he was not prepared to give.

'Go straight home now,' he said, and kissed her awkwardly. '*Au 'voir. A demain.*'

A slight smile crossed her face. '*Oui, à demain,*' she responded. 'See you tomorrow.'

Outside in the street, she was thankful for the early winter darkness which hid her tear-stained face, and on the bus she scrambled for a seat near the window, turning her head away from sympathetic glances, her long hair providing a curtain. She knew, though, that once she was home no screen would shield her from Maman's shrewd gaze. She widened her eyes and practised looking cheerful, smiling. '*Mais non,* Maman, nothing is wrong. The cold air has made my eyes red.'

When she arrived home, however, the house was in darkness, the salon windows already shuttered from the night.

The back door was open, but the kitchen was also in darkness, and Christine's heart pounded with panic in the few seconds it took her to fumble for the light switch.

'*Chérie,*' said the note propped against the salt mill on the kitchen table, 'The Charpentiers have kindly called to take me out this evening. There is some *ragoût* of rabbit on the stove which you can reheat. Madame Rouvieux is here to keep an eye on Bon Papa and will stay till I return. She has already eaten, so don't offer her anything. *Gros baisers*, Maman.'

Christine tore up the note into very small pieces and fed it to the boiler. There was no sign of Madame Rouvieux; she supposed she must be upstairs with Bon Papa, but when she went up to see, he was alone.

174

'Bon Papa?'

He stirred, but did not reply.

'Can I switch on the light?'

With the light on, she could see how ill he was. His skin was yellow, translucent as wax, and his eyes were opaque. The flesh of one hand, feebly clutching the duvet, seemed to have melted away, leaving a bony, veined claw, speckled with brown.

'Bon Papa!' Christine was shocked.

He turned his head slightly, but his eyes seemed focused on some distant dimension and did not see her. His mouth was tight with pain; each breath demanded a strength that his straining chest did not have.

'Oh! Bon Papa!' she said again. Her eyes, already sore from weeping, ached as though they would burst. He seemed already to have left her; he was stranded between life and death. Death was waging a war of attrition against him, whittling his strength away by sheer persistence.

She drew up a chair beside him and took the hand very gently, for it was fragile as the dry twigs she snapped underfoot on her way to school. For a time that she ceased to register, she sat there, quite motionless, beside him.

Finally, when she became aware that her bladder was full and her stomach sore with hollowness, she laid the hand very gently on the bed and drew the duvet over it. His eyes, vacant as ice, flickered slightly.

'I'll be back in a minute, Bon Papa,' she told him. She went quickly to the bathroom, then to the kitchen where she cut herself a rough hunk of stale bread and cheese which she crammed impatiently into her mouth, coughing as the dry crumbs stuck in her gullet. She washed it down with a draught of cold water from the tap ('I wish you would not drink tap water, Christine; there are plenty of bottles of Evian in the larder') and went back to Bon Papa.

Again, the clouded eyes were turned vaguely in her direction, and this time the hand dragged itself from beneath the bedclothes, slowly and with great effort, and clasped her warm fingers feebly. He sighed as if in relief and muttered, 'Sophie – at last!' before sinking into a doze.

Much later, returning home, Giselle found them there. Christine had fallen asleep, hunched forward on the hard chair with her head resting on the edge of the bed, her fingers still clutching the frail hand of the sleeping old man.

'*Bon Dieu*!' Maman exclaimed, rousing her. 'This place is like a mausoleum! There is *la vieille* Rouvieux who is snoring away in the salon and you and Grand-père in here.' She glanced at his waxen face and said softly, 'He does not look good, *hein*?'

Christine, cold and stiff, flexed her fingers and stretched her legs. 'He keeps saying "Sophie",' she told her.

Giselle nodded. 'Papa said we should send for her,' she said, adding by way of explanation, 'I called in at the hospital on my way to the Charpentiers'. Gilbert told me I was mad to bother at that hour, but – *que veux-tu*? – I am like that. Papa is coming home tomorrow, by the way. You would think the hospital would have given us more warning.'

'Yes,' said Christine. 'I know. Do you think she would come, Tante Sophie? Bon Papa says she has not much money.'

Giselle looked sharply at her. 'So he talks to you about her? He has hardly mentioned her to me, all these years. I thought he had forgotten her existence. No, the problem is not money, *ma fille*. Papa could reimburse her the fare. The problem is that I do not have her address.'

Christine looked sideways at Giselle, then at the sick, limpid face of Bon Papa. 'But I have the address,' she said.

Twice in the night, Christine awoke screaming.

The first time, she was sliding down a coal shute, like the one in the old school building, down and down into rough blackness, her skin being scraped away as she slid. Down, down, she fell, and the coal fell on top of her, roaring like an avalanche, crushing her under its weight.

Then, miraculously, she was outside on the wide sunlit playing fields, and it was sports day.

It must have been sports day because they were having a tug of war. Papa was on one side and Maman on the other, and Christine was in the middle. They each took one of her arms and pulled her towards them, first one way then the other, while the crowds screamed encouragement.

'*Tirez*! *Tirez*! Pull! Pull harder!'

Henri Trichard was there, and his wife, arm-in-arm with Ma'mselle Dubois of the late list.

'Come on, Giselle! Harder, Jean-Luc!'

Strangers too, with strange faces and open, shouting mouths. 'Stand firm, *la petite*! *Ah, mais il gagne, le grand monsieur*! He is winning.'

Far away, at the edge of the field, she could see Bon Papa being led away by two tall white figures, and she screamed to him for help.

'Bon Papa! Help me, save me, Bon Papa!' But he was too far away; he did not turn his head, and the two marching creatures led him inexorably away, out of her sight.

'Bon Papa! Bon Papa!'

'What is the matter, Christine?'

She sat bolt upright, sweating and shivering.

'Who is it? Who are you?'

Giselle was startled by her fear. 'It is Maman. What is the matter? You were shouting out loud.'

'Bon Papa,' she said incoherently. 'Where is Bon Papa?'

'He is fast asleep,' Giselle said, 'as you should be. You woke me up, with your screaming. You are too old for nightmares at your age.'

Was it a nightmare? Of course. Nothing more. The details of her terror slid together, fusing into a blur sliding away from her as she had slid . . .

'Go back to sleep now, *ma fille*. Lie on your side. It is sleeping on your back that causes nightmares.'

9

In the early hours of the morning, they were awoken by the sound of Bon Papa choking. Something between a shout and a retch, it was repeated over and over again with horrible relentlessness.

Christine was out of bed before she was awake and found herself standing on the landing. At first she thought it was another nightmare, then Giselle, pulling on her dressing gown as she ran, flew past her and into Bon Papa's room.

'Sit up, Papa, sit up,' she urged, shouting at him above his noise. Still in the dark, for she had not stopped to switch on the light, she tugged urgently at him, heaving him upright in bed.

Christine, in the doorway, did not turn on the light either. It seemed callous to flood the suffering man with the harsh electric glare. Also, she was afraid to see him too clearly.

'Call the doctor, Christine,' Maman said. She spoke quickly but with assurance. Maman was good in a crisis. Papa had once said it was a pity they could not live in a constant state of emergency.

Christine's feet barely touched the stairs. She dialled the number which had been thoughtfully taped to the phone. As soon as the receiver was lifted, she gasped, 'Come quick, at once. My grand-père is dying.'

The doctor, sleepy at first, was alerted by the urgency in the child's voice. 'Who is it?' he asked.

'Rochaud, rue Jean-Jacques Rousseau,' she gabbled. 'Please be quick, he can't breathe.'

'I'm on my way.' The phone was slammed down with reassuring violence.

Christine ran upstairs. 'He's coming, Maman.'

'Good.' Giselle was standing by the bed, no longer active, silently witnessing Bon Papa's fight for breath. He looked shrunken, wizened to little more than a bare outline of bone and nerves held together by desperation. On and on he went, forcing air down his worn-out windpipe and uttering those terrible noises.

'What are you going to do?' Christine asked, prompting Giselle to further action.

'Wait for the doctor,' replied Giselle brusquely.

'Can't you do anything else?'

'What?' Giselle asked simply. 'What can I do?'

The hope drained out of Christine. Clutching at Maman's arm she said desperately, 'But you must do something!'

Giselle shook her off violently. 'What do you suggest?' she said, through clenched teeth. 'I am not a miracle worker!'

'No,' Christine moaned, her eyes on the terrible, beloved figure of Grand-père, who had become little more than a breathing machine, a noisy, faulty old air pump. 'No! Please, Maman!'

'I can't do anything!' Giselle almost shouted. 'It's not my fault, Christine!' Christine saw that Maman had tears rolling down her face, but she had pity only for Bon Papa.

'Keep breathing, Bon Papa,' she said. 'Don't give up.' But she said it almost in a whisper, ashamed at asking him to continue the gross charade.

They stood in silence, very still, as though channelling all their energy into his lonely fight. Christine recalled suddenly quite clearly the tug-of-war of her dream and the crowds cheering the protagonists. Now it was Bon

Papa who held grimly on to the rope, a midget holding out against the giant. It was only a matter of time before the giant, finally bored with the charade, tugged imperiously on the rope and summoned his puny opponent across the line. Only a matter of time, but how much time? In her heart, Christine could not wish for the contest to be prolonged, but still she could not bear to relinquish him.

One word from her, she knew with her deepest intuition, one prayer to spare him further suffering and he would be released, slipping from her grasp as easily as water, draining away into the merciful vacuum of peace. But she could not utter that word; even as she despised her cowardice she knew she could not do it. Don't take him, she prayed instead; not just yet.

'Ring the hospital, Christine,' Giselle said. 'Get them to tell Jean-Luc to come home at once.'

'It's four o'clock in the morning, Maman.'

'He can get a taxi!' Giselle said wildly. 'Tell him he must come home. Oh, wait here; I'll do it.' She pushed past Christine with unnecessary force.

'Don't leave me, Maman!' Christine cried, but Giselle had gone.

Standing there with Giselle, Christine had been seeing Bon Papa through Giselle's eyes. Now, left alone with him, Christine saw that Maman had been wrong. 'Fetch the doctor,' Maman had said, but 'What can a doctor do for old age?' was what Bon Papa had said many times.

This was not just another dying old man, though. This was Bon Papa, and he was strong. It was only his machinery that was failing. Christine was weak. She could not hold up the family as he could. But her body was young and strong. If in some way she could give him her strength, as he had so often given her his . . .

On impulse, she climbed on to the bed and straddled

his knees, facing him. Leaning forward, she grasped him by the shoulders and pressed her forehead against his.

'Stop it,' she said clearly, into his face. 'Stop it now. Breathe. Breathe slowly now. Breathe. Breathe.'

She held her own breath. The choking continued. The hands gripped the bedclothes. Christine caught them and raised them to her neck. 'Breathe,' she said. Bon Papa choked and tore his hands away from her. Christine forced them back around her neck. 'If you don't breathe, I won't,' she said. 'I'll die with you.' The hands tried to pull away again, but Christine pulled them back.

This time, when the choking caught him, his hands squeezed her neck.

'Don't be afraid,' Christine gasped. 'Breathe! Don't be afraid. Breathe, Bon Papa. Breathe.'

The hands relaxed. He tried to take them away, but Christine forced them back. He took one shallow breath before the next choking attack. The hands clutched her neck with all their strength. Sweat ran down Christine's face, as it had run down his. A vein hammered in the side of her neck. Harder and harder he squeezed, fighting for breath.

Christine's head pressed against his. 'Breathe,' she croaked. 'Bon Papa!' The clutch of the fingers eased. He managed one breath before he clutched again. It did not give Christine time to breathe. She felt herself go weak. Sweat on her skin made his fingers slip from her neck down to her knees. 'Breathe,' she whispered. 'Breathe.' She pushed his hands up again before she fell forward.

'There's no answer from the hospital switchboard,' Giselle said, coming into the room. 'Oh my God, what are you doing: Christine!'

When Christine did not answer, Giselle grabbed her around the shoulders to pull her away from the dying man, but the frail, long fingers were locked tight around her neck with impossible strength. When Giselle screamed, Bon Papa's eyelids flickered but Christine's face remained lifeless.

'Oh God!' Giselle sobbed. 'Oh God, no!'

Bon Papa's eyes opened and looked straight at her. The death rattle had ceased. He breathed steadily, with no more than his habitual wheeze. The expression on his face, over Christine's shoulder, was one of peace. His eyes closed. As they did, Christine let out a long shuddering breath. Giselle put her arms around her and hugged her convulsively. The child was rigid, fossilized with cold.

'Christine!' she said. 'Christine!'

'Yes,' Christine said. Her lips hardly moved. They were blue.

'Thank God,' whispered Giselle.

Someone rapped loudly on the front door, and she jumped. 'The doctor,' Giselle said. 'Christine! I'll have to go. I'm going to have to let the doctor in.'

She hesitated, then ran downstairs.

When she returned with the doctor, Christine was still immobile. Between them, they pulled her off the sleeping man. Her limbs were stiff and would not straighten. Giselle, sobbing with fright, chafed Christine's arms beween her hands, rubbing back the circulation.

'It's only shock,' the doctor said.

'But you didn't see what she did!' Giselle wept. Used to hysteria, the doctor felt it tactful to ignore her. He bent over Bon Papa, raised the sleeping eyelids and shone a torch into the old man's eyes, piercing the pupils with relentless light. Then he roused him from his slumbers, tapped the chest and pressed the fragile rib cage before dispensing a blast of oxygen into the exhausted body from a black iron cylinder.

'His condition is serious,' he pronounced. 'I cannot hold out much hope.'

Giselle was not expecting hope. 'I'll fetch my purse,' she said.

'The child will be all right,' the doctor said. 'I can give her a sedative, if you like.'

Giselle looked doubtfully at Christine's exhausted face. Christine looked back. 'Do you think a sedative is what she needs?'

'Of course,' said the doctor smoothly, 'the decision is yours.' Anxious to go home to bed, he accepted the note that Giselle thrust into his hand and made his exit with the dignity of a man accustomed to life and death.

Giselle did not accompany him to the door. 'You are all right now, *chérie*,' she said.

'Bon Papa?' said Christine.

'Bon Papa is fast asleep. He is all right now. Though God alone knows how,' she added under her breath.

'I think I'll go to bed,' said Christine faintly.

'No,' said Giselle firmly. 'You will come downstairs and I will make you a hot tisane. You are as white as a sheet.' It was a relief to them both that Maman was back in control.

Christine followed her, on stiff legs. By the time she reached the kitchen, she was shivering uncontrollably. Giselle fetched an old coat of Jean-Luc's from the porch and wrapped it round her.

'You work yourself up into a nervous state,' she scolded. 'That's all it is.' She put the water on to boil and took down a sachet of tisane. The silence of the early morning modified her movements. She closed the cupboard door gently, with none of her usual briskness. 'You had me worried,' Giselle continued. 'Look at you!' Her own words and the tone of voice reassured her.

'I think I'm hungry,' Christine said.

Giselle looked relieved. 'Yes,' she said. 'No doubt that's all it is. Do you want some toast?'

Christine felt happy: it was nice to be pampered by Maman. A mother who would make you toast at four o'clock in the morning could not, after all, be anything else but a good mother who loved her family. Nothing could go wrong with a mother like that. When Jean-Luc was better, he would see that too.

'Can I have some of the stew?' Christine asked, while Giselle was on her side.

'What stew? The one I left you for supper?'

'Yes. I didn't eat it, but I think I will now.'

'Are you mad?' Giselle demanded. '*Ragoût* of rabbit in the middle of the night? You will ruin your digestion.'

Christine tried to look pale. 'I'm very hungry,' she pleaded.

Giselle looked at her. 'Oh, all right. Just don't blame me if you have a stomach ache later on.'

'I won't.'

The tisane, steaming and herby, was put in front of her. Christine sipped, and wrinkled her nose.

'Drink it,' Giselle said in a voice that brooked no argument. Christine drank. 'By the way,' Giselle said casually, turning away from her to stir the stew, 'what were you doing up there in Bon Papa's room?'

Christine sipped the tea. The warmth began to seep through her limbs and the colour revived in her cheeks. 'He wasn't breathing properly,' she said. 'He was too frightened.'

Giselle stared at her. 'But what did you do?' she repeated.

Christine shrugged. 'I told him to breathe.'

'And he did?' Giselle was still looking at her, perplexed. The stew sizzled on the stove.

'I think it's burning, Maman.'

Giselle tipped the contents of the pan on to a plate and set it in front of Christine. 'But how did you . . .?'

Christine picked up her fork and attacked the plate with enthusiasm. Giselle abandoned the subject. Papa was sleeping peacefully now, and there was obviously little wrong with Christine, to judge by her appetite.

'You want some bread?'

'Yes, please.'

It was better not to know, Giselle decided. Some things do not appear normal, and normal life must go on after all.

She handed Christine a piece of bread. 'Eating *ragoût* in the middle of the night!' she said, and Christine looked up and laughed. 'Whatever would your papa say?' Giselle added.

Christine propped her fork against the side of her plate and imitated Papa dabbing at his moustache with his napkin. '*Mais* Giselle!' she said, in a deep voice. 'You know very well that the child will be quite uncontrollable if you allow her to eat stew in the middle of the night!'

Giselle looked as though she would scold her, then burst out laughing. 'You have the right idea,' she said. 'We will not take Papa's reprimands too seriously, *hein*? Life cannot be lived in a state of penitence. We need to have some fun, you and I. It is in our nature.' Then she sighed. 'He will be home tomorrow,' she said.

Christine had her doubts about whether Jean-Luc would come home as he had promised. She kept wondering, at intervals during the school day, what would happen to the flat he had rented. While he still had those keys in his possession, she could not feel sure that he would stay. What if, by his promise to come home 'for a while', he meant only a few hours? He might be sitting in the salon at this very moment, discussing with Maman his plans to leave. By the time Christine came home, he might be standing on the doorstep with his suitcases, ready to go to that flat.

She still could not understand why he had to go and live in some flat by himself rather than stay at home where he belonged, with his family. His explanations were meaningless to her. How could he say that he and Maman did not get on together, as though they were not husband and wife, father and mother, but merely a couple of strangers who had just met and decided they were not suited? It was not right, Christine thought, for her parents to go away and live separate lives; they were part of the same family, limbs of the same body. One limb could not exist independently without the whole body bleeding to death from the severance.

If Bon Papa died, if Maman preferred Madame Trichard's husband to her own, if Papa went to live alone, then what remained of the family? It would seem that only Christine had stayed the same, Christine who never wanted anything to change. Between school and home, her feet hurried to keep pace with her anxious thoughts.

'*Bonsoir*, Christine!'

'*Bonsoir*, Madame Rouvieux.'

'It is becoming colder, *n'est-ce pas*?'

'Yes, it is.'

'Will you come in today, *mon chou*? I have a new packet of those dry butter gâteaux you like so much.'

'*Merci*, Madame. It's very kind of you but my papa was coming home from the hospital today.'

'Of course! I have already seen him, your poor papa. Such a thing to happen, that accident!'

'Is he still at home, Madame?'

'*Mais certainement*, he is still at home! A convalescent does not go on outings so quickly.'

Christine smiled her relief. 'I'll go in and see him then. *A demain*, Madame.'

'*A demain, ma petite.*'

The old woman looked forlorn standing there. Her cheeks were blue with the cold and she hugged herself against the icy wind.

'You look so cold, Madame Rouvieux,' Christine said with sudden compassion. 'Shouldn't you wear your coat?'

'Bless you, *mon enfant*!' Madame Rouvieux exclaimed. 'I have no coat, only an old mackintosh which keeps out the rain but not the wind. But I must look out my thick winter shawl now, it is true.'

'*Au 'voir*, Madame.'

'*Au 'voir*, Christine.'

Christine ran up the path. 'Maman!'

'In the kitchen!'

She pushed open the back door. 'Maman, have you an old coat you don't need? Madame Rouvieux hasn't got one.'

'Christine Rochaud, I despair of you!' Giselle exclaimed. 'Is that all you can say, when your papa has today been allowed home from the hospital? Does it mean so little to you that you had forgotten?'

Christine flushed. 'Of course I hadn't forgotten!' She wished that Maman would keep her voice down, in case Papa should hear her say that. 'Where is Papa?'

'In the salon. Go and say "*Bonsoir*" to him.'

'How is Bon Papa?'

'He has slept all day. He eats nothing, not even his favourite fish which I bought him for lunch.'

Jean-Luc was in the salon listening to the radio. He sat awkwardly upright, his hands lightly gripping the arms of the chair, as though the comfortable old *fauteuil* no longer fitted his shape.

'*Bonsoir*, Christine.'

'*Bonsoir*, Papa. How are you?'

'All right.'

'You got home all right from the hospital?'

'Yes, thank you.'

'In a taxi?'

'Yes.'

Christine ran out of inspiration. She wanted to ask if he was glad to be home, but she was afraid to hear the answer. Instead, she asked, 'Have you seen Bon Papa?'

'Yes. He is in bed still.'

On impulse, she asked, 'Do you think he is going to die, Papa?'

For the first time, Jean-Luc looked her in the eyes. 'I am afraid so,' he said.

The tight knot, which had formed itself in Christine's chest, seemed to tighten itself a notch further. 'Will you be very sad, Papa, if he dies?' It was not the question to ask a convalescent, newly released from hospital, but she wanted someone to share her own pain.

Jean-Luc picked nervously at the threadbare piping on the chair arm. 'Yes,' he said finally, 'I think we shall all miss him greatly. He has done a lot for us. He provides the cement for our brickwork,' he added, under his breath. It was one of those obscure adult remarks that Christine knew she was supposed not to understand, but this time she understood only too well, for it echoed her own private fears.

'You mean,' she said, 'that we will fall apart when he is gone.'

'*Mais non, non,*' Jean-Luc denied. 'Not at all.'

Christine wanted to ask him how long he would stay, but she refrained, feeling that if the subject was not mentioned he might allow himself to forget his intention to leave, and be lulled back to sanity by the ticking comfort of the old house.

If only Bon Papa were well, he might smooth over the cracks as he had done so often before when Giselle and

Jean-Luc turned against each other. By talking with Jean-Luc man-to-man and with Giselle father-to-daughter, he would make each one feel there was someone who understood and, their irritation soothed, they would draw close together again. Christine feared that Papa was right. Without the cement, how long could the bricks stay standing?

Over the days, Christine watched Papa like a hawk, searching for signs that he would leave or signs that he would stay. Bon Papa she saw more rarely. She would sit with him for an hour at a time, holding his hand, but he did not know her, and she felt that he had already abandoned her.

He ate nothing, the old man, and seldom opened his eyes. He had become incontinent, and Giselle cared for him like a baby, changing his draw-sheets and sponging his lethargic body. Christine forced herself to visit him, but in truth she would have rather stayed away. The sick, half-dead man in the room that smelt of urine was not the Bon Papa she knew. She remembered his words, his jokes, his conversations and his patient listening and could not connect him with the parody of his physical being which lay among sweat-soaked pillows. 'I should have let him die before,' she thought. But at least there was no more choking. He breathed and wheezed and slept, day in, day out.

As the days and nights passed slowly by, Christine sank into abstraction. It was noticed at home – 'Christine, I have asked you three times to change out of those shoes. Are you deaf or stupid, I ask myself?' – and also at school. In class she stared out of the window at the greying November skies and at home she gazed unseeingly at the opened textbooks all evening, till bedtime came and she closed them unread.

The day of reckoning at school had been heralded by

many warnings. It fell on a Thursday, the day when everyone looked forward to the afternoon's freedom. To Christine, the days were all the same now and she did not care – indeed she hardly knew – whether she was at school or at home.

'Christine Rochaud, you have not been listening to my classes, you have not done your homework and you have not answered when spoken to. You are wasting not only my time but the intelligence which God has given you. You will go to Madame Scholbert and you will attempt to give her a better explanation for your laziness than the one you have given me.'

So it was that Christine arrived home at eleven o'clock on a Thursday morning, when she should have been studying the reproduction of the rabbit. Jean-Luc, still convalescent, was alone downstairs.

'*Bonjour*, Papa.'

'Why are you home so early? Are you ill?'

'No, I'm not ill. I was sent home.' Her voice and her face were stony, refusing to acknowledge the inner sense of her disgrace.

Jean-Luc looked severe. 'Who sent you home?'

'Madame Scholbert,' Christine confessed.

'The headmistress!' Jean-Luc, unlike Giselle, regarded education as sacred. He was scandalized. 'What have you been doing, Christine, to be sent home?'

'Nothing, Papa.'

'Don't be insolent with me, Christine. I warn you that my patience is very short.'

'No, I mean that I have been sent home for doing nothing, Papa. I have not been working.'

He frowned. 'Why is that?'

She shrugged. 'I can't seem to concentrate. I think that I'm listening and then I find I've missed it all.'

Jean-Luc looked grave. 'But – surely they have not expelled you?'

'Oh no,' Christine denied hastily. 'Madame Scholbert said that it is not a punishment. She just said that I had better stay home for a few days till the situation is more settled.'

Jean-Luc flushed, and Christine feared that she had made him very angry. She did not blame him, for despite Madame Scholbert's assurance she could not believe that she was not being severely punished.

'What did she mean, the situation?' Jean-Luc demanded. 'You told her that things were not well at home between Maman and me?'

'No, of course not.' Christine would not have told anyone else what she could not admit to herself. 'But I told her about Bon Papa.'

'I see.' He looked at her, still frowning, and Christine shrank, awaiting retribution. Maman would certainly be furious too, that she had discussed her home life with Madame Scholbert. 'You must never talk to people about what happens at home,' Giselle had told Christine more that once. 'It is not their business. What we take for granted other people may find strange; every household has its peculiarities.'

Jean-Luc, however, seemed worried rather than angry. 'It may be,' he murmured, 'that you would be easier in your mind if the situation were resolved.'

Christine looked away from him. He made her uneasy.

'The uncertainty,' he continued, 'may be the worst part of the matter.' He looked at her analytically, as though she were a business problem. 'Would it be possible,' he concluded, 'for me to talk to your Madame Scholbert?'

'Oh,' Christine remembered, 'she said that she wanted to see Maman. But I said she was busy and I didn't know if she would come.'

'Anyone home?' Giselle called. The back door crashed open. 'Come and help me with these bags, Jean-Luc.'

They both rose and went into the kitchen.

'Christine has been sent home early,' Jean-Luc explained, to Christine's relief. Unexpectedly, Papa seemed to be taking her side.

'Is she ill?' Giselle demanded.

'She has been unable to work, with the problems at home. I think I should see her teacher,' Jean-Luc said.

Giselle made a contemptuous sound. 'What problems at home?' she said scornfully. 'If anyone has problems at home it is not Christine.'

'Giselle, you astound me!' Jean-Luc exclaimed. 'You think no one suffers but yourself. You are a complete egoist.'

'Me!' Giselle screamed. 'Me, an egoist! You are joking, *mon cher*. I laugh at you!'

Christine flinched. Just at the time when Papa was, figuratively speaking, hovering on the doorstep, uncertain whether to stay or to go, Maman was slamming the door and drawing the bolts against him.

'All the same,' Jean-Luc said steadily, 'I intend to go and discuss the situation with Madame Scholbert. It is not fair that Christine's education should suffer because of our difficulties.'

'Our difficulties!' Giselle snorted. 'Yours are purely imaginary, *mon brave*, and mine you are totally unable to see.'

'No,' Jean-Luc said, and Christine was surprised to hear that his customary sarcasm was completely lacking. 'I am not unable to see them, in fact I think that some solution must soon be reached.'

'I am glad to hear it,' Giselle told him, 'but if you think that Christine will benefit by your visiting Madame

Scholbert and telling tales about me, you are very much mistaken, Jean-Luc.'

'I have no intention – ' Jean-Luc began.

But Giselle interrupted, 'For a start, she will have no idea who you are. Have you ever visited the school, ever taken the slightest interest in what Christine has been doing?'

Jean-Luc was stung at last. 'Have you?' he retorted.

Christine hated to be the focus of their arguments. 'It doesn't matter,' she said. 'I told Madame Scholbert you probably wouldn't go. She is not expecting you, Maman.'

In response, however, Giselle raised her hand suddenly and struck Christine across the cheek. 'That will teach you,' she shouted, 'to be disloyal to your maman. How dare you tell Madame Scholbert about your home life as an excuse for your shirking, you lazy little animal!'

Christine was stunned. She stared at Maman in disbelief. Tears seemed to well up from below her ribs, but she had no breath to let them rise.

'Giselle!' Jean-Luc expostulated. 'I will not tolerate this! I warn you – '

'No one asks you to tolerate anything!' Giselle screamed. 'What have you to tolerate, you who are never here? Husband!' she spat at him. 'Father! Pah! What have you ever done for any of us?'

'No, Maman!' Christine whimpered. 'No'!

Giselle turned on her. 'Get out of my sight!' she roared. 'Get out, both of you!' She flung herself down on a kitchen chair and sobbed noisily, her head resting on her arms and her shoulders heaving.

Christine went upstairs and, by instinct, made straight for Bon Papa's room. The curtains were drawn back and she sat in the dim November light, watching through the window the tossing tree tops with their sparse yellow leaves hanging on by a thread in the tugging winter wind.

194

By her side, the old man breathed and blew, breathed and blew, with frail persistence.

Later, Maman went out, slamming the door and leaving Papa and Christine to eat their lunch alone. Christine went downstairs.

'Shall we eat in the kitchen, Papa? It's warmer in there.'

'The places are set in the dining-room,' he said.

They spooned their soup and ate their cheese in silence.

'More bread, Papa?'

'*Merci*. But help yourself.'

The wind blew through the trees, gasping and sighing like the old man upstairs.

'Do any of the leaves manage to stay on the trees, Papa?'

'No, they will all fall, sooner or later.'

'Doesn't just one ever stay on?'

'No. The old leaves must die so the new ones can grow. You cannot alter the course of nature.'

Christine sighed and put down her knife. 'I don't want any more.'

'You may go then.'

'Shall I make your coffee, Papa?'

'No, I can do it.'

'I'd like to,' she said. 'Really.'

'All right,' he agreed. 'Don't burn yourself.'

She washed up their plates and Jean-Luc, for once, came and dried them.

'Don't bother, Papa. We can do it.' The 'we' slipped out automatically, as though Bon Papa were still at her side. She kept looking for him. Every time someone opened a door she would look up, expecting to see his face, as though the man upstairs were some stranger who had borrowed his bed for the night, along with his body.

'What are you going to do this afternoon, Christine?'

'I don't know.' She didn't do much these days, except sit and wait. It made little difference to her where she did it.

'Do you want to go for a walk?'

'We can't leave Bon Papa alone in the house.'

'Ah, of course not.'

They finished the washing-up in silence, then Jean-Luc retired to the salon and Christine to her bedroom, where she sat watching the trees, focusing on one leaf at a time, until it fell, whipped by the wind, to join its fellows. She stayed till the light failed and the windows of the houses down the street shone out in yellow squares.

Then she went downstairs and stretched out on the floor before the bright bars of the ancient electric fire, while Papa listened to the political talk on the radio and watched her waving feet.

'Why don't you read something?' he said suddenly.

She twisted round to look at him. 'I'm all right,' she said, surprised.

'Or play a game?' he suggested. 'You used to like Scrabble, *n'est-ce pas*?'

'It's boring on your own,' she dismissed the idea.

'I will play with you, if you wish.'

'Really?' She was astounded. 'Are you sure, Papa?'

'Fetch the board,' he said. 'You will have to teach me the rules.'

'Oh, I will.'

They pored over the board while she explained. 'You make a good teacher,' he complimented her.

She smiled at him. 'That's what I want to be,' she told him.

'Really?' he said. 'I didn't know.'

He played well, not deliberating too long as she had feared he might, but choosing the words and the squares with intelligence.

'You are nearly as good as Bon Papa,' Christine commented. 'You only lack practice.'

'Yes,' he said. 'I know I do.'

When Giselle came home, they were so engrossed in the game that they did not hear her till she stood at the salon door. They looked up, half-ashamed, as if they had been caught in some crime.

'Well, what an unexpected scene!' Giselle declared. Her nose and her cheeks were pink from the wind and her eyes were bright. 'I bought an apple tart,' she told Jean-Luc. It was Giselle's way of saying she was sorry.

Christine watched Jean-Luc, anxious for his reaction, but he only said, 'Good,' and kept his eyes on the game.

'Can we have a piece now?' Christine asked, and Giselle assented, returning with three large slices on a plate and three forks.

'Not for me,' Jean-Luc refused, but when their faces fell and Christine urged, 'Go on, Papa. We'll feel greedy on our own', he gave in. 'Well, just a small piece then.'

Giselle wiped her fingers on her handkerchief. 'Still no word from Sophie,' she said.

'She may not have received the telegram,' Jean-Luc said. 'There is a postal strike in England.'

'Surely that wouldn't affect telegrams?' Giselle asked, but Jean-Luc did not know.

'Let's hear the news,' Giselle said.

Jean-Luc switched on the radio again, and Christine cleared away the Scrabble pieces.

'Who won?' Giselle asked, and Christine said, 'No one. We didn't finish.'

'You can always have another game,' Giselle said, but Jean-Luc and Christine were silent.

The truce lasted through supper and until bedtime. When Christine said goodnight, Giselle was still talking and Jean-Luc was answering her. Christine hoped fervently that it would last.

She peeped round Bon Papa's door on her way back from the bathroom. '*Bonne nuit*, Bon Papa,' she whispered.

The room smelt close and sour even from the doorway, but on impulse she went to him and kissed him on the forehead. His skin was clammy, damp with sweat. '*Dors bien*, Bon Papa,' she said tenderly. 'Sleep tight.'

She closed the door softly and went to bed.

She awoke at midnight, hearing noises outside the door, and stumbled out drowsily to see what was happening. Jean-Luc, in his day clothes and with a dark shadow round his chin, stood on the landing.

'What is it, Papa?'

'Nothing. Go back to bed.'

'You're not leaving?'

'No, I'm not leaving. I haven't gone to bed yet.'

'Is anything wrong, Papa?'

'No, nothing. Go back to sleep, Christine.'

She crept back into bed, pulling the covers over her head to muffle the sounds of the footsteps and the whispering. When she slept, she dreamed that the roof had blown off and that two black crows swooped down and bore the sleeping Grand-père away in their claws.

In the morning, Giselle came in to waken her and told her that Bon Papa had had another attack in the night, and had been taken to the hospital. 'He is dead, *chérie*,' she said.

10

Christine took the news surprisingly calmly. In fact, as Giselle remarked to Léonie, it was slightly unnerving that the child showed no emotion at all.

Christine did not think she would ever feel anything again. All her senses were numb. Like an automaton she went about the house, helped Giselle with the housework and answered when spoken to, mechanically and without interest. But beneath her dry-eyed calm she could hear her own voice screaming and screaming and screaming. No one else could hear it, of course, so they all treated Christine quite normally and went on behaving as though nothing had happened. If she wondered occasionally how her parents could be so uncaring, they wondered the same about her.

'I mean, we all knew he had to go sometime,' Giselle reasoned. 'Let's face it, he was eighty-three and he'd been just hanging on for years. We all tried to warn Christine so that she wouldn't be too upset when it happened. But all the same, she was fond of the old man – you would expect her to cry or something.'

'You never know with children,' Léonie agreed. 'They can be amazingly callous. Fabienne is just the same: one week she is bosom friends with a child at school and the next week she doesn't want to know her.'

As Christine was not upset, they did not consider it necessary to be tactful for her benefit. Bon Papa's name was mentioned freely over the next few days.

When friends and neighbours called round to sympathize, Giselle and Jean-Luc and Léonie – who was spending a lot of time at the house – talked about their memories of Papa. He had not been an easy man to look after, they agreed with a tolerant smile, but they had had a great affection for him and would feel the loss very greatly. When the priest came to discuss the funeral arrangements, they talked about Papa's goodness, despite his faults, and reassured themselves of his happiness at being reunited with *chère* Maman. When they were on their own, they talked about invitations and drink and dress for the funeral and wondered which of the neighbours they could avoid inviting.

Christine listened to it all in silence, but every time they mentioned his name the screaming inside her grew louder. When they referred to him as 'the old man' it took on the pitch of a sawmill, searing her brain and shutting out all other sounds.

Each time she saw Papa, too, the noise seemed to increase, for the very sight of him would recall their whispered conversation on the landing. 'You will stay now, Papa?' she had asked. 'Surely you will stay?' But he had looked grave and shaken his head. 'The situation has not changed, Christine.'

'Sometimes,' remarked Léonie, when she had asked Christine the same question three times, 'I wonder if that girl is all right in the head.'

'They say she is clever at school,' Giselle laughed, 'but I think she must undergo a transformation on the way home.'

'Perhaps her father's witty repartee is too much for her,' suggested Pierre, who was using his father-in-law's death as an excuse for taking a few days off work. He refused to stay at home with René, who was perfectly happy with the neighbour, he said, and was enjoying a holiday enhanced by Giselle's cooking. 'It must be an awesome thing to have a brilliant father,' he added.

Jean-Luc looked at him over the top of his newspaper. 'You seem very hungry,' he said pointedly, as Pierre scooped the last handful of cashew nuts out of a bowl which had not left his side since being filled. 'Didn't you have any breakfast?'

'My wife starves me,' said Pierre cheerfully, winking at him. 'I shall make up for it at lunch time, though; something smells marvellous.'

'Has anyone seen Christine?' Giselle enquired. 'She was meant to be helping Léonie and me with the lunch.'

'Judging by the delicious aroma, you are managing quite well on your own, *chérie*,' Pierre consoled her. 'Don't let my wife near the food, though, or we will all be poisoned; just let her do the washing-up. Jean-Luc, how did a grumpy old devil like you manage to find a wife who has a flair for cooking as well as a perfect figure?'

'Really, Pierre, you are impossible!' said Giselle and went back to the kitchen, smiling.

Jean-Luc rustled the paper disapprovingly. 'I must say,' he remarked, 'that with all the relations mustered here, I am surprised that Sophie has not put in an appearance. We did cable her, you know, several days ago.'

'Not always very reliable, those cables,' Pierre replied. 'And nor was Sophie, if I remember rightly, *hein*? Besides, she might not think it worth the journey if she's been cut out of the old boy's will.'

'As far as I know, no one is cut out of the will,' said Jean-Luc stiffly. 'The house he left to us, as you know, and a lump sum to Léonie. Whatever other provision he may have made is not our business. It is in the hands of Papa's solicitor.'

'Oh well,' said the irrepressible Pierre, 'I suppose Sophie could always claim travel expenses from you for summoning her on false pretences from the wilds of

Angleterre. Ah! There is your errant daughter, wandering about the garden. Hey, Christine!' he yelled, flinging open the window and making Jean-Luc mutter under his breath, 'If you're going to take up residence in the garden, at least pull up some of the weeds while you are there.'

'That's a very good idea,' contributed Jean-Luc, over his shoulder.

'Would you believe that?' Pierre marvelled. 'Your father actually agrees with me. Go on, get the tools out. Your generous papa will give you a *centime* for every thousand weeds, so mind you find a lot.' He pulled faces at her through the window, watching and applauding as she listlessly fetched the gardening tools from the shed and began the work.

'*Formidable*!' he cheered, as she tugged at a thistle. 'Don't let the bastards get the better of you . . . that's right . . . you're winning! We'll make a wrestler of you yet.'

'Do shut the window, Pierre,' said Jean-Luc, at the end of his patience. 'You are causing a terrible draught.'

'You ought to be grateful, *mon vieux*; I have just found you some very cheap labour. One *franc* a month: it's even less than you'll earn on unemployment insurance when Parnassier sack you for eccentric driving!'

Jean-Luc flung down his newspaper and left the room, and Pierre chortled happily to himself. 'Pompous ass,' he murmured.

Christine was not sorry to be given something to do. Although it was difficult to concentrate on anything, she was afraid that if there was nothing to distract her from all the screaming inside her head, she might easily go mad.

It was possible that she had already begun to go mad,

for she had started to forget things. There were two whole days, for instance – the past two days – about which she could remember nothing at all, not the slightest detail, and this frightened her. It frightened her so much that she could not tell anyone about it. If she told Maman, she thought, Maman would look horrified, and then would brush the matter aside, as she did with all unpleasant things. So she kept quiet, and the rival horrors of grief and fear fought it out behind her expressionless face.

Giselle came out into the garden to tell her that lunch was ready and she replied politely that she was not very hungry, thank you. 'Well, I am not making you anything special later on,' Giselle warned.

Christine heard the clatter of plates and the babble of conversation as the family sat down to eat, and then Oncle Pierre called out of the window that if she didn't come in immediately, he would eat all her *ragoût* as well as his own.

'You can if you want,' she called back. 'I don't want any.'

'You won't earn any more by skipping your lunch breaks,' he returned. 'Money-mad, these Rochauds!' And then she was left in peace.

After all the icy days, the November climate had turned suddenly mild and as she worked, Christine began to feel hot. Standing up to peel off her coat, she noticed a woman walking down the road. She carried a small suitcase and walked slowly, as if she were tired. As she passed each house she peered at it through her glasses.

Christine watched her without curiosity until she stopped suddenly at their own gate and began fumbling with the latch. Christine went to help her. 'It's a bit rusty,' she apologized. 'You really have to force it.'

The woman smiled and the tiredness vanished from her face. 'You must be Christine,' she said.

'Yes,' said Christine simply, and stared at her.

The woman looked back at her, taking in the girl's white face, the nervously fidgeting hands and the look of blank despair in her eyes.

'Oh no,' she said helplessly. 'I had a feeling I would be too late. Papa has died, hasn't he?'

Considering that they had not seen her for years, the family gave Sophie a rather cool reception, Christine thought. The long-lost relative, summoned in the heat of the moment, was redundant now that the crisis was over, and everyone seemed embarrassed by her arrival. Even the normally effusive Giselle was at a loss to know how to treat her. They sat her down at the lunch table and stared at her as though she had come from another planet. Christine thought it was rude.

'You must be terribly hungry,' she said. 'Have you been travelling for a long time?'

Sophie smiled at her gratefully. 'I am a bit tired,' she admitted in her funny French-English accent. Christine thought she looked near to tears. 'It's been a long journey.'

Jean-Luc cleared his throat. 'You should have telephoned from the airport,' he said. 'I would have come and fetched you.'

'I didn't come by plane. I took the boat-train.'

'*Mais non*!' everyone exclaimed simultaneously.

'Why ever didn't you fly?' Giselle asked. 'It's much quicker.'

'Perhaps it's difficult to get tickets at such short notice,' Léonie suggested.

'*Mais non*,' Jean-Luc claimed. 'I quite often used to fly

to London at a moment's notice and at this time of year there is never any trouble in obtaining tickets.'

'But Sophie doesn't live in London,' Giselle pointed out.

Why don't they ask her, Christine wondered, instead of talking about her as if she weren't here?

'But you had to travel to London first, in any case,' Pierre informed her.

'No. I came Southampton-Le Havre.'

'No, no, that's no good,' Pierre said. 'I will tell you the best way: train to London, taxi to the airport, plane to Paris, taxi to here . . . it would have taken no time at all.'

Sophie said nothing.

'Well, I wouldn't fly,' Léonie asserted. 'The very idea of it terrifies me.'

'You're not afraid of flying, are you, Sophie?' Pierre teased. 'A pioneer like you!'

'No,' said Sophie quietly. 'It is just that the fare is a bit expensive.'

'For the sake of a few pounds,' Giselle expostulated, 'you must have wasted hours of travelling time!'

'Never mind, *chérie*,' Léonie consoled her. 'You wouldn't have got here in time anyway.'

'When did he die?' Sophie asked. Her hands tightened round the handle of her bag till the knuckles turned white.

'A few nights ago,' replied Giselle vaguely. '*Mon Dieu*! I have just thought, Jean-Luc. Where are we going to put her? There's is Papa's room, of course,' she told Sophie, 'but we haven't cleared it out yet.'

'Christine's room, I suppose,' said Jean-Luc. 'You'll only have to make up the bed. The spare bedroom is full of boxes,' he explained to Sophie. 'We usually use Christine's room when people come to stay.'

'Would you mind, Christine?' Sophie asked apologetically. 'Is there room for two beds in there?'

'Oh no, don't worry,' said Giselle airily. 'It will be far easier if you have Christine's bed and Christine sleeps at Léonie's.'

Christine's face registered dismay.

'Oh, but I wouldn't dream of turning Christine out of her own room,' said Sophie hastily. 'Couldn't I stay with you instead, Léonie?'

'*Chérie*, it would be far too cramped for you,' protested Giselle.

'I'll sleep on the sofa,' said Christine loudly. 'I don't mind at all.'

'I cannot see what all the fuss is about,' said Giselle. 'It's much the easiest thing for Christine to go to Léonie's.'

'No,' said Christine firmly. 'I would prefer to sleep on the sofa.'

Everyone stared at her, and Léonie turned an unattractive shade of red.

'Well, that is settled then,' said Giselle lightly. 'Sophie, I expect you would like a wash after your long journey. If you'll take your things up to Christine's room, I will find you some clean sheets.'

Sophie picked up her case. Jean-Luc stood up and moved to help her.

'No, please,' she said. 'I can manage it quite easily. Don't leave your lunch.'

'There is no point in everyone letting their food go cold,' Maman agreed. 'I will put yours in the oven, Sophie, and you can have it when you come down.'

'I'll take the suitcase,' Christine offered, suiting action to words.

'If you are going up, Christine, will you take some sheets out of the cupboard on the landing?' Giselle called

206

after her. 'And there is a spare bolster in Bon Papa's room.'

'I'm sorry that nothing is ready,' said Christine awkwardly, pushing open her bedroom door with her foot. 'They didn't know if you would come.'

'The telegram only arrived yesterday,' said Sophie faintly. 'I've been travelling all night,' she added, 'and after all, I am too late.' She burst into tears. 'Oh dear,' she said. 'I'm sorry.'

'Come and sit down,' said Christine practically, taking her by the elbow. She cleared the clothes off her bedroom chair, and placed a box of tissues within Sophie's reach. 'Would you like a drink or something?' she asked hesitantly.

'Oh, no,' said Sophie in a choked voice. 'I'll be quite all right.'

'Or a cup of tea?' Christine suggested, on a sudden inspiration. The English drank a lot of tea.

Sophie laughed through her tears. 'You must be psychic,' she said. 'I would love one. That's what comes of living in England!'

Christine skipped downstairs. She would make Sophie some sandwiches too, she thought. Maman's warmed-up meals were always horrible.

When Christine returned with the tray, although Sophie's eyes were red and the waste-paper basket held several crumpled tissues, she appeared to have recovered her composure. 'I'm sorry,' she apologized again. 'I hope I haven't upset you. You must have done quite enough crying yourself.'

'No,' said Christine stonily. 'I haven't cried.'

Sophie looked at her and believed it. 'Sometimes,' she said, attacking a crusty cheese sandwich, 'It's worse if you can't cry.'

'Yes,' said Christine, standing to attention by the door.

'In fact,' Sophie continued, not looking at her, 'the most horrible thing of all is that feeling of crying inside.'

'Yes,' said Christine again, indistinctly. Her hands twisted together.

'Do come and sit down,' said Sophie companionably. 'I never thanked you for those lovely letters. You are just as I imagined you, you know, only much prettier. Very like Giselle when she was your age.'

'Bon Papa said,' Christine said, keeping her voice determinedly steady as she spoke his name, 'that I was like you.'

'Did he?' Sophie smiled at her. 'Poor old you!'

Christine giggled faintly.

'That's better,' Sophie approved. 'Do come and eat one of your sandwiches; they're very good.'

Christine shook her head. 'I'm not hungry,' she said.

Sophie looked sorrowful. 'I feel such a pig,' she said, 'eating on my own.'

Christine smiled. Tante Sophie had such a funny way of talking – not only the accent but the words themselves – more like a schoolgirl than an adult, she thought.

Sophie caught her amusement. 'Is my French terrible?' she asked. 'I haven't spoken it for years, you know. I can't even remember the words for some things, and my slang must be very old-fashioned by now.'

'Do you think in French?' Christine enquired. 'Or in English?'

'In English,' Sophie confessed. 'I am having to translate everything before I say it.'

'But you are French?' Christine was uncertain.

'Oh yes,' Sophie assured her. 'I didn't change. But I feel more English than French now, I must admit. Hence the tea!' She raised her cup to Christine. 'I suppose you think it's horrible.'

'Horrible,' agreed Christine fervently. 'Maman and

Papa never drink it. We just keep some in the house for Bon Papa occasionally.' There it was again – his name just kept slipping out!

'Are you sure you don't mind me sleeping in your room?' Sophie asked, standing up and brushing the crumbs from her skirt carefully on to the tray.

'Of course not,' Christine told her. 'I can easily sleep on the *canapé* in the salon. It's just that I didn't want to go to Tante Léonie's.' She clapped a hand over her mouth, afraid that Sophie would think her rude, but Sophie only said, 'Couldn't we fit a camp-bed in here? There is plenty of room.'

'But you're a visitor!' Christine said, shocked. 'You must have a room to yourself.'

Sophie laughed. 'I am also one of the family,' she said. 'So you don't have to treat me like a proper visitor.'

"Of course you are,' said Christine. 'I was forgetting.'

'There have been times,' Sophie said, 'when I have forgotten too.' She stacked her plate neatly beneath the cup and saucer on the tray.

'Christine!' Giselle called. 'Come down and make the coffee – we are all waiting.'

'You go down,' Sophie said. 'I'll just wash my face and hands, then I'll come and ask Giselle about the camp-bed. Thank you for the lunch, Christine. It was delicious.'

'*De rien*,' said Christine, embarrassed at being thanked. 'It was nothing.'

When she took the coffee into the salon, Christine found them all discussing Grand-père's possessions.

'Of course, there may be special bequests in the will,' Léonie was saying, 'and naturally I wouldn't want to take anything valuable . . .'

'Naturally,' echoed Pierre.

'. . . but I would like some little memento – something for the children rather than for myself.'

209

'Well, make up your mind what you would like, *chérie*, and we can get on with clearing out the room, if you will give me a hand,' Giselle said. 'Though I expect we can throw most of the stuff away. There is nothing there of any value, except his watch perhaps, if anyone wants that.'

'I was thinking,' said Léonie, 'that I might take that little set of ivory elephants he always kept on top of the bureau. Not that they would be worth much, but – '

'No,' said Christine suddenly. 'You can't have those.'

They all stared at her.

'Christine!' exclaimed Giselle.

'Bon Papa gave them to me,' Christine explained, trying to control her voice. 'He wanted me to have them. He told me to put them in my room, but I said no, I would leave them there. They've always been there, on the bureau,' she added, on a hiccup.

'Christine,' said Giselle in an ominous tone, 'you will stop this nonsense immediately. Your aunt is entitled to have anything she wants. Provided, of course, that it doesn't belong to us,' she stipulated hastily.

'But he gave them to me!'

'You can have something else, *chérie*,' Giselle said firmly. 'Now, pour the coffee, will you?'

Christine went straight out through the dining-room and up the stairs.

Léonie sat and listened for a few seconds. 'That child has gone to Papa's room,' she said.

'Oh, forget the bloody elephants, Léonie!' said Pierre, embarrassed. 'What does it matter? The kids would only break them, anyway.'

'No!' said Giselle, tight lipped. 'It is the principle that is important. Christine has no right to contradict me in such matters.' She stood up and made for the door.

'I will deal with this, Giselle,' Jean-Luc said. 'We will

work out some compromise. If Papa promised her the elephants, after all . . .'

'Don't you start going against me as well, Jean-Luc!' Giselle warned. 'I have enough troubles as it is.' She pushed past him, followed by Léonie.

Jean-Luc hesitated, then followed them. Pierre guffawed. 'Isn't it amazing?' he marvelled. 'All over a couple of bloody ornaments!'

Christine was standing by the open bureau in Bon Papa's room. As Giselle came in she caught her breath and clutched something to her chest.

'You wicked child!' Giselle thundered. 'Give that to me at once!'

'No,' she croaked, backing away. Giselle caught hold of Christine's arm, but she turned and flung herself on the bed.

When she started to scream, they all jumped, startled – all except Christine herself, who had been screaming silently for so long that she scarcely noticed the difference. Giselle pulled her up roughly, but when she caught sight of Christine's desperate, staring eyes she let her go, half-afraid, and the unearthly, agonized screams continued.

'The child is sick!' said Léonie, shocked. 'She has gone mad!'

Christine gathered up the duvet from Bon Papa's bed and cradled it in her arms. The screams redoubled and tears poured down her face.

'Christine!' said Giselle. 'Stop this at once, do you hear me?' But her voice shook. Jean-Luc stood in the doorway, appalled.

Sophie, appearing suddenly, took charge. 'Go away,' she said firmly, 'all of you.'

They departed, too stunned to argue.

Sophie sat on the bed next to Christine. 'You poor old thing,' she said. 'You've just had enough, haven't you?'

She put an arm lightly round Christine's shoulders and sat in silence beside her. Gradually the screams subsided into sobs, and Christine hiccuped out a few words.

'No, don't talk yet,' Sophie advised. 'There will be plenty of time later. You have a good cry, and then I think it is really time that you had something to eat and a rest.'

Christine buried her head in the duvet and sobbed bitterly. Finally, exhausted, she was quiet. Her shoulders relaxed, though one hand still tightly clutched the object she had purloined from the bureau.

'I think,' Sophie said, 'that we will put you to bed now.' She helped Christine to her feet and led her to her room. Christine sat dully on the edge of the bed and blew her nose.

'Get undressed and right into bed,' Sophie ordered, 'and I will bring you some food and a drink.'

As Christine began to unbutton her clothes, she unclenched her hand to put down the object she had been holding all this time. It was not, after all, one of the ivory elephants, but an old tobacco tin.

It was Giselle who brought in Christine's tray.

'If you had eaten your lunch with the rest of us, we wouldn't have had all this trouble,' she said. 'Making all that noise, and with poor Papa just out of hospital!'

Christine turned her head away.

'You must realize, *chérie*, that we are all as upset as you are about Bon Papa,' Giselle said more gently. 'But life has to go on, you know.'

'Not for him,' Christine said, the tears beginning again.

Giselle put the tray down. 'You couldn't expect him to live for ever,' she reasoned. 'Everyone has to die. Now sit up properly, will you, and eat this.'

Christine muttered into the pillow.

'What was that?' Giselle asked.

'Nothing.'

'*Au contraire*,' Giselle claimed. 'You quite definitely said something. Now tell me, please, what it was.'

Christine sat up, her face red and her eyes puffy. 'I said,' she repeated indistinctly, 'that I just wish he had died in his own bed, like he wanted, that's all.'

Giselle put her hand on her hips. 'So that's it,' she said. 'That is what all the fuss is about? You think it is my fault that he was taken to the hospital to die.'

'No,' Christine protested. 'I didn't say that.'

'I suppose I should have guessed,' continued Giselle acidly, 'that I would be blamed for it one way or another. Thank you very much, Christine.'

Christine felt too tired to argue. 'I'm not blaming you,' she said listlessly. 'I just thought I would be with him, perhaps, when he died.'

Sophie came up the stairs. 'Everything all right?' she said hesitantly. Giselle ignored her. 'So,' she resumed bitterly, 'that is all the thanks I get for trying to spare you Grand-père's death. I can assure you, *mon enfant*, that death is not such a pleasant thing to witness. You did not miss any great spectacle.'

Christine did not answer. Sophie looked from one to the other. 'What is the trouble?' she asked.

'My daughter,' said Giselle coldly, 'is blaming me for the death of her grand-père . . .'

'No!' Christine said again, shaking her head.

'Apparently,' Giselle continued, 'we should not have taken him to the hospital but left him to die in his own bed in order that Christine could be there. She thinks, it seems, that no one could look after him, no one care for him, except her.'

Christine started to weep again, without any effort. The tears plopped on to her hands.

'I think,' Sophie said, 'that we are all upset at the

moment, but Papa would not want us to quarrel over him, *n'est-ce pas?*'

'I am not quarrelling,' said Giselle. 'But if Christine thinks it was my fault . . .'

'I don't!' Christine wept.

Giselle looked at her, lips pursed, but said simply, 'Eat the food that I have brought you,' and abruptly left the room.

Sophie perched on the end of the bed.

'Will you stay for a while?' Christine pleaded.

Sophie nodded. 'But eat while we are talking.'

'I'm not hungry,' Christine said, but she started to eat.

'You wanted to be with Bon Papa when he died?' Sophie asked.

Christine nodded. 'He always said he wanted to die at home and not in a hospital,' she exclaimed. 'But they took him to the hospital in the middle of the night. I didn't even know he was going.'

Sophie considered. 'I suppose that your parents were trying to give him one last chance,' she said. 'After all, more can be done for a sick person in hospital than anywhere else. You can't blame them for wanting to do as much as possible for him.'

'No, it's not that I blame them for that,' Christine explained. 'It's just that . . .' Her lip trembled. '. . . that I didn't say goodbye to him.'

Sophie patted her hand. 'You said goodbye the last time you saw him,' she said, 'but without realizing it. Can you remember what you said to him, that last time?'

Christine thought back. It was a relief to talk about Bon Papa. When she had kept her grief locked up inside her she had felt that it was choking her, but now it was as though the iron band around her chest and throat had been released. 'I think,' she said slowly, remembering, 'that I just kissed him and said, "Goodnight, sleep well."'

Her face brightened. 'That is almost like saying goodbye, isn't it? But I don't think he really knew who I was.'

'I expect he did really,' said Sophie comfortingly, 'but people get confused sometimes when they are ill.' She sighed. 'I wish I could have seen him before he died,' she said.

Christine leaned forward. 'But that's it!' she said. 'He thought it was you there. He kept calling me Sophie.'

'Did he?' Sophie asked. She smiled, but Christine noticed that she was also holding back tears. 'Well then,' she said, 'it seems that he was saying goodbye to both of us at once.'

Christine smiled too. She pushed her plate away and looked down at it suddenly. 'When did I eat all that?' she exclaimed in amazement, and Sophie began to laugh, so infectiously that Christine joined in. Giselle, coming upstairs, heard them and paused for a minute outside the door. Somehow, she never seemed to be the one who shared Christine's jokes.

It was agreed that the date of the funeral should be brought forward, as Sophie had to go back to England. Giselle was not happy about the arrangement. 'Talk about indecent haste!' she exclaimed. 'It is terribly short notice for everyone. Half the people invited won't be able to come. What is the point of cooking special dishes for a mere twenty or so?'

'Did Papa still have so many friends?' asked Sophie in surprise.

'Most of them are our friends,' replied Giselle stiffly. 'Naturally, Papa knew them quite well.'

'I really don't know how we'll find time to prepare half the food you have planned, anyway,' said Léonie plaintively. 'I think we should cut down on the menu. People won't expect much at such short notice.'

'It wouldn't be short notice if the funeral was held on the original date,' Giselle returned, exasperated. 'Really, Sophie, I cannot see why you have to rush back. It's not as though you see us every day. We expected you to stay at least a few days longer.'

'It's very sweet of you to want me,' said Sophie, without a trace of sarcasm, 'but I promised that I would be back by Wednesday.'

'Promised who?' Pierre enquired. 'Who is the mystery man?'

'You don't think I would tell you that!' Sophie teased. 'No, it's just that I have to go back to work. There is no one to teach my class at school.'

'But for a few days,' Pierre expostulated, 'surely someone can take your place. You are not indispensable, *hein*?'

'At the moment, unfortunately, I seem to be,' Sophie said. 'One teacher has left and his replacement has not yet arrived.'

'For a father's funeral,' Giselle said, 'they must expect to make allowances. Phone them, Sophie, and explain.'

'I promised I would not stay longer than absolutely necessary,' said Sophie firmly, and all further attempts to persuade her were in vain.

The day of the funeral dawned clear and mild. Christine felt that even the weather was indifferent to her grief. It should be dark and stormy, she thought. She had been crying ever since she awoke.

'I look hideous,' she said dismally, staring in the mirror at her swollen eyes and blotchy cheeks.

'Dab on some powder; it will cover the redness,' Sophie suggested. She gave Christine a quick hug. 'Are you sure you want to go? Funerals can be a bit harrowing, you know.'

'Maman said I ought to go,' Christine said. 'She said

that everyone was equally upset but that they were hiding their feelings and that I should do the same. But I can't,' she sobbed. 'Now that I've started crying I just can't stop.'

'You are making yourself ill,' said Sophie gently. 'Come on, come down and have some breakfast and then you won't feel quite so bad.'

Giselle was issuing instructions and took in the new arrivals as soon as they reached the bottom of the stairs. 'Now Sophie, just so that you know what is happening: the hearse is coming here first, straight from the mortuary, and the funeral cars will follow it, so everyone must be ready by the time the hearse arrives. Jean-Luc! Have you got the armbands? Where are they then? Well, tell Pierre to keep one for Sophie. Oh – and Christine had better have one too. Christine! *Nom de Dieu* – what on earth are you wearing? You should be in black; you are not going to a party, you know. Go and put on your black skirt.'

'I've grown out of it, Maman.'

'What do you mean, grown out of it? You wore it quite recently.'

'It's too small. I can't even do up the waistband.'

'Nonsense! Put it on and let me see.'

Christine turned resignedly and went back upstairs.

'And for heaven's sake put some powder or something on the face,' Giselle called after her.

'I already have.'

'*Bon Dieu!*' Giselle looked at Sophie and raised her eyes to heaven. 'You are lucky you haven't a daughter. When they get to this age . . .'

'That,' said Pierre, coming in, 'must win prizes for the most tactless remark ever made.'

Giselle flushed and stammered, 'I'm sorry, Sophie, I

217

didn't think!' but Sophie stopped her. 'It doesn't matter,' she said.

Christine plodded downstairs, wearing a mutinous expression and a short, tight black skirt.

'What is the matter now, Christine?' Giselle asked, glad of the distraction. 'Oh, the skirt – well, I suppose it will have to do.'

'Maman, the zip isn't even done up! I've had this skirt since I was ten.'

'Christine, you really are the limit!' Giselle exploded. 'Why couldn't you have thought of this before? Everything is left to the last minute in this house. And do try to stop crying! Jean-Luc, are the cars here yet?'

Jean-Luc wandered in, looking severe in a sombre suit and black armband. 'Is there any coffee, Giselle?'

'There's not time for breakfast,' said Giselle irritably. 'And you are meant to be fasting anyway. We will be going to Communion.'

'Oh, bad luck, Jean-Luc,' Pierre sympathized. 'Breakfast is cancelled for fear of sacrilege. You would have to phone the Pope for permission, and by that time the coffee would be cold anyway.'

'Do be quiet, Pierre,' Léonie scolded. 'Your jokes are in very poor taste, considering the occasion.'

Fabienne bounced in behind Léonie, wearing a new ruched black dress with white lace. 'Maman, René has wet himself. Isn't he naughty? Ooh look, Christine's face is all red!'

'Pierre, put René into a clean nappy, will you? And take Fabienne into the salon.' Léonie stubbed out a cigarette and lit another one.

'Léonie, I am not changing nappies in this suit. I will be covered in damp patches.'

'Well, what about my dress?'

'Let Christine do it,' said Giselle. 'You watch for the cars arriving, Léonie.'

'Giselle, what on earth have you dressed Christine in?' Pierre enquired. 'You must have only paid for half that skirt: they've claimed the other half back!'

'The hearse is here,' said Sophie.

Giselle started organizing again. 'Jean-Luc, you and Pierre go in the first car and Léonie and I will follow with . . . no, there will be too many of us. Look, if Christine rides in the hearse . . . where is she? Christine! We are all ready to go. How should I know where the clean nappies are? Ask Tante Léonie. And HURRY UP!'

The funeral cortège set off. Giselle pursed her lips into a suitably mournful expression and issued innumerable instructions to the undertakers, in a distressed whisper.

Jean-Luc and Pierre and the other pall-bearers stood round outside the church door, smoking a final, hasty cigarette, while everyone else trooped in to their pews.

Christine's throat was constricting so tightly again that she thought she would choke. It's Bon Papa in that box, she thought with a sudden shock. He'd dead and they've put him in a box and I'll never see him again.

'Are you all right?' Sophie whispered.

Christine nodded. The pall-bearers marched solemnly in with the coffin, and the service began.

Christine did not join in the hymn, nor did she hear a word of the priest's condolences to the family. Her limbs began to stiffen and freeze, and her heart thumped violently against her ribs. I've felt like this before, she thought confusedly, when was it? Her forehead and the palms of her hands were damp with cold sweat. She had a sudden image of Bon Papa lying, wheezing and gasping, in a narrow, rumpled bed . . . no, in a narrow wooden box . . . fighting for air, choking with a ghastly rattling sound . . .

'Aren't you well, Christine?' Sophie whispered again. Giselle frowned at her reprovingly. Sophie leaned across and tapped Giselle's arm. 'The child is not well,' she said. 'I'll take her out.'

Giselle nodded. 'Wait for the next hymn to start,' she hissed, but Sophie pretended not to hear. Taking Christine by the arm she led her out of the church. 'Is that better?' she asked, when they were outside. Christine looked through her. 'Look, sit here and recover for a minute,' Sophie said, 'and then we'll go over to that café opposite. We will still be able to see when everyone comes out.'

Christine's head began to clear. 'I'm all right now,' she said.

'Well, you'll be better out in the open air, anyway,' Sophie said. 'All that incense is enough to make anyone feel peculiar.'

Christine felt a great tide of relief at missing the funeral. 'Do you want to go back?' she asked Sophie.

'No, I'll stay out here,' Sophie said. 'We can say a prayer for him just as well outside.'

They took down a couple of chairs from one of the café pavement tables and the waiter came out to take their order. Sophie explained the situation and he took a personal interest, recommending thick hot chocolate and freshly-baked croissants as a certain cure for faintness. Christine watched Sophie as she was speaking. She was not pretty, thought Christine judicially, but she had a nice face. In her way, she was just as attractive as Maman. Maman could be charming when she wanted to be, but there was something about Sophie that made you like her even before you knew her, Christine thought.

The hot chocolate when it arrived was creamy and delicious. Christine took a huge bite of croissant. 'This is good,' she said indistinctly, and then, 'Papa will be furious.'

'I expect he won't even realize we've gone,' said Sophie consolingly. 'He is right at the front.'

They sat for some time in silence. Sophie ordered more croissants and watched the colour gradually come back to Christine's cheeks.

'Do you know,' said Christine suddenly. 'I can't remember anything for two days? I mean, I can't remember what I did or anything, for two whole days.'

Sophie put her cup down. 'It happens sometimes,' she said gently. 'I shouldn't worry about it if I were you. Sometimes when unpleasant things happen, your mind just shuts them out until you are able to cope with them better. When you start feeling less upset it will all come back to you.'

'Tante Léonie said she thought I'd gone mad when I screamed like that.'

'I think you do go a bit crazy when you lose someone you love,' said Sophie soberly. 'I did the most peculiar things after Nicky died. I wasn't myself at all.'

'Your daughter?' Christine asked timidly, and Sophie nodded. 'Did you get over it?' Christine asked. 'Maman says I'll soon get over it, but I don't think I will.' Her lip trembled.

'No – how can you get over it?' said Sophie in a matter-of-fact tone. 'A part of your life disappears and it is never the same again. But you do get used to it,' she added. 'It takes quite a long time, but one day you find you can think about the person without it hurting, and from then on it is never quite so bad.'

Christine digested this thought in silence. It was somehow more comforting, she thought, then Maman's blithe reassurances.

'Of course, the first time you lose somebody close is

always the worst,' Sophie continued. 'After Nicky, I thought I would never be happy again – but I am, you see, and so will you be.' Christine looked at her. Certainly, tucking into hot croissants, Sophie did not look unhappy. Neither, thought Christine in some bewilderment, did she look in the least wicked. It was a thought that had occurred to her several times since Sophie's arrival.

'Tante Sophie?' she began diffidently.

'Yes?'

'If it is not terribly rude to ask,' Christine said carefully, 'what did you do that was so bad? Not that I believe,' she added hastily, 'that you could do anything really bad.'

Sophie smiled. 'It was bad because it was irresponsible,' she said. 'It was having Nicky. You see, I wasn't married, and it is not a good thing to have a baby without giving it a proper father.'

Christine digested this information. 'Is that why you left home?' she asked.

'Yes. It was a great disgrace then – and I suppose it still is, only people tend to be more tolerant now – a great disgrace to the family, to have an illegitimate child.'

Christine frowned. 'But you didn't have to leave home, did you?'

Sophie sighed. 'Maman was willing for me to go away till the baby was born, then leave it to be adopted and come home again as though nothing had happened. She wanted to tell everyone I had gone away to study. But I wouldn't agree to that.'

'It would be deceitful,' Christine said, nodding.

'Yes,' Sophie agreed, 'but the main thing was that I didn't want to give the baby away, I couldn't bear to think of strangers looking after my baby, however kind they might be.'

Christine looked at her with wide eyes. 'But wouldn't Grand-mère let you keep the baby?'

'No – at least, not to bring it home. I did keep the baby, as you know, but I went to England to have it because Nicky's father was English and he wanted to go back home. His mother lived there too,' she said, and her face hardened a little, 'but after he left me she wouldn't have anything to do with me.'

'Why did he leave?' Christine asked. She felt that she was asking a great many questions, but Sophie did not seem to mind.

'I don't think,' said Sophie slowly, 'that he wanted to take on the responsibility either for the baby or for a homeless French girl who spoke very little English. Every time I asked him he said no, he was not worried, he was quite happy. Then one night he just didn't come back and I never saw him or heard from him again.' Even now, the corners of her mouth dipped slightly as she remembered it.

'How awful!' said Christine, shocked. 'What did you do?'

Sophie smiled. 'Oh, I was very brave,' she said, 'for at least a week! I had to leave the flat and James's mother refused to help me. Eventually I managed to contact a charity organization and once they grasped what I was trying to say in my awful English they arranged for me to go to a mother-and-baby hostel. But I never got there.'

'Why not?'

'Well, that's where my bravery left me,' Sophie said. 'I got as far as the door, and then I lost my nerve.'

'So what did you do then?' Christine prompted.

'I rang Papa,' Sophie said. 'I reversed the charge – all the way to France! – and rang him at his office, and then once I was put through I couldn't even say anything. I just cried and cried! But Papa realized it was me and he made me tell him where I was.

'He gave me the name of a business colleague in London and told me to ring him up in half an hour's time. In that time Papa said he would ring the man himself and explain the situation and ask him to give me some money which Papa would then refund him.'

Christine frowned. 'But surely,' she said, 'Bon Papa would never have let you leave home like that? Not Bon Papa?'

Sophie hesitated. 'He was very much ruled by Maman – your Grand-mére,' she said gently. 'It was she who made all the decisions and she was very strict. None of us ever dared go against her, not even Papa.'

'But you did,' Christine pointed out.

'Yes, I did,' Sophie said sadly, 'and I knew that she would never forgive me or let me come home again. And she never did. But Papa – he was different. It was a very difficult position for him, you know. I know it broke his heart when I left, but he didn't have much choice, I suppose. He didn't want to split the family.'

Christine licked her finger and dabbed up the crumbs on her plate. 'So, did Papa's friend help you?' she resumed.

'Oh, he was marvellous,' Sophie said. 'Instead of just giving me money he took me into his own house and he and his wife looked after me till Papa arrived.'

'Bon Papa arrived? In England?' Christine exclaimed. 'I never knew that Bon Papa had been to England.'

'No one knew,' Sophie told her. 'Maman thought he had been called away on business to Marseilles – he often had to go there. Even in later years, he never told anyone he had seen me. And Maman never knew he sent me money.'

'Did he do that right from the beginning?' Christine asked. 'Before I was even born, was that?'

'Yes, even before then,' Sophie smiled. 'And then later, when I found out that Nicky was . . . that she would never be able to walk, he told me to find a ground-floor flat, with a garden, and he bought it for me. Maman had died by that time, but I know he told Giselle and Léonie that he had lost the money in a business deal.'

Christine was open-mouthed. 'But he could have told Maman!' she said. 'It wasn't Maman or Tante Léonie who had made you leave home, was it?'

'No,' Sophie said. 'No, and I thought he could have told them really. He was afraid it might cause trouble. I suppose, the prodigal daughter being given so much, though he did help both of them too when they married.'

'Couldn't you have gone home then?' Christine pursued. 'If Grand-mère was dead . . .'

'I could have done,' Sophie agreed. 'It was mainly pride, I think, that prevented me. Nicky was quite severely handicapped, you know. The friends I had made in England were very kind and no one ever implied that it was my fault or that I shouldn't have had her, but I thought that if I came home, perhaps . . .' Her voice tailed off.

'Maman might have said it was a judgement on you,' Christine said soberly. She had heard Giselle say that about a neighbour whose baby had died at birth.

'Exactly,' Sophie said quickly. 'I couldn't bear anyone to think that Nicky was some kind of punishment. She was a great joy to me, you see. Those six years may have been difficult but we also had a lot of fun.'

'I wish I had known her,' Christine said.

'I wish you had. She would have loved you.'

Christine smiled.

225

'I have a photo of her,' Sophie said. 'I keep it in my handbag.'

'Can I see it?' Christine pored over the old black-and-white photo in its plastic envelope. A little girl, with strangely distorted limbs but a laughing face, rolled on a pocket-sized lawn with a shaggy-coated dog.

'She looks very happy,' Christine said.

'Yes, she was always a happy child,' Sophie said. 'Right till the end really.'

Christine looked at Sophie with great respect. 'How could you bear it, when she died?' she asked.

'If you have to bear something, then you do,' said Sophie simply. 'Sometimes it is easier, sometimes harder, but the time passes just the same. You'll see, it will be the same with Bon Papa. You will always be able to think of him with affection, but without the grief.'

Christine could not help but believe her. 'I wish you didn't have to go home yet,' she said. Once Sophie had gone, Christine realized, she would be all alone, with only Giselle and Jean-Luc's arguments for company.

Sophie leaned forward and patted her hand. 'Listen,' she said. 'I was going to leave it to Giselle to ask you this, but I have spoken to your parents about your coming to stay with me, and they are quite willing. As long as you would like to come, that is,' she added as Christine, unaccountably, hesitated.

'Now?' Christine asked. 'When you go back, you mean?'

'I thought so, then there would be no problems about your travelling. I work during the day, of course, but you could always come into school with me. They are only the very smallest children and you could either help with them or else join in the class of your own age group. We would have the evenings and the weekends free. But perhaps you would be bored.'

'Oh no,' Christine said. 'No I wouldn't, not at all.' But still she hesitated.

'Why don't you think about it?' Sophie suggested diplomatically. 'You don't need to decide till tonight. You already have a passport, so Giselle said.'

'Yes,' said Christine. Suddenly she burst out, 'I would love to come, Tante Sophie, but I can't now!' Her face contorted with misery.

'Because of Bon Papa?' Sophie enquired.

'No,' Christine said wretchedly. 'Because of Papa. I can't go, you see, because . . . because I don't know what would happen at home while I was away.' She stopped.

'Between Maman and Papa?' said Sophie.

'Yes.' Christine stared at her fingers, twined together like one of the rope puzzles that Marie-Lousie brought to school.

'What do you think might happen?' Sophie asked.

Christine felt disloyal, but she wanted to tell someone, and Sophie was one of the family after all. 'I am afraid,' she said, almost inaudibly, 'that Papa is going to leave.'

'I see,' Sophie said, and Christine was glad that she did not dismiss the possibility out of hand as Maman would have done ('You always imagine things, Christine'), but considered her statement seriously. 'Has he said that he will leave?' Sophie asked.

'Yes,' Christine replied. 'But I don't think that he has told Maman. He has taken a flat, you see, a flat of his own. He was going to go there before, but I asked him to come home. Maman didn't know.'

'If he didn't go before, when you asked him . . .' Sophie began, but Christine shook her head.

'No,' she said dully. 'He said he would just put it off for a short time. And Maman has not been nice to him. I know he will go.'

Sophie turned her empty cup round and round in its saucer. Finally she said, 'Look, Christine, they are all coming out of the church now. We will have to go. But try not to worry, and we will talk about it again this evening. *D'accord*?'

'Okay,' Christine echoed. The situation could not be said to have improved, and Tante Sophie, after all, would not be able to change Papa's mind once he had made it up. Things were no better then they had been before, but now, somehow, at least she did not feel so alone.

11

'Léonie should keep those kids under control,' said Jean-Luc, tossing down the damp tea towel. 'It was sheer madness to bring them to the funeral. They are totally undisciplined.'

'They were over-excited,' Giselle excused them. 'It's been a long day, and it's not over yet.' She yawned. 'Still, the lunch party went off very well, don't you think so, Sophie?'

Sophie was spared the necessity of answering, for Giselle did not wait for a reply.

'Let's go and sit down,' she said. 'I think we deserve a drink after all that washing-up.'

Under Giselle's supervision the last vestige of the visitors, the last glass, the last ashtray, had been removed from the salon, though the smoke still lingered. Cleared so recently of its crowd, the room felt unnaturally empty.

Jean-Luc brought in the drinks on a tray.

'Aren't you having one?' Giselle asked.

'I have had enough,' he said. 'I have a headache.' He sat in his usual armchair and lit a cigarette.

'This room is already quite smoky enough,' Giselle said, 'and I've taken away all the ashtrays to clean them.'

'I'll fetch one,' Christine said quickly. Several times it had occurred to her to warn Maman to be careful, not to upset Papa, but Maman would want to know the reason for such an unnatural request and Papa had said that Maman must not know.

If Christine was worried about Giselle's reaction to the news that Jean-Luc would be leaving, she was far more worried that she would find out that Christine already knew. Christine was pinning all her hopes on Sophie, praying that Sophie would think of some solution before she went home tomorrow. In the moments when she looked at the situation dispassionately, however, Christine had to admit that even Sophie's diplomacy would be inadequate here. What was needed was a miracle, and Christine did not honestly feel that she was entitled to one.

Sophie was talking, when Christine returned with the ashtray, about Jean-Luc's accident. 'I had no idea,' she was saying. 'It was your neighbour, the old lady, who told me at the funeral party.'

'We had almost forgotten about it,' Giselle said, 'with Papa's death coming so soon afterwards.'

'But you are better now, Jean-Luc?' Sophie asked. 'You must only just have come out of hospital?'

'Yes,' he said, 'I am better now.'

Christine did not think he looked better. If anything, he looked worse than he had that first day in the hospital. His face was pinched and white, and there were lines of strain around his mouth. His hands were ceaselessly on the move, tugging nervously at a loose thread in the chair or tapping non-existent ash from his cigarette.

'How did it happen, the accident?' Sophie enquired, and Giselle stood up abruptly and went to straighten a picture on the wall. There was an uneasy pause.

'You will have to forgive me,' Jean-Luc said. 'I suffered concussion from the accident and I find it difficult to remember now quite how it happened.'

Giselle sat down again and crossed her legs. 'It is something which is better forgotten,' she said pointedly, and Sophie sipped her drink and was obediently silent.

'Well!' said Giselle brightly. 'After this dismal topic of

230

conversation, I am glad to say that we have some good news, for you at least, Christine.'

Christine, who had been sitting on the carpet idly tracing the pattern with her finger, looked up. 'For me?'

She felt apprehensive. Maman's way of presenting bad news was invariably to disguise it as good, in the hope of avoiding unnecessary emotion.

When she was very young, Christine remembered, Giselle had met her from school one day with the news, 'We are going to buy you a kitten, Christine. Aren't you a lucky girl?' Christine had been doubtful for it seemed disloyal to Mimi, the Rochaud's ancient tabby, who had one ear and a strange predilection for sleeping on Bon Papa's boots. 'Mimi might not like a strange kitten,' Christine had pointed out, and Giselle had said quickly, 'Well, unfortunately, *chérie*, Mimi has been run over. But you will like the new kitten even better, I know.'

So now Christine waited, alert and suspicious, for the 'good news'.

'See if you can guess!' Giselle continued brightly. 'A long journey, a change of scene, new friends . . .'

Christine sprang up. 'You're sending me away to boarding school!' she cried 'Maman, you promised that Papa would only send me if I was disobedient and I haven't been! I haven't, Papa!'

Jean-Luc looked at Giselle. 'What is all this?' he asked.

'Don't be silly, Christine!' Giselle admonished. 'Whoever mentioned boarding school?'

'You did,' Christine insisted. 'You said that if I didn't do as I was told, Papa would send me . . .'

'What nonsense!' said Jean-Luc. 'There was never any question of boarding school. Giselle, what have you been saying?'

Giselle had flushed an angry shade of red. 'It was only a threat,' she said, 'when Christine was being difficult. Of

231

course I didn't mean it, Christine! Do try not to jump to conclusions.'

Christine sat down again. 'I'm sorry,' she said, feeling ridiculous.

There was silence.

'Well?' said Giselle. 'Don't you want to know after all, Christine?'

'Oh,' said Christine. 'Yes.'

'Tante Sophie,' said Giselle triumphantly, 'has invited you to go back to England with her!'

The announcement did not meet with the response she had expected. Christine looked uncertainly at Sophie, who said quickly, 'I have already asked Christine, Giselle. I am sorry, I should have told you. I thought it best to check with Christine whether it was convenient for her.'

Giselle laughed, annoyed. 'Well, of course it is convenient for her!' she said.

'No,' said Sophie, 'I was wrong to ask her to come now, in the middle of term. Of course, Christine must not miss school.'

'Oh, that doesn't matter,' said Giselle confidently. 'She will soon catch up on a few weeks' work, and there are no exams this term.'

'All the same,' Sophie said, 'I am sure the holidays would be a better time – perhaps at Easter? I shall be on holiday then too and I'll be able to take Christine around more.'

'But Christine won't expect a lot of fuss,' Giselle objected. 'As you said yourself, she can go into school with you during the day. She'll soon make friends – she's not shy.'

Sophie looked at Christine. 'But perhaps Easter would be a better time,' she repeated, and Christine, grateful for her intercession, nodded agreement.

'But the whole idea,' said Giselle crossly, 'was that

Christine should travel with you. You suggested it your-self, Sophie. It wasn't my idea.'

'I know,' Sophie agreed, 'but I'm afraid that I probably didn't give the matter enough thought. It would not be very interesting for Christine, after all, if I was working all the time.'

Giselle's suspicions were aroused. 'Is this what you have said, Christine?' she asked. 'That you would not find it interesting?'

Christine hung her head. 'No,' she said.

'There is no need to make a great issue of it, Giselle,' Jean-Luc interposed. 'If Sophie feels that Easter would be a better time – '

'If Sophie feels!' Giselle snorted. 'Believe me, it is not Sophie who has changed her mind but Christine who is being difficult. Isn't that the case, Christine? Answer me.'

'Giselle, we will discuss this later,' Jean-Luc said. 'We will not have arguments in front of a guest.'

'Sophie is family,' said Giselle dismissively. 'And you don't realize, Jean-Luc, that there is no time to discuss it later. Sophie leaves tomorrow and if Christine is going with her – '

'I'm not,' Christine told her. 'I will go at Easter instead. It is decided.'

'So, it's decided!' Giselle cried, and Jean-Luc said again, 'Giselle, we will talk about it another time!'

Sophie stood up. 'If you will excuse me,' she said politely, 'I think I will just go and do my packing, to save time tomorrow.'

'Shall I come and help you?' asked Christine hopefully.

'You will stay here, Christine,' said Giselle grimly, and Sophie gave Christine a small, apologetic smile and went out alone.

'Giselle, you are very rude,' Jean-Luc remonstrated, but Giselle countered, 'I am not so rude that I would refuse an invitation without even consulting my parents. How could you be so ungrateful and offend your aunt like that, Christine?'

'I haven't offended her,' Christine protested. The words struck home, however. Was Sophie offended, she wondered. But no, surely she had understood?

'I am sure it is not true that Christine does not want to go,' Jean-Luc said.

'Well, perhaps Christine will tell us,' said Giselle inflexibly.

Christine looked steadily at her feet, 'It's just that it's not a good time for me to go,' she said.

'Not a good time for you!' Giselle exclaimed. 'For sheer arrogance, Christine Rochaud . . .'

'Wait a minute,' said Jean-Luc. 'Christine, is this because of Bon Papa? Because if so, I think it would be good for you to go away for a while, to have a break, even if you feel that you don't want to. And as Madame Scholbert has already given you leave from school . . .'

'Of course you must go, Christine,' Giselle affirmed. 'Once you are in England, in a new place, you will soon forget all about it.'

'It's not because of Bon Papa,' said Christine.

'Then what is it?' demanded Giselle, exasperated.

Christine looked Jean-Luc straight in the face. You know what it is, her expression said. Help me.

Jean-Luc heaved a deep sigh and went to stand by the window. 'Is it because of me?' he asked.

'Of course it's not because of you!' Giselle snapped. 'Why should it be?'

'Yes,' said Christine simply.

Giselle, taken off guard, looked from Christine to Jean-Luc. 'What is all this?' she asked.

Jean-Luc turned to face her. 'If I understand it correctly,' he said, with his usual deliberation, 'Christine does not want to leave home in case, on her return, there is no home to come back to. Is that it, Christine?'

'Yes,' said Christine in a tiny whisper.

Giselle stared at Jean-Luc and the colour drained from her cheeks. Christine wished she were somewhere else.

'What do you mean, Jean-Luc?' Giselle asked, in a voice from which all the sharpness had fled.

'I am sorry that this had to come out so soon after Papa's death,' said Jean-Luc formally, 'but we have to face the fact, Giselle, that our marriage has hit a very rough patch recently.'

'Christine,' said Giselle, 'go and help Tante Sophie to pack.'

'No,' said Jean-Luc. 'Christine has a right to hear what affects her equally. I shall be leaving, Giselle. I have taken a small flat.'

'Leaving?' said Giselle, and her voice came out in a whisper. 'Leaving me?'

He nodded.

'But why?' she said.

Jean-Luc looked at her. 'You ask me why?'

'But Jean-Luc . . .' she went over to him, put her hands on his shoulders, 'all marriages have their problems. As you say, a rough patch! But isn't it better to stay and sort it out?'

'I hope we can sort it out, Giselle,' he said gravely. 'But just at the moment – you must excuse me – I cannot live here.'

She looked at him with a kind of hopeless amazement. Christine could see her selecting and rejecting arguments, one after another. Finally Giselle said, 'And so we are to give up a marriage so easily, after one problem? You know, Jean-Luc, you are not being fair. I have been under a great strain recently, with the illness and the death of Papa – '

'Yes,' he interrupted, 'I know. I am sorry, Giselle. I cannot say more than that, but I cannot live in this house with you, sleep in that bed . . .' His voice cracked, and he turned away.

Christine wanted to turn him back to face Giselle, to push them together, to lock all the doors, so that neither of them could leave, but the scene was unfolding with a relentless fatality and she could do nothing but watch.

'You can't just leave, like that!' Giselle said in desperation. 'After all these years of marriage, to let it all go to waste! It is wrong, Jean-Luc. We are Catholics, after all.'

His mouth curled and he shook his head with sad irony. 'Not very good ones,' he said. 'It would appear that we have failed in all the important things.'

'If you talk of failure,' Giselle cried, on the defensive, 'You should consider how much time you have actually devoted to your family since you sold your soul to Parnassier, the great God of the business world!'

'Yes,' Jean-Luc agreed. 'That is my failure. I am aware that it is much too late, Giselle, but all the same you can believe me, I regret it more than I can say.'

Giselle clenched her hands together till the knuckles turned white. With great effort, she said, 'It is not too late, Jean-Luc.'

He looked at her. Christine knew that he understood the effort it cost Giselle to say that, but he only said gently, 'But yes, I regret that it is.'

Giselle sank into a chair and gave way to convulsive sobbing, the anguish on her face unshielded by her hands which clutched frantically at the front of her blouse. Christine, frightened, moved near to the chair and watched her.

'Christine,' said Jean-Luc, 'I think it would be best if you went out for a little while. Can you take Sophie for a walk?'

'Yes,' she said.

He looked at her with pity in his eyes. 'Will you be all right?' he asked.

A mixture of emotions filled her mind, struggling for precedence over one another. She looked at Papa, and at the hysterical grief he had caused in Maman, and she did not know what she felt for him.

'Try to understand, Christine,' he pleaded, and he looked so bleak and alone that she said, almost without thinking, 'Yes, I do understand.' Then she burst out, 'But how could you do that to Maman?' and saw the pain quickly cloud his face, and he turned away from her.

Christine wanted to comfort him, and to comfort Giselle, but she could not. Instead she went out, closing the door.

Sophie was upstairs, looking out of the window. When Christine came in she turned quickly and said, 'What has happened?'

'He is leaving us,' said Christine heavily, and sat down on the bed.

'Oh, no!' Sophie sat beside her and put an arm round her. 'When?'

'I don't know,' Christine had not thought to ask when but it had seemed to her to make little difference. He had already abandoned them. 'Papa said could we go out for a walk,' she added dully.

'Yes, of course,' Sophie said, but added hesitantly, 'I suppose there is nothing I can do?'

Christine shook her head. 'It is too late, Papa said.' Her eyes, still sore from crying over Bon Papa, squeezed out a few painful tears.

'Come on,' said Sophie. 'We'll go for a walk.'

They went out, arm-in-arm, into the chill November evening.

'Where shall we go?' Christine said hopelessly.

'How far is your school?' Sophie asked.

'Not far.'

'Will you show it to me?'

Christine was surprised. 'Do you want to see it?'

'Yes, I'd like to. Then when I'm back in England I'll be able to think of you in your own surroundings.'

Christine was cheered by the idea that someone would think of her. 'I could write to you, when you go home,' she suggested.

'I hope you will,' Sophie said. 'I don't want to lose touch again. It's not every day that one discovers a long-lost niece.'

'Two long-lost nieces and a nephew,' Christine reminded her.

'Yes, that reminds me – is the school a long way from Léonie's?' Sophie asked. 'I said I would either pop in or telephone to say goodbye before I left.'

'It's about half an hour's walk,' Christine told her. 'Or there's a bus.'

'Which would you prefer? Are you tired?'

'No,' Christine said. 'Not if you aren't.' She did not know if she was tired or not. Her senses seemed to have gone numb recently, so that she hardly knew what time it was, or even what day.

'We'll walk then,' Sophie decided. 'It will blow away the cobwebs.'

Christine thought she was right. As they walked the familiar route from home to school, she began to feel more normal. 'I will go back to school soon,' she said, 'If Maman will let me.'

'Did they give you time off for the funeral?' Sophie asked.

'Not just for the funeral,' Christine said. 'Madame Scholbert – our headmistress – told me to go home till

238

things were more settled. I kept being sent to her,' she explained. 'I wasn't working.'

'I see,' Sophie said. 'But I heard you were doing so well at school.'

'I was,' Christine admitted. 'But I can't seem to concentrate recently.'

'You will have to work,' said Sophie seriously. 'Try to keep home things out of your mind, Christine, while you are at school. It will make it easier for you to cope, as well.'

'Yes, I know,' Christine agreed. It would be much nicer, she thought, to be able to give her whole attention to school while she was there, to worry about nothing more important than solving the next maths problem, or beating Marie-Louise at skipping. Only how could she concentrate on such things when at the back of her mind she was forever wondering what she would find when she went home?

'You have quite a long way to walk every day,' Sophie said.

'I like it,' Christine told her. 'It gives me time to think. Look, here is the wall where Bon Papa used to rest sometimes on the way.'

'Did he walk you to school every day?' she asked.

'Yes. We were usually late,' Christine said, then added hurriedly, 'only it wasn't his fault, of course. It's difficult to get ready quickly when you're old.'

They stopped in front of the school gates, barred and locked at this time of the evening. 'What time is it?' Christine asked, and when Sophie replied, 'Just after seven,' exclaimed, 'I thought it was much later than that!'

'It seems a long time since this morning,' Sophie agreed and Christine said sadly, 'It's because so much has happened.' Since this morning, they had said goodbye to Bon Papa and to Papa, and tomorrow they would say

239

goodbye to Sophie as well. Christine would not have believed that the world could change so much in so short a time.

'I wish Papa had not told her,' Christine said. 'Suppose he had just been going to forget it after all, and I pushed him into it?'

'I don't think you could push him into something like that,' Sophie said. 'It is not the sort of thing one does on impulse, and he had obviously been thinking it over for some time.'

'Papa doesn't do things on impulse,' Christine agreed.

She remembered that she was meant to be showing Sophie the school. 'My classroom is that one, third window from the left,' she told her. 'You can't see out of it much, when you're in there.'

'And a good thing too,' said Sophie severely, making Christine laugh. 'You see, you were forgetting that I am a schoolmistress,' Sophie said. 'I can be very strict.'

'You couldn't be as strict as Ma'mselle Dubois,' Christine said, but Sophie assured her, 'Oh, but I am, much worse!'

'But you don't stare at people over the top of your glasses and say, "Christine Rochaud, if you are late again, I shall be forced to speak to your parents,"' Christine said.

'No, much worse than that,' Sophie said.

Christine looked slightly anxious. 'Do they have corporal punishment in girls' schools in England?'

'Oh, we have capital punishment,' Sophie told her. 'If anyone is late we guillotine them immediately.'

Christine giggled. 'You wouldn't have many pupils left!' she said.

'No, it is a means of keeping the class small,' agreed Sophie solemnly. 'It proves very effective.'

* * *

Before they were halfway to Léonie's house it began to drizzle with depressing persistence. 'How can such fine drops be so damp?' Sophie exclaimed. She turned up her coat collar and fished in her pocket for a headscarf. Christine noticed that she knotted it sensibly under her chin, so that her hair was covered. Maman would have folded it into a tiny triangle and tied it at the back, or wound it round her head like a turban. It would not have kept the rain off but it would have looked very chic.

'I wonder if Maman is all right,' Christine said.

'When we get to Léonie's I will phone and tell her where we are,' Sophie said. 'Then if she wants us to go back we will.'

The front door of the house in which Léonie and Pierre had their apartment was of heavy oak which had warped over the years. Now, in the damp night air, it stuck fast.

'Push!' cried Sophie, and they hurled themselves at it till suddenly it swung open and they hurtled into the hall, laughing a little hysterically. After the long day of grieving it was good to laugh. But tomorrow, Christine thought, we will be mourning again for Papa as well as Bon Papa, and Sophie will be gone. She could not foresee much laughter in the days ahead.

The hall light had gone, so they struggled up the stairs in the dark. Hearing footsteps coming down, they stood to one side and a shadowy figure brushed past them.

'It's only the man who lives below Tante Léonie,' said Christine. 'It's a bit ghostly in the dark like this, *n'est-ce pas*?'

'Ghosts don't wear cologne,' said Sophie.

Christine sniffled. 'It was a bit strong,' she agreed. 'Papa doesn't wear cologne. Aftershave, sometimes, but it smells quite nice. This is the last flight.'

'However does Léonie manage to get the children up all these stairs?' Sophie marvelled.

'She wanted to move to a ground floor flat,' Christine told her, 'but Oncle Pierre said this house had unique character. It's historical or something.'

'That must console Léonie when she's carrying up the bags of shopping?' Sophie said.

Tane Léonie and René were alone in the apartment.

'Pierre has gone out,' she announced as she led them into the salon. 'He said that funerals made him miserable and he had to go and cheer himself up, though for my part I thought he was quite cheery enough this afternoon. So I told him, you can go but you can take Fabienne with you. I have had enough of her for one day.'

René was lying on the floor, his face streaked with tears.

'He is being infernal, too,' said Léonie. 'Only, thank God, he is never as bad as Fabienne even at his worst.'

Sophie smiled at him. 'It was a long day for the children,' she said.

'It was a long day for all of us,' said Léonie. 'Still, at least it's over, I can't bear funerals. I never have been able to stand them.'

She spoke, Christine thought, as though everybody else went to funerals for amusement.

'You and Giselle worked wonders to plan that lunch for everybody,' Sophie said, settling herself into a chair.

'The food was good,' Léonie admitted. 'Giselle did most of the actual preparation, of course. With two small children, it is not possible for me . . .'

'Of course not,' Sophie agreed.

'Actually, Sophie did a lot of it,' Christine told Léonie. 'Maman was off having her hair done yesterday afternoon.'

'Tante Sophie,' Léonie corrected her. 'You are not so informal with me.'

René sat up and began to take an interest in the

visitors. He picked up his toy monkey and waved it hopefully at Christine. Christine laughed. 'You remember, *hein*?' she said. 'You remember the game we had last time?' She went to sit with him on the floor and René chuckled in anticipation.

'I must just ring Giselle if I may, Léonie,' said Sophie. 'We came out for a walk and she doesn't know we are here.'

'Oh, Giselle won't worry,' Léonie said. 'She'll be glad to have the house to herself for a while, I expect.'

'All the same,' Sophie said, 'I'll just let her know where we are.'

The phone was in the hall and Léonie stayed out there while Sophie rang. Christine strained her ears to hear, above René's clamouring, but Sophie seemed to be confining her conversation to sympathetic murmurs. Poor Sophie, thought Christine suddenly: everyone tells her their problems and no one asks about hers.

'Come and sit down,' Léonie said, coming back into the room, 'and we will have a good tête-à-tête. I have hardly seen you to talk to since you arrived.'

Christine looked enquiringly at Sophie, and she nodded reassuringly. 'We needn't go back yet,' she said. 'Everything is all right.'

'I should hope you won't go back yet!' Léonie exclaimed. 'You've only just arrived. Giselle can't monopolize you, you know. Do you want a drink, Sophie?'

'No, no,' Sophie said hastily. 'I shall be afloat if I drink any more.'

'Have a cup of tea?' Christine suggested, and Léonie glared at her.

'You can have tea if you want it, of course,' she said jealously. 'You can make it, Christine, if you are so keen to offer.'

'All right. Do you want one, Tante Léonie?'

'Not for me!' Léonie shuddered. 'It is terribly bad for the health you know, Sophie.'

'Is it?' Sophie sighed. 'All the nice things are bad for you, aren't they? Never mind, everybody needs one vice.'

Léonie reached for her cigarettes. 'It's the tannin that's dangerous,' she warned. 'It is a stimulant, you see.'

Sophie laughed. Christine, in the kitchen, heard her and smiled. Sophie's laugh was infectious. 'Perhaps I need stimulating, at my age!' she said.

Léonie snorted. 'You are no great age,' she said. 'Only a few years older than me, after all, and younger than Giselle. You would look younger, too, if you took care of yourself as she does.'

'Giselle is so *soignée*,' Sophie agreed. 'I am too lazy to take the trouble, I suppose. You always look very elegant too, Léonie.'

'If I can take the trouble, with two kids, then you can,' Léonie said severely. 'Without children, one has so much more time.'

Christine, thinking of Sophie's lost daughter, winced. Tante Léonie was not the soul of tact, sometimes. She went into the salon.

'Where are the sachets, Tante Léonie?'

'If we have any,' Léonie said pessimistically, 'they will be in one of the cupboards. You will have to look. What was I saying, *chérie*?'

Christine found two sachets of tea at the bottom of a tin. She sniffed doubtfully. They were a bit musty. Most of the food in Tante Léonie's house had been there a long time; either that or it wilted as soon as it was brought into the house, defeated by the dark little kitchen and Léonie's uninspired cooking. If it were her kitchen, Christine thought, she would paint it bright yellow, like sunshine, and put jars of flowers on the wide windowsill where the half-empty jars of carrots and the tubs of sunflower margarine now mingled with a pile of ironing.

She carried the tray into the salon.

'No milk,' said Léonie triumphantly. 'I am sure Sophie drinks tea with milk, *à l'anglaise* – *n'est-ce pas*, Sophie?'

'If you have some,' Sophie admitted.

Christine was crestfallen. She had not thought, earlier, to offer Sophie milk in her tea.

'It is nice without, too, sometimes,' Sophie said. 'The tea is different here anyway – it makes a change.'

'I expect it is better here,' said Léonie complacently. 'How do you bear the food in England, Sophie? All that tasteless overcooked meat and half-raw vegetables!'

'The English home cooking is very good, once you get used to the change of style,' Sophie said. 'And much simpler to prepare on the whole.'

'Greasy chips,' said Léonie gloomily, 'and jam with the meat! And heavy puddings – not that you ever put on weight, Sophie. You could always eat like an ogre and it never showed.'

'Oh, I still do,' Sophie said. 'Mind you, with school lunches you need to eat well in the evenings.'

'And I suppose you have the English breakfasts,' said Léonie scornfully.

Sophie laughed. 'The English breakfast is mostly corn-flakes or toast these days,' she said. 'English people have to rush off to work in the mornings, too, you know. Bacon and egg is for the weekends, if at all.'

'Well, I don't know how you can live there,' said Léonie, 'among those people.'

Christine giggled. 'They are human, Tante Léonie,' she said. 'They don't have little green horns!'

Sophie smiled, but Léonie retorted, 'And what do you know about England?'

'Nothing,' admitted Christine, but the corners of her

mouth quivered. At least I know they don't have little green horns, she thought. If Maman had been there, she would have been scolded for baiting Tante Léonie, but without Maman the temptation was at times too great to resist.

'Tell me about yourself, Léonie,' said Sophie quickly. 'It is so long since I had any news. You know, I didn't even hear that you had had René till long afterwards. I would have written if I had known.'

'Well, if you will exile yourself in some foreign place,' Léonie grumbled. 'Besides, I expect Papa would have been angry if you had written. He never mentioned you, you know, in all those years.'

Sophie sipped her tea and her mouth looked as though it did not much like what it tasted.

'What a time I had with René!' Léonie exclaimed. 'It was as well you didn't know perhaps, Sophie, it was a near thing. The doctor told Pierre he was lucky to see me alive.'

'Poor you,' said Sophie sympathetically.

'So I told Pierre – no more, I said, that is the last one,' Léonie recounted, and her face hardened at the memory.

'Did Pierre want more children?' Sophie enquired.

'Oh, it was not the children he wanted,' Léonie declared, 'Just the creation of them – *tu m'entends*? It never seemed to occur to him that I paid for his amusement with nine months of torture.'

Sophie glanced pointedly at Christine, whose face was expressionless as she flicked through one of René's picture books with him.

'Oh, they don't listen,' Léonie assured her. 'It means nothing to children, after all. Anyway, you have no idea, Sophie, of how selfish Pierre can be. In the end I told him, I said, "If you want nothing but your amusement you can look elsewhere, *mon chou*. I have a house to run and children to look after. You cannot expect everything, you know. I need my sleep.'"

'Oh, Léonie!' said Sophie.

'You needn't tell me "Oh Léonie",' Léonie said defiantly. 'I have the right to a little consideration too. It's not even as though I enjoyed it,' she added. 'I am not like Giselle.'

'What a beautiful picture that is,' said Sophie hastily. 'It is from home, isn't it?'

'*Hein*? Oh, yes, it used to hang in the salon,' Léonie said. 'Papa let me have it when we got married. Anyway, as I was saying about . . . ah, that mutual friend of ours. You heard all about it, I suppose?'

'About what?' Sophie asked.

Léonie lowered her voice to a conspiratorial whisper. 'The affair!'

René let out a peal of laughter. '*Oton!*' he crowed, as Christine turned the page to reveal a smiling pink pig.

'Yes,' Christine agreed. '*Cochon!*' She said the word so vehemently that Léonie hesitated.

'Christine, why don't you take René to Fabienne's room and play there?'

Christine stood up. '*Viens*, René.'

But René stood his ground. '*Non!*' he roared, '*Non, non!*'

'He won't go,' Christine said.

'Oh well, leave him then,' said Tante Léonie. 'Well, you see, Sophie – '

'Shall I put some music on?' said Christine loudly.

'If you want,' Léonie said, annoyed at the interruption. 'It's mostly classical, though – Pierre's choice,' she explained to Sophie.

'Let me look,' Sophie said. She knelt by the music cabinet and she and Christine looked through the records.

'I don't really know any of them,' Christine said. 'Oncle

Pierre put on something good when I was here before. Do you know what that was, Tante Léonie?'

'I have no idea,' said Léonie huffily. 'It does not interest me, music.'

'Mendelssohn!' exclaimed Sophie delightedly. 'You will like this, I should think, Christine.'

'What is it?' Christine asked.

'"Fingal's Cave". It's a piece of music written about a cave in Scotland, surrounded by sea. If you listen you will hear the waves crashing on the rock.'

Christine settled back to listen, gently restraining René as he attempted to grasp the revolving turntable.

'*Non*, René. Look, here is your tractor.'

'So, do you want to hear about this affair, Sophie, or not?' said Léonie sulkily.

'Is it over now?' Sophie enquired.

'Oh yes, since the accident, of course . . .'

'Then I think not,' said Sophie apologetically.

Léonie was taken aback. 'Why not?' she said.

'I haven't seen you all for such a long time,' Sophie explained. 'I would like to leave the past alone and hear all about how you are now. What have you been doing, Léonie? do you still make your own clothes?'

'Some,' said Léonie shortly.

'You used to make such beautiful things,' said Sophie persuasively. 'Dresses with little lace collars and mother-of-pearl buttons . . .'

'I made this one,' said Léonie, mollified. 'The one I am wearing.'

'You are so clever, Léonie,' said Sophie sincerely. 'How ever did you get all those pin tucks so even?'

The record turned and the notes rose and fell, rose and fell.

* * *

René grew sleepy; he leaned against Christine and put his thumb in his mouth. The music soared and crashed and subsided again. Christine thought not of water breaking on the rocks, but of Sophie calming the grief of those around her. If only she would stay, Christine thought, I think I could exist even without Bon Papa.

For a fleeting moment, she thought she would tell Sophie that she had changed her mind, that she would go to England with her, now that the situation at home was at last, and unhappily, resolved. Then she saw Maman, sobbing and hysterical, and she rebuked herself for her selfishness. She could not leave Maman now, she thought, and perhaps she would not be able to for quite a long time. Besides, even at Easter, would there be any money to spare for sending Christine to England?

Surely, thought Christine, Papa would not leave them destitute? Would Maman have to work to keep them? The thought of poverty, a condition unknown to Christine's nearly twelve years of life, sent shivers of apprehension down her spine. As well as Papa's money of course, there had been Bon Papa. 'Grand-père does not pay me for his keep,' Giselle used to say, when someone remarked on their luck in being provided by the old man with a free home, but the fact remained that Bon Papa had frequently made presents to Giselle.

'A little gift,' he would say, pressing some rustling notes into her hand. 'Buy something nice for yourself and for Christine.' And Giselle would spend a day combing the expensive shops on the Rive Droite, returning with something sensible for Christine and something frivolous – perfume or a little brooch or a silk scarf – for herself. Her eyes would sparkle as she unfolded the treat to show Papa. 'Look, Jean-Luc, how delicate,' she would say, fluttering the silky fabric between her fingers. She would toss the scarf around her shoulders or over her head and pout like a mannequin, making them all laugh.

With Bon Papa gone, there would be no more presents, and with Jean-Luc leaving too – would there be no more food? Christine drew in her breath sharply, so that Sophie looked at her and said, '*Ça va*, Christine? Perhaps we had better go soon, Léonie. I think everyone is tired.'

'You can wait for Pierre if you like, to drive you home,' Léonie said, 'though I can't tell you what time he will be back, even with Fabienne with him.'

'Where has he taken her?' Sophie enquired.

'Oh, he will be in a bar somewhere with his so-called friends,' Léonie said. 'They will all make a great fuss of Fabienne and spoil her with sweetmeats and sugar cubes and God knows what else, and she will no doubt be sick in the night.'

Sophie rose. 'We will let you get René to bed,' she said. 'He is fast asleep, poor lamb. *Au 'voir*, Léonie. It has been lovely to see you again.' She put her arms around her sister and kissed her affectionately.

'You will have to come again,' said Léonie gruffly. 'Don't leave it so long, next time.'

'I won't,' Sophie promised. 'I would invite you to England too, Léonie, only my flat is so tiny. But Christine is coming on her own, at Easter, *n'est-ce pas* Christine?'

'Yes,' Christine said, 'I hope so.'

She kissed Tante Léonie dutifully and Léonie, in return, pursed her lips and brushed Christine's cheek with her ear. '*Au 'voir*, Sophie . . . Christine.'

'*Au 'voir*,' they responded, looking back over their shoulders as they descended the stairs. '*A bientôt* – see you again soon!' Sophie cried, and her voice floated eerily up the dark stairwell.

Out in the street, the cold wind pounced on them like an angry lion. '*Ouf*!' Christine exclaimed. It lashed their faces, making their eyes stream and their cheeks tingle. Christine's coat flapped about her legs, tugging her sideways as she walked.

'Run, to keep warm!' Sophie shouted, and they ran a few paces but the wind ran against them, filling their lungs with icy breath, and they gave up, gasping.

Round every corner the wind lurked, like an urchin waiting for them. Spitefully, it whipped their unprotected legs, howling gleefully in their ears as they recoiled. Drops of rain, borne on the icy gale, became splinters of glass which stung their hands and faces. The lid of a dustbin clattered noisily down the street, caught in the wind, and they jumped aside to avoid it before it fell to rest in the gutter.

Ahead in the dark, the lights of a café-bar glowed. 'Shall we have a break?' Sophie shouted, and Christine nodded gratefully.

Inside, despite the chatter and the laughter, it seemed suddenly quiet after the noise of the wind. Several heads turned to look at the newcomers and Christine was uncomfortably aware of their dishevelled appearance. Sophie, unperturbed, found a free table and ordered two hot chocolates. She undid her scarf and shook her hair free of her coat collar, rubbing her hands together to warm them.

'There is Oncle Pierre,' Christine said suddenly, and Sophie turned to see him amid a crowd of well-dressed men and women, drinking Ricard and making more noise that the other patrons together.

'*Ecoutez, écoutez, mes enfants!*' Pierre cried. '*Je vais vous raconter . . .*' It was his party cry: 'I am going to tell you something . . .' and the story was always well told and aroused laughter and applause.

Sophie smiled. 'He must have an endless fund of

stories,' she said. 'I would have thought he had run out of them, after this afternoon.'

'He makes them up as he goes along,' Christine said. 'He used to tell Fabienne and me stories about an imaginary man called Monsieur Foutu. Tante Léonie hated them. She used to keep saying, "Couldn't you even give the man a decent name, Pierre?"'

'Where is Fabienne?' Sophie said. 'She is not with Pierre.'

They looked round.

'There!' said Christine. 'Sitting on the bar eating chocolate, with that fat man.'

'Who is he?'

Christine shrugged. 'I don't know. He doesn't seem to be with Oncle Pierre's group.'

'Léonie would have a fit,' Sophie said.

'She would if it was René,' Christine said. 'I don't think she worries so much about Fabienne.'

Sophie drank her chocolate. 'By the way,' she said, 'when I rang Giselle she said that your papa was staying tonight. He will leave tomorrow.'

'Everyone is leaving tomorrow,' Christine said sorrowfully.

Sophie patted her head. 'I shall write you lots of letters,' she said, 'and I shall be looking forward to Easter. You will come, won't you?'

Christine looked wretched. 'There may not be enough money,' she said. 'I know Bon Papa would have paid for me, but now . . .'

'Don't worry about the money,' Sophie said. 'If that's the only problem, then I'll raise it somehow. I borrowed the money to come here; I'm sure I can do it again.'

'Are you very poor?' said Christine sympathetically.

Sophie laughed. 'No, not very poor. I get a bit panicky over the mortgage and the bills sometimes but I can afford the necessities, if not the luxuries of life. I shall miss Papa's money, though, I admit.'

'I suppose we will be poor, when Papa goes,' said Christine fearfully. She sipped her chocolate and the froth left a white rim on her upper lip.

Sophie frowned. 'You may have to economize a little,' she admitted. 'Jean-Luc will give Giselle money, though, I am sure. He won't leave you penniless.'

'Won't he?' Christine was relieved. 'You think Maman won't have to go out to work?'

'I don't know,' Sophie told her. 'It's a little soon, I suppose, for her to think about things like that. Would you mind if she did?'

Christine looked doubtful. 'I don't know. I can't see Maman going out to work, somehow. She always says that running the house is a full-time job, but now she has no one to run it for, has she?'

'Poor Giselle,' said Sophie soberly.

'Why can't he stay with us?' Christine burst out. 'Even if Maman has done something wrong, why can't he forgive her? I would forgive her, if it was me. And don't tell me I'm too young to understand,' she added fiercely.

'You are not,' said Sophie simply. 'But troubles between a husband and wife can never be understood properly by anybody except the two people concerned – not you, not me, nor anyone else. Even if you forgive someone, too, sometimes it's not easy to go on living with them.'

Christine shook her head. 'He has lived with her for all these years,' she said. 'Why can't he now? Maman is still the same person – she hasn't changed.'

'Perhaps the circumstances have changed,' Sophie suggested. 'A marriage can change, you know, even if the people don't. Perhaps their careers become too demanding, or their friends move away, so the couple become overworked, or lonely, or maybe just bored. Or they can become too rich, or too poor, or have too many children, or not enough. All sorts of things can cause trouble in a marriage.'

'Look who it is!' Pierre cried, lurching against the table so the cups clattered in their saucers. 'What are you doing here, my chickens? My wife sent you to spy on the reprobate, *hein*? Or did you just come to get drunk?'

'We came in out of the wind for a few minutes, on our way home,' Sophie said.

'The story of my life!' exclaimed Pierre. 'That's the reason I am here too. But now I am going back to a storm far worse than the one outside. Come with me, Sophie, and shield me from the thunder and lightning of Léonie's temper.'

'You couldn't give us a lift home, Oncle Pierre?' Christine suggested hopefully.

Pierre staggered theatrically. '*Mon chou*, you know I would give you a lift anywhere, especially if the lovely Sophie came too, but unfortunately I am very slightly . . . how can I express it?'

'Drunk,' supplied Christine.

Pierre clicked his tongue reprovingly. 'How can you say such a thing? But yes, I must admit, you would both be safer on foot, and probably quicker too. I would hate to follow in your father's tradition of arguing with brick walls.'

'I will say goodbye to you then, Pierre,' Sophie said. 'I am leaving tomorrow afternoon.' She extended a hand, but Pierre ignored it and kissed her full on the lips.

'You must return,' he said, 'very, very soon.'

'Oh, I will,' Sophie assured him. 'Just as soon as I am invited.'

He wagged an unsteady finger at her. 'Now that is

unfair,' he chided. 'Very naughty, Sophie. Not my fault you were cast into exile by your wicked papa.'

'It wasn't Bon Papa's fault!' Christine cried.

'Don't forget to collect Fabienne, before you go home,' Sophie reminded Pierre.

'Fabienne! *Nom de Dieu*, I had forgotten the brat completely!' Pierre giggled. 'Imagine Léonie's face if I returned home without her, *hein*?' He mimicked Léonie's voice. 'Now, Pierre, you really are too careless! Not only do you forget my cigarettes, but you have also forgotten my daughter. Go back at once and buy another packet. *Au 'voir, mes enfants*,' he finished, in his own voice. 'Come, Fabienne! We're off!'

When Fabienne, enjoying her stardom, protested, he plucked her from the bar and tucked her under one arm, kicking and screaming and trying to bite his hand.

'*Au 'voir, tout le monde*!' Pierre cried, benefiting from the audience his daughter had gained him. '*En avant*!' And he exited at a run, leaving the doors to crash dramatically behind him.

'He is mad,' said Christine admiringly. 'It's a pity he couldn't give us a lift home, though.'

Sophie threw her damp scarf over her head again. 'We had better start walking,' she said, and they set off again into the wind, battling their way home to their own particular storm.

12

In the dark, the house lights glowed invitingly, casting a bright path for the homecomers. Christine felt warmed at the sight even while the icy wind wrenched the gate from her grasp.

Once inside, however, the promised welcome was exposed as an illusion, as cruel as that of the desert oasis which the weary traveller finds to be a mirage.

Giselle was in the salon, sitting where Christine had left her, staring into space. She looked up without interest as they came in.

'There's some food in the kitchen,' she said, 'if you want it.'

'Where's Papa?' Christine asked.

'Packing,' said Giselle shortly, and Christine, without warning, burst into tears. 'Oh, for God's sake!' said Giselle. 'Go somewhere else if you're going to do that, Christine. I have had enough.'

Christine went upstairs and found Jean-Luc crumpling his neatly ironed shirts into a suitcase.

'Shall I fold them for you, Papa?'

'It doesn't matter,' he said.

'But you will go to work all creased,' she said. 'Let me.'

'All right,' he agreed.

Christine folded them as Giselle had shown her – sides in, sleeves back. 'Who will iron them for you?' she asked. 'Will you bring them home to Maman?'

'No!' he said. 'I will do them myself, I suppose.'

'Do you have an iron?' Christine enquired, surprised.

'I will have to get one,' he said wearily. 'I will have to learn to iron. I will have to learn to do a lot of things.'

Christine looked warily at him. It was worth one more try, perhaps. 'Do you really want to go, Papa?' she asked diffidently.

'No, I do not want to,' he said heavily. 'But I cannot stay, either.'

Christine wanted to ask if she would be able to see him, but she was afraid that he would not want her. Did Maman want her, she wondered? If she had to go and stay with Tante Léonie, she would run away, she decided.

'Will I be staying here,' she asked, 'with Maman?'

He looked at her in surprise. 'But of course,' he said. 'Where else?'

Christine went on folding shirts.

'You know,' Jean-Luc said, to reassure her, 'there was really never any question of your going to boarding school.'

'I wouldn't have gone anyway,' said Christine defiantly. 'You can't make me go to places. I won't go to Tante Léonie's either. If Maman doesn't want me, I shall just stay anyway. She can't make me go.'

'She doesn't want you to go!' Jean-Luc said, scandalized. 'She will need you now more than ever, Christine. You must take care of her.'

Christine threw the shirt into the suitcase. 'And who is going to take care of me?' she demanded.

'Maman, of course,' he said shortly.

Christine picked up the brown shirt with the little stripes, the one Papa wore to work with his dark tie. 'And what are you going to do?' she said rudely. 'Who are you going to be looking after? Just yourself?'

He flinched. 'Yes,' he said. 'Unfortunately.'

'Unfortunately for us,' persisted Christine, twisting the knife in the wound. 'Bon Papa would be very upset, you

257

know, if he knew that the minute he died you would go away and leave us.' She knew she was hurting him, but she wanted to hurt someone.

'It is not like that!' Jean-Lùc shouted, his apathy evaporating in the face of such an assault. 'Don't go on, Christine! You are as bad as your mother.' He stopped, but it was too late. Christine froze. The shock in her eyes wounded him.

'I didn't mean it,' he said roughly.

Christine stared at him in horror. As bad as your mother, he had said. He did not love Maman any more, and he did not love her either. He was leaving, not just because Maman had done something wicked, but because he hated her – hated Maman and hated Christine. He hated them so much that he could not bear – what had he said before? – could not bear to live in the same house with them. Her shoulders shook, and she pressed the brown shirt to her eyes.

'Don't,' said Jean-Luc. 'Don't, Christine.'

'You hate us,' she wept, but he did not catch her words.

'What?'

'You don't love us any more,' she sobbed incoherently. It was incredible, she could not believe it. That Papa should not love them! Granted, he had always been remote, severe, but that was just his way. Had he hated her all along? 'Jean-Luc would have taken more interest in a son,' echoed Giselle's voice. Had he never wanted her from the day she was born? 'It is my fault!' she cried. 'It is all my fault.'

'No,' he said. 'It had nothing to do with that argument over your holiday with Sophie. I was going to tell Giselle anyway, once the funeral was over. It made no difference. It was not your fault.'

'You hate me,' she said again, more clearly.

'No!' he said. 'Of course I don't hate you. Whatever gave you that idea? This is nothing to do with you, Christine – do you hear me?'

She shook her head, inconsolable. 'You don't love me,' she said, with conviction. 'You don't want to see me any more.'

He sat down on the bed, heavily. 'Oh, God,' he groaned. 'What kind of a father have I been?'

A breath of compassion stirred in Christine. 'You wanted a son,' she said, to show that she understood.

'No!' he said again. Then he held out his arms to her. 'Come here,' he said.

She went, wondering.

'Sit down,' he said, 'and listen to me. I don't know if you will understand all this, Christine, but you will hear Maman's side and I want you to hear mine. Even if you don't understand it,' he said fiercely, 'you are to listen.'

She nodded.

'I know,' Jean-Luc began, 'that we have not been as close as some fathers and daughters and, believe me, Christine, I have often regretted it. At first I think it was simply because a baby – a boy or a girl – has to be looked after by its mother. The father is perhaps a little afraid of the baby. It is so small, he does not know how to hold it and he fears he will drop it. A woman seems naturally better at these things.'

'Then, as you became older, there was Grand-père, of course, who was at home while I was out at work. He had more time for you, more patience perhaps. He used to make things for you – a dolls' house, I remember.'

'And a cradle,' Christine prompted, 'and a new seat for the swing.'

'And he used to invent all sorts of games,' Jean-Luc continued. 'Story games and word games and little rhymes. Things that I had not the imagination to do.

259

There was not much, I felt, that I could do for you. Between Grand-père and Giselle you were well cared for, mind and body.'

'You took me to see the Tour Eiffel,' Christine reminded him. 'And those fountains, and the boats on the river.'

He looked pleased. 'You remember that, *hein*? You were only quite small. Giselle said I had exhausted you.'

'It was wonderful,' Christine said dreamily. 'We walked such a long way. I had never walked so far.'

Uncharacteristically, he put his arms round her and gave her a quick hug, and she jumped up and flung her arms round his neck. 'Oh, don't go, Papa!' she pleaded.

He cleared his throat. 'Let me finish,' he said, and obediently she sat down again.

'Then as my career progressed, I spent less and less time at home,' he said, and his voice grew bitter. 'I became a stranger to my own family. I was a bad father and a bad husband. My child learned to do without me and my wife . . . my wife too, learned to live her own life. I have only myself to blame that eventually she found a . . . a replacement.'

'You are talking about Monsieur Trichard?' Christine asked uncertainly.

'Yes,' he said painfully. 'Monsieur Trichard, who managed to keep not only his own wife happy but another man's as well, while I could not even look after my own.'

'Monsieur Trichard never made anyone happy,' said Christine contemptuously. 'Maman said he was a waster,' she lied.

He looked at her. 'Giselle said that?'

Under his gaze, Christine faltered. 'Or else it was Bon Papa,' she amended.

Jean-Luc sighed. 'However,' he said, 'it is because of that man that I am leaving, Christine. I tell you this not because I want you to understand these things or because I think it suitable, at your age, for you to know them, but because you must understand that my decision to leave is in no way your fault. I do not want to leave you,' he said with an effort. 'I had always thought that when Bon Papa went, I would . . .' he shrugged hopelessly, '. . . become more of a father, certainly not less of one.'

Christine spread her hands in despair. 'But why,' she said, repeating the question she had asked herself so constantly, 'why do you have to go? You don't want to, Maman doesn't want you to, and I don't. How can Monsieur Trichard make you go if you don't want to?'

'Monsieur Trichard cannot make me do anything,' he declared, stung by this remark. Then he shrugged, and added, 'Except indirectly, I suppose.'

'But if Maman promised not to see him any more,' Christine pleaded, 'couldn't you forgive her?'

'I do forgive her,' he said quickly. 'It was not her fault. It was mine.'

'Then can't you forgive yourself?' Christine said. She was puzzled by his situation. It was so much easier to forgive yourself for things than to forgive someone else. Christine had done it many times. It had taken Maman weeks to forgive Christine for that ink blot on the salon carpet, but Christine had absolved herself at once, and her conscience had not troubled her. It was an accident, she had consoled herself, an accident can happen to anyone.

Jean-Luc shook his head. 'It is not so easy,' he said. 'One can forgive and one can understand, but how can one go on living with the memory of one's betrayal? That is the problem.'

'Even if you forgive someone, it may not be easy to go on living with them,' Christine said wisely, and he turned his head sharply.

'You are very shrewd,' he said, 'for your age.'

'Not really,' Christine confessed. 'It was Sophie who said that.'

'You talked to Sophie about it?'

'I didn't mean to,' said Christine defensively, 'it was just that I didn't understand. But she said that no one could understand, anyway, except the two people concerned.'

Jean-Luc sighed. 'And perhaps not even them,' he said. Then, as Christine's stomach rumbled intrusively, he said, 'You had better go downstairs now. Have some supper and then go to bed. It has been a long, sad day for us all.'

She was reluctant to leave. 'Will I see you again?'

'I will still be here in the morning.'

'I know,' she said, 'but after that?'

He shook his head. 'It will depend on Maman,' he said. 'I do not know if she will think it good for you to be divided between one parent and the other. A conflict of loyalties is not a pleasant thing.'

As she was silent, looking down at her hands, he said forcefully, 'It is not that I do not want to see you, Christine. It is simply that I do not wish to cause you more trouble than I already have.'

'You won't,' she said. 'You could see me if you wanted to.'

He squeezed her shoulder to make her understand. 'You need never doubt that I want to,' he said. Then, hurriedly, and in a voice that was almost ashamed, he muttered, 'I shall miss you a great deal.' As she turned to answer, he said quickly, 'Go downstairs now and ask Maman for something to eat.'

There was a knock at the bedroom door.

'May I come in?' said Sophie.

'Please,' said Jean-Luc.

'Giselle sent me up to ask what you'd like to eat.'

Jean-Luc and Christine looked at each other blankly. It was unprecedented for Maman to ask them. Normally, she simply provided food and they were expected to eat it.

'Anything,' mumbled Jean-Luc. 'Here, Christine, I forgot.'

He took a small package out of the dressing-table drawer. 'The set of ivory elephants. Pierre says you are to have them after all.'

Christine was overwhelmed. 'Did you ask him?' She started to cry again.

'Yes,' he said. He turned his back on them both and went on packing.

'Did you know the story behind those elephants, Jean-Luc?' Sophie said.

'*Hein*? *Non*,' he said gruffly.

'Bon Papa said he was given them by a friend,' Christine recalled.

'A friend called Jacques Duvier, that's right,' Sophie agreed. 'Monsieur Duvier and Papa were at school together, and their first job after leaving school was in the same firm.'

Sophie was telling this story, Christine realized, to calm them down. Jean-Luc knew this too, she could see. Everyone knew, but still it was working. Jean-Luc's shoulders relaxed, and Christine perched on the edge of the bed.

'But then,' Sophie said, 'Duvier had an ambition to travel. He wanted Papa to go with him to Africa. He had great plans for their future out there but Papa by that time had met Maman, your grand-mère, Christine. He said that he would go out to Africa for a year and then return, but Maman refused to hear of it. She said that unless Papa stayed in France she wouldn't wait for him,

263

she would marry someone else. So Papa stayed and Duvier went to Africa on his own, rather disgruntled. He wouldn't stay in France long enough to attend Papa's wedding, and the whole thing caused a rift between them. They wrote only a couple of times in the next four years.

'By the time Duvier returned, they were both older and wiser. The elephants were a kind of peacemaking gift, I suppose. Maman never liked them, and she never liked Duvier either. So Papa lent me the elephants and I kept them in my room, on the mantelpiece. I used to like them better than toys. I would play with them for hours, lining them up and marching them through imaginary jungles, pulling down trees.

'Then Duvier came for supper one night. He had some friends staying with him from Germany, and he asked if he might bring them too, and Maman said yes. She liked to entertain and to meet new people, and I think she was relieved not to have Duvier alone. He was very amusing company and used to make Papa laugh, and they would stay up very late and get a bit drunk, and I think Maman was jealous perhaps.'

'Why?' Christine asked.

'Oh, she felt left out, I suppose, of their conversation about the old days, and their jokes. Duvier used to tease her, rather like Pierre teases Léonie, and she never got used to that.'

'So, what were the friends like?' Christine prompted.

'Very nice,' Sophie said. 'Monsieur and Madame Bernstein. German Jews. They had a little girl about Léonie's age: she would have been about seven then, I suppose. We all played quite happily together and the Bernsteins and Duvier went home very late. They were going back to Germany the next day.'

'Bernstein,' said Jean-Luc suddenly, as though he had

only just started listening. 'Wasn't that the child in the rue Saint Marc?'

'That's right,' Sophie said. 'You know the story, then?'

'Only second-hand. A man was shot by the Nazis in the rue Saint Marc for harbouring a Jewish child in his house. It was the first such incident in this area. The troops made an example of him, *n'est-ce pas*? Some atrocity with the body . . .'

'That was Duvier,' Sophie said quietly. 'The child was Sarah Bernstein. The parents returned to Germany alone, to clear up some business affairs, leaving Sarah in Duvier's care. I suppose it was strange to leave a child with a bachelor who had no experience of children, but Duvier was their only friend in France. And I think it reassured them meeting us. Maman said that Sarah was welcome here any time, to play with us. She felt sorry for Sarah. It wasn't easy for children growing up in Germany at the time.'

'She was bitter about the whole thing afterwards,' Jean-Luc recalled. 'The first time I met my prospective mother-in-law, I remember someone saying something about Jews and she got ferocious.'

'Yes, she felt that the Bernsteins had planned to leave Sarah indefinitely,' Sophie recalled. 'But of course they hadn't. If they had had any idea of what was going to happen they would never have gone back to Germany for those couple of weeks. At that stage people were still dismissing the European war talk as rumours. I suppose they were playing safe in leaving Sarah here but, heaven knows, they would never have gone back home knowing that they would be arrested by the Nazis.'

'What happened to Sarah?' Christine asked.

'She stayed with Duvier,' Sophie said. 'I think she was happy there and she came here to play every day, but she used sometimes to cry in the evenings. She was only a child and she missed her parents.

'We never heard for certain what happened to them, until the war was nearly over, and by then it was too late for Sarah anyway. Duvier was terrified for the child and for himself, when the occupation forces came. Terrible penalties were threatened for anyone sheltering Jews.

'Sarah never came here any more, and Duvier became almost a recluse. Papa used to go and see them, though Maman said he must leave them completely alone, and he said it was pitiful how pale and drawn the child had become, from being always indoors.

'And then they found her. Whether someone informed or whether it was a routine house search, I don't really know, but little Sarah was found and poor Monsieur Duvier was executed, degradingly, in the street.

'Papa was broken-hearted. He shut himself in his room for three weeks and wouldn't eat. I remember going in to see him, and he was staring at the wall and wouldn't look at me. When he came out he just picked up the threads of his life as though nothing had happened, and I never heard the subject mentioned again. The only thing that changed was that the elephants disappeared out of my room and appeared in the salon, and Maman allowed them to stay there this time. But both Maman and Papa had an unreasonable prejudice against Jewish people, and that never changed.'

'Understandable, in the circumstances,' Jean-Luc said.

'More understandable to have hated the people who did such things to Jews,' Sophie said. 'Even if the Bernsteins did plan to save Sarah by leaving her in France, how terrible to be so afraid of other human beings that you would abandon a much-loved only child to strangers in a foreign country.'

'Yes,' Jean-Luc admitted, 'yes.'

They were all silent for a moment, staring at the ivory elephants with their yellowed tusks. When Giselle came in, they were startled.

'I have laid out a cold supper in the dining-room,' she said, 'since no one came down to say what you wanted.

Sophie stayed up with Giselle till the small hours of the morning. At breakfast, she looked exhausted, with dark-ringed eyes outlined against the pallor of her face.

Giselle's exhaustion took the form of nagging. 'Don't crumble your bread so, Christine. Don't drip jam on the table.'

Jean-Luc ate nothing, but sat with his head lowered, staring at the last wisps of steam rising from his coffee.

'What time do you have to be at the station, Sophie? What time will you have to leave?' asked Christine.

'The taxi is ordered for an hour's time,' Sophie told her.

'I doubt that you will get there in time,' Giselle said dourly. 'These taxis are always late. You had better ring them, Jean-Luc, and ask them to send it earlier. Jean-Luc?'

He looked up. '*Hein*!'

'He doesn't care,' said Giselle bitterly, to no one in particular. 'He thinks he is already free of us.'

'What did you ask, Giselle?' he said.

'To order the taxi earlier,' she repeated.

'It is already ordered. I did it yesterday.'

'But earlier!' she cried impatiently. 'It will not get her there in time.'

'*Mais si*,' he denied. 'It will leave plenty of time. Any earlier and Sophie will be hanging about the station for ages. The boat train is invariably late.'

'I don't know why you're not flying, Sophie,' said Giselle petulantly. 'It would be so much easier.'

'Sophie has a return ticket for the boat,' Christine defended her.

'Eat your breakfast, Christine. Jean-Luc, your coffee must be quite cold by now.'

'I am sorry.' He pushed the bowl away. 'I don't think I want it.'

'What is wrong with my coffee?' demanded Giselle. Her voice cracked on the indignant high notes. Christine regarded her uneasily.

'Nothing is wrong with it,' said Jean-Luc patiently.

'I shan't make you any more,' said Giselle furiously, 'if you let it get cold.'

They held their breath, waiting for her to realize what she had said. For a second, before her own words sank in, she continued to gather up the coffee bowls. Then she crumpled, laying her head on the tablecloth and sobbing noisily, like a child.

Jean-Luc picked a strand of her hair out of the coffee. 'Come, Giselle,' he said, more embarrassed than compassionate.

'I have said that it may not be irrevocable. We will regard it as a trial separation, *hein*?'

'Why have you packed so much?' she cried. 'All your clothes, so many books? You are determined never to return!'

'We will have to see,' he said awkwardly. 'One cannot tell at present. Who knows,' he added, in an attempt at light-heartedness, 'in a few weeks I may come crawling back and you will be having such a good time that you will not want me.'

She struck out at him wildly, catching him on the chin. 'You insult me!' she shouted. 'You have a very poor idea of me if you think I am only interested in a good time! It was not a good time that I wanted, only a good marriage. All I ever wanted,' she repeated in a bitterly reproachful voice, 'but you would not give it to me. No, you could not spare the time.'

Sophie sat with her head down, eyes averted from Giselle's contorted face. Christine clutched her plate to her chest, the crumbs tipping into her lap, and watched Maman with fearful eyes. Jean-Luc cleared his throat and scraped back his chair.

'We have been over this ground so many times,' he pleaded. 'Let us leave it now, Giselle. I do not want to part on these terms.'

'You do not want!' she screamed at him. 'You don't care what I want, *hein*? You have never cared, never, never . . .' She covered her face with her hands and rocked with misery, back and forth like the doll in the mechanical rocking-chair that Bijouets, the toyshop, displayed in its window. Jean-Luc edged his way out of the room.

'If he cared for me,' Giselle wept, 'the tiniest bit, he would never leave me like this, all alone.'

Christine put her arm round Giselle's shoulders. 'You still have me, Maman,' she said. 'I'll look after you.'

Giselle shrugged her off. 'It is I who will have to look after you,' she said tearfully. 'To bring you up all on my own, with no support. He thinks he can give me money and end his responsibility there.'

'He has agreed to give you money, has he?' Sophie asked anxiously.

'Of course – he knows he has to,' said Giselle contemptuously. 'I should not have to pay for his desertion, I hope.'

'At least you have that,' said Sophie, a trifle wistfully. 'You will not have to struggle financially.'

'Finance is the least of my worries,' said Giselle loftily. 'Money means little to me. All I crave is the affection of my husband, and that he has never given me, Sophie!'

Sophie took Giselle's hand. 'But you have the affection of your family, Giselle,' she said gently. 'Of Christine, and Léonie and Pierre, and me. You will not be alone, I promise you. Don't give up.'

'I don't want anyone else!' cried Giselle wildly. 'I only want Jean-Luc.'

Christine rose quietly and went out to the bathroom. As she closed the kitchen door behind her, she heard Sophie say, 'Try to keep going, Giselle, for Christine's sake. It is hard for her too, you know,' and heard Maman's reply, 'She will not miss her father. It was Grand-père who was a father to Christine.'

As a special treat, Christine was allowed to go with Sophie to the station. The ride was an anxious one, for an accident on the arterial road had caused a traffic jam, much longer than the usual rush-hour one, and they arrived at the station with only minutes to spare.

Sophie gave Christine a hasty hug as the taxi pulled up. 'Until Easter, then,' she said. 'Don't let things get you down, Christine. I will write as soon as I get home – okay?'

'Okay,' Christine responded, but her heart contracted as she watched Sophie through the back window as the taxi pulled away. Case in hand, she was running towards the station entrance, but she paused for a second to look back and wave a hasty goodbye. When she disappeared from view, Christine felt that her only support had gone forever.

'Where's she going then?' the taxi-driver enquired cheerfully. 'England?'

'*Oui*,' responded Christine mournfully. 'It is a long way.'

'Well, rather her than me,' said the driver with feeling. 'Cold, foggy place this time of year. And the food is terrible, of course. Why doesn't she pick a better place for a holiday?'

'She lives there,' Christine told him.

'Oh?' he raised his head to scrutinize her in the driving mirror. 'She's not your mother then?'

'No,' said Christine, 'not my mother,' but for a fleeting shameful moment she wished that Sophie was.

Thinking of her own mother, she asked the driver to drop her at the end of the road, so that she could delay her return by walking the rest of the way.

'No tip?' said the taxi-driver in pained surprise.

'I have no money,' Christine said. 'My papa gave you a tip in with the fare, before we left.'

The driver spat scornfully on his hand and drove away in a cloud of exhaust. Like the wizard at the pantomime, disappearing in a puff of smoke, Christine thought, but the comparison was spoiled by the thought that the man did not like her. It would not have bothered her much, except that without Bon Papa or Papa or Sophie, the people who liked her were becoming thin on the ground. Christine was afraid to lose any more friends however transient, lest she should be left with no one at all.

When she got home, Jean-Luc had gone.

'He didn't say goodbye to me,' she said.

'He thought it was best,' Giselle said. 'He said he had said goodbye to you last night. Not that I heard him.'

'When can I see him again?' Christine asked.

'God knows,' said Giselle, 'when any of us will see him again.' She had stopped crying but was still in her dressing gown, the white embroidered one. There was a coffee stain on the front of it.

'You have spilt coffee on your best dressing gown,' Christine told her.

Giselle shrugged. 'Who is going to see me now?'

Christine thought of saying that she would, but thought

better of it. Maman meant, she realized, that no one important, no man, would see her now. Not that poor Bon Papa had ever been able to see very much, with his cloudy eyes.

The absence of Bon Papa struck her anew each morning. It was normal, after all, for Papa to be out at this hour, claiming his place in the early traffic war between the streams from rival *arrondissements*. But a morning without watching Bon Papa shave, without taking up his shoes from their warming-place beside the boiler, without urging him, 'Come on, Bon Papa; we will be late,' and without hearing his familiar hacking cough as he wheezed his way down the stairs was still unbearable.

'If only Bon Papa were here,' she said longingly, 'nothing would be so bad.'

Giselle nodded. 'It would never have happened,' she said, 'if he had not died. Jean-Luc would never have dared to do such a thing while Papa was around.'

Christine was about to point out that Jean-Luc had planned his departure even before Grand-père's death, but she stopped herself in time.

'Jean-Luc respected Grand-père's judgement too much,' Giselle continued, 'and Grand-père would never have let him do it. Oh!' she wept, 'if only I had listened to him! Oh Papa, what have I done?' She leaned against the kitchen mantelpiece and wept with real sorrow. 'I told him it was his fault,' she sobbed, 'but it was mine too. I should never have let things get so bad. Oh, *cher* Papa, what am I going to do?'

For the first time, Christine forgave her unreservedly. She put her arms round Maman and hugged her. 'I am sure Bon Papa understands,' she said.

Giselle shook her head. 'I can't believe he still sees us,' she said. 'He is dead and gone, and wherever he is gone he is far away from us.'

Christine frowned. 'But you can talk to him,' she said, 'like you pray to God. Father Delfarge says . . .'

'I don't believe all that,' said Giselle impatiently.

'But I talk to him,' Christine said, her lip trembling, 'I tell him things. I'm sure he hears. He promised that he would.'

'You can believe it if it helps you,' said Giselle with a shrug, 'but for my part I think the dead are dead, and better off that way. Why should they bother about us? I would not, if it were me. I would congratulate myself on a lucky escape,' she said bitterly.

'But if you believe in God,' Christine pursued, bewildered, 'then surely . . . ?'

Giselle pursed her lips. 'I don't know any more,' she said. 'I just don't know.'

Christine did not like it when she talked like that. 'I had better go and get ready for school,' she said.

Giselle looked at her. 'You're not going to school today!'

'Why not?'

'The day after the funeral of your grand-père? The school will hardly expect it.'

Christine remembered Sophie's advice to think only of school things whilst she was there, and thought longingly of the haven of the overcrowded classroom, with its noise and work subduing truant thoughts. 'I would rather go to school,' she said.

'It is not respectful, Christine,' Giselle objected. 'It does not express proper sorrow for a family death.' As she saw Christine's mouth open to disclaim, she added, 'Besides, would you leave me all alone now when your father has just deserted us?'

Christine relinquished all thoughts of escape. 'No,' she said, resigned. 'I will stay at home today.'

'Well, I am not staying in,' Giselle declared. 'I shall

only mope and be depressed. This house is unbearable when one is miserable. It closes in on you.'

'Where are you going?' Christine asked. Surely, if Maman were to go to Tante Léonie's, Christine could just as well go to school?

'I have not decided,' said Giselle, 'but there is no point in having freedom and not using it. Thousands of women would envy me, after all.'

Christine followed her upstairs. The double bed in Giselle's room had been slept in on one side only.

'Thousands of women,' Giselle continued, 'with boring, overworking husbands who never take them anywhere, or drunken spendthrift husbands who consort with dirty women . . .' – she rummaged in a drawer for a clean pair of stockings – '. . . or cruel husbands who beat them black and blue and give them endless babies, would be delighted . . .' – she threw open the wardrobe and took out one dress after another, inspecting it against the light – '. . . delighted to be in my situation.'

'But Papa is not like any of those,' Christine objected.

'Who mentioned Papa?' Giselle snapped. 'And let me tell you, Christine, a child has very little idea of a man's faults, even though he lives in the same house. A father and a husband are different things entirely. Not,' she added, shaking herself into a silky slip, 'that he was such an agreeable father. One could hardly blame you, Christine, if you were glad to see him go.'

'Well, I'm not,' Christine retorted. Her sympathy with Maman evaporated. When she was in this mood, defiant and self-righteous, Christine could almost see why Jean-Luc had left. Had it happened like this with him, she wondered. Had he sat here, on the edge of the bed, listening to Maman reviling him and the world at large, and suddenly felt that he did not want to be with her? The idea frightened Christine, for if she now felt as he had felt, what guarantee was there that she would not go on, as he had done, to feel that she could not love Maman, could not live with her any more?

In the past, there had been times, certainly, when Christine had not felt that she liked Maman very much. But the incidents had never bothered her, for Maman was Maman and one naturally loved one's family, however bad-tempered they might be sometimes. But now her eyes were opened to the fact that one could have a family – a wife, a husband, a mother or a father – whom one found, suddenly, that one could not love.

If someone had told Christine, even a few weeks ago, that Maman and Papa could cease to co-exist, to be a couple, a pair of parents, a composite entity of two-in-one, she would have ridiculed the very thought. Ever since she had learned to talk, there had been the ever-present dual personage, Maman-et-Papa, as immutable and invulnerable as the stars above the earth.

But now the earth had been displaced, it seemed, and the stars torn from their stitches in the sky, and all the natural laws were law no longer. Like Giselle who felt that if Bon Papa were dead to them then God was also dead, Christine feared that if the ties between mother and father could be broken so easily, then parent and child could be separated by the same force.

So now she asked anxiously, 'But you do still love me, Maman?'

But when Giselle answered, predictably, 'Yes, of course I do', Christine did not feel reassured.

'But will you love me forever?' she persisted.

'Forever and a day, and a day longer,' said Giselle blithely.

The question Christine wanted answered, she could not ask. She could not bring herself to say: But will I love you forever? Or: If you hate me when I'm difficult and love me when you're lonely, which will I remember when I'm old?

'I will take you,' Giselle said, 'for a day out. We will go on a spree, you and I, and treat ourselves to a tour of the Rive Droite. Then, elegant and chic in our new attire, we will astound the populace with our beauty as we lunch exotically in some imaginative little bistro.' She waltzed round the room in her slip and stockings, coming to rest in front of the long mirror where she dropped a gracious curtsey.

Christine looked dubious. Apart from the unlovely prospect of spending the day, listless as she was, running to keep up with Maman as she elbowed her way through the crowds in search of that 'perfect little dress' she felt sure existed, Christine felt that if going to school was disrespectful after a funeral, then going shopping would be even more so.

'What is the matter?' Giselle demanded, registering her doubt.

Christine hesitated. 'Nothing,' she said.

'Then go and get ready,' Giselle instructed. 'And don't be too long.' Her gaiety evaporated and she said with a shudder, 'I can't bear to stay in this house today. It is full of death.'

On the bus, Maman talked of what she would buy. Christine looked out of the window and hoped that they would not encounter anyone from school. Oh, the disaster, too terrible to be imagined, if Ma'mselle Dubois were to see her!

'Why were you not at school yesterday, Christine Rochaud?'

'It was my grand-père's funeral the day before, Ma'mselle.'

'So?'

276

'My mother said it would be disrespectful to go back to school straight afterwards.'

'Ah-hah!' And here Ma'mselle would play her trump card, 'Then what were you doing, Christine Rochaud, on the Elysées bus yesterday morning?'

'Going to buy a new dress, Ma'mselle.'

It did not sound good, even to Christine's ears. She was not happy about it. Unable to believe that Bon Papa had completely abandoned her on his death, she could imagine him now, in his new state of unity with God and with Grand-mère, still keeping a grandfatherly eye on her. If the thought had comforted her before, it disturbed her now. 'What are you doing, Christine, the day after my funeral?' she could hear him say, peering at her through the spectacles that never would sit straight on his nose. 'Are you managing all right without me?' And she would have to answer, casually, as though it were the accepted thing to do, 'Oh, I'm going shopping with Maman to buy a new dress.'

'. . . with long sleeves,' continued Giselle, making a slicing gesture at her wrist, 'so that it will be warm enough for all those winter parties in cold houses. Elegant, but slightly *risqué* too. Nothing too prim and proper. Or perhaps separates would be better. What do you think, Christine?'

'Yes,' said Christine.

'Yes to which?'

'Either,' Christine said. 'It sounds very nice either way.'

'That is not much help, it must be said!' Giselle frowned.

'Well, maybe the dress then.' A dress, being only one item, would not take so long to buy. Then they could go home and Christine could think of Bon Papa, and of Papa, without having to bite her lip to hold back the

277

tears. If only the shopping trip were not too long, she would not disgrace herself and Maman in public but could hold in her dual griefs until, in her own room, she could fling herself face down on the bed and cry and cry until she was empty of all the tears that were building up inside.

The shops were full of Christmas things already. In the window space of the Galeries Lafayette, three women and a man were setting up a snow scene with moving puppets. Christine lingered to watch.

'Keep up, Christine! I'm holding the door open.'

Christine followed. 'Will Papa be home for Christmas?'

Giselle did not answer.

'Maman, will Papa – '

'Christine, I am not even thinking of Christmas yet.' She added, under her breath, 'It will be quite enough if I get through today.'

Maman did not look at price tags when she chose dresses. She simply held them at arm's length, half closed her eyes, then said, 'No, not suitable,' or 'Possible, but I doubt it will hang properly.' If it was not suitable she handed it to Christine to put back on the hanger.

'Come along, Christine. There is nothing here.'

Downstairs, the perfumeries sent out a heavy aroma. Christine looked at the gifts, the decorations; she trailed her fingers through a pile of tinsel – blue, cerise and gold.

On the way out, Giselle remembered, 'We have not looked at dresses for you. Do you want to? The children's department is not very good here.'

Christine shook her head. 'I have enough dresses, anyway. I don't really need one.' It would not be disrespectful to Bon Papa, surely, if she merely accompanied Maman rather than actually buying clothes for herself.

'Really, Christine,' said Maman crossly. 'This is meant to be a treat. You are very ungrateful. Well, we will get my dress first,' she conceded, 'and then if there is time we can look for you.'

The sales ladies at the next couple of shops admired Maman's decisiveness. 'Madame knows what she wants.'

Madame tried on, considered herself in the mirror, pirouetted, criticized, rejected. It was a pity, when Madame knew just what she wanted, that the shops did not seem to have anticipated her needs.

'What about this one, Maman?'

'No, Christine, that is far too old for me. Old and prim. Find something a little more *risqué*.'

Christine found a flowered dress with a plunge neckline and slit sleeves. 'Vulgar,' said Giselle, with a sharp shake of her head.

The sales lady brought a slim black dress with shoulder ties and a rolled neckline.

'*Chouette*,' Christine approved.

'It fits Madame beautifully,' said the sales lady.

Giselle took it off and turned it inside out to see the seams. 'Badly made,' she said.

The next shops were more expensive.

'Maman, have you seen the prices on these?' Christine whispered.

'I deserve it,' said Giselle grimly. 'I need spoiling at the moment, if anyone ever did.'

She smoothed her hands over her hips. 'Is this dress unflattering?'

'No, it's very nice,' Christine said. Bored, she peeped between the curtains and watched, through the gap in the opposite cubicle, a fat lady struggling into a low-slung evening dress.

'Then it is my figure,' said Giselle critically. 'I have put weight on my hips.' She swivelled round to see the back view. 'My bottom was never that size before,' se said. 'Christine!'

Christine popped her head back. 'What?'

'Don't say "What"! Do you agree that I have put on weight, here?'

'I don't think so. Why?'

'This dress makes my bottom look enormous,' Giselle pulled the offending dress over her head and inspected herself again, in her slip. '*Bon Dieu*!' she moaned. 'What a sight!'

Christine could see nothing wrong. 'What's the matter, Maman?'

'Obscene!' Giselle wailed. 'Grotesque! My figure is quite ruined. That is what happens when one gets old. Who would ever look twice at me, like this?'

'You look all right, Maman,' said Christine. A backside seemed a funny thing to get upset about. Christine hoped that Maman would suggest lunch soon. She was getting hungry. 'Shall we go now?'

'We may as well,' Giselle said. She put her own clothes on again, peering over her shoulder as they left the cubicle, to watch her retreating rear view.

'Can we eat soon, Maman?'

'We will just try this little boutique, Christine. These department stores are no good when you want something special.'

The lady in the boutique wore make-up like a mask, with eyelashes as thick as combs and a perfume that took the windpipe by surprise. She smiled with her lipstick.

'May I help you, Madame?'

'A little cocktail dress,' Giselle said. 'Chic, a little *risqué*, simple without being plain.'

'Of course, Madame.' The mascara did not flicker. 'Here we have a very special little number, beautifully cut, quite simple . . .'

Giselle fingered the fabric. 'Rather too flimsy, for winter.'

'Perhaps. Well now, Madame, this one may suit you better. A very unusual design, as you see – a Zoèbe.'

'Really?' Maman was impressed.

'We have a good selection always from the Zoèbe collection, Madame. Priced a little above the rest, of course, but they are made in very limited editions. You will not see all the world wearing this dress.'

'How much is it?' Christine asked. When the lady answered, addressing the reply over her head to Giselle, Christine whistled.

'Would Madame like to try it on?' the lady asked, ignoring Christine's vulgarity.

'Yes,' said Giselle slowly. 'I think I will.'

In the changing room, Christine hissed, 'You can't pay that much for a dress!'

'I am not paying,' said Giselle grimly. 'I think Jean-Luc owes me one good dress, *n'est-ce pas*?'

The good dress, Christine was relieved to see, looked horrible.

'It doesn't suit you, Maman.'

Giselle surveyed her reflection in despair. 'It's my terrible figure,' she said. 'I look old and flabby and quite past it in this.'

'It's not you,' said Christine consolingly. 'It's the dress.'

'How can it be the dress?' snapped Giselle. 'It is a Zoèbe!'

'It can't suit everybody,' said Christine sagely, 'whatever it is.'

'How is it?' crooned the sales lady, parting the curtains. 'Oh, very pretty, Madame. The colour – very suitable for your complexion.'

'It doesn't suit me,' said Giselle flatly.

'You don't think so, Madame? It is not everyone who can wear such a dress, but in my opinion, Madame, you are – '

'It makes me look old and ugly,' Giselle said. To Christine's horror, she put her hands over her face and gave a dry sob.

The sales lady, after a secondary lowering of the mascara fronds above the eyes, rallied to the occasion.

'But not at all, Madame!' she cried. 'Madame has a very elegant and youthful figure! Wait, I have just the gown for you – *très mignonne*, very flattering – not that, of course, Madame needs it, but if Madame feels . . .' She fluttered away, her pointed shoes tottering on the deep-pile moquette.

Giselle continued to sob. 'These clothes are for beautiful young girls,' she said. 'I am no longer young or beautiful, me. Jean-Luc will start again with some fresh-skinned young girl with firm breasts and a tight bottom . . . !'

'Sssh!' Christine agonized, as the painted lady tottered back, moving with surprising briskness despite her corseted bulk.

But Giselle could not be consoled. 'My husband has left me,' she sobbed to the uncaring mask. 'He took my youth and my beauty and cast me aside, like an old . . . an old doll.'

The lipstick pouted in momentary sympathy. 'Men!' said the dragon. 'They are all the same. They use one and exploit one and then run off to some immature young girl.' She glared at Christine as though youth were an offence. 'What you need, Madame, is a special little treat to cheer you up. Treat yourself to something very chic and elegant to restore your confidence. There will be other heads that will turn to look!' Invitingly, she held out an armful of gowns.

Giselle continued to weep, without tears, hiccuping drily into her hands. Christine was reminded of Bon Papa, gasping and coughing and clutching at breath.

'Let's go home, Maman,' she pleaded, tugging at Giselle's sleeve.

Giselle rose obediently, let Christine help her, like a child, out of the expensive dress, and dabbed powder on her eyes before allowing herself to be led past the silent fury of the *vendeuse* and into the callous street.

White and expressionless, unflinching in the jostling crowd, Giselle, on Christine's guiding arm, waited uncomplainingly at the bus stop, paid the fare, alighted, and walked the length of rue Jean-Jacques Rousseau. Madame Rouvieux, seeing her, forbore to call a greeting.

Without fumbling, Giselle found the key, opened the back door and entered the kitchen with a slow, measured pace. Then she collapsed, falling like a rag doll on the cold, hard floor, her eyes closed and her hair escaping from its tight chignon.

'Maman!' Christine screamed. She shook the lifeless figure, then ran, still screaming, down the garden path.

Madame Rouvieux was across the road before Christine reached the gate. 'What is it?'

'Maman!' Christine cried. 'She has fainted.'

She took the old woman's arm and hurried her up the path. 'Come quickly, Madame!'

The old woman bent over Giselle, and she stirred as if in protest. 'Some cold water,' ordered Madame Rouvieux, and Christine fetched her a glass. She dipped her handkerchief into it and dabbed it on Giselle's brow, as tenderly as if it had been her own daughter.

'Will she be all right?' Christine breathed.

'Don't worry,' Madame Rouvieux assured her. 'When she comes round we will put her to bed and she will be fine.'

Giselle opened her eyes. '*Ah, non!*' she muttered, as if in despair at finding herself in such a situation.

Madame Rouvieux helped her to sit up. 'Rest quietly a little while, *ma chère*,' she said. 'You will be all right.'

'Let me get to bed,' Giselle said faintly. 'I must lie down.'

They pulled her to her feet, supporting her when she swayed. 'How foolish,' she whispered. 'I should not be so weak.'

'It is not to be wondered at,' said Madame Rouvieux staunchly. 'It is only to be expected.'

Christine looked at her and wondered how much she knew. But of course she knew everything, Madame Rouvieux.

Giselle seemed relieved to be in bed. She lay back against the pillows and closed her eyes with a deep sigh.

'You are very pale, Maman,' Christine said anxiously.

'Leave me to sleep,' Giselle said. 'Sleep is what I need.'

Madame Rouvieux went out, but Christine lingered a moment. 'You're not angry that I called her?' she whispered. 'I know you don't like neighbours interfering but truly, Maman, I didn't know what to do.'

Giselle moved her head from side to side. 'It doesn't matter,' she said wearily. 'Let her stay. We need someone to look after us, just now.'

Christine found Madame Rouvieux washing up the breakfast bowls. 'Please don't bother,' she said. 'I can do that.'

'No-bother, *mon enfant*.'

'It is very kind of you,' said Christine and added, 'Maman is grateful too, but she is too tired to say so now.'

'Bless you!' Madame Rouvieux turned and beamed at her. 'I've known your maman for years; you don't need to tell me.' She heaved a sigh. 'And I knew your grand-père, God have mercy on his soul, since he was a young married man.'

Christine hoped she was not going to talk about Bon Papa. The tears kept themselves ready, these days, to well up at a moment's notice. Already she could feel the dreaded prickling sensation at the back of her eyes.

'He was a good man, your grand-père,' Madame Rouvieux said, pausing in the act of swilling out Papa's untasted coffee. 'We will all miss him greatly, *hein*?'

Christine gave a sudden explosive sniff. You cry baby, she admonished herself, at least wait till Madame Rouvieux is gone.

'That's right,' said the old woman, unperturbed. 'Crying is the best thing. The body's way of easing the mind. You cry, *mon lapin*, don't mind me.'

Christine fled into the dining-room and returned, pink-eyed but calmer, as Madame Rouvieux was putting away the last clean dish.

'Thank you so much for helping us,' Christine said formally. Then, her composure crumbling, 'Do you have to go home yet?'

Madame Rouvieux shook out the tea towel and hung it over the boiler. 'Not if you want me to stay.' She cocked a hopeful eyebrow. '*Tu veux*?'

'If it isn't too much trouble,' said Christine humbly.

13

'I'm the Virgin Mary, I'm the Virgin Mary!' Fabienne caught hold of Christine's skirt and twirled it round and round her.

'Yes, I know; you told me.' Afraid she had sounded unenthusiastic, Christine added, 'Congratulations, anyway.'

'You have told Christine at least ten times this afternoon,' said Tante Léonie. 'Anyone would think you were appearing at the Opéra instead of just in the school nativity play.'

'It's going to be the best nativity play the school has ever done,' Fabienne asserted. 'Were you ever in a nativity play, Christine?'

'Yes, when I was in your class.'

'But you weren't the Virgin Mary?' said Fabienne jealously.

'No, I was an angel.'

'The Angel Gabriel or an ordinary angel?'

'An ordinary one, in the choir.'

'I'm not in the choir,' said Fabienne complacently. 'I don't sing. I just sit there with the Baby Jesus and look holy.'

Tante Léonie snorted. 'Do they give you a mask to wear?'

Fabienne looked puzzled. 'Of course I don't wear a mask, I am the Virgin Mary. But listen, Christine, the others sing this, while I'm looking holy. They sing, "*Adeste Fideles, Laete triumphantes* . . ."' She stopped singing. 'That's German,' she said instructively.

'Latin,' Christine corrected.

'No, German. Listen: *Ades-te Fide-les, Lae-te tri-um-phantes . . .*'

'I have to go home now,' said Christine. 'Thank you for having me, Tante Léonie.'

'Are you sure Giselle will be back yet?' Léonie asked.

'Oh yes, she asked me to come home at four,' Christine explained. 'She said she would be back from the hairdresser's by four at the latest and could I come home then. Maman doesn't like to be in the house alone, since Papa left.'

'She will have to get used to it sometime,' Léonie said. 'It's three weeks now. Have you seen him?' she added curiously.

'No.'

Léonie's nose twitched, as it always did when she scented an interesting piece of news. 'Don't you want to see him?'

'Maman doesn't let me,' Christine said. 'She won't tell me where he's living.'

Léonie sniffed. 'I suppose she knows best,' she said. 'I shouldn't think I would want anything to do with my husband either, if he had behaved like that.'

'Maman, will you stop talking and listen to my song!' said Fabienne.

'It wasn't all Papa's fault,' Christine defended him.

Léonie eyed her. 'Taking sides?'

Christine flushed. 'No, I'm not. But there is Papa's side as well as Maman's.'

'Oh, I suppose you know all about it,' said Léonie disparagingly.

'It would be difficult not to,' said Christine frigidly, 'when everyone talks of nothing else.'

Léonie shrugged. '*Eh bien.* Give my love to Giselle.

Tell her to pop in any time she feels miserable. Not that I can do much to cheer her up, with all my problems.'

'I'll tell her,' Christine promised. '*Au 'voir*, Tante Léonie . . . Fabienne.'

'Just stay a minute longer,' Fabienne begged, 'and listen to my song.'

'It is not even your song,' said Tante Léonie. 'You are not going to be singing it.'

'Everybody is going to sing it *to me*,' said Fabienne with emphasis, 'because I am the Virgin Mary.'

'You don't say!' said Tante Léonie.

'Listen, Christine, please!'

'Well, all right, but then I must go. I promised Maman I would be back.'

'Just half a quarter of a minute,' Fabienne promised. '*Ad-es-te Fid-e-les* . . .'

When Christine got outside, a light sprinkling of snow had fallen, outlining the trees and the parked cars with a silvery rim. Underfoot, the careless passers-by had trampled the silver into slush.

Fearful that Maman would think she had forgotten her promise, Christine began to run, but the wet pavements were slippery and she was forced to settle for a rapid walk.

It was almost December, she thought; her birthday and then Christmas. She hoped that no one would remember her birthday. It had been bad enough last year with everyone trying to be jolly, though Maman had had a row with Papa just before the rest of the family arrived. The forced smiles. The kisses. The card with 'To our darling daughter' on it, with both signatures in Maman's handwriting. The present from Tante Léonie: 'It's not much, I know, but Pierre gives me so little money.' Oncle Pierre pinching her thigh: '*Incroyable*! Our little niece is growing up quite beautiful, Léonie.' Tante Léonie, black as thunder: 'Oh, do stop mauling her about, Pierre! You can see the child doesn't like it.' Maman, dabbing lipstick on her mouth, painting on the smile: '*Venez, venez, tout le monde!* We are going to play a game.'

Bon Papa had been there too, shuffling out of the way of Fabienne who, pretending to be an Indian, was waving the poker like a tomahawk. 'I will come down when the presents are opened, Giselle,' he had said. 'Call me then.'

Christine had sneaked up to his room later, on the pretext of fetching something. 'Are you all right, Bon Papa? Is it too noisy for you?'

'No, no.' He had given her a hug as she leaned against him. 'Are you having a good birthday?'

'Oh yes,' she had lied, but he had looked at her in that quizzical way and they had both laughed. She had hugged the laughter to her like a shared secret throughout the afternoon, and after that nothing could spoil the day, not even when René was sick over her new game.

This year, however, there would be no one to make her laugh, and Christine prayed that there would be no party either. How terrible if Maman, despite her efforts to put on a good face, broke down in the middle, as she had done in the dress shop three weeks ago!

'*Bonsoir*, Christine!'

'*Bonsoir*, Madame Rouvieux.'

'You are home late for a Thursday. Didn't you have your half day?'

'I went to my Tante Léonie's,' Christine explained. 'But not for the whole afternoon because Maman wanted me back at four. I'm a bit late.'

'I saw your Maman come home twenty minutes ago,' Madame Rouvieux agreed. 'But she has gone out again now.'

'She can't have done!' Christine realized it was rude to

289

contradict the old woman. 'Perhaps she's back now,' she amended. '*Au 'voir*, Madame.'

'*Au 'voir, mon lapin.*'

The back door was open. Christine kicked off her shoes in the porch and opened the door to the kitchen. 'I'm home, Maman!'

No answer. On the kitchen table, a note. 'Sorry to miss you, *mon chou*. Madame Bénaud has kindly invited me round for an early apéritif as I was feeling a little depressed. I shall not be later than 9 P.M. Eggs in the fridge, or go to Madame Rouvieux. Big kisses, Maman.'

Christine read it in disbelief. '*Merde!*' she said, under her breath. The word relieved her feelings. Bon Papa would never have let her get away with it, but there was no one to care about her language now. '*Merde!*' she said again, loudly. '*Merde! Nom de Dieu! Espèce de con!*' Then, greatly daring, but in a quieter voice, '*Foutre!*'

She crumpled the note. '*Je m'en fous!*' she told the boiler, adding the paper to its flickering embers. Automatically, she picked up the coal scuttle and refilled the stove. What am I going to do for five hours, she wondered. She watched the clock, imagining its hands revolving five times, but the movement was so slow as to be imperceptible. Even the ticking seemed to be slower than usual.

Christine leafed through the other papers on the table. A cheque from Papa, but no letter. If only she knew where he was! She could have spent this evening with him, if only she had known. Perhaps he did not know that Maman had not given her the address. Perhaps he was wondering why his daughter had not come to see him. An idea struck her. She went to the telephone, but hesitated. Then she remembered Maman's note, and began to dial the number.

'Parnassier S.A. May I help you?'

'Can I speak to Monsieur Rochaud, please.' Her heart thumped uncomfortably. Suppose he was angry?

A pause, then the switchboard girl returned. 'I am sorry but Monsieur is in a meeting. Shall I put you through to his secretary?'

'No. Yes. No, I don't think so,' Christine babbled.

'Is that his daughter?' The voice enquired. It sounded kind.

'Yes, it is.'

'Would you like me to tell him that you called?'

'Yes. Yes, please. Tell him that . . . that I can come and see him if he likes.'

'All right. *Ciao*, Christine.'

'*Au 'voir*, Madame.'

How did the switchboard lady know her name? Perhaps Papa talked about her. Would he be cross about the message? Christine went hot and cold at her tactlessness. Suppose the people at Papa's office did not know that he was no longer living at home? 'Your daughter rang, Monsieur Rochaud, to ask if she might come and visit you.' His boss might be there. 'What is this, Rochaud? Why does your daughter have to visit you?' And then perhaps, 'We do not want men who leave their wives, Rochaud. You had better look for another situation.'

No, that was ridiculous. Papa's boss called him Jean-Luc and came to the house for dinner sometimes. 'An excellent dinner, Giselle.' 'Thank you, Philippe.'

Christine returned to the kitchen and examined the contents of the fridge. After due deliberation, she selected a wedge of Camembert and the remains of a packet of dates and accompanied them with an apple from the larder.

Sitting at the kitchen table to eat them, she saw an unopened letter that she had missed among the papers. Addressed to her and with an English stamp – Tante

Sophie! Christine ripped open the envelope. There was a short letter for Giselle and a longer one for Christine. '*Ma bien chère Christine,*' it read, 'Thank you so much for your lovely letter. I am sorry to hear that the situation at home is no better, but glad that you have managed to catch up on your work at school.'

Christine skimmed the rest of the letter for the answer she had requested. Here it was. 'As to your question about seeing your father . . . it is a difficult one for me to answer, Christine, and I would hesitate to go against your mother's instructions. But, after all, he is your father and if you want to see him then I think you have a right to do so. Don't be furtive about it, though. Tell Giselle honestly and I am sure that she will in the end understand.

'One further word of advice, Christine. If you go to see your father, don't be a "go-between". What I mean is, don't let either Papa or Maman give you messages to pass on to the other, or ask you for information about each other. It may be hard to refuse, I know, but their conflict is not yours and you must not let yourself become a part of it.'

There followed an amusing account of Sophie's attempt to buy a suitable hat for the school speech day, and a note about the nativity play she was rehearsing with her infants' class: 'The girl chosen for the Virgin Mary,' she wrote, 'got the part by virtue of her long hair. In character she is the noisiest little tearaway you ever encountered, and this has caused some indignation among the other parents, who claim that whoever cast Susie in the role is guilty of grievous blasphemy.'

Christine thought of Fabienne and chuckled, but she returned to the part about Papa. 'After all, he is your father.' Of course. Of course he was. She, his daughter, had a perfect right to ask to see him. She felt a great sense of relief. It could not be such a crime to ring him at his office, whatever Maman would say when she found out.

Christine was quite used to Maman's scoldings anyway. There had been that bad one a few weeks ago.

'So you knew before I did that your father intended to leave? And you never thought to inform me?'

'He told me not to.'

'And you put your father's wishes before your mother's happiness?'

Christine had cleared her throat uncomfortably. 'I thought it might not happen,' she extemporized. 'I thought he might change his mind.'

In the end, however, Maman had given up. '*Eh bien*, what difference does it make?' she had said wearily. 'He has left me and I do not hold out hopes of his returning.'

'Do you think that if you asked him, Maman . . . ?'

'I am not asking him, me! He is the one who left. Do you think I am going begging to him, on my knees?'

'You could just let him know that we miss him,' Christine had suggested, but Maman retorted, 'Do we? I don't know that I do.'

Later that night, though, Christine had heard her crying and had silently popped her head round the bedroom door, and there was Maman with her arms round Papa's abandoned pillow, sobbing, 'Jean-Luc! Oh, Jean-Luc!' over and over again.

When it grew dark, Christine turned on all the lights to make the house feel less empty. She was not afraid, for she did not feel alone. The kitchen clock ticked reassuringly and the coals glowed a comforting red behind the little window in the grate, and the furniture was solid and familiar, standing where it had always stood. Once or twice, too, when she was not listening, Christine's mind registered the low cough of Bon Papa. It was only when she raised her head to listen that she realized that she must have been mistaken.

Once, barely convinced by her own logic, she went upstairs to his room but it was empty, as she had known it would be, the mattress bare and the bureau cleared of his possessions. The little clock had gone to Papa and the ivory elephants to her own room. The rest – the razor and the little shaving brush, the papers and the book of crossword puzzles – Maman had thrown away. 'No point in keeping them,' she said.

The old tobacco tin stayed safely under Christine's pillow, where it felt bumpy under her ear when she turned over but warded off any evil spirits that might lurk around her in the night.

Several times, Giselle told Christine she had found her in the middle of the night in Bon Papa's room, asleep but with her eyes open. 'When I asked you what you were doing,' Giselle recounted, 'you said, "Looking for Papa." Bon Papa, you must have meant.'

Christine kicked idly against the leg of the chair and thought about starting her homework. The telephone rang.

'Christine?'

'Papa!' she said joyfully. 'Where are you?'

'At the office. I received a message that you had rung.'

'Yes.' Was he angry?

'Is anything wrong?'

'No. Nothing is wrong.'

There was a pause. Christine could sense him searching for words.

'You just rang for a chat?' He did not sound cross.

She took a deep breath. 'Maman is out till nine o'clock,' she said. 'I thought, if you agreed . . . that is, if you wanted me to . . . I could come and see you.'

There was a moment's silence at the other end of the line. 'Now?' he said.

'Oh no,' she said hurriedly. 'I know that you're working. Whenever suits you.'

'Does Maman know?' he asked.

'Maman is not here,' Christine explained patiently. 'She asked me to come back from Tante Léonie's at four o'clock – it's Thursday, you see, half day – but when I got home there was a note saying she would be out till nine.'

'In case she comes home early,' he said, 'you had better leave a note to tell her where you are.'

'OK.' She rejoiced silently. He had agreed!

'What if she phones up to see if you are all right?'

'She won't,' said Christine confidently. 'She never does.'

'I don't want her worried.' He sounded worried himself. 'Listen, I will ring Léonie and tell her that you are with me. If Maman should ring home and be anxious that you don't answer she is sure to phone Léonie.'

'OK.' Christine repeated happily. She did not care what arrangements he made. Papa wanted to see her!

'I shall be over in about half an hour,' he said.

She was disappointed. 'Can't I come and see your flat?'

'Yes, that is what I intend. I shall come and collect you.'

'In half an hour?' The thought registered. 'But you work till at least six.'

'I can leave early,' he said, 'for once. *Au 'voir*, Christine.'

'*Ciao*, Papa.' Christine replaced the receiver and waltzed around the room, hugging herself. He was leaving work early – for her. She wondered if there was any reason for it. Perhaps he wanted her to do something for him. She could not imagine what. But she could not imagine either that he would want to see her, just like that, without a reason. Papa always had a reason for things.

When he arrived, she asked him. 'Did you leave work early just to see me?'

He closed the car door carefully and started the engine. 'Yes.'

She beamed. 'But why?' she asked.

He frowned at her. 'Does there have to be a reason?'

Christine considered. 'Yes,' she said.

Jean-Luc laughed suddenly. 'I wanted to see you,' he said and sounded only slightly embarrassed. 'All right?'

'*Mais oui*,' she assented. 'But why?'

'Why not?' Then, as she still waited, he said quickly, 'Because I have missed you.'

'Really?' She was delighted. '*Vraiment-vraiment*?'

'*Vraiment*,' he said solemnly. 'Unbelievable, isn't it?'

She giggled. 'What is your flat like, Papa?'

'Wait and see.'

'Do you like it?'

'Of course.' But involuntarily he grimaced.

'You don't!' she said triumphantly. 'I can tell.'

'You can tell a great deal more than is good for you,' he said.

Christine peered out of the window, relishing the adventure. 'Where are we now? In the Quartier Latin?'

'Not too far from there. You left a note for Maman?' he asked suddenly.

'Yes. And you rang Tante Léonie.'

'For my sins,' he said grimly.

'Why, what did she say?'

'She seemed to think,' he said drily, 'that I was some kind of criminal. Kidnapping my own daughter, or some such nonsense.'

Christine laughed. 'I'm surprised she minded, then,'

she said cheekily. 'Didn't she ask you to take Fabienne as well?'

He glanced at her. 'Even kidnappers have their standards,' he said, straight-faced.

She searched his face, unused to jokes from him. 'Are you joking, Papa?' A corner of his mouth twitched. She relaxed.

'You seem different,' she told him frankly.

'Ah?' he said. 'In what way?'

She thought about it. 'More . . . well, a bit like Bon Papa really,' was the nearest she could get.

He turned to look her full in the eyes. 'Thank you,' he said simply.

'Brake, Papa!'

He slammed his foot on the brake, avoiding a collision with the car in front which had stopped suddenly at a crossing.

They drove on in silence.

'After your accident,' said Christine, 'weren't you afraid to drive?'

'I was a little nervous,' he admitted. 'That is one reason why I moved nearer to work.'

She regarded him reproachfully.

'Not a reason why I left home,' he clarified. 'Just a reason for choosing a flat here and not elsewhere.'

He had pulled up by the kerb. 'Jump out. This is it.'

It was an old, tall house rather like Tante Léonie's, only dirtier, shabbier and more cramped. There was an impressive array of doorbells.

'What a lot of apartments in one house,' Christine commented.

'When you see the size of them,' Papa said, 'You will understand why.'

Papa's flat was on the second floor. He unlocked the

door and pushed it open. 'Here we are,' he said, without enthusiasm.

She went in and looked around. There was one small sitting room with dingy curtains, dark-painted walls and a square, faded carpet which did not fit the shape of the room: it climbed up the chimney breast and missed out the alcoves, which had to make do with cracked brown lino.

The kitchen was the size of the larder at home. A few tins of ravioli and *cassoulet* stood on the single shelf, with a jar of chicory coffee, a packet of dried milk and a bowl of sugar.

'Is that all you have to eat?' Christine asked.

'I eat at midday,' he said. 'In a restaurant near the office. I do not need much in the evening.'

'You are thinner,' she said critically.

'That is not a bad thing,' he suggested, but she shook her head.

They returned to the salon.

'Where do you sleep, Papa?'

'On the sofa. It opens into a bed.' He pulled it out to show her. 'The duvet and the pillow are kept underneath.'

'And the sheets?'

'I don't bother with sheets.' He smiled at the disapproval on her face. 'So you don't like my flat, *hein*?'

She tried to be polite. 'It could be more comfortable,' she said guardedly.

'How?' he asked.

'There could be some cushions, perhaps.'

'There is one here.' He pulled out a small squashed object from the side of the chair. Christine regarded it with distaste.

'Where is your bathroom?'

'On the landing downstairs. The toilet is shared with

three other people and one can only have a bath at one's allotted time.'

Christine looked at him in silence.

'Yes,' he said heavily. 'I agree with you. It is a squalid way to live.'

'Papa,' she said, 'why don't you come home?'

He heaved a deep sigh. 'It is not so easy, Christine.'

'But don't you want to?'

'Yes,' he said. 'In many ways.'

'In what ways don't you?' she pursued.

He hesitated. 'I would have to be sure,' he said, 'that it was what we all wanted.'

'But Maman didn't want you to leave in the first place,' Christine pointed out. 'It was you who did.'

He nodded. 'But Giselle may well change her mind,' he said soberly.

Christine shifted from one foot to the other. 'What do you mean?'

Jean-Luc cleared his throat. 'I am sorry,' he said. 'I did not mean to begin such a heavy discussion.'

'No, tell me!' Christine pleaded. 'Please, Papa.'

He sat down on the edge of the sagging chair. 'Giselle had already begun to make her own life, before I left,' he said, in a voice that almost stayed firm. 'I want to give her a few months to discover whether she actually prefers things that way.'

'But she doesn't!' Christine protested.

'Perhaps not now,' he allowed. 'It was undoubtedly a shock for her. But when she becomes accustomed to life on her own or with . . . with her friends, she may well decide that my decision was a blessing in disguise for her.'

Christine kicked the leg of the sofa. 'Does that mean you are never coming back?' she said harshly.

'Not necessarily. But if I came back I would have to be sure that Giselle wanted it.'

'She does, Papa!' Christine claimed. 'I assure you!' She could not tell him about Maman sobbing herself to sleep, for that would be disloyal, and what had Tante Sophie said? 'Don't give information about one to the other.'

'Ah, but . . .' He spread his hands. 'Is it for the right reasons?'

'What are the right reasons?'

He shook his head. 'I do not think I can explain,' he said helplessly.

'I am not,' said Christine ominously, 'too young to understand.'

Jean-Luc smiled wryly. 'No,' he agreed, 'but I think that perhaps I am. Come, we will go out and find something for you to eat.'

She eyed him suspiciously, debating whether to allow herself to be side-tracked. Jean-Luc stood up and moved towards the door with an air of purpose.

'All right,' she assented. She followed him down the stairs. 'What shall we get?'

'Anything you like.'

'I had Camembert and cooking dates before I came out,' she told him.

Jean-Luc was not impressed. 'Perfectly disgusting,' he said severely. 'I hope we can do better than that.'

They did considerably better. Christine, toiling up the stairs again, said, 'Papa, we're never going to eat all this.'

'We can try,' said Jean-Luc imperturbably, and she grinned.

It was a good meal. Christine insisted on setting it all out properly on the rickety table, though the slices of quiche had to stand on their wrappers because there were not enough plates.

Jean-Luc cut the sausage into satisfyingly large chunks

300

– 'Vulgar,' Giselle would have said – and they used their forks to spear the pickled gherkins which bobbed evasively in their sea of brine.

'I don't think,' said Christine in despair, 'That I will have room for the cherry tart.'

They had been eating stolidly and, if not silently, at least without conversation. Jean-Luc, incongruous in the setting of this picnic meal, licked his fingers fastidiously, giving a comic dignity to the process.

Christine burst out laughing.

'What is the matter?' he enquired.

Christine held her side. 'You,' she gasped, 'licking your fingers!'

He half smiled, infected by her amusement but unsure of its cause. 'So?'

'You always use a knife and fork,' she hiccuped, 'and wipe them on your bread – so, and lay them down, just so, and wipe your mouth, so.' She imitated Jean-Luc's usual deliberation.

'Do I?' he said. 'How very boring of me.'

In case he should be hurt, she got up and kissed him.

'You smell of gherkins,' he complained.

'You smell of garlic,' she retaliated. It was safe to say anything to Papa today.

'What about that cherry tart?' he asked.

Christine shook her head regretfully. 'I just can't,' she said. 'I've eaten too much already. Look.' She slid a finger under her waistband to show him how little space there was.

'In that case,' he said, 'we will have to walk it off, and then you can come back and start again.'

She began to re-wrap the leftovers.

'Leave it,' he said.

'It will go dry,' said Christine reprovingly. 'You can have it tomorrow for supper if you keep it covered.'

'*Oui*, Madame,' he said meekly, and she giggled. He patted her shoulder with unprecedented affection.

'Oh, come back home, Papa!' she said suddenly.

He flinched as though she had struck him, and turned away. 'We will walk as far as the river,' he said.

They walked in silence, taking the small streets to avoid the rush-hour crowds.

'We have chosen the wrong time for a walk,' Jean-Luc said. 'Usually I go later in the evening, about nine. The streets are full of couples then,' he said austerely, 'dressed up and excited, going out for the evening.'

Christine stole a glance at him. 'Do you go out because you don't like staying in the flat?'

He looked startled. 'Why do you say that?'

'It's what Maman says,' she said simply. 'She keeps going out because she can't bear to be in the house.'

Papa frowned. 'Who looks after you?'

Christine was afraid she had been disloyal. Was this what Sophie had warned against? 'Oh, I'm all right,' she said hastily.

Jean-Luc looked worried. 'I don't like to think of you in the house alone,' he said. 'It's not right.'

Christine nearly said that Bon Papa was keeping an eye on her, but he would think her fanciful or mad. 'I'm all right,' she repeated.

They stood on the bridge for a long time, between the reflections of the lights ahead of them, bobbing in the water among the dark outlines of the buildings, and the hooting, crawling rush-hour cars at their backs.

'You are cold?' Jean-Luc said finally, when Christine shivered.

'Not really.' But he began to walk back anyway.

She was not really cold. The shiver was at the sense of desolation that suddenly overwhelmed her. As though she had been watching strangers, she saw the two of them standing on the bridge, solitary figures in the deepening dusk, alone amid the swarming, faceless traffic and the swift, uncaring flow of the water: static amidst the action, directionless among the purposeful; alone, abandoned, unbelonging.

'Tomorrow, will you go to work, Papa?'

'Of course. Tomorrow and the next day and the day after that and again the day after that.' He seemed to pick up some of her hopelessness.

'And on Sundays what do you do?'

He averted his face from her enquiring gaze. 'I read the paper,' he said. 'Tidy the flat. Go for a walk, perhaps.'

She thought of his Sundays at home. 'Listen to concerts on the radio?'

'There is no radio in the flat. I sit in the car sometimes and listen to that one.'

'I could bring the radio from home. Maman never listens to it,' Christine suggested, but he shook his head. 'No.'

'What else do you do?' she asked.

'I go to church,' he said.

Christine was surprised. 'Every Sunday?'

'And sometimes during the week,' he confessed.

'You are a practising Catholic now?' she said. Before, Papa had never bothered. 'I can pray just as well at home,' he used to say before dozing off behind his newspaper.

'I need it,' said Jean-Luc grimly. 'We ignore God, you see, until we want to make use of him, and then we remember to take notice of him again.'

'Well,' said Christine comfortingly, 'he's always there, isn't he?'

'Yes,' Jean-Luc conceded, 'but we forget how to find him, through sheer lack of practice.'

Christine slipped her hand through his arm. 'I expect he'll find you,' she said. 'He knows where you are.'

The flat was cold and depressing when they returned.

'A home should be welcoming,' Jean-Luc said. 'It should meet you with warmth and relief. "Aha," it should say, "you are back!"'

It was strange, Christine reflected, that she had never before noticed how like Grand-père Papa could be. Perhaps it was because Grand-père's way of talking, his comparisons and his jokes and his flights of fancy had always been there whereas Papa, as merely a part-time resident, had always been in his shadow.

'It should make welcoming noises,' Christine said, to show she understood. 'It should creak and tick.'

'And smell of food cooking in the oven,' said Jean-Luc longingly.

'There is always the cherry tart,' Christine consoled him.

He refused it, preferring coffee, so she ate his portion for him.

'It smells funny, that coffee,' she said critically.

'It is the chicory,' he said. 'Instant stuff.'

'Is the good coffee too expensive?' she sympathized.

'Not the coffee itself,' he said, 'but I would have to buy a grinder and filter and papers. I haven't bothered, so far.'

'Maman has a spare filter at home,' Christine said. 'Shall I . . . ?'

But he forestalled her: '*Merci. Non.*'

Too soon, it was a quarter to nine.

'I will take you back,' Jean-Luc said.

'Maman will be late,' Christine pleaded. 'She is usually late. We needn't go yet.'

'No,' he said. 'It is important to return you at the proper hour, the first time.'

Christine brightened. 'Will there be other times?'

'I hope so.'

'I hope so too,' she said.

He stooped suddenly and caught her in his arms, brushing his moustache against her hair. 'Don't make it too long until next time,' he said. 'You can ring me at work if you like. Leave a message with Yvette if I am not there.'

They drove home in silence. The car, warmer than the flat they had left, purred in the dark. Christine's eyes closed, and opened, and closed again. She yawned.

'Tired?'

She smiled. 'Not at all. It was a nice evening.'

'Go to bed when you get home,' he told her. 'You have to be up for school tomorrow.'

The house lights shone out in the darkness.

'Giselle must be home,' said Jean-Luc.

'I left all the lights on,' Christine confessed. 'I thought burglars would see them and think there was someone in.'

'Go in and see if she is back,' he told her. 'If not, you can wait in the car till she comes.'

'Won't you come in, Papa?'

'No,' he said. 'You go.'

Christine used Jean-Luc's key to open the back door. 'Maman!'

No answer.

'Ma-maan! Are you there?'

Silence.

She checked the salon, ran upstairs and looked in the bedroom. No one.

'Not back yet?' Jean-Luc said when she rejoined him.

'No.' She got back in the car. He switched on the car radio and lit a cigarette.

'You don't have to wait, Papa. I don't mind.'

'I will wait,' he said.

'Is it a nuisance?' she asked anxiously.

He blew a cloud of smoke. 'I have no pressing engagements,' he said ironically.

'. . . an economic alliance which does not and cannot ever benefit the French,' said the radio vehemently. 'A policy which every responsible citizen should repudiate, reject utterly, as harmful and even unpatriotic . . .'

Jean-Luc turned the knob. A burst of music assailed them. Christine hummed along, tapping her knee.

'You know this song?' Jean-Luc asked.

'It's Number One, Papa! Everybody knows it.'

It was followed by a recording of carols sung by a German choir: '*Stille Nacht, Heilige Nacht, Alles schläft, Einsam wacht . . .*'

'Christmas soon,' said Christine.

Jean-Luc turned the knob again. 'I know,' he said. He found another discussion programme and turned up the volume.

'To my mind, de Gaulle was not a hero, never could be a true hero of the people. Even in the eulogies which inevitably follow the death of a great public figure . . .'

'Maman is late,' said Christine.

At twenty minutes to ten, the Bénauds' grey Citroën turned into the rue Jean-Jacques Rousseau.

'There she is,' Jean-Luc said. 'Hop out now. *Au 'voir, ma fille.*'

'Aren't you even going to speak to her, Papa?'

'Not this time,' he said. She closed the door and he drove off, crashing the gears.

'Was that Jean-Luc?' Giselle demanded, meeting Christine at the gate.

'Yes.'

'He called to see me?' she asked.

Christine hesitated. 'Not this time,' she said.

When the inquisition was over, she went to bed. It was all right for Sophie to offer advice from the safety of the other side of the Channel, Christine thought. Sophie did not realize how thorough and relentless Maman's questioning could be. How many chairs were there, what colour carpet had he, what kind of *saucisse* had they bought, what kind of tart, were the olives green or black, stuffed or stoned? Christine's head reeled. Finally, after the trivia, came the heavyweights. Who was with him, how many bedrooms were there, how many pillows on the bed, how many toothbrushes in the bathroom? What time did his secretary leave work? Did he give his secretary a lift home, his colleagues' secretaries, the receptionist, his colleagues' wives?

'I don't know!' Christine shouted finally. 'I don't know and I don't care!'

'What time did he drive you home?'

'I don't know,' sullenly, now.

'You must know what time he brought you home, Christine!'

'Six o'clock, eight o'clock, midday, midnight,' retaliated Christine, deliberately infuriating. 'Today, tomorrow, yesterday, next week.'

'Oh, go to bed,' said Giselle wearily. 'I have a headache.'

'You have drunk too much,' Christine told her, watching Giselle's efforts to tuck the protruding corner of a scarf into her handbag.

'So what if I have?' Giselle retorted. 'It is I who will have the hangover in the morning and not you.'

She did indeed have a hangover in the morning.

'Bonjour, Maman.'

''*Our*,' she responded groggily, shielding her eyes against the crack of light from the landing.

'Some coffee for you, Maman.'

'*T'es gentille*. Thank you.'

'I am going to school now. *Au 'voir*, Maman.'

'*'Voir*.'

'Don't forget to drink your coffee.'

No answer.

'Happy birthday, Christine,' Christine prompted.

'*Hein*?' Giselle opened her eyes, then shut them again hastily. 'Oh yes. Happy birthday, *mon chou*. I will buy you a present later – *d'accord*?'

'Okay.'

'You won't hate me for forgetting it, *hein*? In the circumstances . . .'

'No. That's all right.'

'Christine – one more thing.'

'Yes?'

'Bring me the bowl from the kitchen, will you?'

14

'*Au revoir*' to the grumpy school porter; through the gates, down the hill and round the corner . . .

It was nice of Carine and her mother to invite both Christine and Giselle for the evening, in honour of Christine's birthday. 'A day late,' Carine apologized, 'but we didn't know.'

Véronique had made her a birthday card and gave it to her, with the paint still slightly wet, at break time, and Marie-Louise had actually spoken to her and given her a bite of her brioche and a look at a whole new set of photographs taken by her father. 'You can choose which one you like,' she offered. 'Any one at all, and I will ask Papa to print it for you large – or even extra large, if he will.'

So Christine, glad to let past frictions ease, had pored over the set and had let Marie-Louise advise her on the best choice. 'This one, or else that one,' instructed Marie-Louise. 'This one is the best of me in profile, but here the light is prettiest on the hair.' Christine had admired and had reserved judgement, till Marie-Louise decided, 'If you'll take large and not extra large, I'll let you have them both.'

Christine gave an involuntary skip, and swung her school bag joyously against the hydrant. Past the news-stand with its pouting nudes and shouting headlines; across the road to the Bar Vichy, its pavement tables stored away now for the winter, its red printed canopy faded and torn. An evening out! A night out with Maman, with Carine. A treat! An invitation specially for her birthday.

Mademoiselle Javine had found the words, '*Bon Anniversaire*, Christine,' scrawled across the blackboard and had ordered it rubbed off, but when it was done she had looked across at Christine and almost – almost – smiled. 'Happy Birthday, Christine,' she had said. 'I hope you will not allow it to interfere with your concentration,' and Christine had lowered her eyes and promised, '*Non*, Mademoiselle,' hardly able to believe her luck.

Round the corner and into the final home stretch; she covered the route in half the time today: rue Jean-Jacques Rousseau, number 18, with the new front door, smooth and brightly coloured green, contrasting with the stained wood, panelled one next door. Number 14 with its twin, number 14 *bis*, and finally home. Pushing open the rusty gate, with a kick and a shove to encourage the worn-out hinges. And round to the back kitchen door. Home. Christine's heart fell. She had forgotten, yet again, that home no longer meant Bon Papa.

She took a deep breath. 'Are you there, Maman? I'm home.'

'Don't take too long, Maman; we'll be late.'

Giselle dabbed perfume on her wrists and rubbed them together. 'There is plenty of time,' she said. 'Besides, it is polite to be late, unless one is invited for a meal.'

Christine could not see how that could be so. 'Well, there is going to be food, Carine said.'

'It is such a peculiar time for an invitation,' Giselle complained. 'I don't know what to wear at this hour. What are we invited for anyway, if it is not apéritifs or dinner?'

'I told you, Maman,' Christine said patiently, 'that

Carine and her mother often invite their neighbours in to play Monopoly or Scrabble or . . .'

Giselle swung round on her dressing-table stool. 'I hope you are joking, Christine!'

Christine was hurt. 'No, I'm not.'

'Do you mean to say that we are going to spend an entire evening with people we don't even know, playing children's games?'

Christine did not know which part to answer first. 'No, the neighbours are not going to be there tonight. It is just us. And you do know Carine's mother.'

'I have met Madame Legrand once, for two seconds, if you call that knowing her!'

'We have to go, Maman,' Christine pleaded. 'We were invited and we said yes. They are expecting us.'

'If I'd known what it was,' Giselle grumbled, 'I certainly would not have said yes. All right, Christine, don't make a fuss; we can hardly avoid going now, but I warn you, I am not going to play board games!'

Christine left it. If Carine's mother suggested it, then Giselle could hardly refuse, after all. At least, Christine hoped that she could not. With Maman in her aggressive mood these days, one never knew.

'Well,' Giselle challenged, 'what am I going to wear, then? Perhaps I had better borrow something of yours, Christine,' she said sarcastically, 'as it is a children's party.'

Christine bit her lip. 'It was nice of them to ask us,' she said. 'It's the first time I've been invited there properly, in the evening.'

Giselle relented. 'Don't worry,' she said. 'I'll behave myself. But just tell me, will you, what I should wear?'

Christine opened the wardrobe. 'The blue dress is pretty,' she said.

'That's a cocktail dress!' Giselle objected. 'Far too

formal. What will Carine's mother be wearing? Does she dress up, for these occasions?'

'I don't know,' Christine shrugged. 'Ring and ask her.'

'Don't be silly,' Giselle dismissed the idea. 'Well, what is she like, then?'

'Quite nice, I thought,' Christine said.

'I mean, what does she look like? Elegant, dowdy? Fat, thin? I only saw her in the car, remember.'

Christine wrinkled her nose. 'Medium-size,' she said vaguely. 'Not terribly smart but not dowdy either.'

'Beautiful?' said Giselle jealously.

'She's old!' Christine said. 'She is Carine's mother.'

'So one is too old to be beautiful just because one is somebody's mother?' Giselle accused. '*Merci beaucoup*, Christine!'

Christine sighed. 'Couldn't you just wear what you have got on?'

'I suppose I could,' Giselle surveyed herself. 'After all, no one is going to look at me, *n'est-ce pas*?'

'No, of course not,' said Christine comfortingly. 'It won't matter what you wear. Only, could you hurry a bit, Maman?'

Knowing Maman, Christine did not ring to order the taxi until she said she was quite ready. Even so, they kept the driver waiting while Giselle ran back to change her earrings.

'Going somewhere nice?' said the taxi-driver good humouredly.

'No,' Giselle retorted, exasperated by what she called 'all that hurrying'. 'Not really.'

On arrival at the Legrands' apartment, she paid the fare in small coins from her purse. 'I hope they offer us a lift home,' she told Christine, 'I can't afford all these taxis.'

They were given a warm welcome by Carine's mother.

'*Chère* Madame!' she effused. 'What a pleasure to receive you!'

Giselle thawed visibly. 'And how very charming of you to invite us, Madame,' she responded.

Christine relaxed. It was going to be a good evening after all. The only possible cause for alarm was that Carine's mother was wearing a very frilly dress with a great deal of jewellery, but she exclaimed so loudly and so enviously at Giselle's woollen ensemble that it appeared that it was the hostess who had overdressed and not the guest who had been too casual.

Carine herself, Christine was glad to see, looked just as usual in an old jumper and skirt and with wispy hair escaping from ribboned bunches. She hugged Christine as though she had not seen her just two hours ago. 'It is so good to see you,' she enthused. 'Shall I set out the Monopoly, Maman?'

'We will have a drink first,' her mother decreed, 'and make ourselves comfortable. Madame Rochaud, take this chair, please. It is the best.'

Giselle, gratified at being made the guest of honour, accepted a gin and vermouth. 'A very small one.'

Attentive to her role of hostess, Carine's mother poured a generous measure and kept the bottles on the table – 'for topping up.'

For Christine, Carine mixed a special cocktail, lovingly invented and carefully poured. 'Just so much orange juice,' she instructed Christine, 'with a squeeze of real lemon, lots of ice, and then Cola up to the top of the glass.'

'Don't drink it if you'd rather not, Christine,' urged Madame Legrand. 'There is plenty of ordinary squash. I have tried it,' she told Giselle. 'A simply disgusting mixture!'

Christine and Carine exchanged pitying glances. 'It's

lovely,' Christine said, sipping appreciatively. As if anyone would prefer plain squash to an exotic drink!

Carine's mother offered cigarettes.

'My favourite brand,' said Giselle with pleasure. She tapped her own packet self-consciously. 'I have only recently resorted to these.'

'So much better value,' approved Madame Legrand. 'Still I find it hard to do without my little extravagances!'

'Of course,' sighed Giselle, 'if one can afford them. Also, in present circumstances, I have to reduce my standards.'

Oh God, prayed Christine, please not the 'my husband has left me' speech; they don't even know her. Giselle's tendency to pour out her heart to total strangers appalled Christine. Admittedly, people gave freely of their sympathy, but what did they say afterwards, Christine agonized? Did they laugh and nudge each other and say, 'Funny woman – no wonder he left!' Maman did not seem troubled by this possibility.

Madame Legrand clicked her tongue understandingly. 'How well I know the situation, *chère* Madame Rochaud, from my own experience. It is just two years, you know, since my own husband left.'

'*Vraiment*?' Giselle began to take an interest. 'But you work, Madame Legrand, you have a job?'

'But yes! I am quite the career woman,' Carine's mother declared. 'Yet, a few years ago, if anyone had told me, "Violette, in two years you will be an administrator, in charge of your own office", I assure you I would have laughed in that person's face. "I am a housewife," I would have said, "What do I know of the business world?"'

Giselle was impressed but not convinced. 'But you obviously have a flair for it,' she said. 'One is born with such talents.'

'But, *chère* Madame, how does one know what talents one has until one begins to exploit them? I declare,' she declared, 'that the divorce was the best thing that ever happened to me. If Robert was still with me today, I would be still a housewife, with no more pressing concern than what to buy for supper or whether to do the ironing before the cleaning.'

Christine and Carine sipped their drinks and looked from Madame Legrand to Giselle, awaiting her reply.

'But now,' Giselle said, a little demoralized by this sweeping résumé of a housewife's concerns, 'you manage all these things in addition to doing a full-time job?'

Carine's mother spread her hands. 'Before,' she said, 'I had a large house to run, with many rooms to clean and with dinner parties, entertaining, all the time. Now, you see, we live more modestly, just the two of us. The chores are quickly done. We eat our main meal at midday, Carine at school and I at work, and make do with a simple snack in the evening. So, my mind and my energies are free for my work.'

'But surely,' Giselle said wistfully, 'you miss all the parties and the entertaining, cooking special meals and so on?'

Madame Legrand looked at her daughter and they both laughed, as if at a shared joke. 'Oh, dear Lord, no!' Madame exclaimed, still chuckling appreciatively. 'I was never of the opinion, Madame Rochaud, that a woman's role was to boost her husband's status. And all those dinner parties, you know, were just for show – to impress, to acquire influential friends and to further his business interests.'

'I suppose one does hold dinner parties for one's husband's sake,' said Giselle, inspired by this free-thinking attitude. 'Jean-Luc used to boast of my cooking.'

'You see!' Madame crowed. 'All part of the plot to

keep one in the kitchen. Now, you tell me, Madame, whether he would have boasted of his wife's skill as an entrepreneur, had you set up your own business, or of her adventurousness, had you left him to his own devices while you pursued a sales contract in the Middle East?'

Giselle laughed, 'No,' she said. 'I doubt that.' She held her glass steady while her hostess refilled it.

'Men,' said Carine's mother philosophically. 'They are all the same. While they keep us in the subservient role they can delude themselves that we cannot live without them. But, of course, we can.'

'Of course,' Giselle echoed. Then she said, with a touch of anxiety, 'You think it necessary for a woman on her own to get a job, even if there is no financial necessity?'

'But absolutely,' Madame Legrand affirmed. 'How can one respect oneself, I ask you, Madame, if one is forced to depend for one's livelihood on the man who has betrayed one?'

'Ah yes,' said Giselle faintly.

'"You can give me the house," I told him, "but I will not accept your payments, except for Carine. I can manage without you," I said. "I can live very well on my wits."'

Giselle regarded her with admiration. 'What did he say?'

Madame Legrand sighed and clasped her hands to her bosom. 'He did not care at that stage,' she said. 'He was glad to be spared the expense. Even the house he begrudged me because it left less for his mistress.'

Giselle flinched.

'I see,' Carine's mother declared, 'that the very mention of the word upsets you. Forgive my lack of delicacy, *chère* Madame, I have forgotten what it is to be wounded by such behaviour since I now no longer think of him.'

'You have got over it then,' said Giselle eagerly, 'in two years?'

'Oh, long before!' said Madame Legrand. 'As soon as I knew of the affair I said to myself, "Violette, you will not demean yourself by competing with this bitch." (Excuse me, Madame.) "You will not weep or plead or beg him to stay. You will relinquish him as though he meant nothing to you." And that is what I did. From that day I looked forward to my new life, and never backwards to the one I had left.'

Giselle was open-mouthed. 'But surely there were times . . .' she said.

Christine and Carine drained their glasses and fixed their eyes on Madame Legrand's face.

'Oh, of course,' Madame conceded. 'In private, there were the tears, the regrets, the sleepless nights. But in public, and in front of him – never! Never once did I give him the satisfaction of saying that I could not do without him. "My life has just begun," I told him, even before I believed it myself. I could not have held up my head, *chère* Madame, if I had made a spectacle of myself, grovelled or pleaded with him. I do not know how any woman can do such things.'

'No,' said Giselle, 'to be sure.' She gave Christine an anxious glance from the corner of her eye.

'One must retain one's pride,' asserted Madame Legrand, 'especially when one's husband has done his best to humiliate one by going off with another woman.'

Christine felt it was time to set the record straight. 'But my Papa never went off with another woman,' she said.

Giselle glared at her. Madame Legrand caught and interpreted the look. 'Carine,' she said smoothly, 'take Christine next door and set out the Monopoly board, *chérie*. All this grown-up conversation must be tedious for you girls.'

As they left the room Christine heard her say, in a lowered voice, 'How wise of you not to let Christine know all the sordid details, *chère* Madame.'

'Maman,' Carine said, 'will you be joining us for the game?'

Madame Legrand looked at Giselle, whose face betrayed not a trace of enthusiasm. 'No,' she said. 'You go ahead. We will stay here and have a cosy chat, Madame Rochaud and I.'

'Giselle,' said Giselle, 'Please.'

Carine's mother beamed. 'And you must call me Violette,' she said.

'I wasn't bored by the conversation,' Carine said. 'Were you? I love to listen to grown-up talk.'

'Your Maman seems to like it,' Christine said. 'Living without your Papa, I mean.'

'She says it was the best day of her life when the divorce came through,' said Carine proudly. 'She says that now she has truly found herself.'

Christine arranged the pieces on the Monopoly board. 'I think,' she said, 'that my mother has just got lost.'

They left the Legrands' house later than intended. Giselle, shrugging herself into her coat, swayed and stumbled in the doorway.

'*Oh là!*' she exclaimed, 'your hospitality was too lavish, Violette!'

The two women giggled, their comradeship strengthened by the copious gins. Violette hiccuped. 'I am only glad,' she said, 'that I have no stairs to climb to bed!'

They both laughed again. They laughed when Violette, reversing the car to turn it, forgot to change gear to go forward and backed instead against the bumper of the car behind. They laughed at silly jokes on the journey home, and laughed recalling earlier jokes when they said goodbye.

'A marvellous evening!' Giselle called, from the garden gate. 'You must come to us, next time!'

In answer, Carine's mother blew the horn – toot, toot-toot, toot – and Giselle laughed again, kissing her hands and waving as the car drew away.

'What a scream that woman is!' she said.

Christine opened the door for her.

'I couldn't have found the keyhole!' Giselle thanked her.

Once inside, she flung her coat down on a chair and blew a soundless whistle. 'What an evening!' Then she put her hands to her head. 'Make me some coffee – *hein, chérie*? Black. It will keep me awake, I know, but if I don't drink it I will have such a headache in the morning.'

Sitting on one kitchen chair, she manoeuvred another one round with her foot and kicked off her shoes. 'Violette,' she said, putting her feet up, 'seems very happy living on her own.'

Christine struggled to open a new packet of coffee beans. 'She has Carine,' she pointed out.

'On her own, without a husband, I mean,' Giselle clarified. 'She said that leaving him was the best thing she ever did. That is encouraging for me, *hein*?'

'She didn't like him anyway,' Christine told her. 'Or so Carine said. They never spoke to each other. She used to say he bored her to tears.'

'I know how she feels,' said Giselle, yawning.

Christine tipped the beans into the coffee grinder and pressed the switch.

'Oh, my head!' Giselle shouted, above the noise.

'What?' Christine switched it off.

'My head!' Giselle repeated. 'The noise!'

'I can't help it,' said Christine unhelpfully. She set the

319

machine to life again, whirring and clattering. When it stopped, she said, 'Papa is not boring. You can't say that he is.'

'Can't I?' Giselle said lazily.

Christine emptied the grinder, refilled it and started it up again.

'For the love of Christ!' Giselle exclaimed. As Christine did not react, she shouted, 'Switch the damned thing off, Christine!'

'I'm doing some for the morning,' Christine shouted back. 'The jar is empty.'

'Leave it!'

'I'll just fill up the jar!'

'I said leave it, Christine!' Giselle jumped to her feet and dragged Christine away from the table. 'Turn it off!' To save time, she turned it off herself. 'Are you deliberately annoying me?'

'Papa is not boring,' said Christine stubbornly.

'All right, no, fine,' agreed Giselle, exasperated. 'Papa is not boring. Make the coffee now.'

Christine fetched the filter. 'You don't really think he is, do you?' she asked. 'Not really?'

'No couple finds each other fascinating every minute of the day,' Giselle said.

'No,' Christine allowed, 'but in general – '

The rap at the door made them both jump.

'Who can that be?' Giselle whispered. 'At this time of night?'

Christine was equally frightened. 'Not Papa,' she said. 'He has a key. Don't answer it, Maman.'

The knock came again.

'I shall have to,' said Giselle. 'Anyone can tell that we are in.'

Christine followed close behind her as she opened the door to a familiar smiling face.

'Henri!' Giselle exclaimed. 'What on earth are you doing here at this time?'

His smile broadened. 'I am paying a social call,' he said. 'I see you are not yet in bed.'

'Only because we have been out,' said Giselle shortly. She did not, Christine thought, sound particularly pleased to see him.

Henri, unasked, stepped into the porch. 'Anyone nice?' he asked amiably.

'Yes, thank you,' said Giselle with hauteur.

'Carine and her mother,' Christine enlightened him. Giselle frowned forbiddingly. Christine turned to go but Giselle restrained her.

'Stay and make the coffee, Christine.'

'Two sugars for me,' said Henri, pulling up the chair Giselle had been using as a foot-rest. 'No milk.'

No coffee either, if it had anything to do with me, Christine thought grimly. She poured the coffee and set it on the table then stood over them, like a guard dog watching its charge.

'Must be your bedtime, Christine,' said Henri easily. 'I am sure Marie-Louise is asleep by now.'

'Congratulations to Marie-Louise,' said Christine rudely. Giselle said nothing but stirred her coffee thoughtfully.

Henri turned his back on Christine. 'So,' he said conversationally, 'the two merry widows have been discussing their plight, *hein*? Thinking up some names for the heartless race of man?'

'Oh, not the whole race,' Giselle assured him. 'There are, I believe, some men who are quite human.'

Henri chortled. 'I am flattered, *ma chérie*.'

'There is no need to be,' Giselle said sourly.

'Can it be,' Henri teased, 'that you are confusing me with Jean-Luc, Giselle?'

'That,' said Giselle, 'is hardly likely, I think.'

Christine looked from one to the other. She had the impression that they were enjoying this cross-talk.

'I think so too,' agreed Henri.

'But you need not think,' Giselle flared, 'that any comparison favours you.'

Henri raised one eyebrow and sipped his coffee with the utmost delicacy. 'Don't tell me,' he said, 'that you have decided to canonize Jean-Luc by virtue of his leaving. For that,' he chuckled, 'must surely be the first virtue he has displayed.'

Giselle slammed her coffee cup into its saucer. 'Jean-Luc has many virtues,' she said, 'which you are totally unable to recognize.'

'Ah, yes,' said Henri smoothly. 'Let me remember: insensitive, wasn't it, and boring, and callous and – '

'*Taisez-vous*!' said Giselle furiously, addressing him formally. 'Shut up!'

'*Calme-toi, chérie*,' Henri soothed, persistently keeping his speech intimate. 'Perhaps my memory misled me.'

'It certainly does,' Giselle said angrily. 'It must be the approach of old age, perhaps!'

'*Tiens, tiens*!' Henri scolded. 'This is beginning to sound like old times, you know, with our little fights.'

'Out!' Giselle shouted, rising to her feet. 'Get out of my house!'

Henri caught hold of her upraised arm. 'That's better,' he encouraged. 'A few sparks, my little one, are so much more fun than mere indifference!'

'Get out!' Giselle screamed. 'Get out of my sight!' She struggled to pull away from him, but he held her fast.

'But where would I go?' he reasoned. 'It so happens that I have no bed for the night, you see, and . . .'

'Well, you are not sharing mine,' Giselle spat. 'You have done enough damage already to my life. I never,

NEVER want to see your smirking, self-satisfied face again, MONSIEUR Trichard!'

'Come now!' said Henri, tightening his grip and smiling more persistently. 'Come now, Giselle . . .'

'You must go now,' said Christine, very quietly. Turning, he saw that she had taken the poker from the boiler. The tip was red hot.

'What's this?' he said, still smiling, but his voice wavered. Giselle, released, rubbed her wrists.

Christine made a jab at him with the poker and he started back.

'Leave Maman alone,' Christine threatened.

'It was a joke,' Henri protested. 'An adult joke. You are too young to understand, my child.'

Christine glanced at Giselle, but Giselle shook her head and said, 'Not much of a joke, Henri.' She opened the door for him. 'Go.'

Henri, after a second glance at the waving poker, went, slamming the porch door behind him.

'Horrible man!' Giselle said furiously. 'How dare he?'

Christine replaced the poker carefully. Giselle watched her curiously. 'Would you really have burned him?' she asked.

Christine put her head on one side. 'I don't think so,' she said honestly.

Giselle began to laugh, slightly hysterically, and Christine joined in, reluctantly at first and then wholeheartedly. Giselle put her arms round her and kissed her.

'I am sorry, *chérie*,' she said soberly. 'I have not set you a very good example as a mother. But, if it is any consolation, I do love you.'

Christine hugged her. 'Do you really not like him now?' she asked.

Giselle shuddered. 'I detest the man,' she said fervently. 'What arrogance! How I never saw it before, I shall never know.' She hesitated. 'It was not true, what he said about Jean-Luc,' she said. 'I never said he was boring – certainly not to Henri, believe me.'

Christine found no difficulty in believing her. It was, after all, inconceivable that Papa was boring. Had she not said as much just before Henri's arrival?

'I remember,' said Giselle dreamily, swilling the now cold coffee round in the cup, 'the first time I met Jean-Luc. The attraction, the excitement when he spoke to me, the dressing up to go out with friends, knowing he would be there.' She sighed. 'It doesn't last,' she said wistfully. 'He used to send me flowers, you know – little bouquets of red roses, when I knew he couldn't afford them. And there was always a little note, hidden down among the stems where Maman couldn't see it.'

'What did they say, the notes?' Christine asked. She poured Giselle some more coffee and began idly to pull the soft, crumbly centre from the remains of the morning's loaf. 'Were they love letters?' she said, with her mouth full.

'No,' said Giselle. 'At least, not at first. Just a few lines saying "See you on Thursday" or "Wear your blue dress to the Duponts" – something like that.'

Christine was disappointed. 'Why did he write a note, just for that?' she said. 'He could have said it to you when he saw you.'

Giselle smiled. 'I suppose so,' she agreed. 'It was the fact of receiving those notes at all that was exciting. In those days, you see, it was not done to exchange notes with someone who was not your fiancé, much less to go out with him alone.'

'Did you go out with him alone, though?' Christine asked, intrigued. It was strange to connect this romantic young couple with her own parents.

'Oh yes,' Giselle said. 'We used to meet up with a

group of friends and then go off together. At the end of the evening we would rejoin the group and a couple of them would see me home, to keep Maman happy.'

'Was Grand-mère very strict?' Christine asked.

'Very,' said Giselle feelingly. 'It was not a good thing, I think. Both Sophie and I rebelled in our own way. I always thought Maman was so hard on Sophie not because of the baby but because she considered the man to be unsuitable. In my case, she probably suspected that Jean-Luc and I were . . . meeting each other, but she approved of him and so she turned a blind eye.'

'What was he like – Papa?' Christine asked, fascinated. 'What did you first like about him?'

Giselle looked into space, thinking. 'He made me feel important,' she said. She smiled slowly, remembering. 'I was only nineteen. I was used to going round with a crowd of friends. We all knew each other very well. I was "one of the gang", if you like. Jean-Luc treated me as though I was different, special. He picked me out of the crowd.'

'Why did he pick you?' Christine asked. She cupped her chin in her hands, leaving the bread untouched on the table.

'Oh,' said Giselle softly, 'he said I was so bright, always laughing, talking, dancing. Vivacious. He said I brought a glow to his heart.' She paused. 'Yes,' she repeated, 'a glow. That is what he said.' She fumbled in her bag for her cigarettes, and lit one.

'But what was *he* like?' Christine pursued. 'Was he good-looking?'

Giselle got up to fetch an ashtray. 'Not handsome,' she said thoughtfully, 'though he had nice eyes. It was not until he began talking that you noticed he was attractive. He was shy really – reserved. But once I got him talking he would forget his self-consciousness and he was . . . yes, very attractive.'

'And what – ' Christine began, but Giselle interrupted her.

'It was not until later,' she said, 'that I realized who he reminded me of. I knew he seemed vaguely familiar; that was why I felt so at ease with him, but at the time I didn't see how like Papa he was. I suppose that was why Maman liked him too.'

'Like Bon Papa?' said Christine, surprised.

'Yes, haven't you ever noticed?' Giselle said. 'Through living in the same house for so long, of course, they grew more alike, if anything, over the years.'

'I had noticed it,' Christine said slowly, 'just recently. I don't know why, but I never saw it when Bon Papa was here.'

'You were too engrossed with Bon Papa to notice anyone,' Giselle said. 'One would have thought, to see you, that he was the father and Jean-Luc was some outsider. You never took much notice of him.'

Christine was shocked. 'You always said he never took any notice of me!'

'Who can say,' said Giselle musingly, 'which came first? Of course, he was never here as much as Grand-père, but also, when he was home, he was so quiet. It was easy to ignore him.'

'I didn't ignore him' said Christine indignantly.

'I think we all did, to a certain extent,' Giselle said. 'He was the kind of man who needed to be drawn out of himself. He could never be the one to show affection; he needed someone to make the first move, to show him he was wanted. I understood that so well when I was younger,' she added wistfully, 'but somehow I must have forgotten it, or just couldn't be bothered later on. I thought he should have been the one to make the effort sometimes. I felt he should have been more demonstrative. But it wasn't in his character.'

'You talk about him as if he were dead,' said Christine brusquely, breaking into Giselle's reverie.

'Sometimes I feel as though he were,' she said dismally. 'For all the difference it makes, he could be at the other end of the world.'

Christine frowned. 'He is living near the Quartier Latin,' she said. 'You know that.'

'I meant,' Giselle told her, 'that I have so little contact with him that he might just as well be at the end of the world – or out of the world.'

Christine thought it was a waste when Bon Papa was actually lost to them, to treat Papa who was alive and well and living a few kilometres away, as though he too were lost. She twisted the bread crust into ugly shapes.

'You know very well,' she said roughly, 'that he is quite near, living in a horrible little flat when he could be at home with us. And you won't ask him,' she said, her voice rising, 'you just won't ask him to come home.'

'He doesn't want to come home,' said Giselle flatly. 'He is the one who has chosen to live in a horrible flat rather than here with us. It is not for me to ask him to do what he clearly does not want.'

'But you want it?' Christine said anxiously. 'You want him to come home, don't you?'

Giselle laid her head down on the table, as though she were suddenly very tired. 'Yes,' she said. 'Oh, yes.'

'Maman!' Christine said urgently. 'It's half past eight!'

Giselle groaned. 'Oh, no,' she said. 'We haven't overslept again?' She sat up and peered at the clock. 'I don't remember turning off the alarm.'

'Have I any clean socks, Maman?'

'Aren't there any in the cupboard?'

'No.'

'Then no, you haven't. Can't you wear yesterday's?'

'I wore them the day before as well. My feet will smell.'

Giselle slumped back against the pillows. 'Have you had your breakfast?'

'No, there isn't time. I'll have to go without it.'

'Are you going now?' Giselle asked.

'When I've found my socks,' she said.

'Kiss me goodbye now, then. I may as well stay in bed a while longer.'

Christine kissed her. 'Aren't you going to get up?' she said anxiously. Maman always got up on time. Only sluts and lazy women stayed in bed, she always said.

'What is there to get up for?' Giselle said listlessly. 'Besides, I have a headache.'

Christine hovered in the doorway.

'What are you waiting for, Christine? I thought you were late.'

'If you're not well,' Christine said, 'I can stay.'

'No, you go,' Giselle told her. 'I shall only sleep. What are you looking at me like that for?'

Christine rubbed one leg against the other. 'You never lie in bed,' she said worriedly.

'I never used to lie in bed,' Giselle corrected. 'I never used to stay in my dressing gown till past midday. I never used to let a week go by without washing the kitchen floor. That was when I had a husband and a father to keep house for. What is the use,' she demanded, 'what is the use now of all that effort?'

Christine did not know. 'You would get up if Papa were here,' she said.

Giselle raised herself on one elbow and said bitterly, 'Well, he is not here, is he? He is not here any more. When will you realize that – *hein*? It is not my fault.'

'You could do something about it,' Christine mumbled.

'Speak up, I can't hear you.'

'You could ask him to come home,' Christine repeated.

'I could ask him to come home and he could say no!' Giselle said. 'And where would that leave us?'

'He thinks you don't want him – because of Monsieur Trichard,' Christine said. 'You could at least tell him you sent Henri away last night.'

'No, I could not.'

'I could tell him then,' Christine offered.

'It's no use, Christine! He doesn't want to come home and I am not going to humble myself again.'

'He does want to!' Christine insisted. 'He said so.'

'Then he knows where to come,' Giselle said.

Christine bit her lip in frustration. 'He won't come,' she shouted, 'unless you ask him!'

Giselle rolled over and turned her back on her. 'You are making this up to suit yourself,' she said. 'If Jean-Luc wanted to come back he would have contacted me by now.'

'He thinks you don't want him!' said Christine desperately.

'You are wrong,' Giselle said coldly. 'It is he who does not want me.'

'No, Maman, honestly . . .'

'Go to school, Christine.'

She left, slamming the door behind her.

She was very late. The first lesson was well under way when she arrived. Even Ma'mselle Dubois, thank God, was no longer standing sentinel at the gates. Only the concierge was there to grunt, 'You'll catch it!' as Christine ran past.

She hid in the lavatories till the first lesson had ended. As luck would have it, the teachers changed today between the first and second period; she would be able to sneak into class undetected during the change. If she mistimed it she would tell the second teacher, she had just come back from the lavatory.

Christine settled herself more comfortably on the seat and silently addressed herself to Bon Papa. It was a habit that had replaced praying recently. At least with Bon Papa she knew who she was talking to.

It's not that I don't want Maman to have a lie-in, if she's tired, she told him; but she isn't really tired, just miserable and a bit hung-over from the night before. I don't like to see her staying in bed just because she can't see a reason to get up. It doesn't seem right somehow. What do you think, Bon Papa? She waited expectantly for him to convey his reply by telepathy or divine inspiration, but no answer came. Christine sighed. It was difficult to believe, sometimes, that he was really listening. If only Tante Sophie were here! Try not to interfere, Sophie had said, in your parents' lives. But it's my life, too, Christine thought. I want Papa back too. It is not just a matter for him and Maman.

Only occasionally did she have the slightest glimmer of doubt. When she had been to see him at his flat, he had received her with obvious pleasure. He had been far nicer to her, she had to admit, than when he had lived at home.

If he came home, would the niceness continue? Had he, as he said, learned to value his family and the time he spent with them? Or would he, on his return, become once more the harassed executive, begrudging the noise Christine made and the social events his wife arranged?

Of course, Christine told herself, it made no difference. However he behaved, she would still want him home. But a tiny doubt niggled at the back of her mind. 'It's much more fun,' echoed her friend Carine's voice, 'when they live apart. They both spoil you because they're afraid you'll love the other one more.'

Ask and you shall receive. But you have to know what you are asking for, thought Christine wretchedly. You have to be sure of what you want, otherwise how can you truly pray to be given it? She buried her face in her hands. Help me, Bon Papa, she cried silently. Do something!

She stayed in that position for some time. The ancient cistern hissed and rumbled to itself, like a monster with indigestion. From a distant classroom came the sound of an upraised voice, the words indistinguishable, teaching something or other. Christine kept very still. She had done all the talking she could do. She had pleaded with Papa and with Maman. She had pleaded silently with Bon Papa and in writing with Tante Sophie. Now she could only plead with God. You're all there is left, she told him. I can't do any more.

Phrases jostled through her mind. Sophie's voice: 'He is your father, after all.' Giselle's: 'I don't know, Christine, I'm so confused.' Papa's: 'If I came back I would have to be sure Giselle wanted it', and her own: 'Come home, Papa! Come home where you belong.'

She saw him sitting on his own in the grim little flat, then fastidiously wiping his fingers after their picnic meal. Then she saw him outside their own house in the old days, getting out of the car, locking and checking it. From the window his daughter waved but did not run to meet him.

Then the scene changed: an old man walked up the path, tired, hesitant, unsure of his step. The girl flew down the path to meet him. She hugged him joyfully. '*Salut*, Bon Papa! I have had such a day; you'll never guess . . .'

She looked lovingly into his face, watching the tiredness disappear and the smile begin. '*Bonsoir, ma petite*. I have had a trying day.' But it was not Grand-père's face she looked into, it was Papa's.

The mists cleared and there was no more doubt. Christine took her hands away from her face. That's it, she said. I know now. I do want him home.

The bell rang and she got up to go. Okay God, she said, I know now. Now you can get on with it.

She felt as though the burden had been lifted from her shoulders. It was no longer her concern. Relieved of the load of anxiety of the past months, she skipped into class.

'Where've you been?' said Carine.

'Wasting time,' Christine answered. 'I slept too long. But I'm here now.'

Carine caught her exuberant mood. 'You'd better have lots of energy,' she said. 'It's gym next.'

Christine mimicked the gym teacher. '"No talking, no dawdling! Changed by the time I count to ten!" *Un-deux-trois-quatre*!'

Giggling, they made their way down to the changing rooms. 'You seem very happy,' Carine said. 'Your papa hasn't come home, has he?'

Christine pulled off her sweater and flung it carelessly on to the locker. 'No,' she said cheerfully. 'Not yet.'

The mood lasted throughout the day. The clock, rejoicing with her, obligingly went faster. She forgot to count the minutes, to chew her pencil or to stare out of the window at the flurrying snow. Instead she worked with placid concentration until the end-of-day bell caught her unawares.

She galloped home at twice her usual pace, oblivious of the cold of falling snow. There was no time to dawdle today, and nothing to worry about. She was eager to be home to see what God had accomplished.

At the end of the rue Jean-Jacques Rousseau, her steps faltered, however, and her pace dropped. What reason had she, after all, to suppose that God had listened to her? How could she expect that without any effort on her part the weeks of unhappiness would suddenly be put right?

Her feet dragged, kicking up the snow which was turning to slush in the dusty Parisian streets. 'The dust here is different from the dust anywhere else in the world.' Suddenly the voice was clear in her ears, the slow, familiar, unmistakable voice. 'Bon Papa!' she said joyfully. The voice continued unfaltering, with its well-remembered brusquerie. 'Nonsense, Christine, of course you can do it. A clever girl like you!' She recalled the incident. There had been a wall in the park along which all the children ran, and she had wanted so much to join them but she had been afraid – afraid, just as she was now, hesitating outside her own back door.

'Go on, go on,' he had encouraged her. 'Don't look back. You will not fall. I am right behind you.'

The voice was so clear that she looked round to see if he was there. No, of course he was not. 'I am right behind you.'

Christine took a deep breath and pushed open the door. Maman, in tears, sat at the kitchen table.

'Maman! What's wrong?'

Giselle, red-eyed, brandished a piece of paper.

'A letter?' Christine asked. Her heart sank.

'A bill!' said Giselle frantically. 'A bill for electricity. I cannot pay it! I have no money. It is only two weeks since Jean-Luc's cheque and it was meant to last the month!'

Christine looked at the bill. 'Perhaps Papa did not give you enough,' she suggested.

'It was enough,' Giselle sobbed. 'It was a great deal more than usual, so I spent it on taxis and on clothes and – oh, on flowers and things. I forgot, you see, that it was

333

not just for housekeeping. I forgot there would be bills. Oh, what a fool I am!'

Christine put her arm round her. 'You're not a fool, Maman,' she said. 'You weren't to know. Papa always did the bills before.'

'I can't do it, Christine!' Giselle wailed. 'I can't cope without him. I don't want to be independent. I want Jean-Luc!'

'Then,' Christine said firmly, 'you must tell him so.'

Giselle looked at her, struck by the confidence in her voice. 'Oh no,' she said, but her voice wavered, 'I can't do that.'

'Nonsense,' said Christine brusquely, in Bon Papa's tones. 'Of course you must do it. It is the only way.'

'You want me to?' Giselle whispered. 'He was always cross with you. You're sure you want me to?'

'Yes,' said Christine, 'Yes. Yes.'

'I must change,' said Giselle distractedly. 'I must do my face.'

'No,' said Christine steadily. 'You must go now. Don't look back.'

Giselle got up, bemused, as if in a dream, and brushed vaguely at her skirt. 'Will you come with me, Christine?'

Christine shook her head. 'It is not for me to go,' she said. 'You must do it yourself. I am right behind you.'

'Call me a taxi,' Giselle said.

They sat in silence till the taxi came. Giselle sat quietly. Her face was composed and her hands, for the first time in months, lay still and folded in her lap. As the clock ticked and the floors creaked, the old house settling itself in its foundations, her foot tapped lightly in time to its rhythmic breathing.

When the taxi came, she went out without a backward glance. 'Don't look back.'

Christine went upstairs to Grand-père's room and looked out as the taxi drew away. The snow still fell, silent and steady on the city streets, burying the dust and grime in the new-born white. It fell on the plane trees, bare now of their leaves, and on the tall three-storey houses with their blistered walls, on the iron-railinged gardens, the pavements and the slow-moving cars – it fell on the Bar Vichy and the sodden newspaper stand. It fell over the whole of Paris. In England too, perhaps, it fell on the towns and the villages and the place where Sophie lived. Christine would go there now, she knew, when Easter came.

'Don't look back. I am right behind you.' The voice came again, so familiar that she did not need to see him to know who it was.

'Ça va, Bon Papa?' she said. 'Did I do all right?'